G-MAN

Cape Crisis

by Chris Giarrusso

Cape Crisis

created, written & illustrated by
CHRIS GIARRUSSO

Savage Dragon appearances illustrated by
ERIK LARSEN

web design, book design & color assists by
DAVE GIARRUSSO

edited by
BRANWYN BIGGLESTONE

www.chrisGcomics.com

IMAGE COMICS, INC.

Robert Kirkman - Chief Operating Officer
Erik Larsen - Chief Financial Officer
Todd McFarlane - President
Marc Silvestri - Chief Executive Officer
Jim Valentino - Vice President

Eric Stephenson - Publisher
Todd Martinez - Sales & Licensing Coordinator
Betsy Gomez - PR & Marketing Coordinator
Branwyn Bigglestone - Accounts Manager
Sarah deLaine - Administrative Assistant
Tyler Shainline - Production Manager
Drew Gill - Art Director
Jonathan Chan - Production Artist
Monica Howard - Production Artist
Vincent Kukua - Production Artist
Kevin Yuen - Production Artist

www.imagecomics.com

International Rights Representative - **Christine Meyer** (christine@gfloystudio.com)

G-MAN, VOL 2: CAPE CRISIS. First Printing. September 2010.
Published by Image Comics, Inc.
Office of publication: 2134 Allston Way, 2nd Floor, Berkeley, CA 94704.

Chapter 1

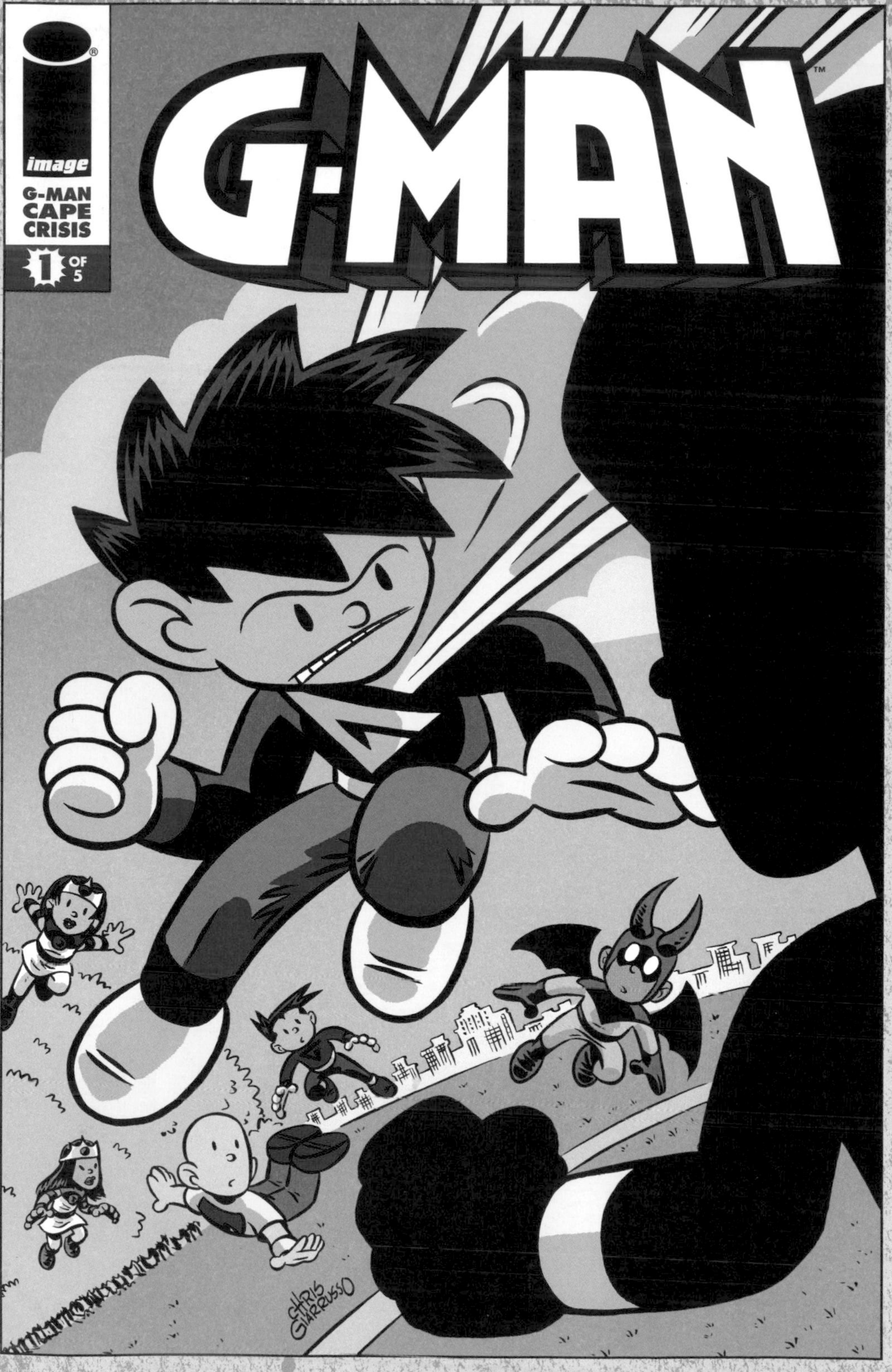

image
G-MAN
CAPE
CRISIS
1 OF 5
G-MAN™
CHRIS GIARRUSSO

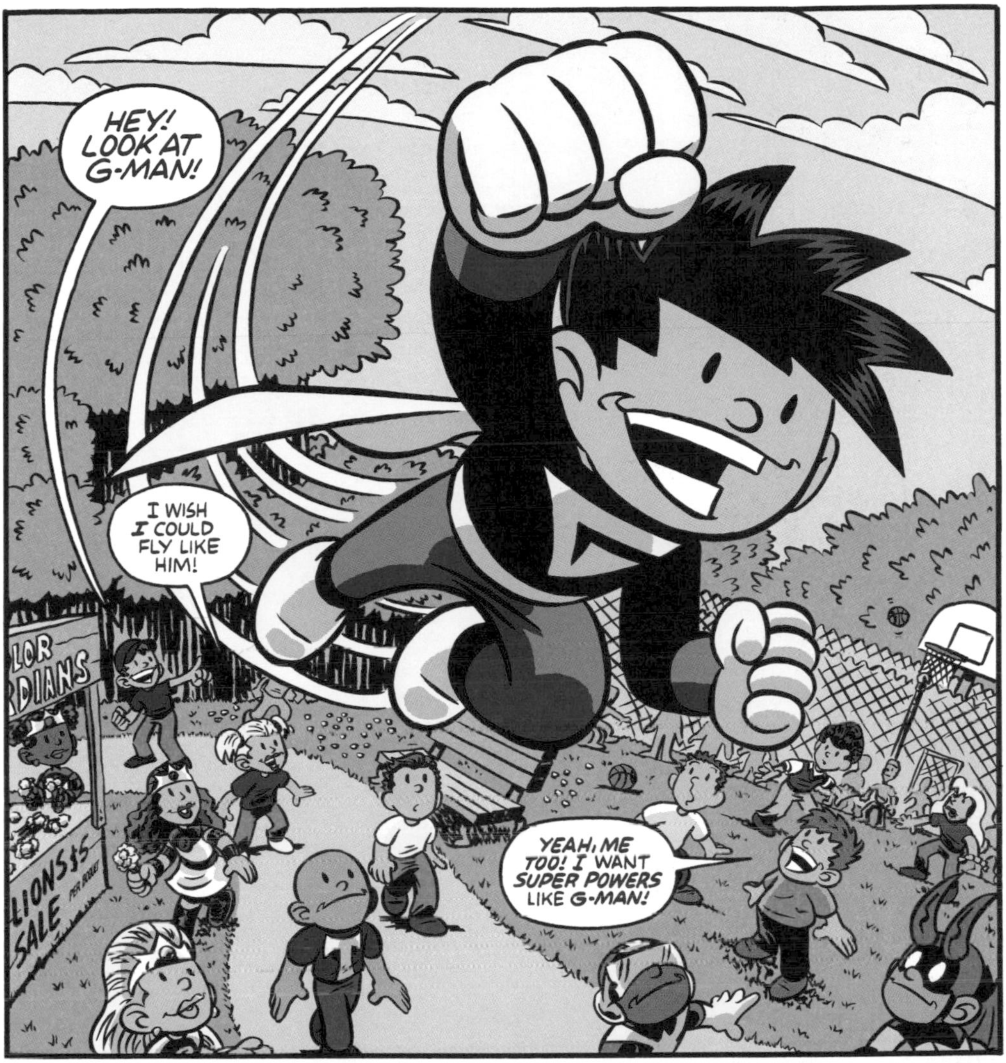
HEY! LOOK AT G-MAN!
I WISH I COULD FLY LIKE HIM!
YEAH, ME TOO! I WANT SUPER POWERS LIKE G-MAN!
LIONS $5 SALE PER BOQUET
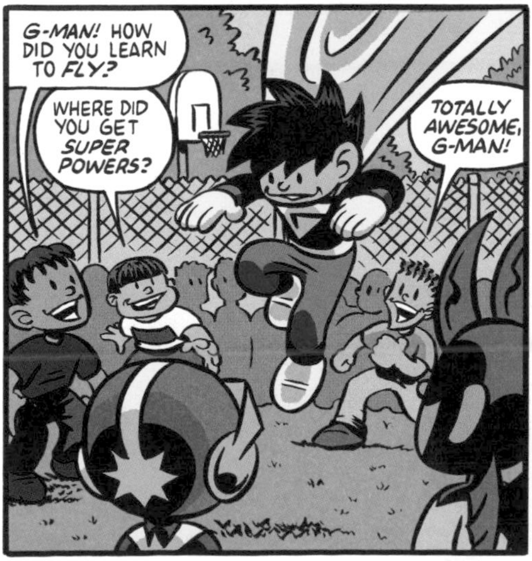
G-MAN! HOW DID YOU LEARN TO FLY?
WHERE DID YOU GET SUPER POWERS?
TOTALLY AWESOME, G-MAN!
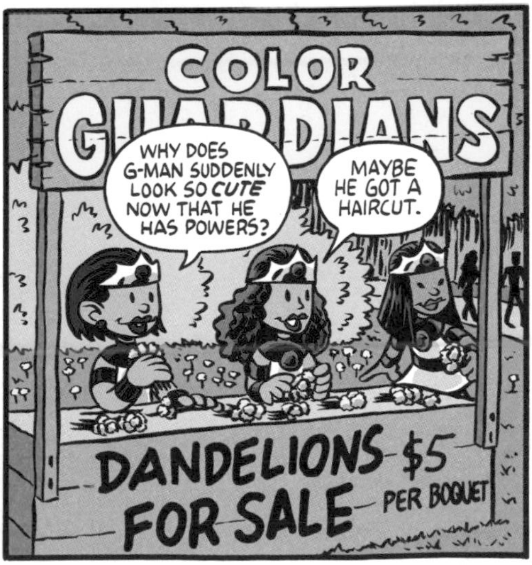
COLOR GUARDIANS
WHY DOES G-MAN SUDDENLY LOOK SO CUTE NOW THAT HE HAS POWERS?
MAYBE HE GOT A HAIRCUT.
DANDELIONS $5
FOR SALE PER BOQUET

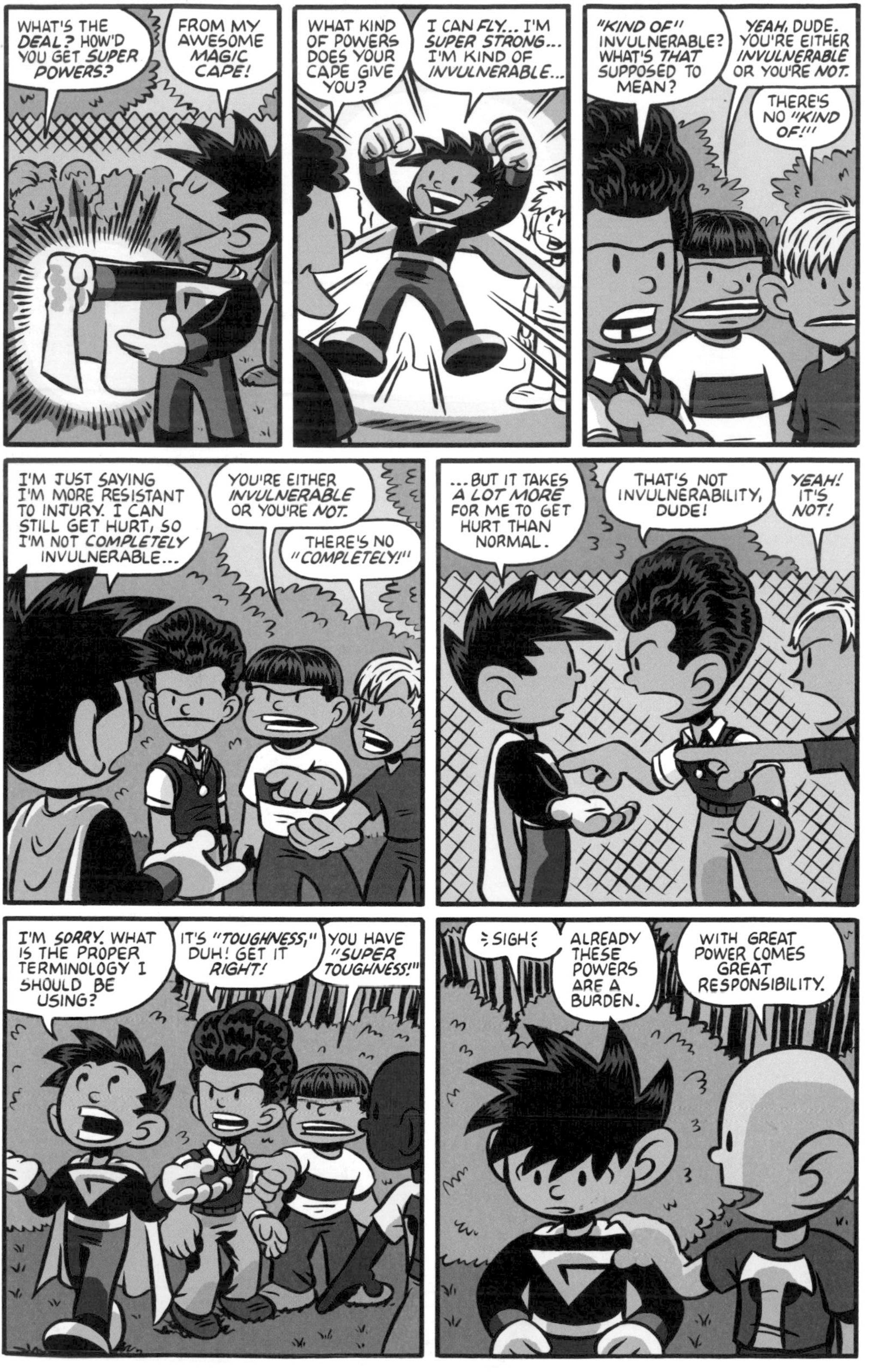

WHAT'S THE DEAL? HOW'D YOU GET SUPER POWERS?
FROM MY AWESOME MAGIC CAPE!
WHAT KIND OF POWERS DOES YOUR CAPE GIVE YOU?
I CAN FLY... I'M SUPER STRONG... I'M KIND OF INVULNERABLE...
"KIND OF" INVULNERABLE? WHAT'S THAT SUPPOSED TO MEAN?
YEAH, DUDE. YOU'RE EITHER INVULNERABLE OR YOU'RE NOT.
THERE'S NO "KIND OF!"
I'M JUST SAYING I'M MORE RESISTANT TO INJURY. I CAN STILL GET HURT, SO I'M NOT COMPLETELY INVULNERABLE...
YOU'RE EITHER INVULNERABLE OR YOU'RE NOT.
THERE'S NO "COMPLETELY!"
...BUT IT TAKES A LOT MORE FOR ME TO GET HURT THAN NORMAL.
THAT'S NOT INVULNERABILITY, DUDE!
YEAH! IT'S NOT!
I'M SORRY. WHAT IS THE PROPER TERMINOLOGY I SHOULD BE USING?
IT'S "TOUGHNESS," DUH! GET IT RIGHT!
YOU HAVE "SUPER TOUGHNESS!"
SIGH
ALREADY THESE POWERS ARE A BURDEN.
WITH GREAT POWER COMES GREAT RESPONSIBILITY.

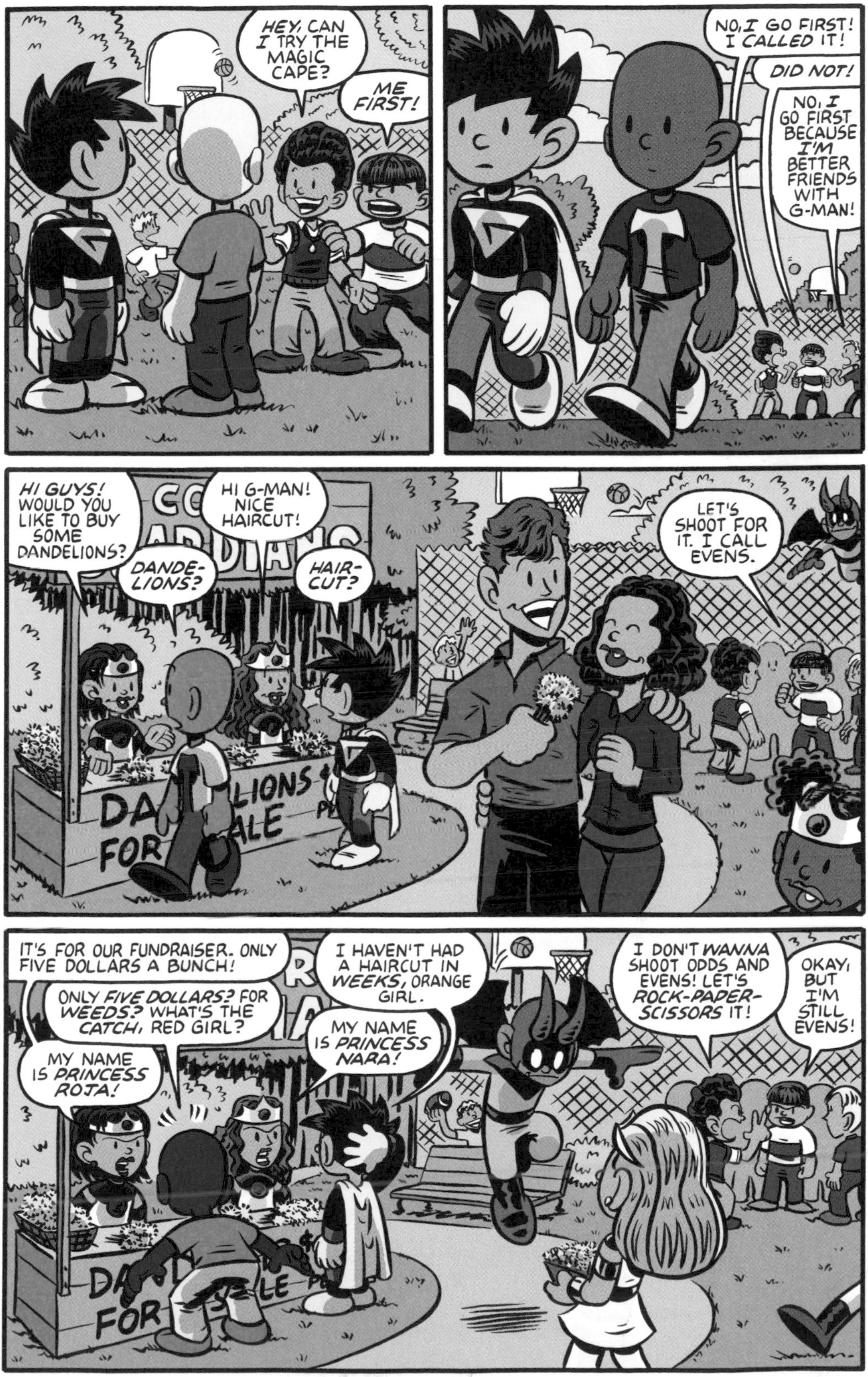
HEY, CAN I TRY THE MAGIC CAPE?
ME FIRST!
NO, I GO FIRST! I CALLED IT!
DID NOT!
NO, I GO FIRST BECAUSE I'M BETTER FRIENDS WITH G-MAN!
HI GUYS! WOULD YOU LIKE TO BUY SOME DANDELIONS?
HI G-MAN! NICE HAIRCUT!
DANDE-LIONS?
HAIR-CUT?
LET'S SHOOT FOR IT. I CALL EVENS.
IT'S FOR OUR FUNDRAISER. ONLY FIVE DOLLARS A BUNCH!
ONLY FIVE DOLLARS? FOR WEEDS? WHAT'S THE CATCH, RED GIRL?
MY NAME IS PRINCESS ROJA!
I HAVEN'T HAD A HAIRCUT IN WEEKS, ORANGE GIRL.
MY NAME IS PRINCESS NARA!
I DON'T WANNA SHOOT ODDS AND EVENS! LET'S ROCK-PAPER-SCISSORS IT!
OKAY, BUT I'M STILL EVENS!

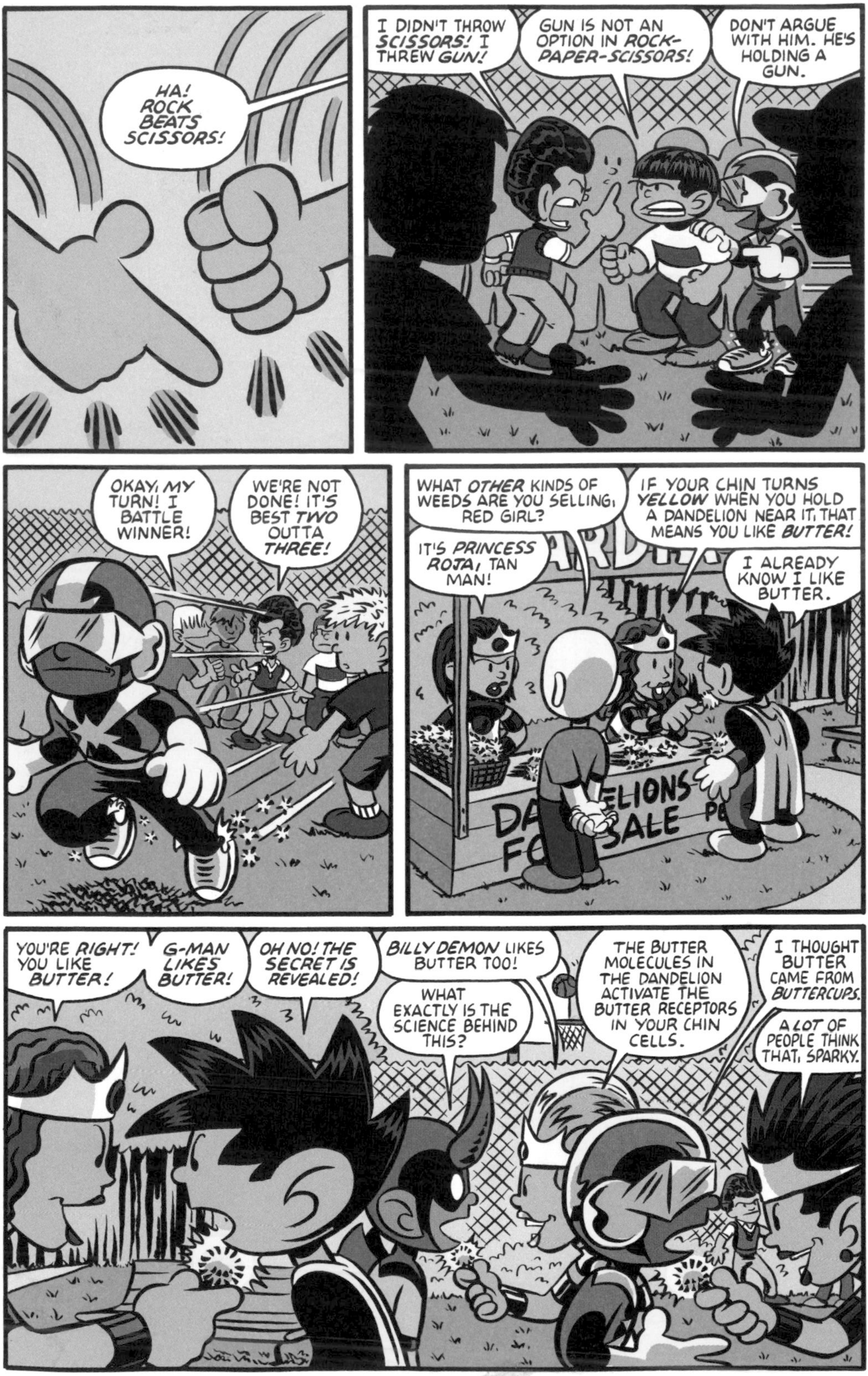
HA! ROCK BEATS SCISSORS!
I DIDN'T THROW SCISSORS! I THREW GUN!
GUN IS NOT AN OPTION IN ROCK-PAPER-SCISSORS!
DON'T ARGUE WITH HIM. HE'S HOLDING A GUN.
OKAY, MY TURN! I BATTLE WINNER!
WE'RE NOT DONE! IT'S BEST TWO OUTTA THREE!
WHAT OTHER KINDS OF WEEDS ARE YOU SELLING, RED GIRL?
IT'S PRINCESS ROJA, TAN MAN!
IF YOUR CHIN TURNS YELLOW WHEN YOU HOLD A DANDELION NEAR IT, THAT MEANS YOU LIKE BUTTER!
I ALREADY KNOW I LIKE BUTTER.
YOU'RE RIGHT! YOU LIKE BUTTER!
G-MAN LIKES BUTTER!
OH NO! THE SECRET IS REVEALED!
BILLY DEMON LIKES BUTTER TOO!
WHAT EXACTLY IS THE SCIENCE BEHIND THIS?
THE BUTTER MOLECULES IN THE DANDELION ACTIVATE THE BUTTER RECEPTORS IN YOUR CHIN CELLS.
I THOUGHT BUTTER CAME FROM BUTTERCUPS.
A LOT OF PEOPLE THINK THAT, SPARKY.

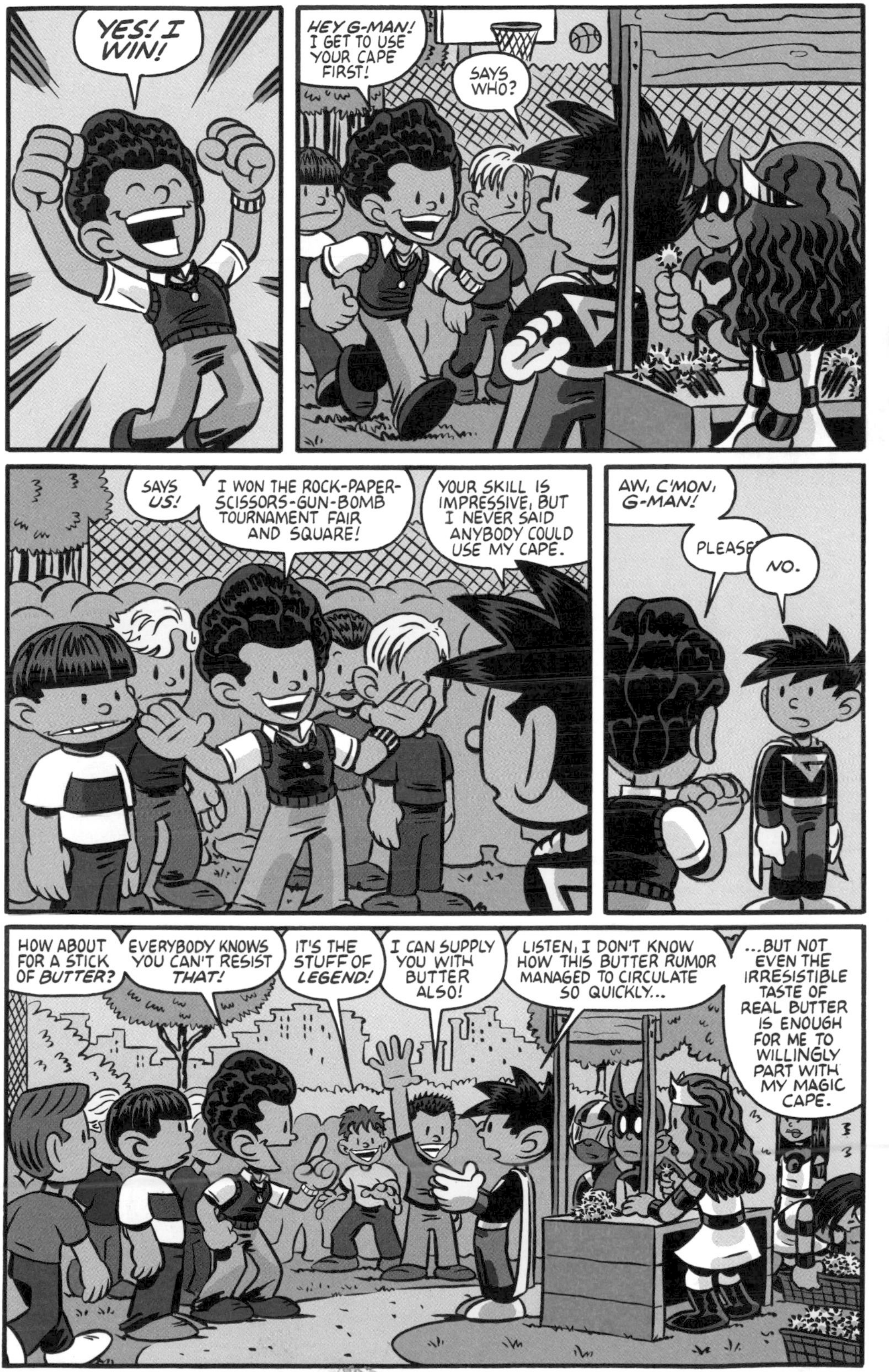
YES! I WIN!
HEY G-MAN! I GET TO USE YOUR CAPE FIRST!
SAYS WHO?
SAYS US!
I WON THE ROCK-PAPER-SCISSORS-GUN-BOMB TOURNAMENT FAIR AND SQUARE!
YOUR SKILL IS IMPRESSIVE, BUT I NEVER SAID ANYBODY COULD USE MY CAPE.
AW, C'MON, G-MAN!
PLEASE
NO.
HOW ABOUT FOR A STICK OF BUTTER?
EVERYBODY KNOWS YOU CAN'T RESIST THAT!
IT'S THE STUFF OF LEGEND!
I CAN SUPPLY YOU WITH BUTTER ALSO!
LISTEN, I DON'T KNOW HOW THIS BUTTER RUMOR MANAGED TO CIRCULATE SO QUICKLY...
...BUT NOT EVEN THE IRRESISTIBLE TASTE OF REAL BUTTER IS ENOUGH FOR ME TO WILLINGLY PART WITH MY MAGIC CAPE.

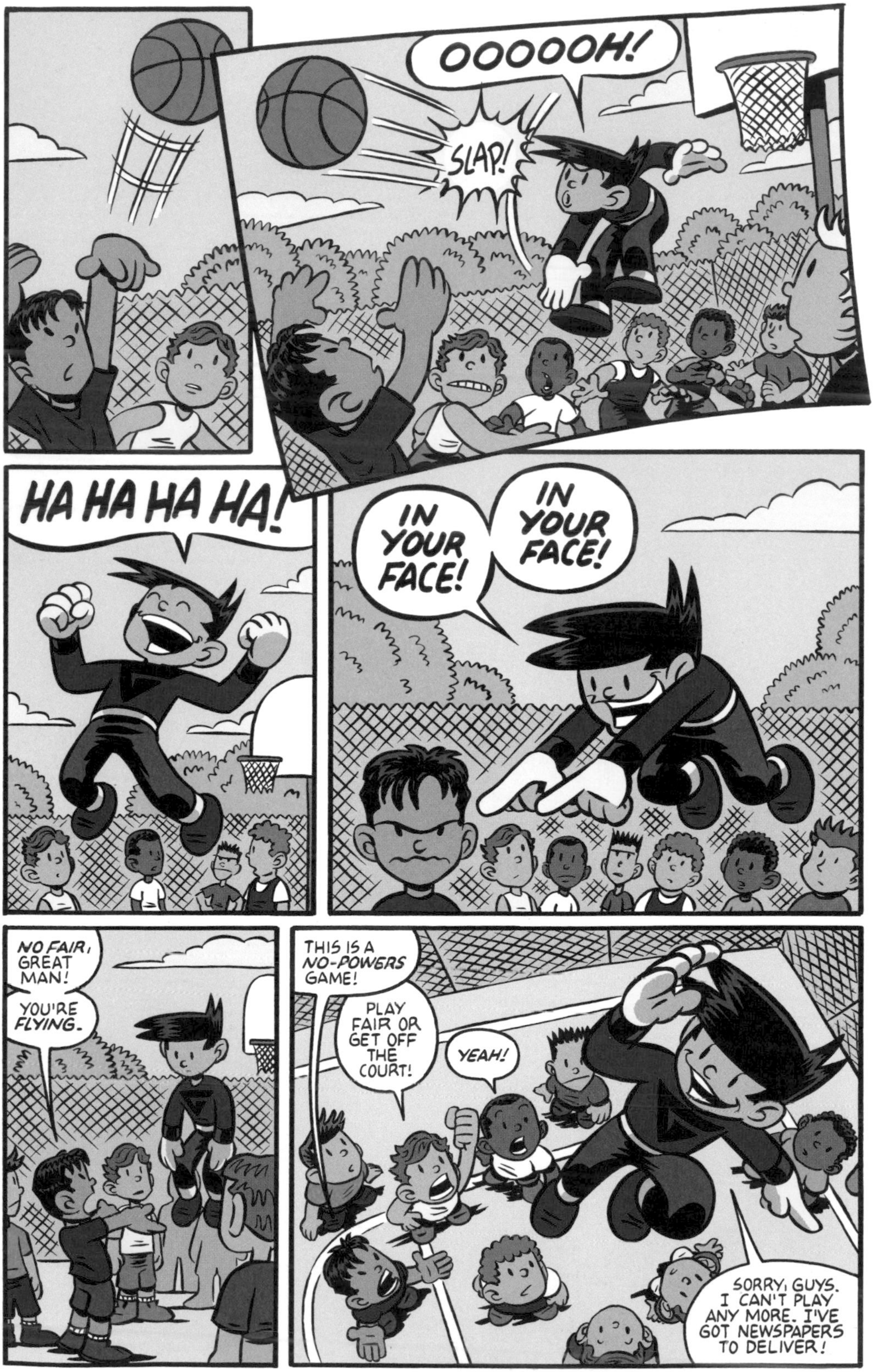
OOOOOH!
SLAP!
HA HA HA HA!
IN YOUR FACE!
IN YOUR FACE!
NO FAIR, GREAT MAN!
YOU'RE FLYING.
THIS IS A NO-POWERS GAME!
PLAY FAIR OR GET OFF THE COURT!
YEAH!
SORRY, GUYS. I CAN'T PLAY ANY MORE. I'VE GOT NEWSPAPERS TO DELIVER!

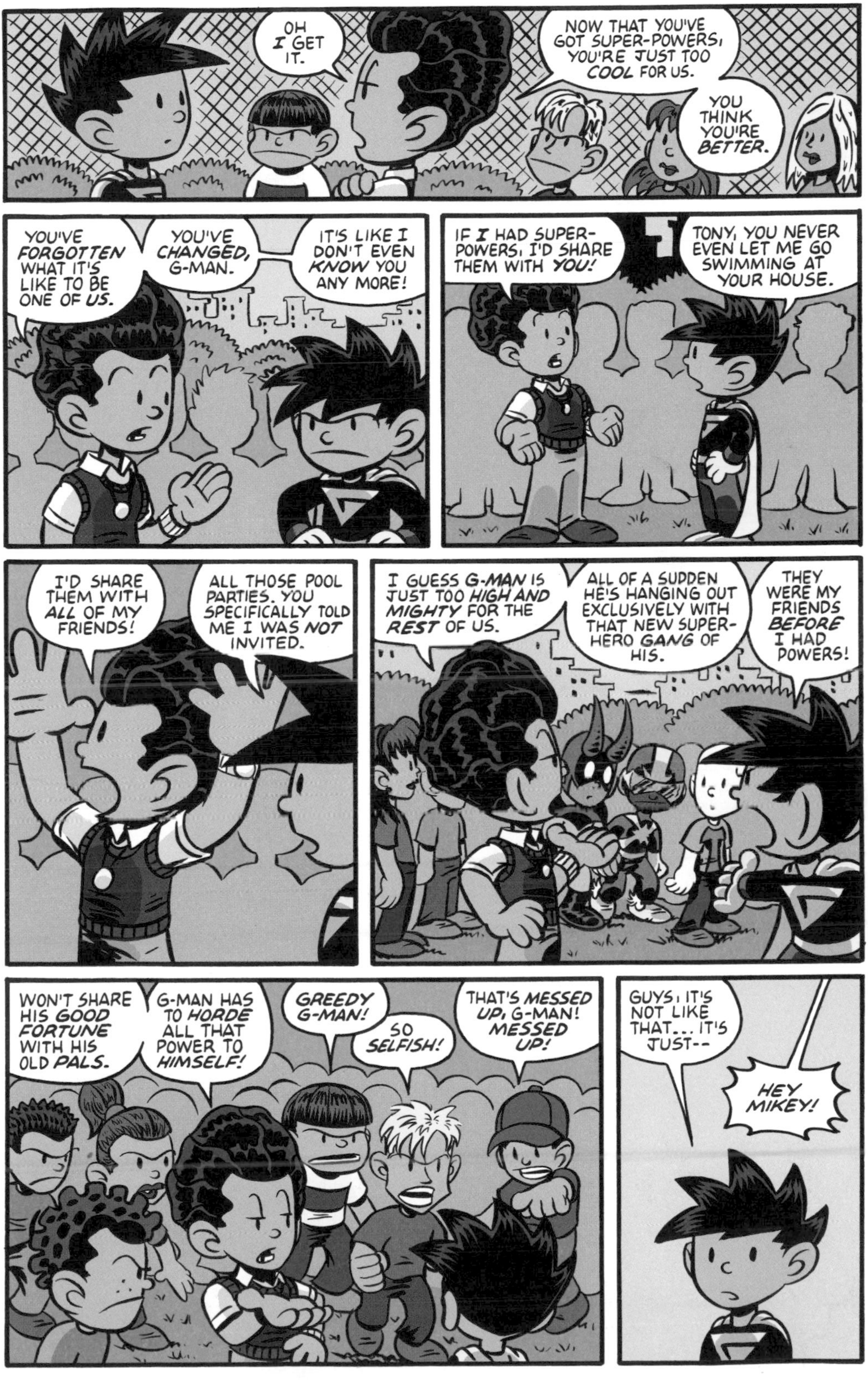
OH I GET IT.
NOW THAT YOU'VE GOT SUPER-POWERS, YOU'RE JUST TOO COOL FOR US.
YOU THINK YOU'RE BETTER.
YOU'VE FORGOTTEN WHAT IT'S LIKE TO BE ONE OF US.
YOU'VE CHANGED, G-MAN.
IT'S LIKE I DON'T EVEN KNOW YOU ANY MORE!
IF I HAD SUPER-POWERS, I'D SHARE THEM WITH YOU!
TONY, YOU NEVER EVEN LET ME GO SWIMMING AT YOUR HOUSE.
I'D SHARE THEM WITH ALL OF MY FRIENDS!
ALL THOSE POOL PARTIES. YOU SPECIFICALLY TOLD ME I WAS NOT INVITED.
I GUESS G-MAN IS JUST TOO HIGH AND MIGHTY FOR THE REST OF US.
ALL OF A SUDDEN HE'S HANGING OUT EXCLUSIVELY WITH THAT NEW SUPER-HERO GANG OF HIS.
THEY WERE MY FRIENDS BEFORE I HAD POWERS!
WON'T SHARE HIS GOOD FORTUNE WITH HIS OLD PALS.
G-MAN HAS TO HORDE ALL THAT POWER TO HIMSELF!
GREEDY G-MAN!
SO SELFISH!
THAT'S MESSED UP, G-MAN! MESSED UP!
GUYS, IT'S NOT LIKE THAT... IT'S JUST--
HEY MIKEY!

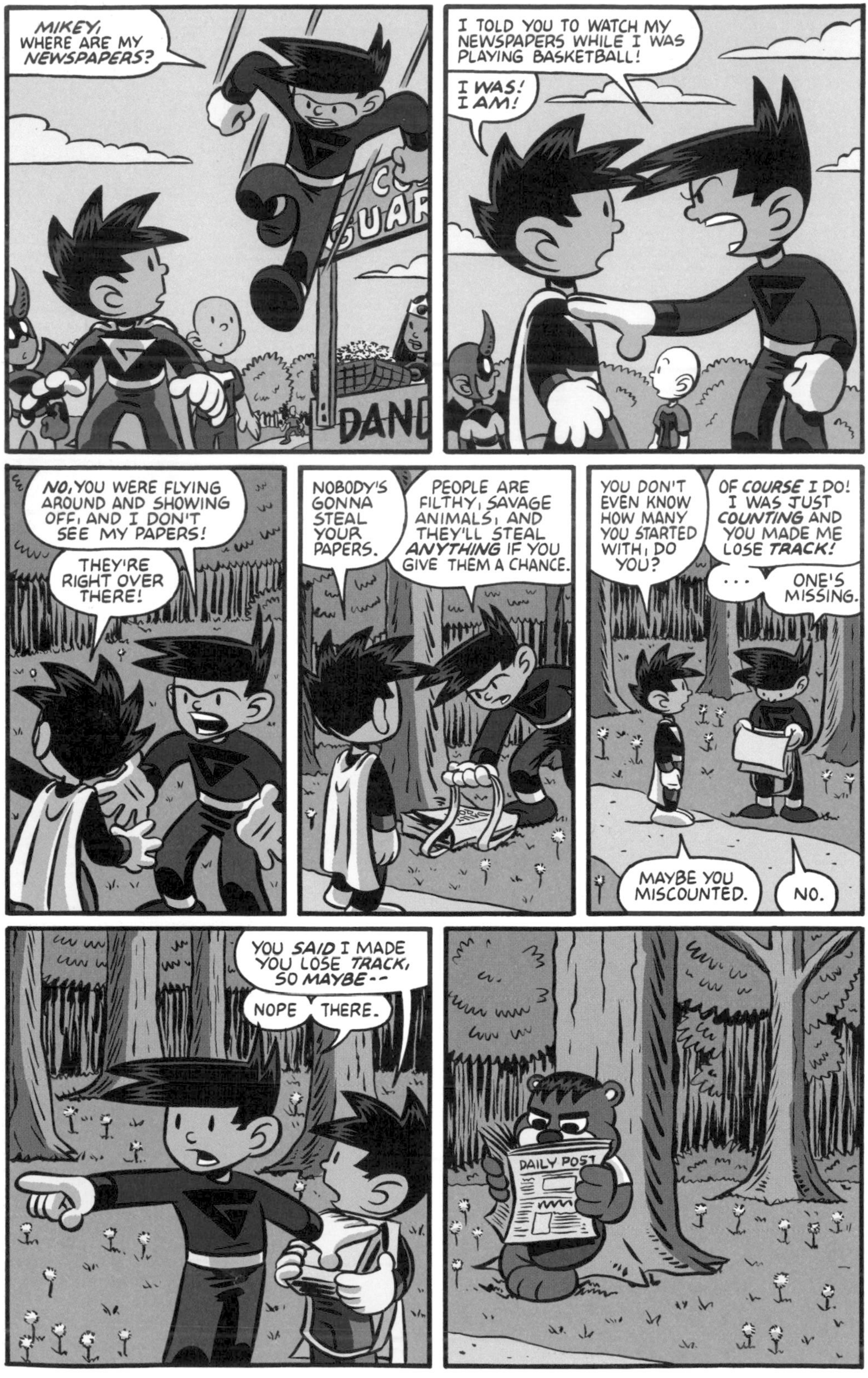
MIKEY, WHERE ARE MY NEWSPAPERS?
GUAR
DAN
I TOLD YOU TO WATCH MY NEWSPAPERS WHILE I WAS PLAYING BASKETBALL!
I WAS! I AM!
NO, YOU WERE FLYING AROUND AND SHOWING OFF, AND I DON'T SEE MY PAPERS!
THEY'RE RIGHT OVER THERE!
NOBODY'S GONNA STEAL YOUR PAPERS.
PEOPLE ARE FILTHY, SAVAGE ANIMALS, AND THEY'LL STEAL ANYTHING IF YOU GIVE THEM A CHANCE.
YOU DON'T EVEN KNOW HOW MANY YOU STARTED WITH, DO YOU?
OF COURSE I DO! I WAS JUST COUNTING AND YOU MADE ME LOSE TRACK!
. . .
ONE'S MISSING.
MAYBE YOU MISCOUNTED.
NO.
YOU SAID I MADE YOU LOSE TRACK, SO MAYBE--
NOPE
THERE.
DAILY POST

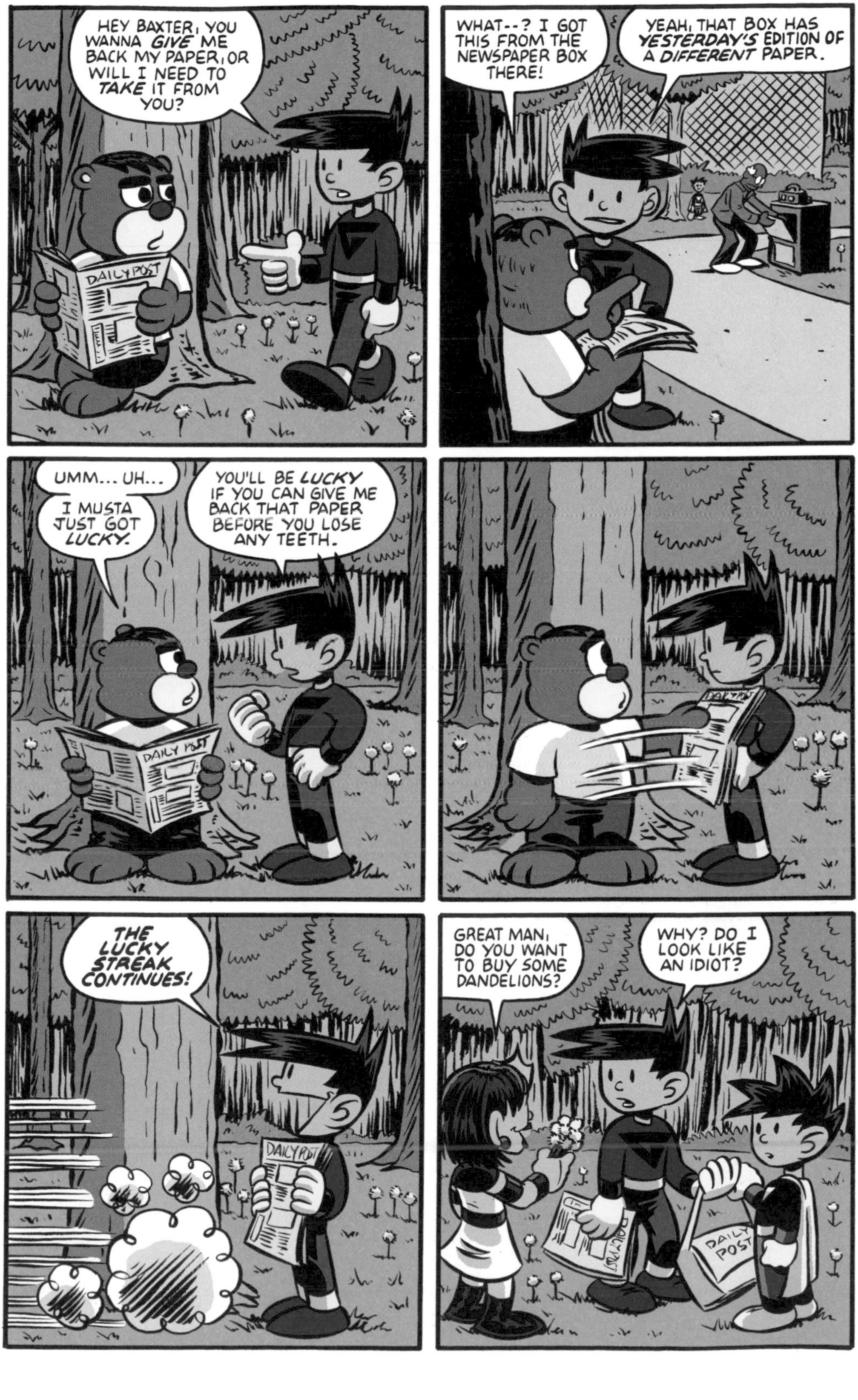
HEY BAXTER, YOU WANNA GIVE ME BACK MY PAPER, OR WILL I NEED TO TAKE IT FROM YOU?
DAILY POST
WHAT--? I GOT THIS FROM THE NEWSPAPER BOX THERE!
YEAH, THAT BOX HAS YESTERDAY'S EDITION OF A DIFFERENT PAPER.
UMM... UH...
I MUSTA JUST GOT LUCKY.
YOU'LL BE LUCKY IF YOU CAN GIVE ME BACK THAT PAPER BEFORE YOU LOSE ANY TEETH.
DAILY POST
THE LUCKY STREAK CONTINUES!
DAILY POST
GREAT MAN, DO YOU WANT TO BUY SOME DANDELIONS?
WHY? DO I LOOK LIKE AN IDIOT?
DAILY POST

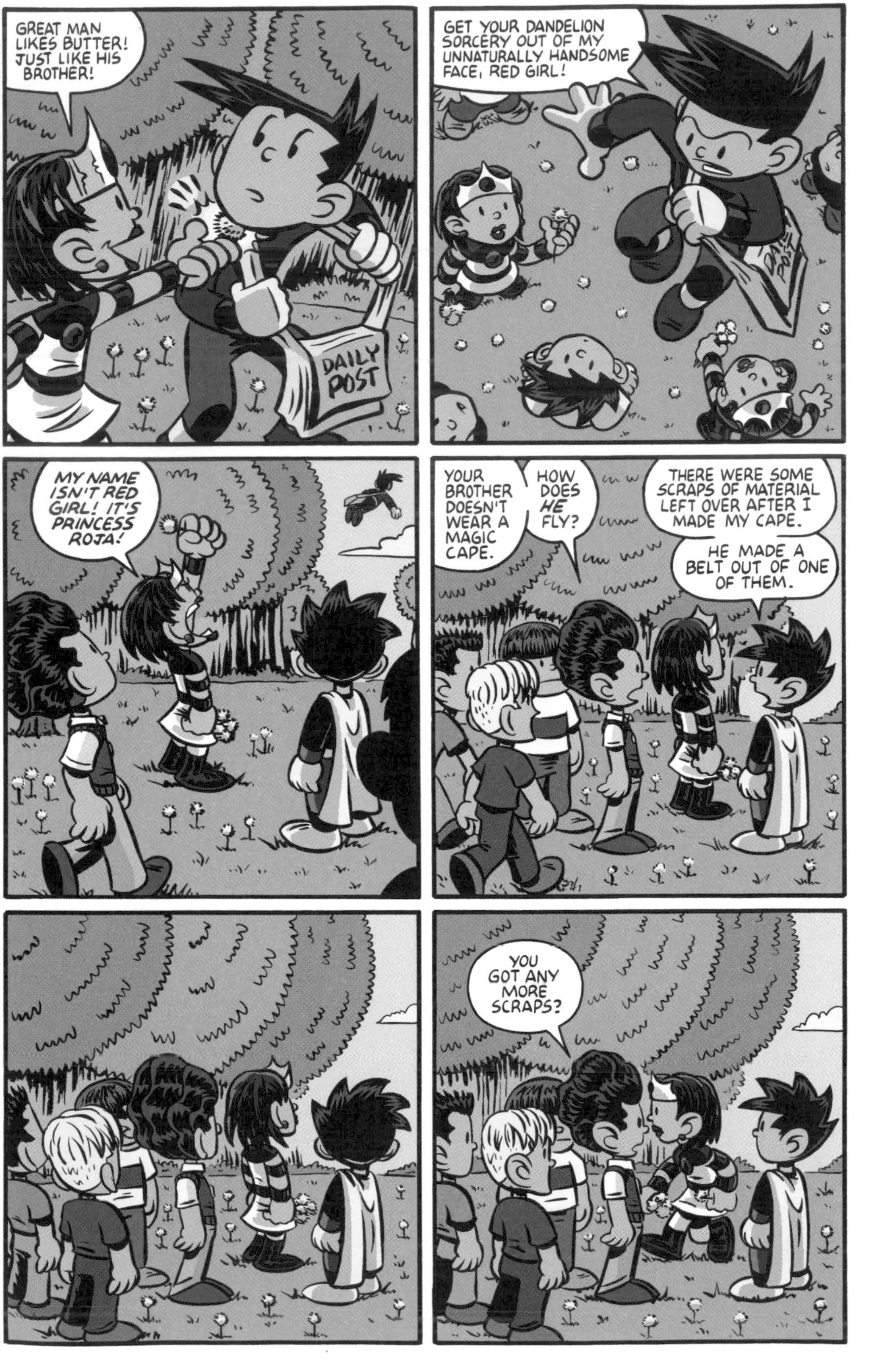
GREAT MAN LIKES BUTTER! JUST LIKE HIS BROTHER!
GET YOUR DANDELION SORCERY OUT OF MY UNNATURALLY HANDSOME FACE, RED GIRL!
DAILY POST
MY NAME ISN'T RED GIRL! IT'S PRINCESS ROJA!
YOUR BROTHER DOESN'T WEAR A MAGIC CAPE.
HOW DOES HE FLY?
THERE WERE SOME SCRAPS OF MATERIAL LEFT OVER AFTER I MADE MY CAPE.
HE MADE A BELT OUT OF ONE OF THEM.
YOU GOT ANY MORE SCRAPS?

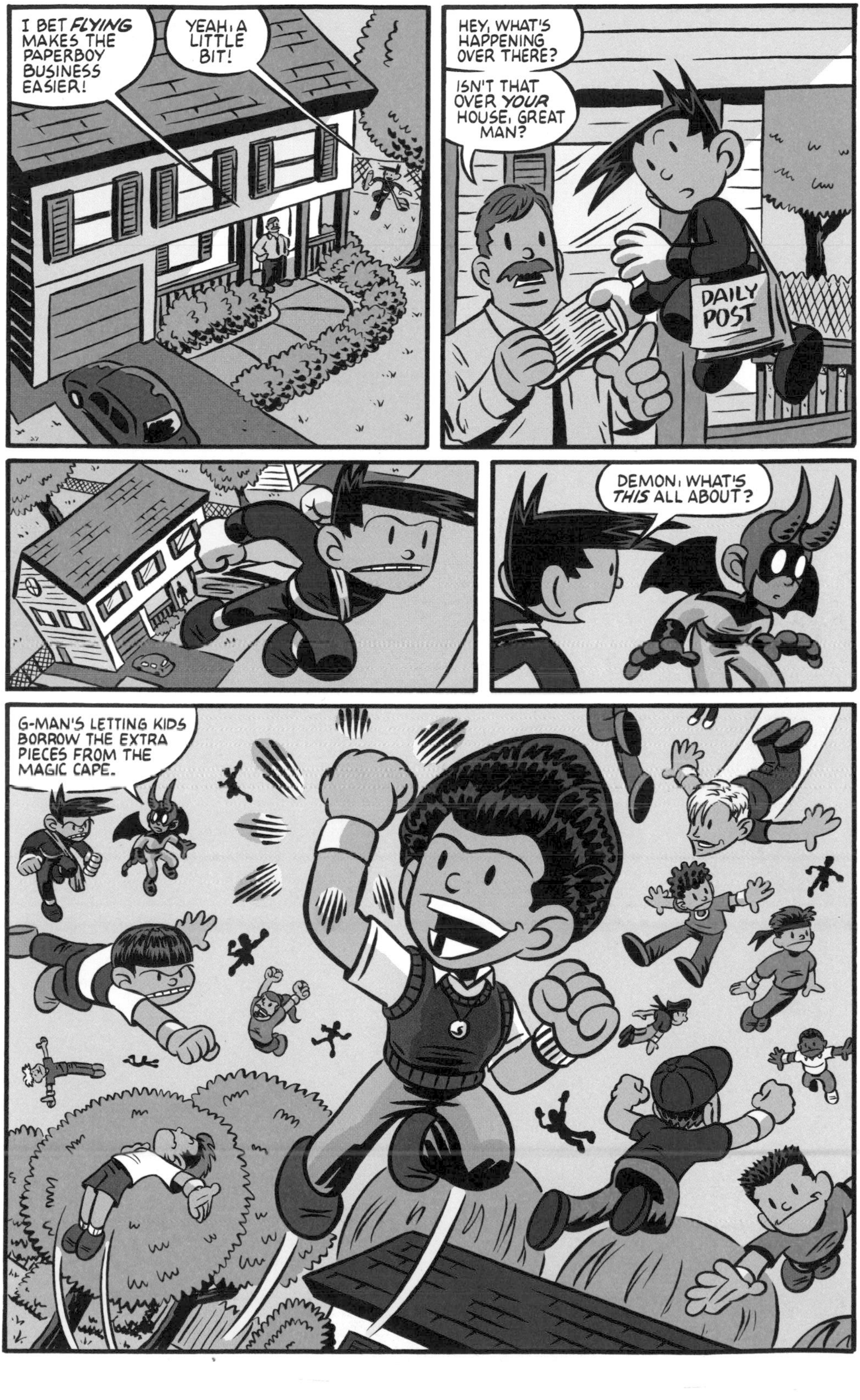
I BET *FLYING* MAKES THE PAPERBOY BUSINESS EASIER!
YEAH, A LITTLE BIT!
HEY, WHAT'S HAPPENING OVER THERE?
ISN'T THAT OVER *YOUR* HOUSE, GREAT MAN?
DAILY POST
DEMON, WHAT'S *THIS* ALL ABOUT?
G-MAN'S LETTING KIDS BORROW THE EXTRA PIECES FROM THE MAGIC CAPE.

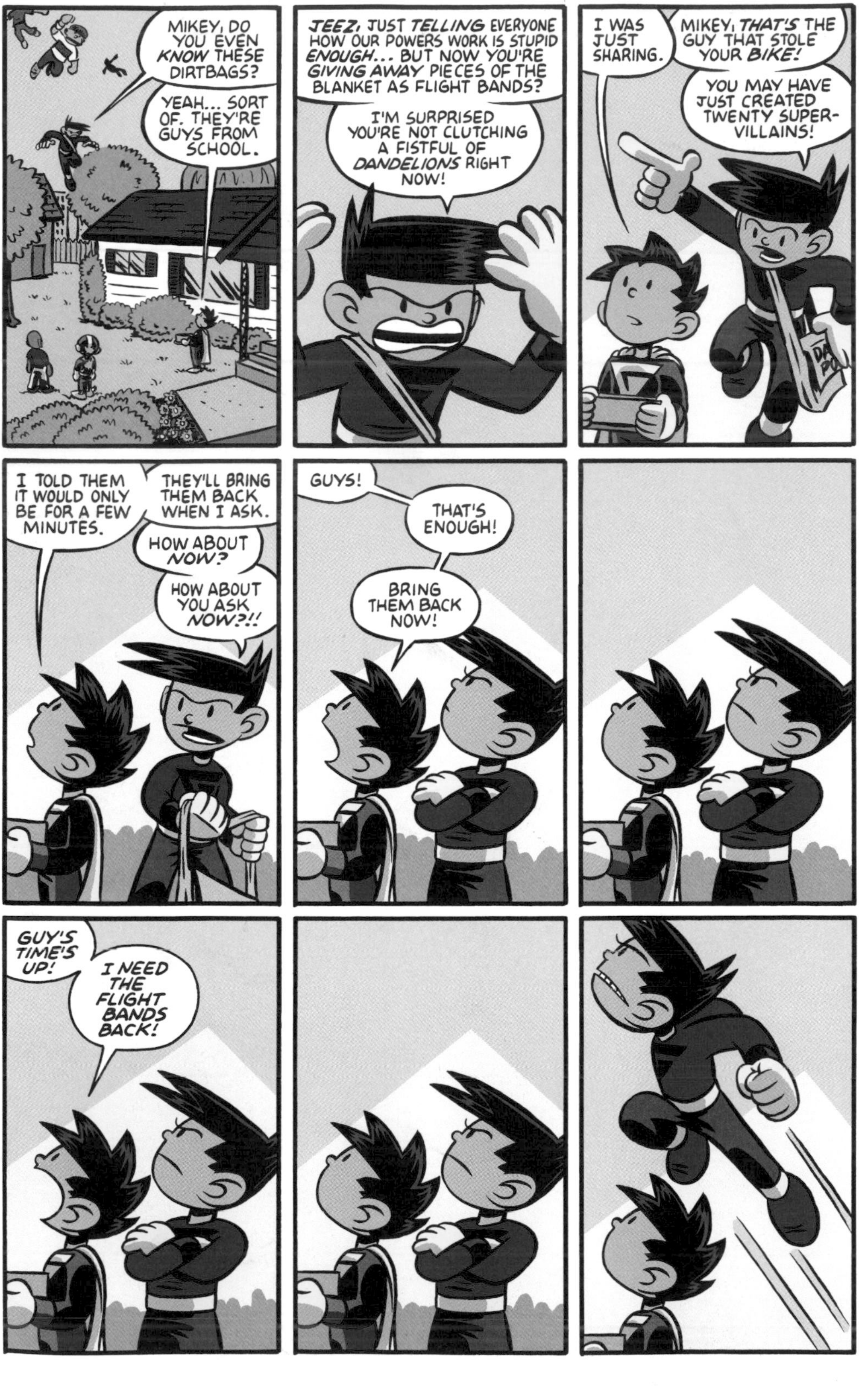
MIKEY, DO YOU EVEN KNOW THESE DIRTBAGS?
YEAH... SORT OF. THEY'RE GUYS FROM SCHOOL.
JEEZ, JUST TELLING EVERYONE HOW OUR POWERS WORK IS STUPID ENOUGH... BUT NOW YOU'RE GIVING AWAY PIECES OF THE BLANKET AS FLIGHT BANDS?
I'M SURPRISED YOU'RE NOT CLUTCHING A FISTFUL OF DANDELIONS RIGHT NOW!
I WAS JUST SHARING.
MIKEY, THAT'S THE GUY THAT STOLE YOUR BIKE!
YOU MAY HAVE JUST CREATED TWENTY SUPER-VILLAINS!
I TOLD THEM IT WOULD ONLY BE FOR A FEW MINUTES.
THEY'LL BRING THEM BACK WHEN I ASK.
HOW ABOUT NOW?
HOW ABOUT YOU ASK NOW?!!
GUYS!
THAT'S ENOUGH!
BRING THEM BACK NOW!
GUY'S TIME'S UP!
I NEED THE FLIGHT BANDS BACK!

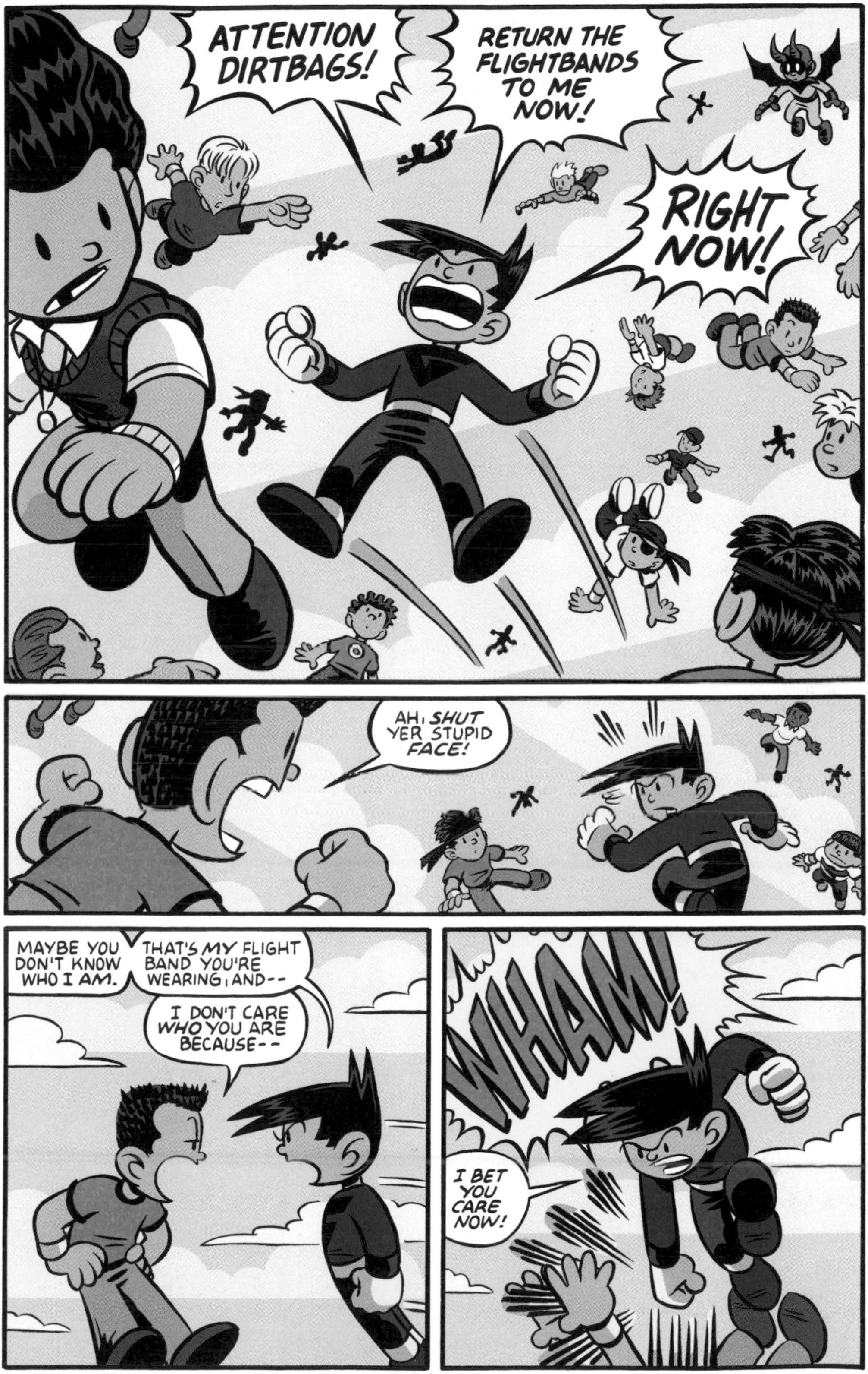
ATTENTION DIRTBAGS!
RETURN THE FLIGHTBANDS TO ME NOW!
RIGHT NOW!
AH, SHUT YER STUPID FACE!
MAYBE YOU DON'T KNOW WHO I AM.
THAT'S MY FLIGHT BAND YOU'RE WEARING, AND--
I DON'T CARE WHO YOU ARE BECAUSE--
WHAM!
I BET YOU CARE NOW!

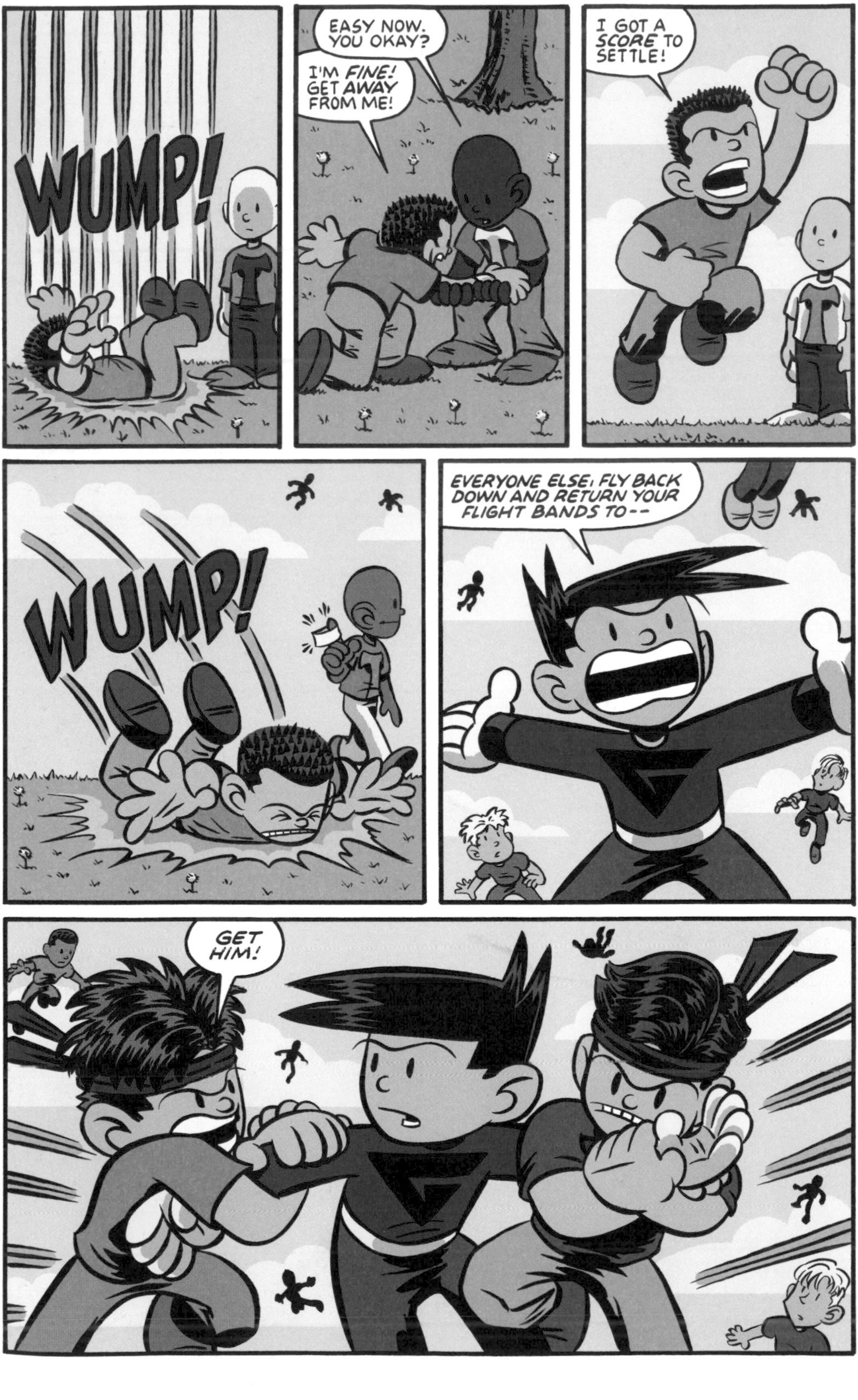
WUMP!
EASY NOW. YOU OKAY?
I'M FINE! GET AWAY FROM ME!
I GOT A SCORE TO SETTLE!
WUMP!
EVERYONE ELSE: FLY BACK DOWN AND RETURN YOUR FLIGHT BANDS TO--
GET HIM!

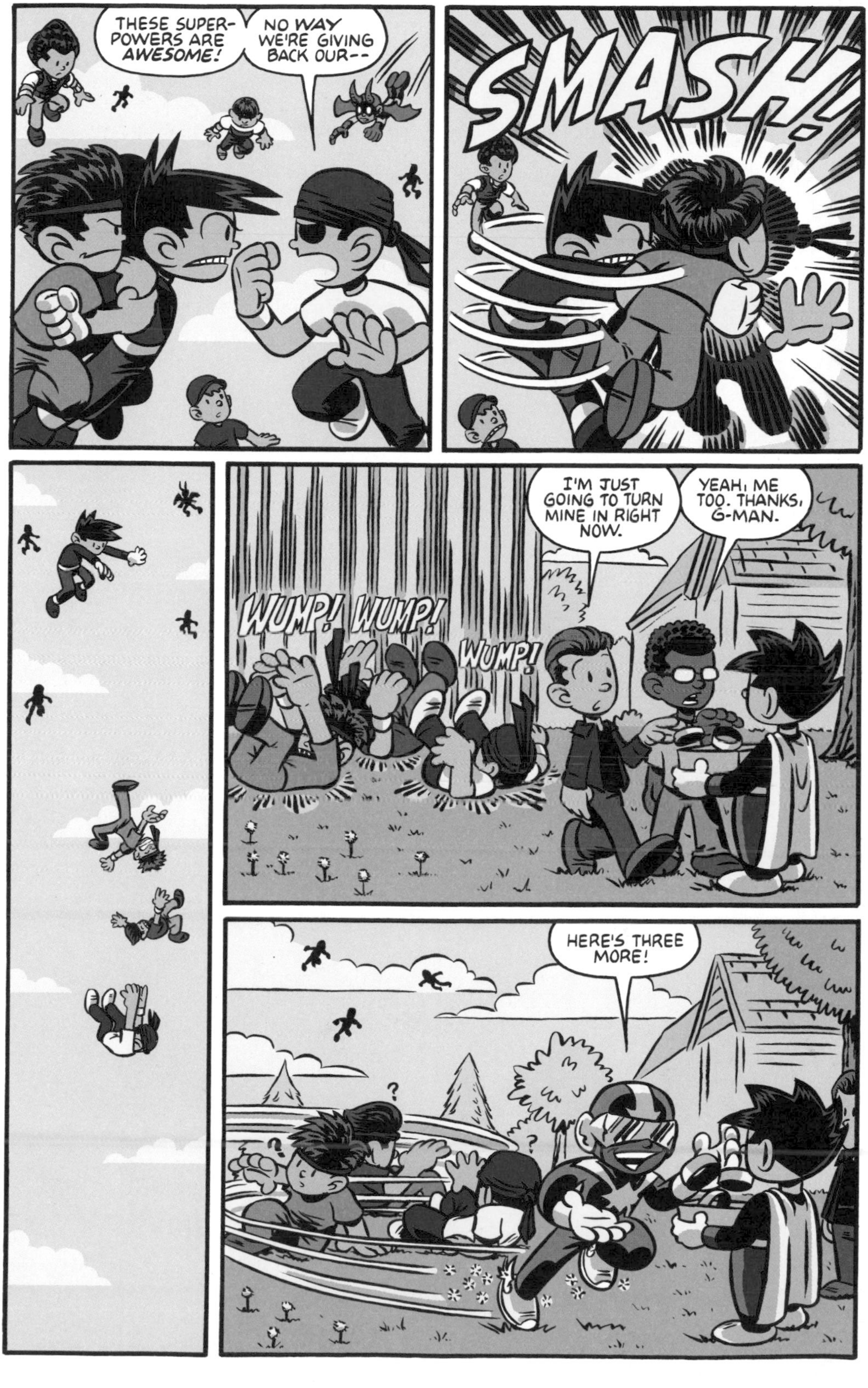
THESE SUPER-POWERS ARE AWESOME!
NO WAY WE'RE GIVING BACK OUR--
SMASH!
WUMP! WUMP!
WUMP!
I'M JUST GOING TO TURN MINE IN RIGHT NOW.
YEAH, ME TOO. THANKS, G-MAN.
HERE'S THREE MORE!

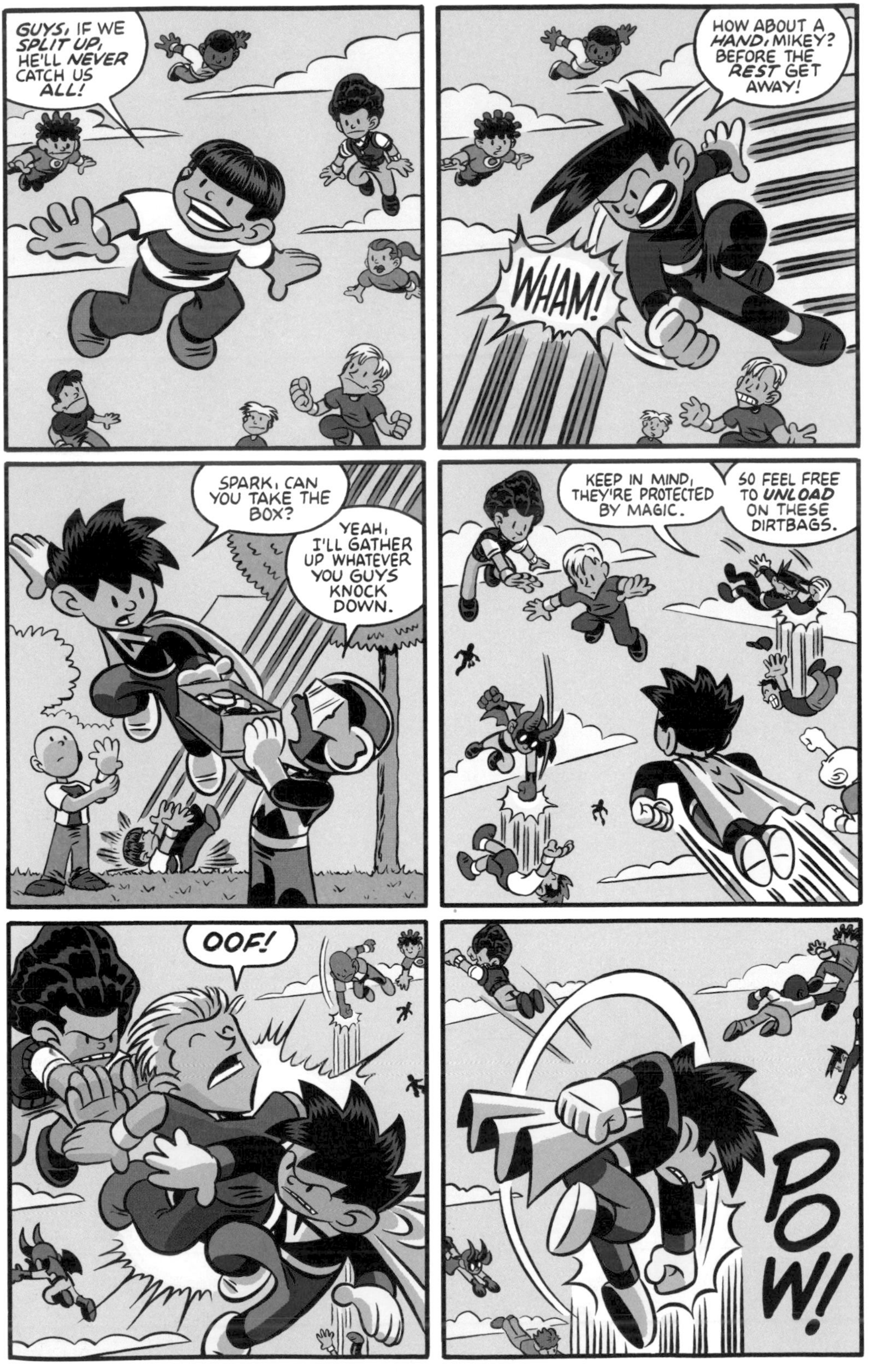
GUYS, IF WE SPLIT UP, HE'LL NEVER CATCH US ALL!
HOW ABOUT A HAND, MIKEY? BEFORE THE REST GET AWAY!
WHAM!
SPARK, CAN YOU TAKE THE BOX?
YEAH, I'LL GATHER UP WHATEVER YOU GUYS KNOCK DOWN.
KEEP IN MIND, THEY'RE PROTECTED BY MAGIC.
SO FEEL FREE TO UNLOAD ON THESE DIRTBAGS.
OOF!
POW!

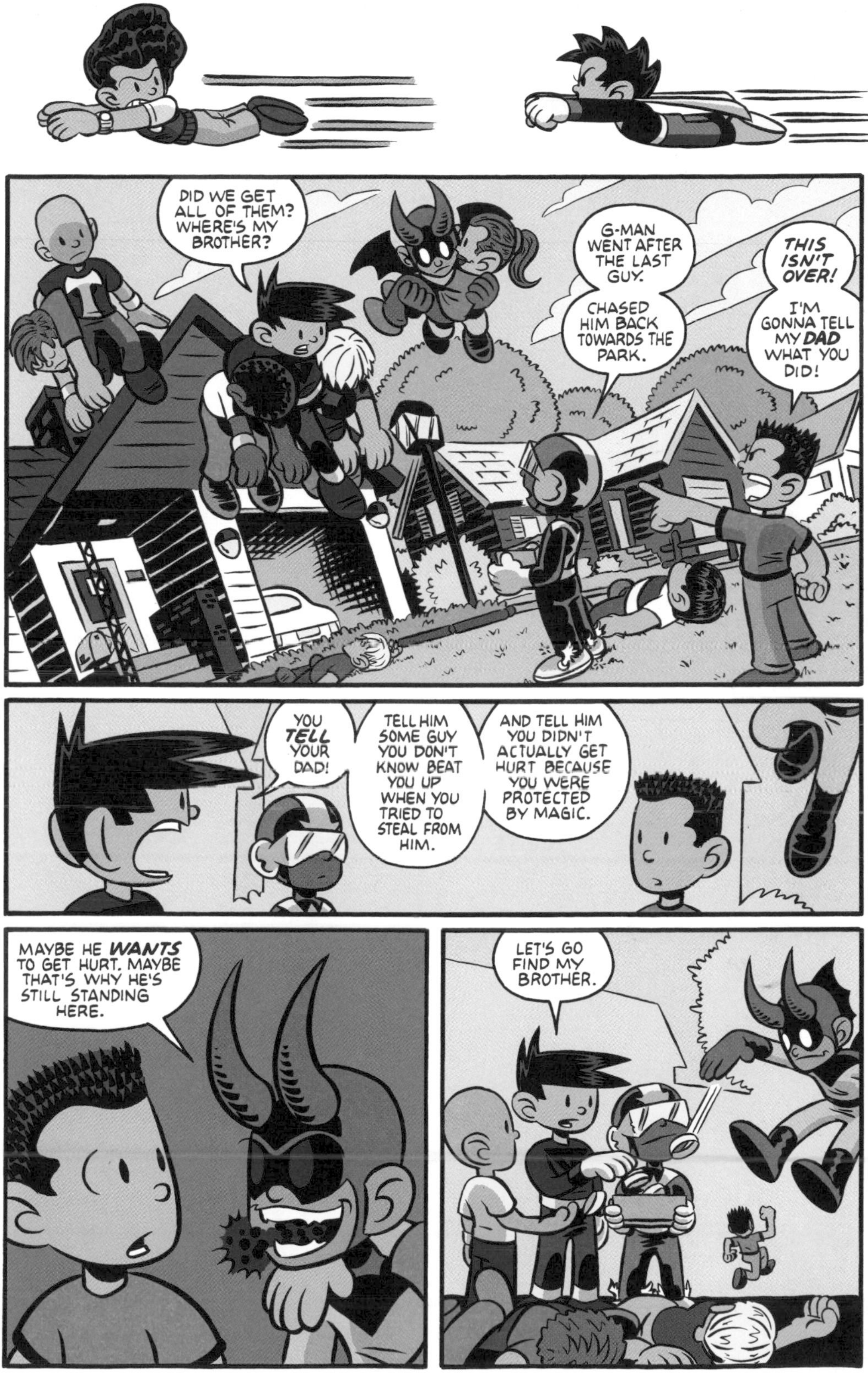
DID WE GET ALL OF THEM? WHERE'S MY BROTHER?
G-MAN WENT AFTER THE LAST GUY.
CHASED HIM BACK TOWARDS THE PARK.
THIS ISN'T OVER!
I'M GONNA TELL MY DAD WHAT YOU DID!
YOU TELL YOUR DAD!
TELL HIM SOME GUY YOU DON'T KNOW BEAT YOU UP WHEN YOU TRIED TO STEAL FROM HIM.
AND TELL HIM YOU DIDN'T ACTUALLY GET HURT BECAUSE YOU WERE PROTECTED BY MAGIC.
MAYBE HE WANTS TO GET HURT. MAYBE THAT'S WHY HE'S STILL STANDING HERE.
LET'S GO FIND MY BROTHER.

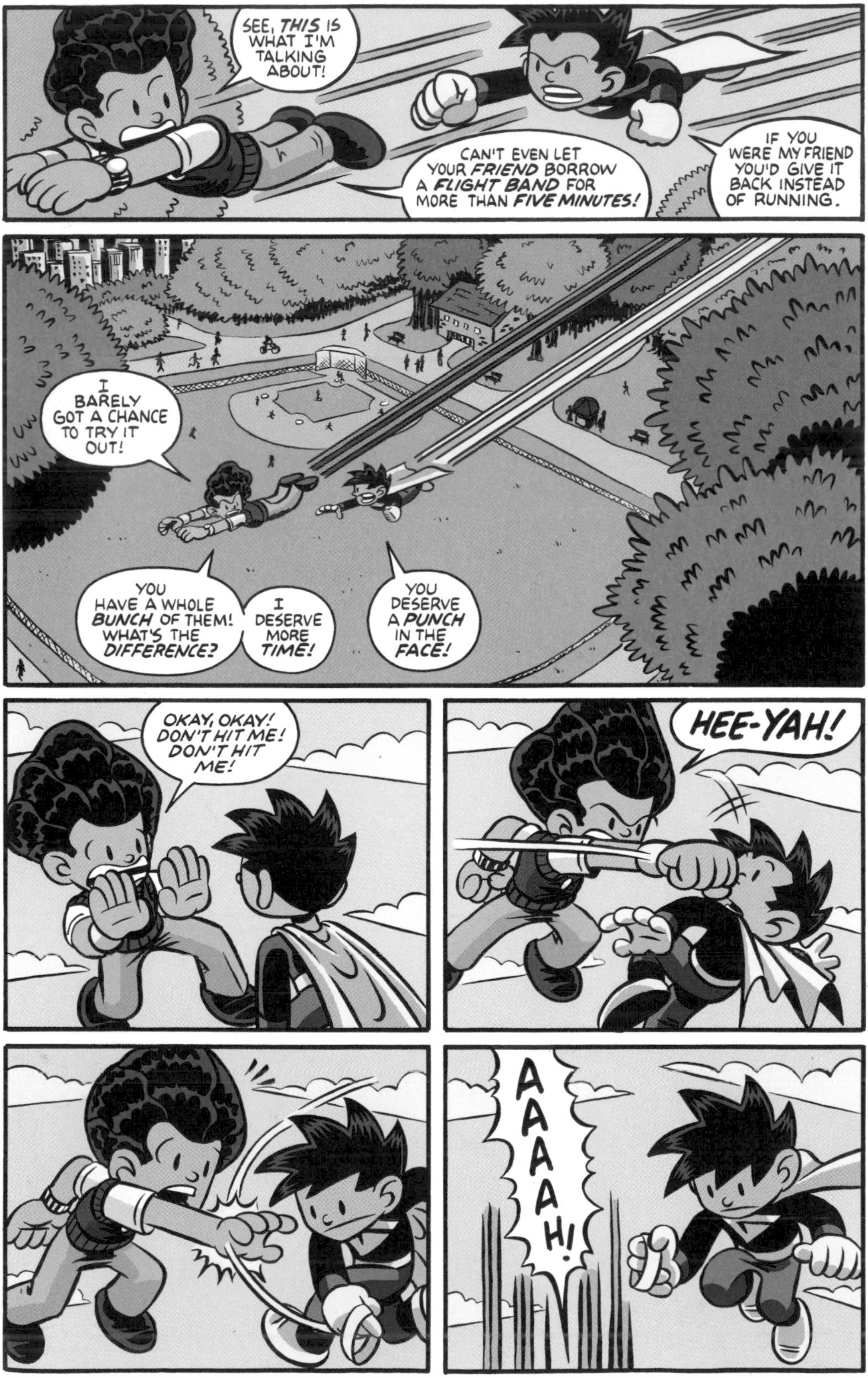
SEE, *THIS* IS WHAT I'M TALKING ABOUT!
CAN'T EVEN LET YOUR *FRIEND* BORROW A *FLIGHT BAND* FOR MORE THAN *FIVE MINUTES!*
IF YOU WERE MY FRIEND YOU'D GIVE IT BACK INSTEAD OF RUNNING.
I BARELY GOT A CHANCE TO TRY IT OUT!
YOU HAVE A WHOLE *BUNCH* OF THEM! WHAT'S THE *DIFFERENCE?*
I DESERVE MORE *TIME!*
YOU DESERVE A *PUNCH* IN THE *FACE!*
OKAY, OKAY! DON'T HIT ME! DON'T HIT ME!
HEE-YAH!
AAAAAH!

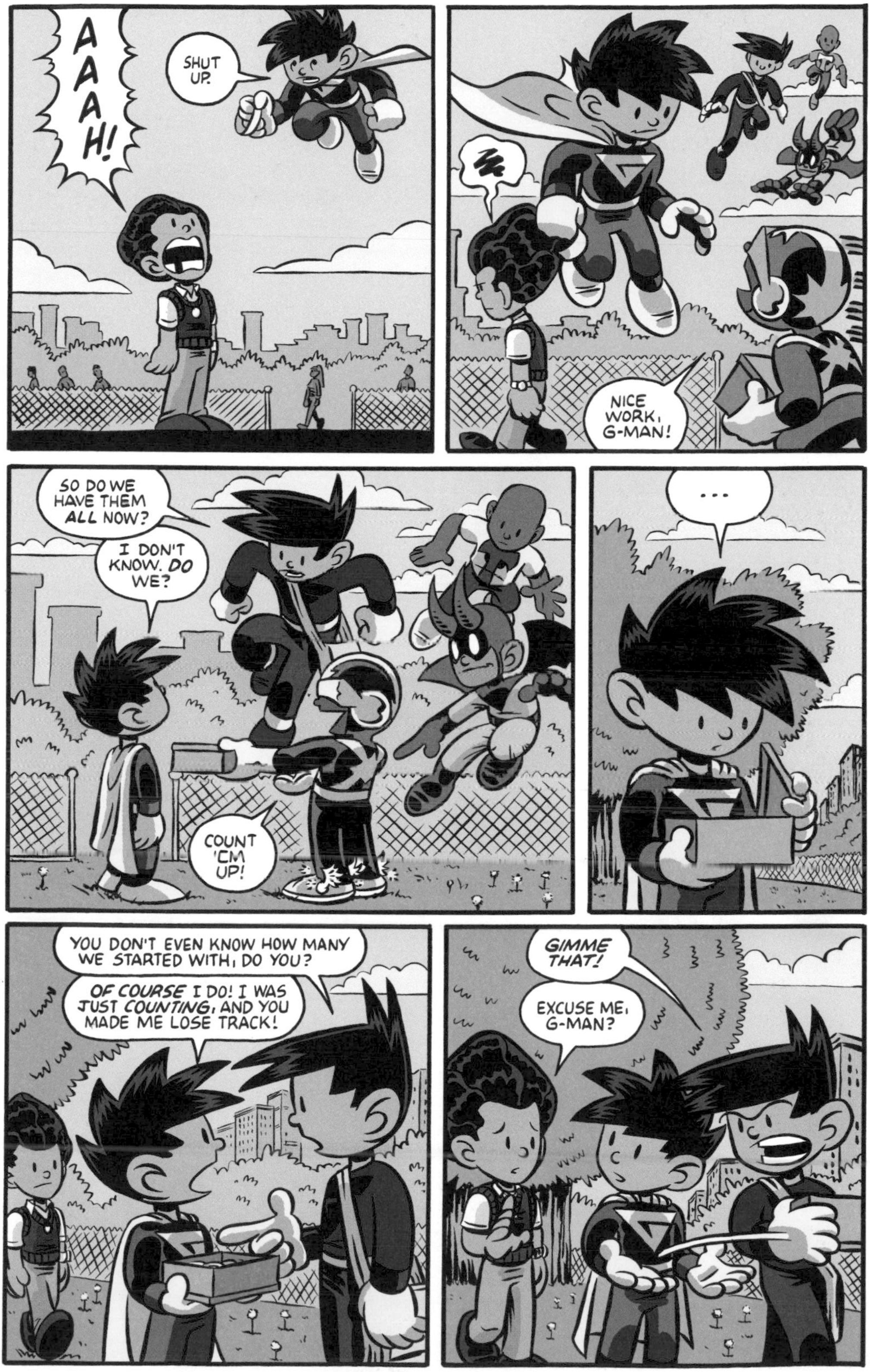
AAAAH!
SHUT UP.
NICE WORK, G-MAN!
SO DO WE HAVE THEM ALL NOW?
I DON'T KNOW. DO WE?
COUNT 'EM UP!
...
YOU DON'T EVEN KNOW HOW MANY WE STARTED WITH, DO YOU?
OF COURSE I DO! I WAS JUST COUNTING, AND YOU MADE ME LOSE TRACK!
GIMME THAT!
EXCUSE ME, G-MAN?

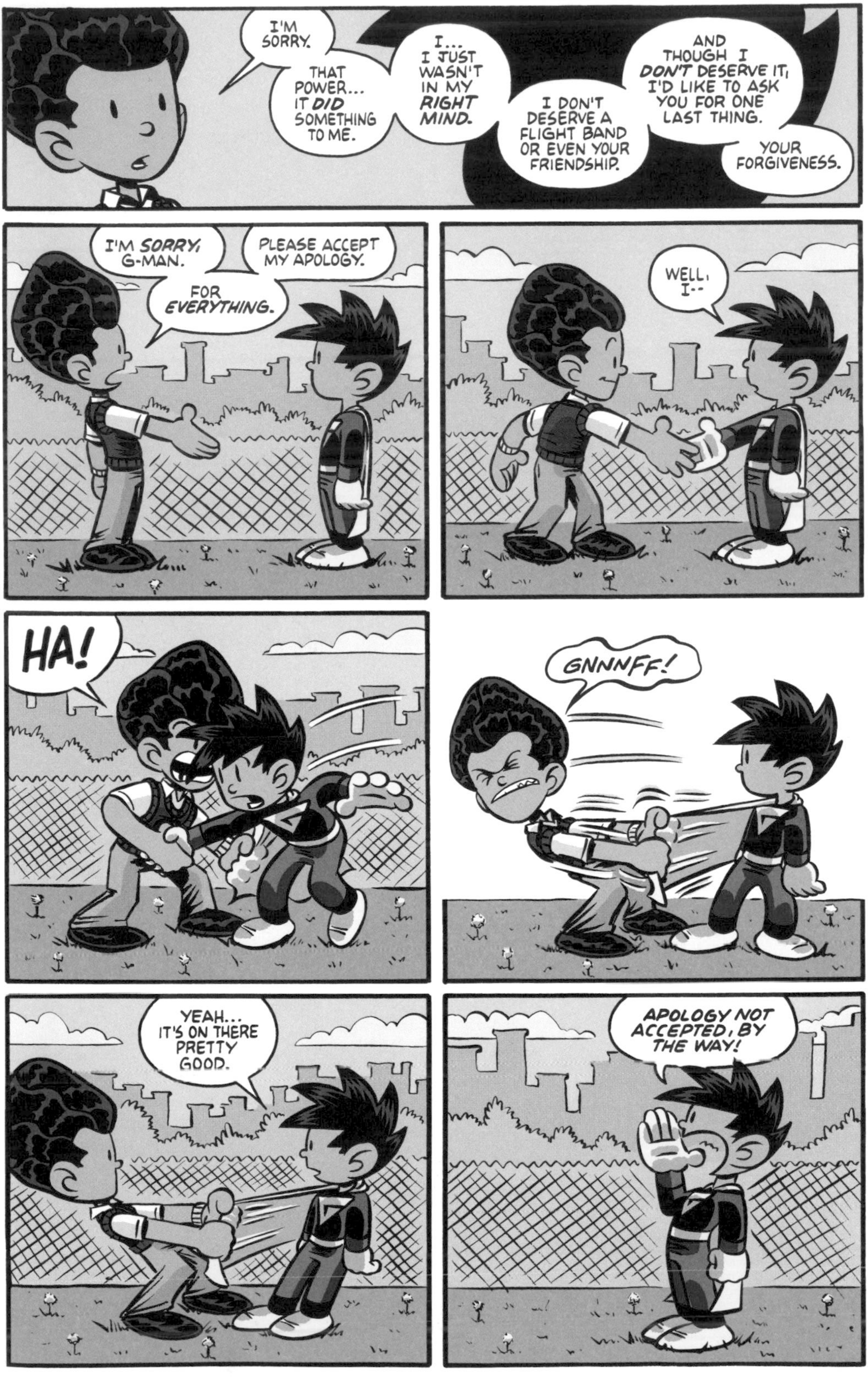
I'M SORRY.
THAT POWER... IT *DID* SOMETHING TO ME.
I... I JUST WASN'T IN MY *RIGHT MIND.*
I DON'T DESERVE A FLIGHT BAND OR EVEN YOUR FRIENDSHIP.
AND THOUGH I *DON'T* DESERVE IT, I'D LIKE TO ASK YOU FOR ONE LAST THING.
YOUR FORGIVENESS.
I'M *SORRY,* G-MAN.
FOR *EVERYTHING.*
PLEASE ACCEPT MY APOLOGY.
WELL, I--
HA!
GNNNFF!
YEAH... IT'S ON THERE PRETTY GOOD.
APOLOGY NOT ACCEPTED, BY THE WAY!

Chapter 2

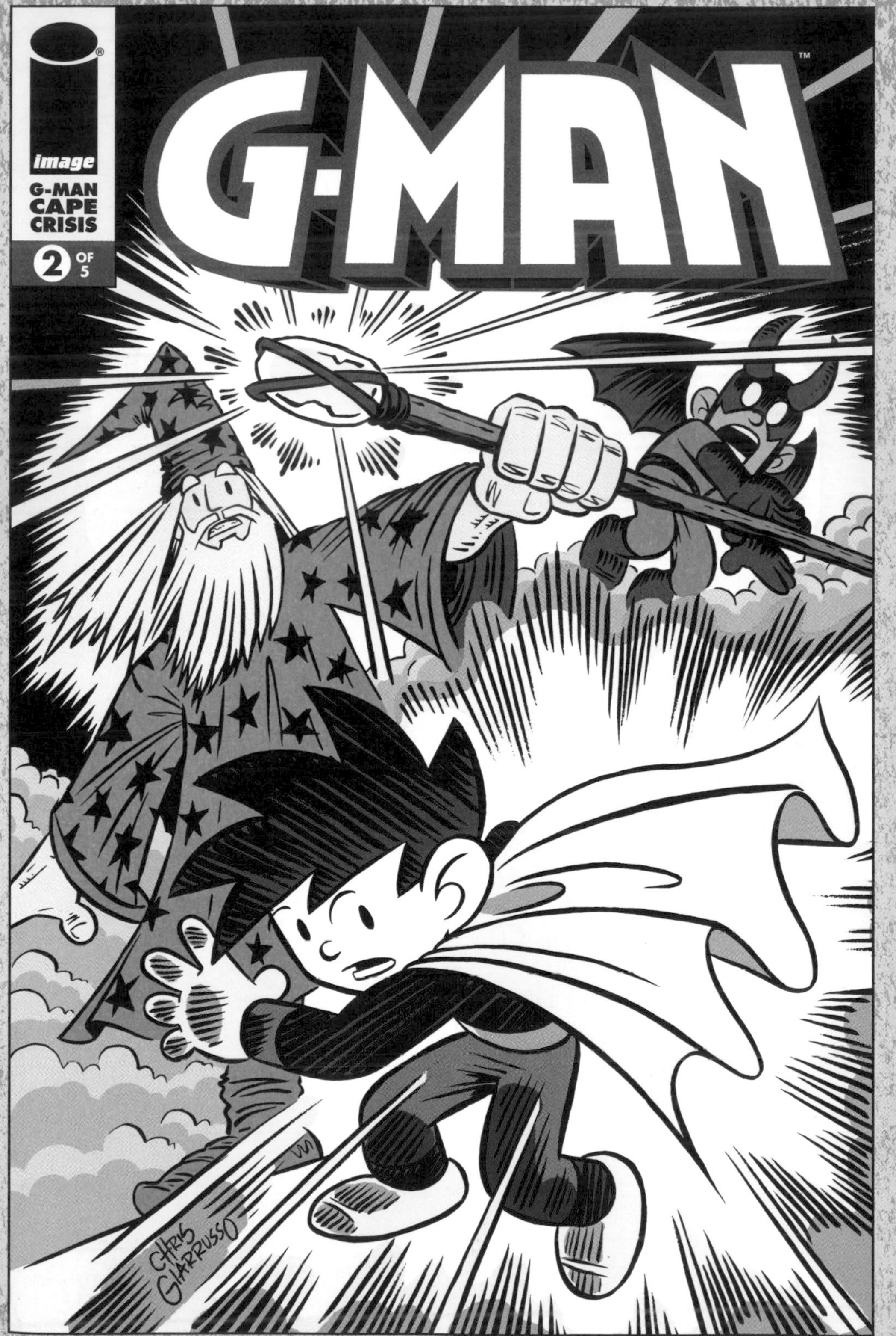
image
G-MAN CAPE CRISIS
2 OF 5
G-MAN™
CHRIS GIARRUSSO

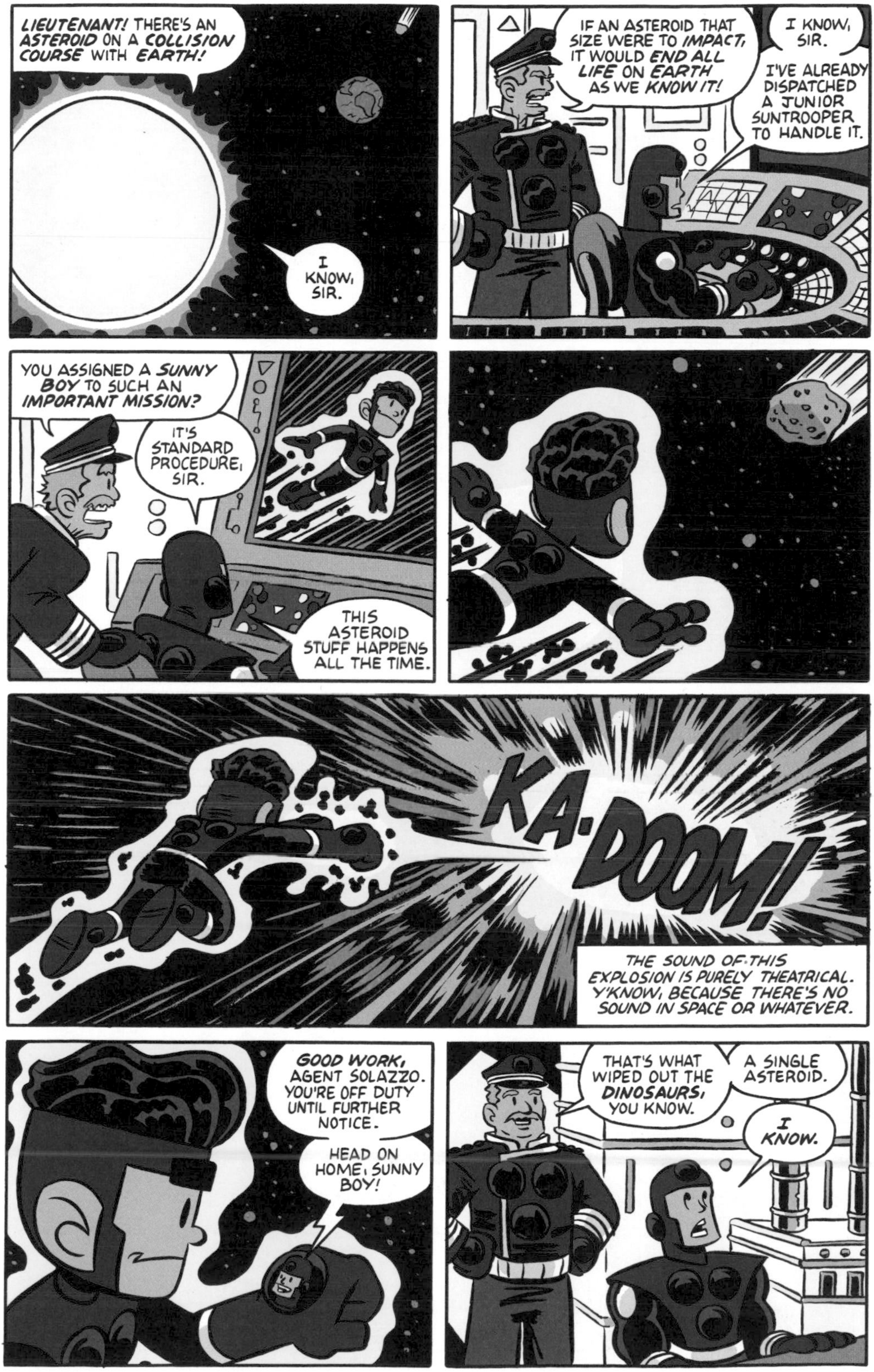
LIEUTENANT! THERE'S AN ASTEROID ON A COLLISION COURSE WITH EARTH!
I KNOW, SIR.
IF AN ASTEROID THAT SIZE WERE TO IMPACT, IT WOULD END ALL LIFE ON EARTH AS WE KNOW IT!
I KNOW, SIR.
I'VE ALREADY DISPATCHED A JUNIOR SUNTROOPER TO HANDLE IT.
YOU ASSIGNED A SUNNY BOY TO SUCH AN IMPORTANT MISSION?
IT'S STANDARD PROCEDURE, SIR.
THIS ASTEROID STUFF HAPPENS ALL THE TIME.
KA-DOOM!
THE SOUND OF THIS EXPLOSION IS PURELY THEATRICAL. Y'KNOW, BECAUSE THERE'S NO SOUND IN SPACE OR WHATEVER.
GOOD WORK, AGENT SOLAZZO. YOU'RE OFF DUTY UNTIL FURTHER NOTICE.
HEAD ON HOME, SUNNY BOY!
THAT'S WHAT WIPED OUT THE DINOSAURS, YOU KNOW.
A SINGLE ASTEROID.
I KNOW.

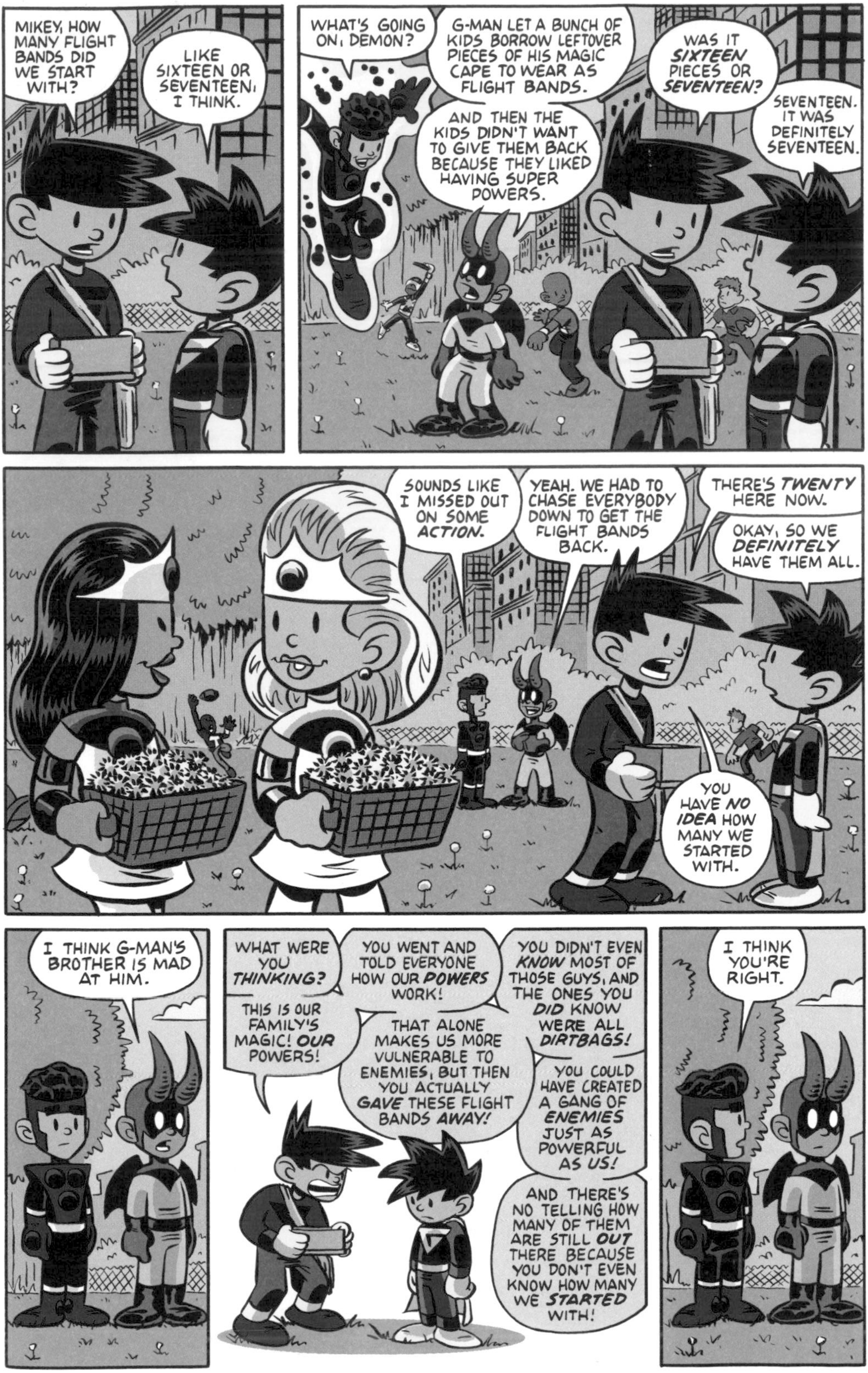
MIKEY, HOW MANY FLIGHT BANDS DID WE START WITH?
LIKE SIXTEEN OR SEVENTEEN, I THINK.
WHAT'S GOING ON, DEMON?
G-MAN LET A BUNCH OF KIDS BORROW LEFTOVER PIECES OF HIS MAGIC CAPE TO WEAR AS FLIGHT BANDS.
AND THEN THE KIDS DIDN'T WANT TO GIVE THEM BACK BECAUSE THEY LIKED HAVING SUPER POWERS.
WAS IT SIXTEEN PIECES OR SEVENTEEN?
SEVENTEEN. IT WAS DEFINITELY SEVENTEEN.
SOUNDS LIKE I MISSED OUT ON SOME ACTION.
YEAH. WE HAD TO CHASE EVERYBODY DOWN TO GET THE FLIGHT BANDS BACK.
THERE'S TWENTY HERE NOW.
OKAY, SO WE DEFINITELY HAVE THEM ALL.
YOU HAVE NO IDEA HOW MANY WE STARTED WITH.
I THINK G-MAN'S BROTHER IS MAD AT HIM.
WHAT WERE YOU THINKING?
YOU WENT AND TOLD EVERYONE HOW OUR POWERS WORK!
THIS IS OUR FAMILY'S MAGIC! OUR POWERS!
THAT ALONE MAKES US MORE VULNERABLE TO ENEMIES, BUT THEN YOU ACTUALLY GAVE THESE FLIGHT BANDS AWAY!
YOU DIDN'T EVEN KNOW MOST OF THOSE GUYS, AND THE ONES YOU DID KNOW WERE ALL DIRTBAGS!
YOU COULD HAVE CREATED A GANG OF ENEMIES JUST AS POWERFUL AS US!
AND THERE'S NO TELLING HOW MANY OF THEM ARE STILL OUT THERE BECAUSE YOU DON'T EVEN KNOW HOW MANY WE STARTED WITH!
I THINK YOU'RE RIGHT.

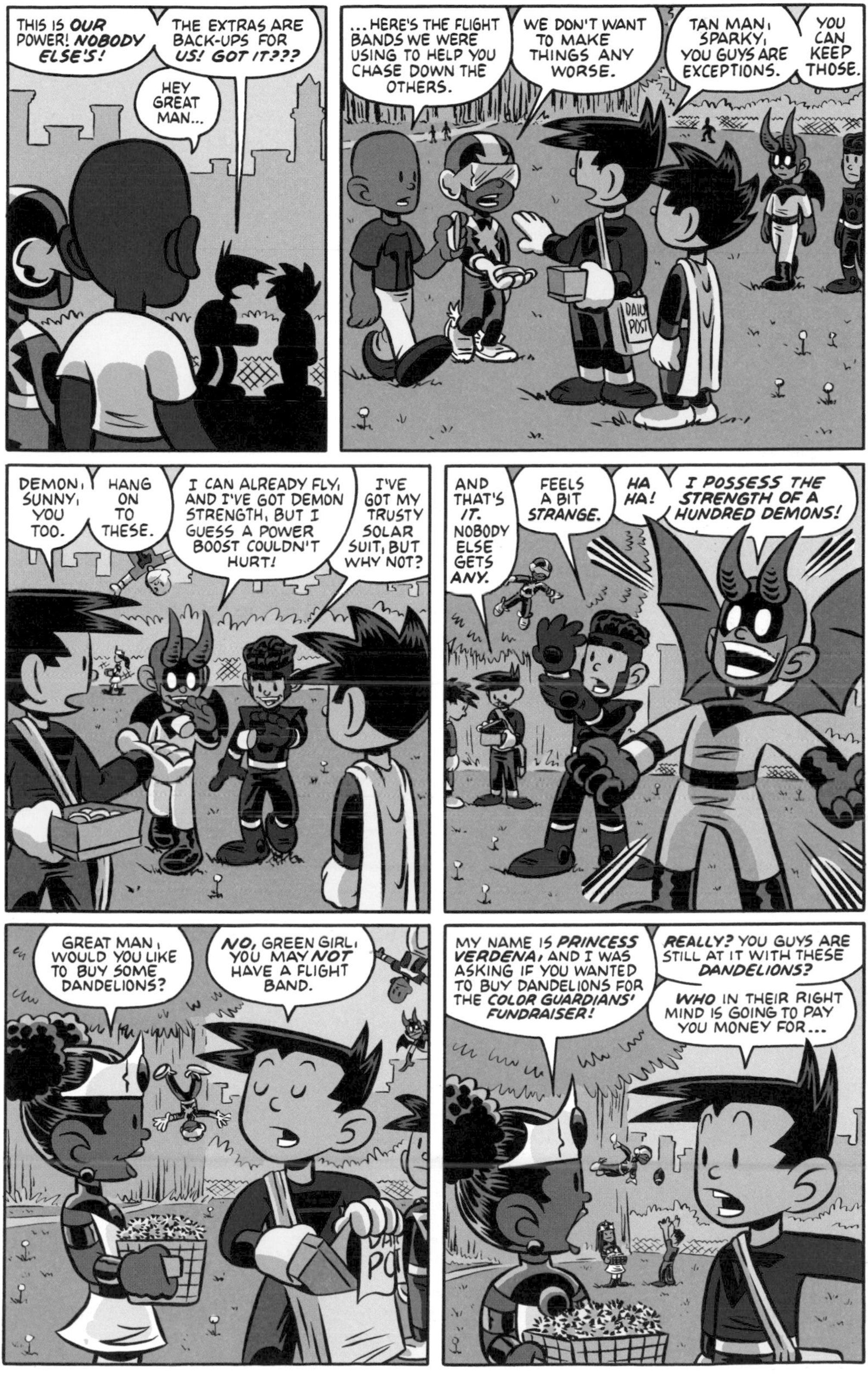
THIS IS OUR POWER! NOBODY ELSE'S!
THE EXTRAS ARE BACK-UPS FOR US! GOT IT???
HEY GREAT MAN...
...HERE'S THE FLIGHT BANDS WE WERE USING TO HELP YOU CHASE DOWN THE OTHERS.
WE DON'T WANT TO MAKE THINGS ANY WORSE.
TAN MAN, SPARKY, YOU GUYS ARE EXCEPTIONS.
YOU CAN KEEP THOSE.
DAILY POST
DEMON, SUNNY, YOU TOO.
HANG ON TO THESE.
I CAN ALREADY FLY, AND I'VE GOT DEMON STRENGTH, BUT I GUESS A POWER BOOST COULDN'T HURT!
I'VE GOT MY TRUSTY SOLAR SUIT, BUT WHY NOT?
AND THAT'S IT. NOBODY ELSE GETS ANY.
FEELS A BIT STRANGE.
HA HA!
I POSSESS THE STRENGTH OF A HUNDRED DEMONS!
GREAT MAN, WOULD YOU LIKE TO BUY SOME DANDELIONS?
NO, GREEN GIRL, YOU MAY NOT HAVE A FLIGHT BAND.
MY NAME IS PRINCESS VERDENA, AND I WAS ASKING IF YOU WANTED TO BUY DANDELIONS FOR THE COLOR GUARDIANS' FUNDRAISER!
REALLY? YOU GUYS ARE STILL AT IT WITH THESE DANDELIONS?
WHO IN THEIR RIGHT MIND IS GOING TO PAY YOU MONEY FOR...

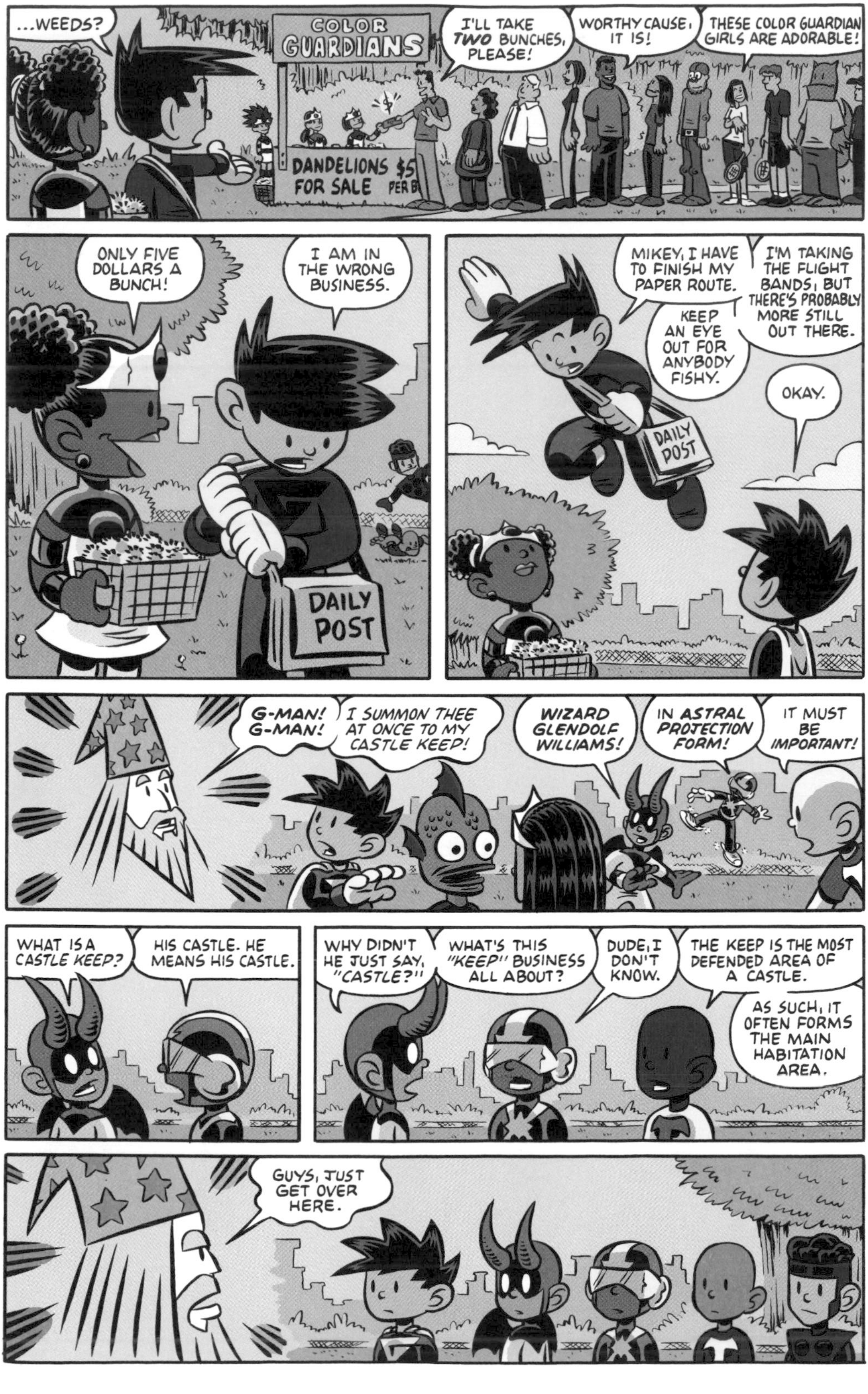
...WEEDS?
COLOR GUARDIANS
I'LL TAKE TWO BUNCHES, PLEASE!
WORTHY CAUSE, IT IS!
THESE COLOR GUARDIAN GIRLS ARE ADORABLE!
DANDELIONS $5 FOR SALE PER B
ONLY FIVE DOLLARS A BUNCH!
I AM IN THE WRONG BUSINESS.
DAILY POST
MIKEY, I HAVE TO FINISH MY PAPER ROUTE.
KEEP AN EYE OUT FOR ANYBODY FISHY.
I'M TAKING THE FLIGHT BANDS, BUT THERE'S PROBABLY MORE STILL OUT THERE.
OKAY.
DAILY POST
G-MAN! G-MAN!
I SUMMON THEE AT ONCE TO MY CASTLE KEEP!
WIZARD GLENDOLF WILLIAMS!
IN ASTRAL PROJECTION FORM!
IT MUST BE IMPORTANT!
WHAT IS A CASTLE KEEP?
HIS CASTLE. HE MEANS HIS CASTLE.
WHY DIDN'T HE JUST SAY, "CASTLE?"
WHAT'S THIS "KEEP" BUSINESS ALL ABOUT?
DUDE, I DON'T KNOW.
THE KEEP IS THE MOST DEFENDED AREA OF A CASTLE.
AS SUCH, IT OFTEN FORMS THE MAIN HABITATION AREA.
GUYS, JUST GET OVER HERE.

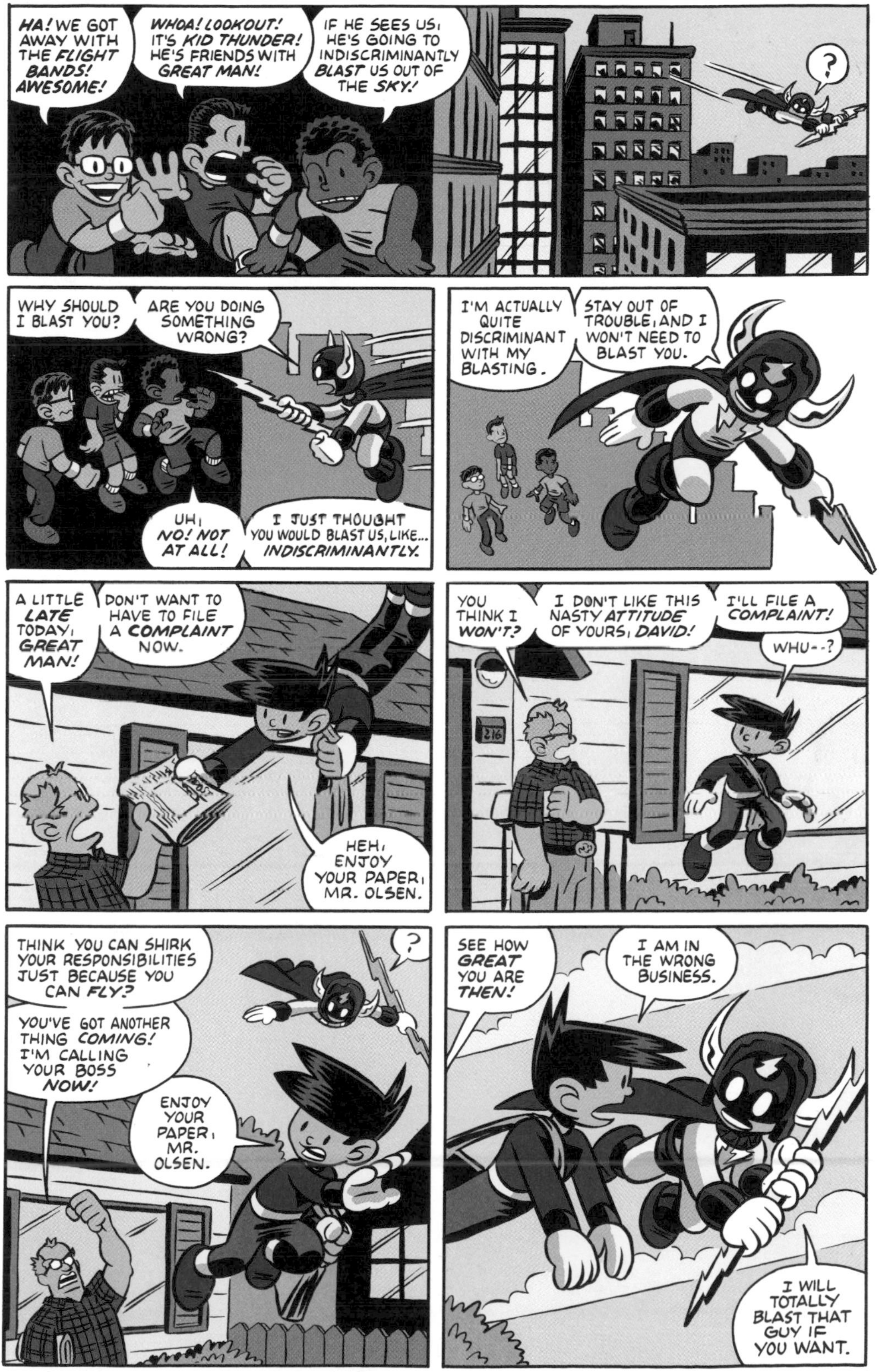
HA! WE GOT AWAY WITH THE FLIGHT BANDS! AWESOME!
WHOA! LOOKOUT! IT'S KID THUNDER! HE'S FRIENDS WITH GREAT MAN!
IF HE SEES US, HE'S GOING TO INDISCRIMINANTLY BLAST US OUT OF THE SKY!
?
WHY SHOULD I BLAST YOU?
ARE YOU DOING SOMETHING WRONG?
UH, NO! NOT AT ALL!
I JUST THOUGHT YOU WOULD BLAST US, LIKE... INDISCRIMINANTLY.
I'M ACTUALLY QUITE DISCRIMINANT WITH MY BLASTING.
STAY OUT OF TROUBLE, AND I WON'T NEED TO BLAST YOU.
A LITTLE LATE TODAY, GREAT MAN!
DON'T WANT TO HAVE TO FILE A COMPLAINT NOW.
HEH, ENJOY YOUR PAPER, MR. OLSEN.
YOU THINK I WON'T?
I DON'T LIKE THIS NASTY ATTITUDE OF YOURS, DAVID!
I'LL FILE A COMPLAINT!
WHU--?
216
THINK YOU CAN SHIRK YOUR RESPONSIBILITIES JUST BECAUSE YOU CAN FLY?
?
YOU'VE GOT ANOTHER THING COMING! I'M CALLING YOUR BOSS NOW!
ENJOY YOUR PAPER, MR. OLSEN.
SEE HOW GREAT YOU ARE THEN!
I AM IN THE WRONG BUSINESS.
I WILL TOTALLY BLAST THAT GUY IF YOU WANT.

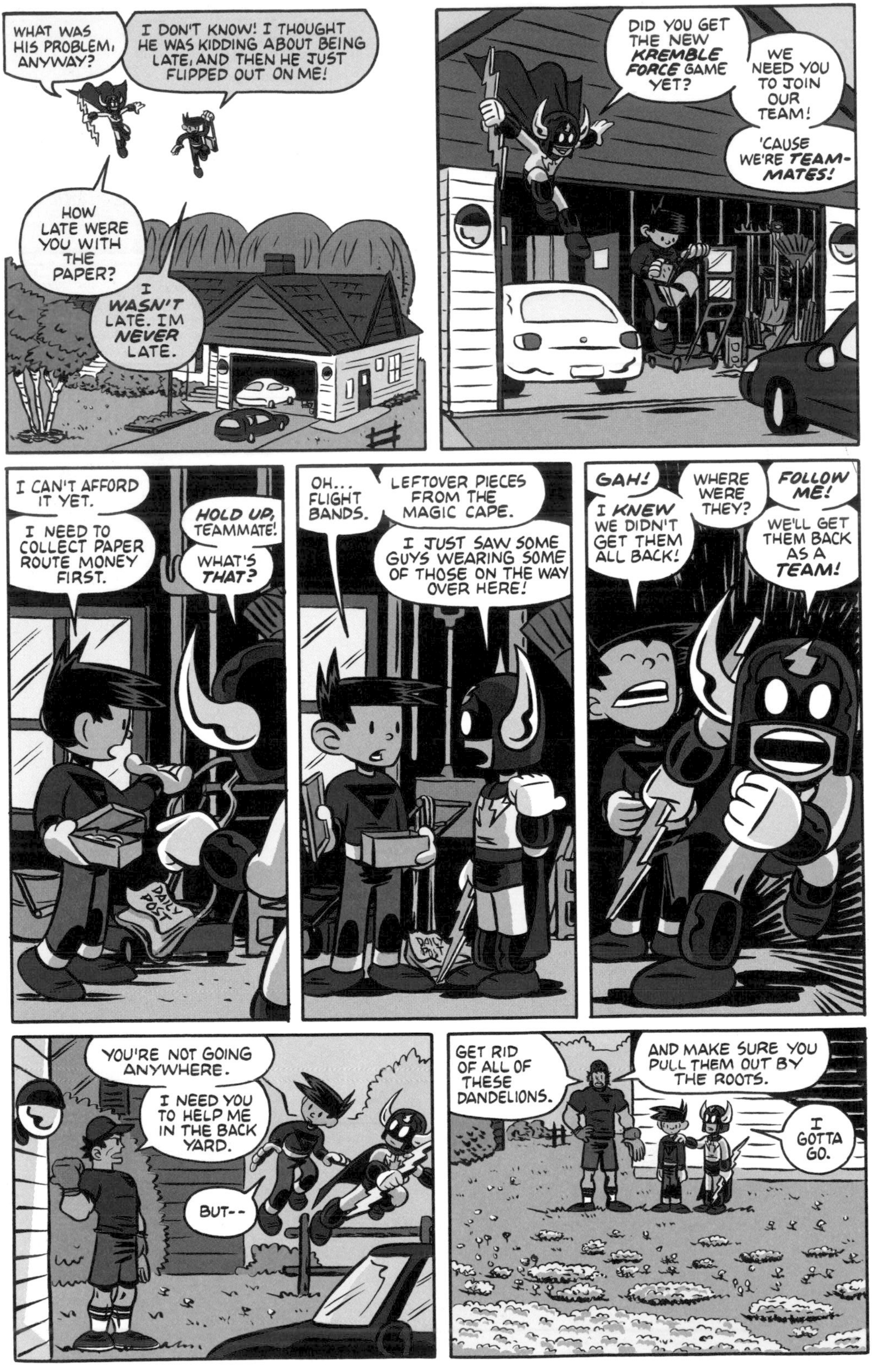
WHAT WAS HIS PROBLEM, ANYWAY?
I DON'T KNOW! I THOUGHT HE WAS KIDDING ABOUT BEING LATE, AND THEN HE JUST FLIPPED OUT ON ME!
HOW LATE WERE YOU WITH THE PAPER?
I WASN'T LATE. IM NEVER LATE.
DID YOU GET THE NEW KREMBLE FORCE GAME YET?
WE NEED YOU TO JOIN OUR TEAM!
'CAUSE WE'RE TEAM-MATES!
I CAN'T AFFORD IT YET.
I NEED TO COLLECT PAPER ROUTE MONEY FIRST.
HOLD UP, TEAMMATE!
WHAT'S THAT?
DAILY POST
OH... FLIGHT BANDS.
LEFTOVER PIECES FROM THE MAGIC CAPE.
I JUST SAW SOME GUYS WEARING SOME OF THOSE ON THE WAY OVER HERE!
DAILY POST
GAH!
I KNEW WE DIDN'T GET THEM ALL BACK!
WHERE WERE THEY?
FOLLOW ME!
WE'LL GET THEM BACK AS A TEAM!
YOU'RE NOT GOING ANYWHERE.
I NEED YOU TO HELP ME IN THE BACK YARD.
BUT--
GET RID OF ALL OF THESE DANDELIONS.
AND MAKE SURE YOU PULL THEM OUT BY THE ROOTS.
I GOTTA GO.

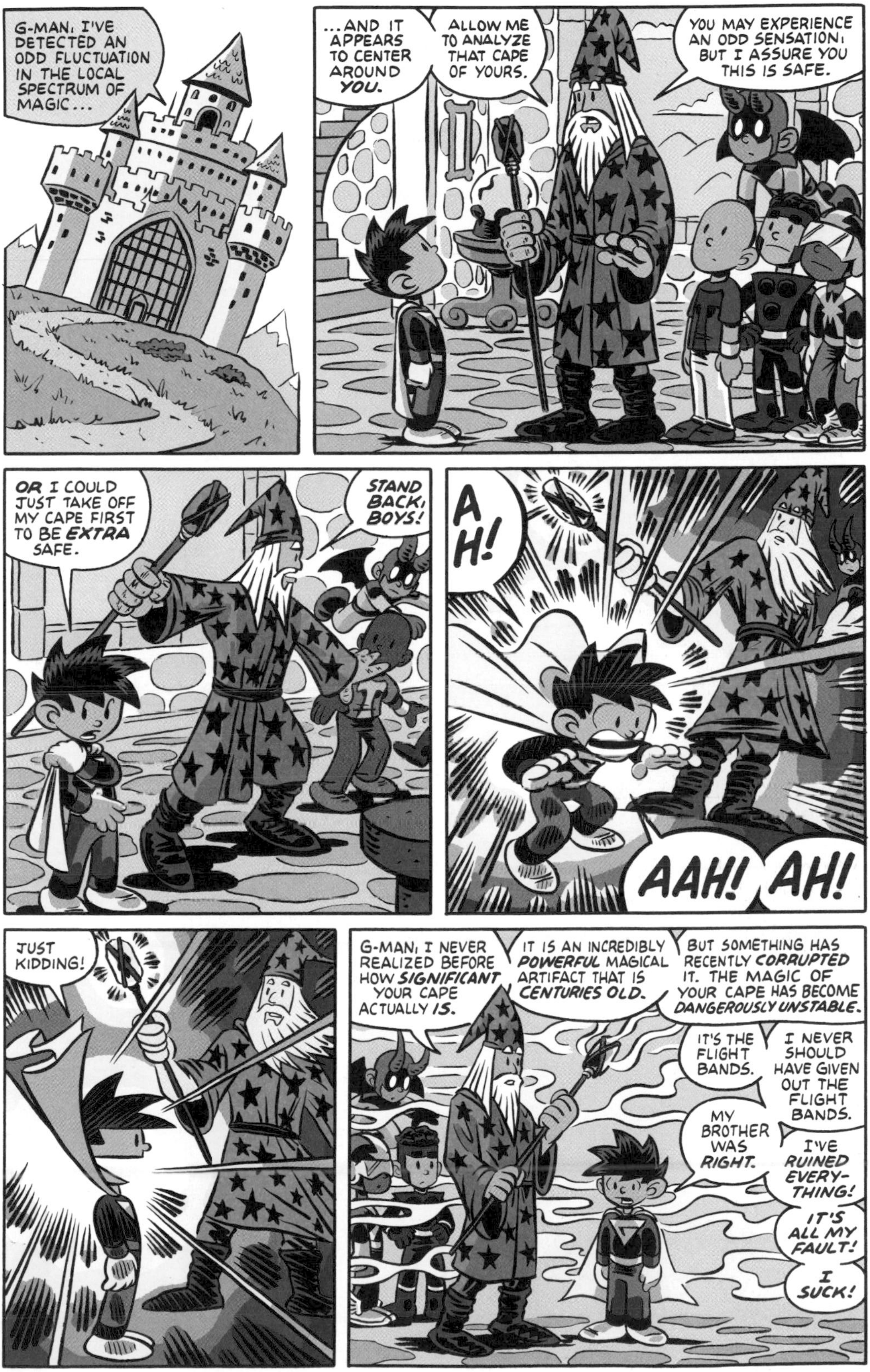
G-MAN, I'VE DETECTED AN ODD FLUCTUATION IN THE LOCAL SPECTRUM OF MAGIC...
...AND IT APPEARS TO CENTER AROUND YOU.
ALLOW ME TO ANALYZE THAT CAPE OF YOURS.
YOU MAY EXPERIENCE AN ODD SENSATION, BUT I ASSURE YOU THIS IS SAFE.
OR I COULD JUST TAKE OFF MY CAPE FIRST TO BE EXTRA SAFE.
STAND BACK, BOYS!
AH!
AAH!
AH!
JUST KIDDING!
G-MAN, I NEVER REALIZED BEFORE HOW SIGNIFICANT YOUR CAPE ACTUALLY IS.
IT IS AN INCREDIBLY POWERFUL MAGICAL ARTIFACT THAT IS CENTURIES OLD.
BUT SOMETHING HAS RECENTLY CORRUPTED IT. THE MAGIC OF YOUR CAPE HAS BECOME DANGEROUSLY UNSTABLE.
IT'S THE FLIGHT BANDS.
I NEVER SHOULD HAVE GIVEN OUT THE FLIGHT BANDS.
MY BROTHER WAS RIGHT.
I'VE RUINED EVERY-THING!
IT'S ALL MY FAULT!
I SUCK!

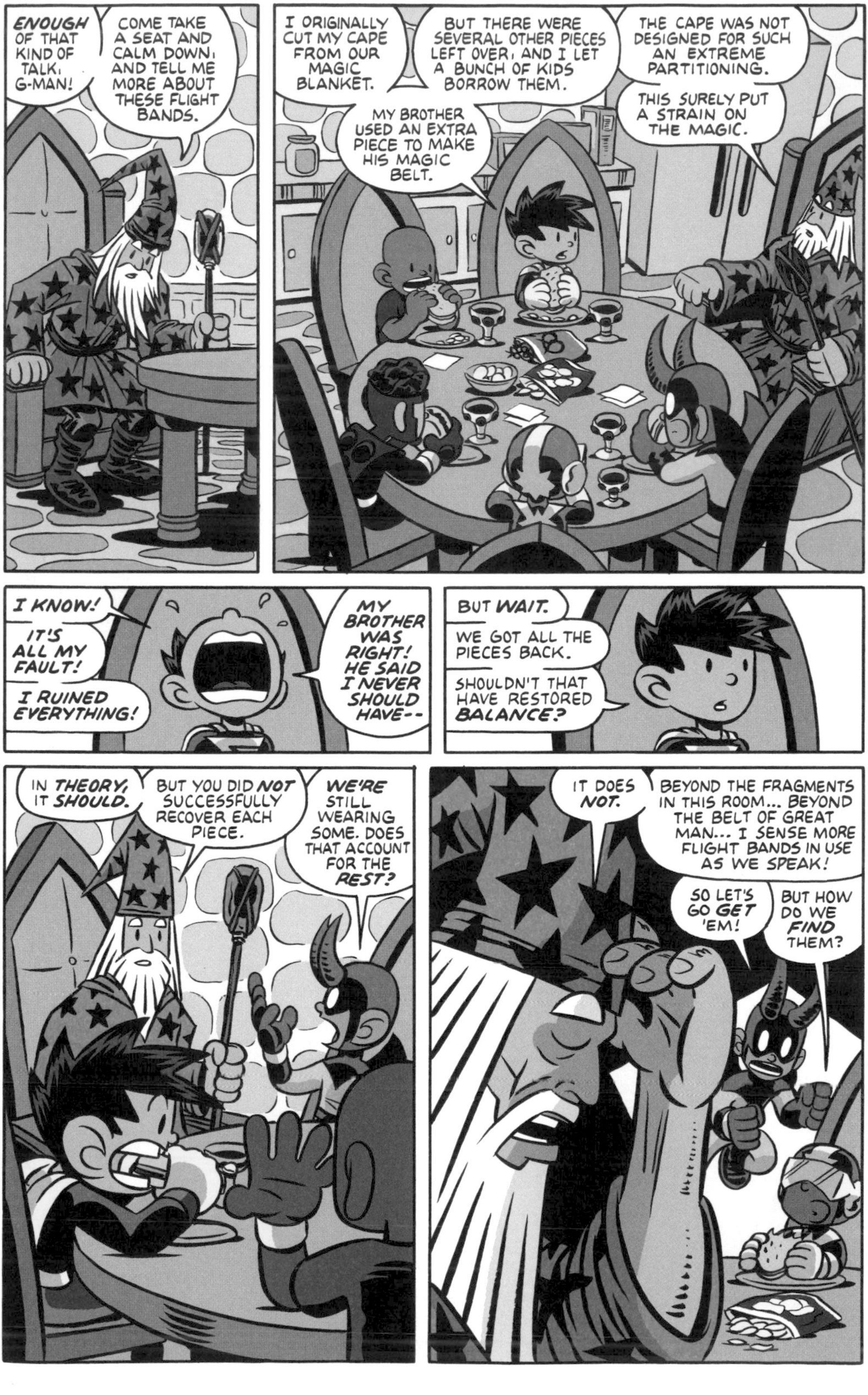
ENOUGH OF THAT KIND OF TALK, G-MAN!
COME TAKE A SEAT AND CALM DOWN, AND TELL ME MORE ABOUT THESE FLIGHT BANDS.
I ORIGINALLY CUT MY CAPE FROM OUR MAGIC BLANKET.
BUT THERE WERE SEVERAL OTHER PIECES LEFT OVER, AND I LET A BUNCH OF KIDS BORROW THEM.
MY BROTHER USED AN EXTRA PIECE TO MAKE HIS MAGIC BELT.
THE CAPE WAS NOT DESIGNED FOR SUCH AN EXTREME PARTITIONING.
THIS SURELY PUT A STRAIN ON THE MAGIC.
I KNOW!
IT'S ALL MY FAULT!
I RUINED EVERYTHING!
MY BROTHER WAS RIGHT! HE SAID I NEVER SHOULD HAVE--
BUT WAIT.
WE GOT ALL THE PIECES BACK.
SHOULDN'T THAT HAVE RESTORED BALANCE?
IN THEORY, IT SHOULD.
BUT YOU DID NOT SUCCESSFULLY RECOVER EACH PIECE.
WE'RE STILL WEARING SOME. DOES THAT ACCOUNT FOR THE REST?
IT DOES NOT.
BEYOND THE FRAGMENTS IN THIS ROOM... BEYOND THE BELT OF GREAT MAN... I SENSE MORE FLIGHT BANDS IN USE AS WE SPEAK!
SO LET'S GO GET 'EM!
BUT HOW DO WE FIND THEM?

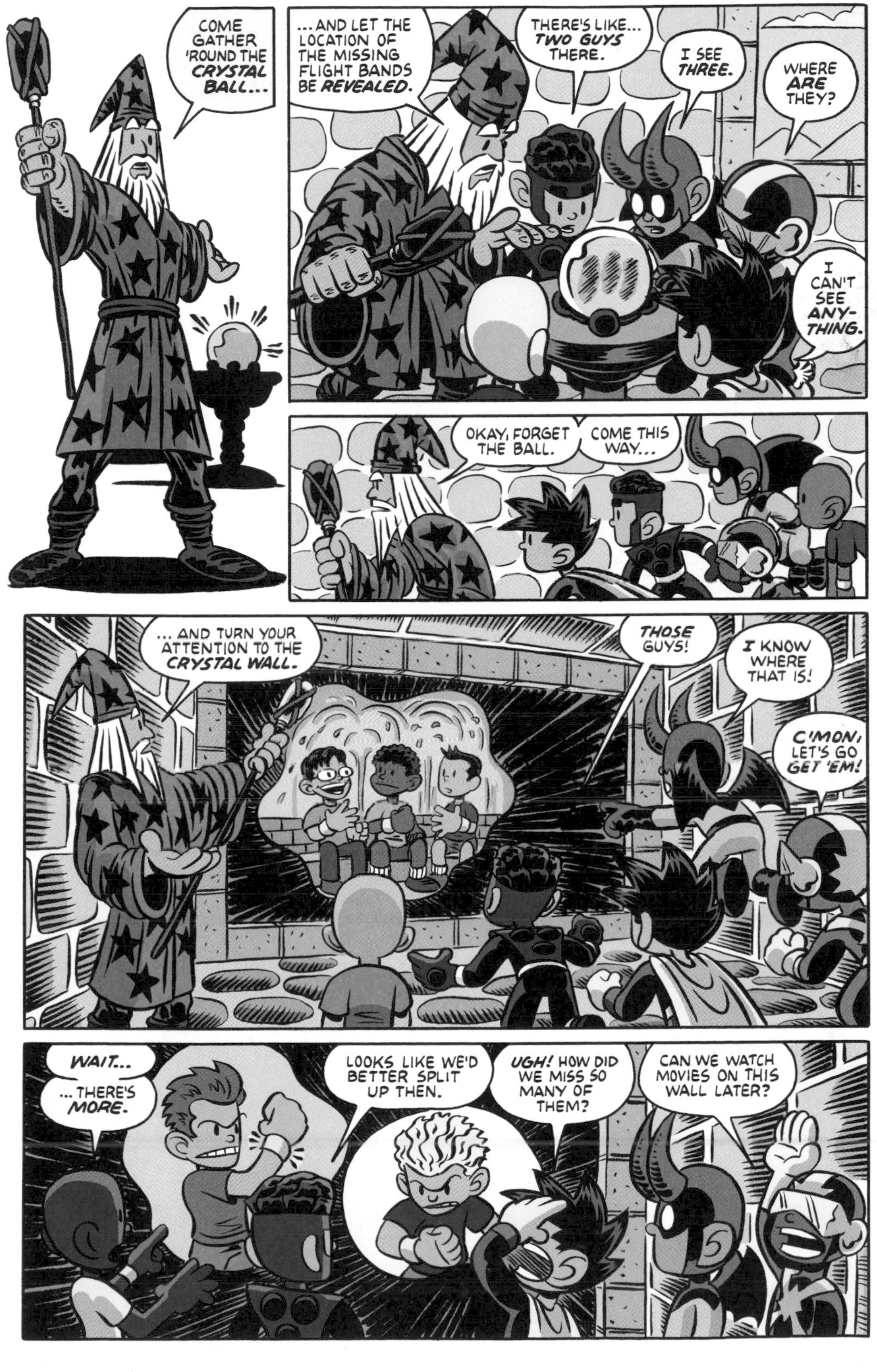
COME GATHER 'ROUND THE CRYSTAL BALL...
...AND LET THE LOCATION OF THE MISSING FLIGHT BANDS BE REVEALED.
THERE'S LIKE... TWO GUYS THERE.
I SEE THREE.
WHERE ARE THEY?
I CAN'T SEE ANYTHING.
OKAY, FORGET THE BALL.
COME THIS WAY...
...AND TURN YOUR ATTENTION TO THE CRYSTAL WALL.
THOSE GUYS!
I KNOW WHERE THAT IS!
C'MON, LET'S GO GET 'EM!
WAIT...
...THERE'S MORE.
LOOKS LIKE WE'D BETTER SPLIT UP THEN.
UGH! HOW DID WE MISS SO MANY OF THEM?
CAN WE WATCH MOVIES ON THIS WALL LATER?

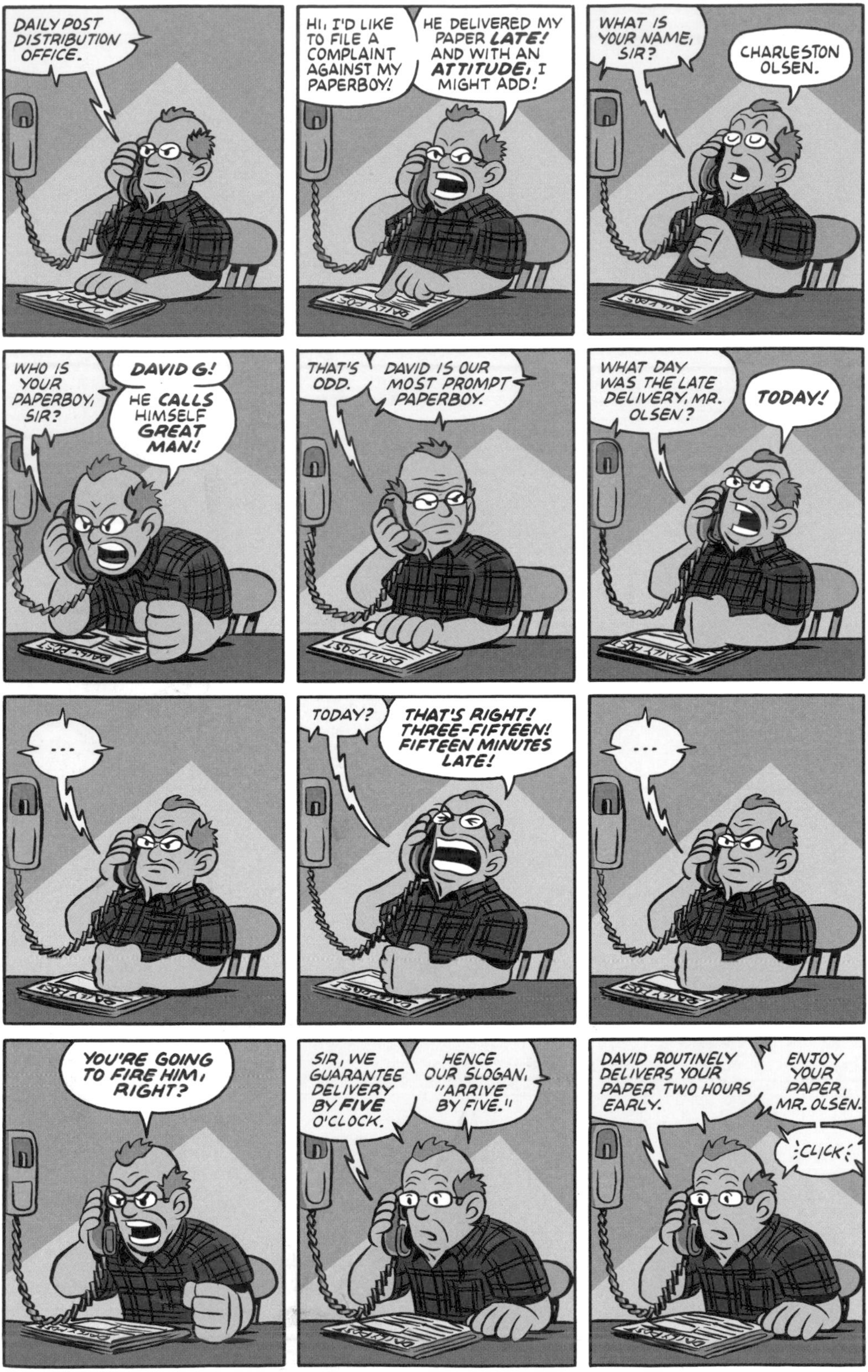
DAILY POST DISTRIBUTION OFFICE.
HI, I'D LIKE TO FILE A COMPLAINT AGAINST MY PAPERBOY!
HE DELIVERED MY PAPER LATE! AND WITH AN ATTITUDE, I MIGHT ADD!
WHAT IS YOUR NAME, SIR?
CHARLESTON OLSEN.
WHO IS YOUR PAPERBOY, SIR?
DAVID G!
HE CALLS HIMSELF GREAT MAN!
THAT'S ODD.
DAVID IS OUR MOST PROMPT PAPERBOY.
WHAT DAY WAS THE LATE DELIVERY, MR. OLSEN?
TODAY!
...
TODAY?
THAT'S RIGHT! THREE-FIFTEEN! FIFTEEN MINUTES LATE!
...
YOU'RE GOING TO FIRE HIM, RIGHT?
SIR, WE GUARANTEE DELIVERY BY FIVE O'CLOCK.
HENCE OUR SLOGAN, "ARRIVE BY FIVE."
DAVID ROUTINELY DELIVERS YOUR PAPER TWO HOURS EARLY.
ENJOY YOUR PAPER, MR. OLSEN.
CLICK

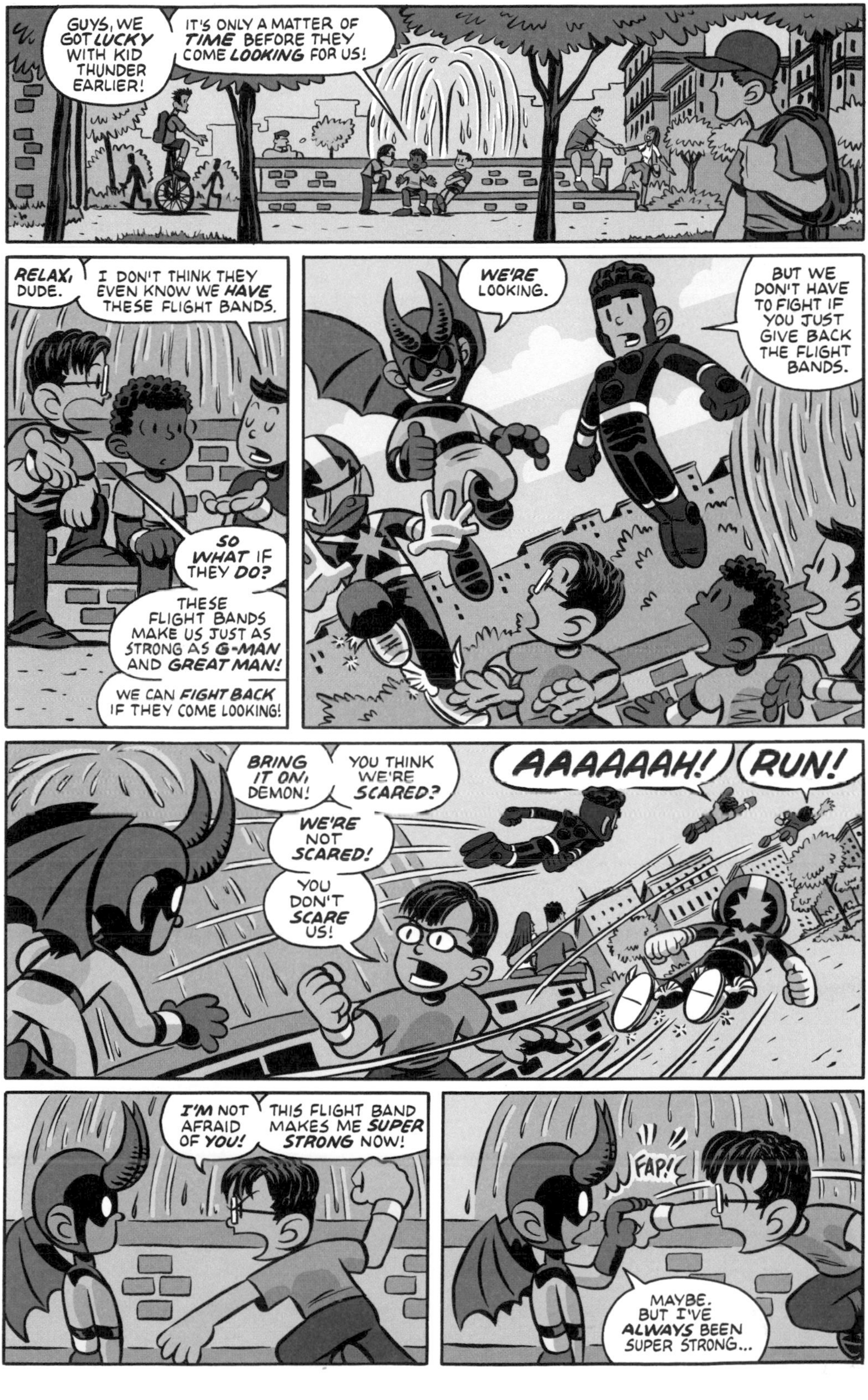
GUYS, WE GOT LUCKY WITH KID THUNDER EARLIER!
IT'S ONLY A MATTER OF TIME BEFORE THEY COME LOOKING FOR US!
RELAX, DUDE.
I DON'T THINK THEY EVEN KNOW WE HAVE THESE FLIGHT BANDS.
SO WHAT IF THEY DO?
THESE FLIGHT BANDS MAKE US JUST AS STRONG AS G-MAN AND GREAT MAN!
WE CAN FIGHT BACK IF THEY COME LOOKING!
WE'RE LOOKING.
BUT WE DON'T HAVE TO FIGHT IF YOU JUST GIVE BACK THE FLIGHT BANDS.
BRING IT ON, DEMON!
YOU THINK WE'RE SCARED?
WE'RE NOT SCARED!
YOU DON'T SCARE US!
AAAAAAH!
RUN!
I'M NOT AFRAID OF YOU!
THIS FLIGHT BAND MAKES ME SUPER STRONG NOW!
FAP!
MAYBE. BUT I'VE ALWAYS BEEN SUPER STRONG...

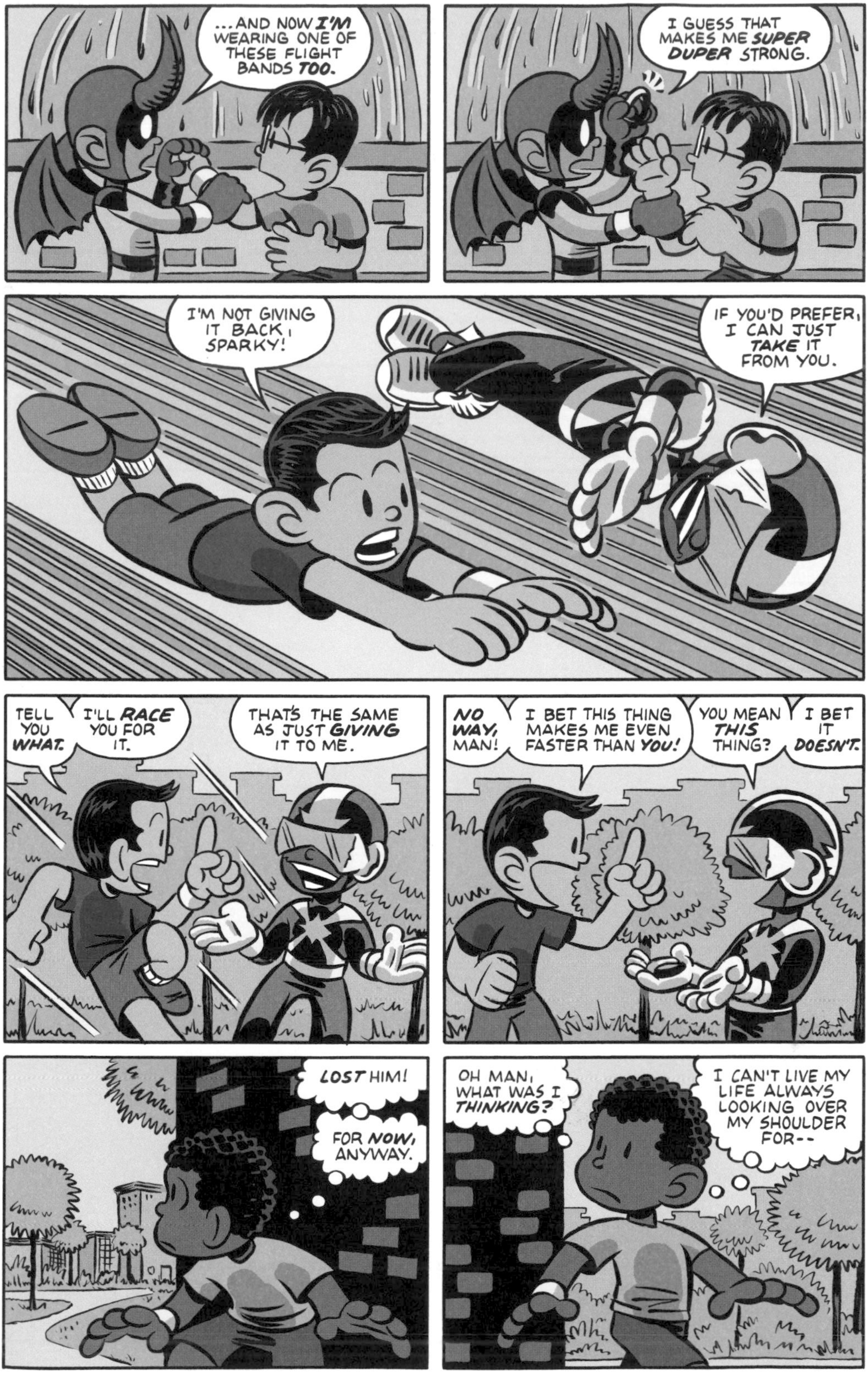
...AND NOW I'M WEARING ONE OF THESE FLIGHT BANDS TOO.
I GUESS THAT MAKES ME SUPER DUPER STRONG.
I'M NOT GIVING IT BACK, SPARKY!
IF YOU'D PREFER, I CAN JUST TAKE IT FROM YOU.
TELL YOU WHAT.
I'LL RACE YOU FOR IT.
THAT'S THE SAME AS JUST GIVING IT TO ME.
NO WAY, MAN!
I BET THIS THING MAKES ME EVEN FASTER THAN YOU!
YOU MEAN THIS THING?
I BET IT DOESN'T.
LOST HIM!
FOR NOW, ANYWAY.
OH MAN, WHAT WAS I THINKING?
I CAN'T LIVE MY LIFE ALWAYS LOOKING OVER MY SHOULDER FOR--

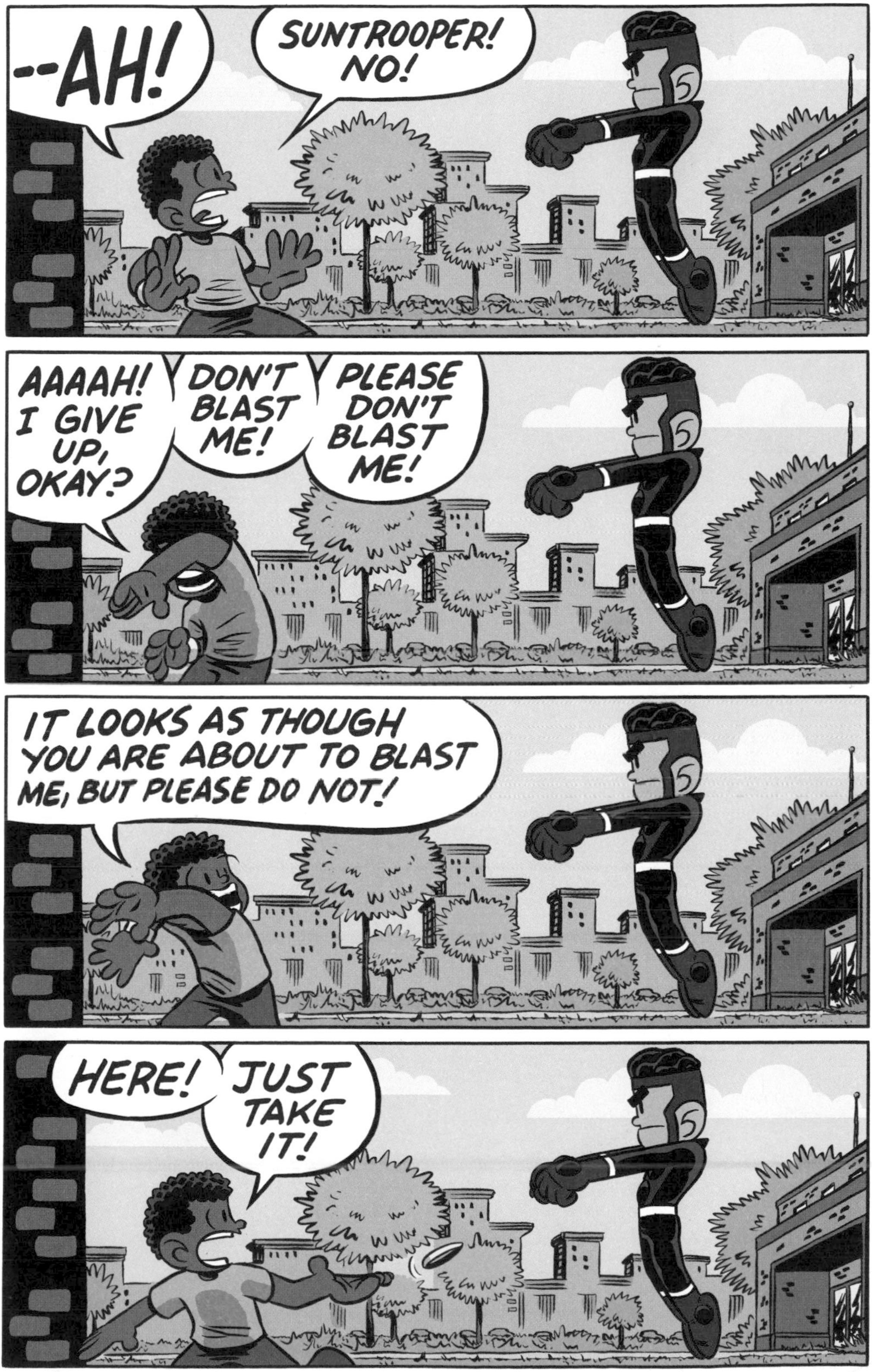
--AH!
SUNTROOPER! NO!
AAAAH! I GIVE UP, OKAY?
DON'T BLAST ME!
PLEASE DON'T BLAST ME!
IT LOOKS AS THOUGH YOU ARE ABOUT TO BLAST ME, BUT PLEASE DO NOT!
HERE!
JUST TAKE IT!

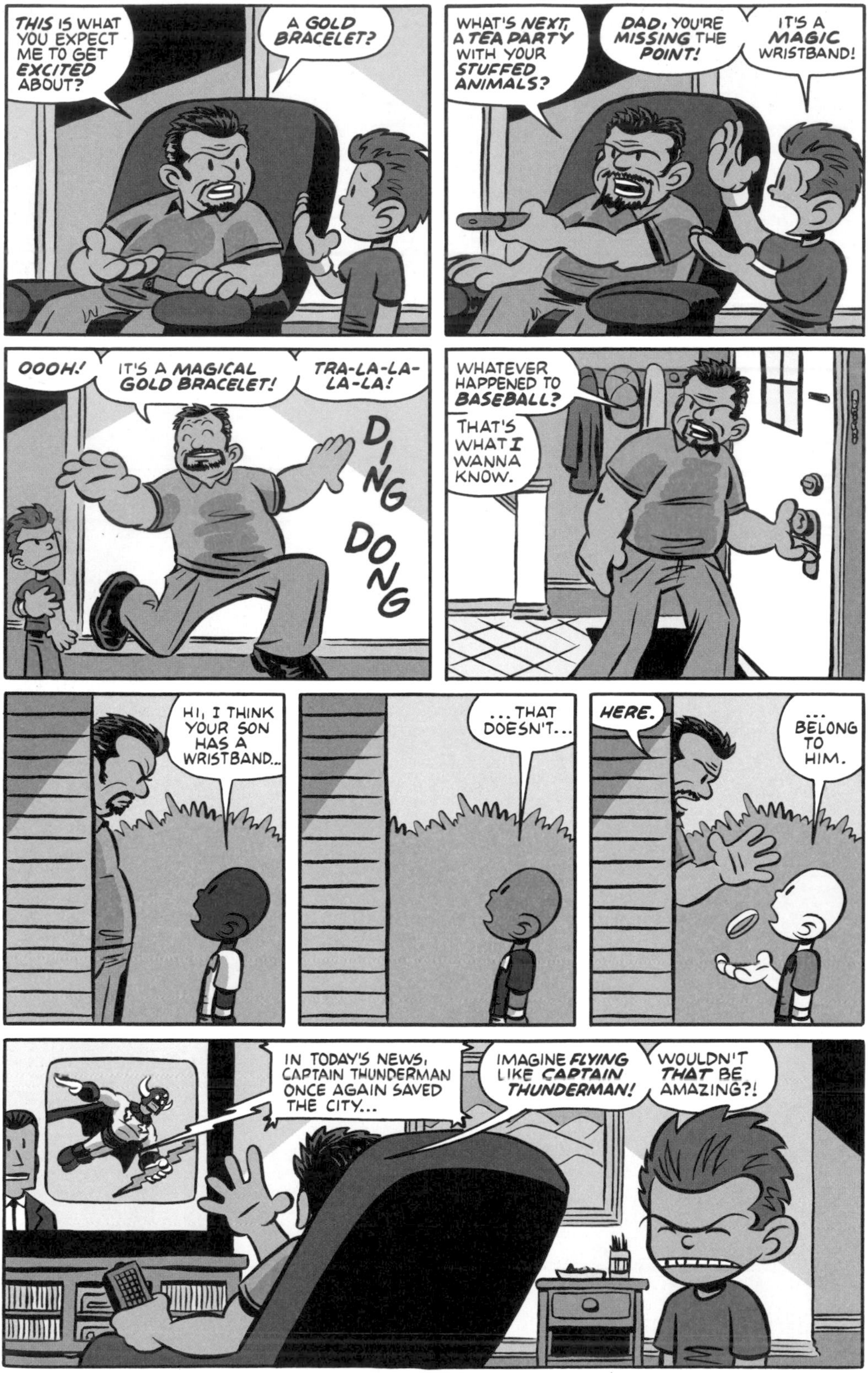
THIS IS WHAT YOU EXPECT ME TO GET EXCITED ABOUT?
A GOLD BRACELET?
WHAT'S NEXT, A TEA PARTY WITH YOUR STUFFED ANIMALS?
DAD, YOU'RE MISSING THE POINT!
IT'S A MAGIC WRISTBAND!
OOOH!
IT'S A MAGICAL GOLD BRACELET!
TRA-LA-LA-LA-LA!
DING DONG
WHATEVER HAPPENED TO BASEBALL?
THAT'S WHAT I WANNA KNOW.
HI, I THINK YOUR SON HAS A WRISTBAND...
...THAT DOESN'T...
HERE.
...BELONG TO HIM.
IN TODAY'S NEWS, CAPTAIN THUNDERMAN ONCE AGAIN SAVED THE CITY...
IMAGINE FLYING LIKE CAPTAIN THUNDERMAN!
WOULDN'T THAT BE AMAZING?!

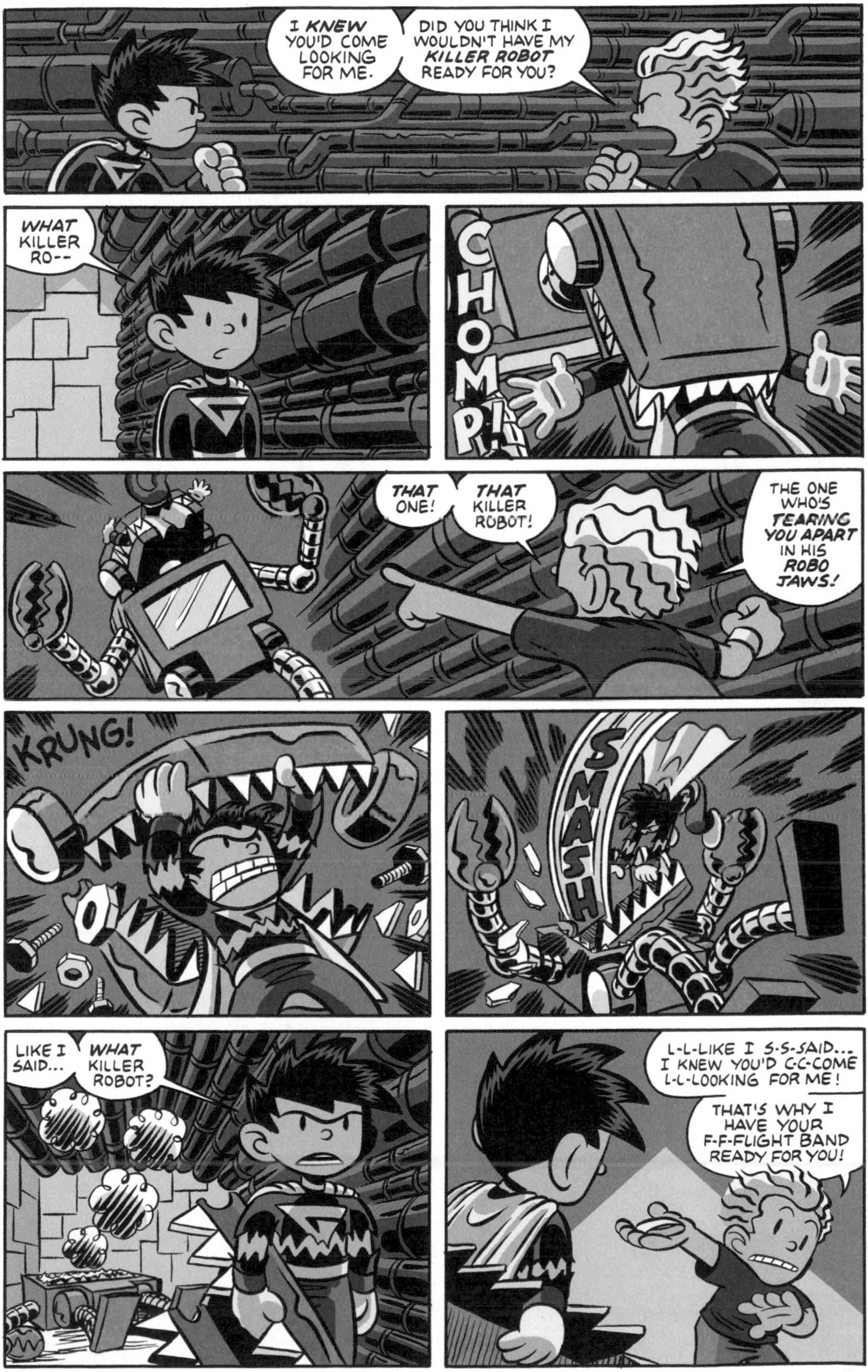
I KNEW YOU'D COME LOOKING FOR ME.
DID YOU THINK I WOULDN'T HAVE MY KILLER ROBOT READY FOR YOU?
WHAT KILLER RO--
CHOMP!
THAT ONE!
THAT KILLER ROBOT!
THE ONE WHO'S TEARING YOU APART IN HIS ROBO JAWS!
KRUNG!
SMASH
LIKE I SAID...
WHAT KILLER ROBOT?
L-L-LIKE I S-S-SAID... I KNEW YOU'D C-C-COME L-L-LOOKING FOR ME!
THAT'S WHY I HAVE YOUR F-F-FLIGHT BAND READY FOR YOU!

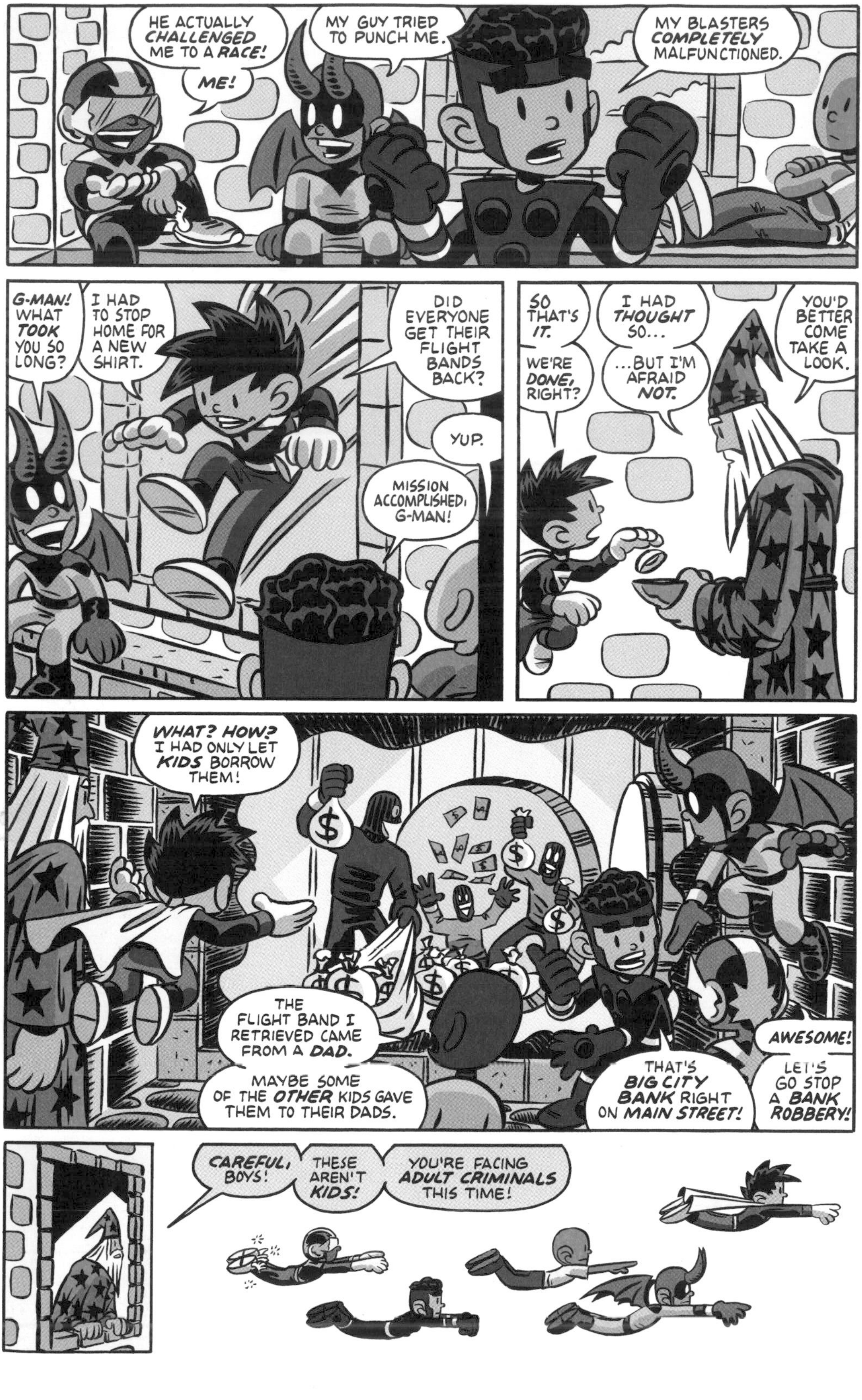
HE ACTUALLY CHALLENGED ME TO A RACE!
ME!
MY GUY TRIED TO PUNCH ME.
MY BLASTERS COMPLETELY MALFUNCTIONED.
G-MAN! WHAT TOOK YOU SO LONG?
I HAD TO STOP HOME FOR A NEW SHIRT.
DID EVERYONE GET THEIR FLIGHT BANDS BACK?
YUP.
MISSION ACCOMPLISHED, G-MAN!
SO THAT'S IT.
WE'RE DONE, RIGHT?
I HAD THOUGHT SO...
...BUT I'M AFRAID NOT.
YOU'D BETTER COME TAKE A LOOK.
WHAT? HOW? I HAD ONLY LET KIDS BORROW THEM!
THE FLIGHT BAND I RETRIEVED CAME FROM A DAD.
MAYBE SOME OF THE OTHER KIDS GAVE THEM TO THEIR DADS.
THAT'S BIG CITY BANK RIGHT ON MAIN STREET!
AWESOME!
LET'S GO STOP A BANK ROBBERY!
CAREFUL, BOYS!
THESE AREN'T KIDS!
YOU'RE FACING ADULT CRIMINALS THIS TIME!

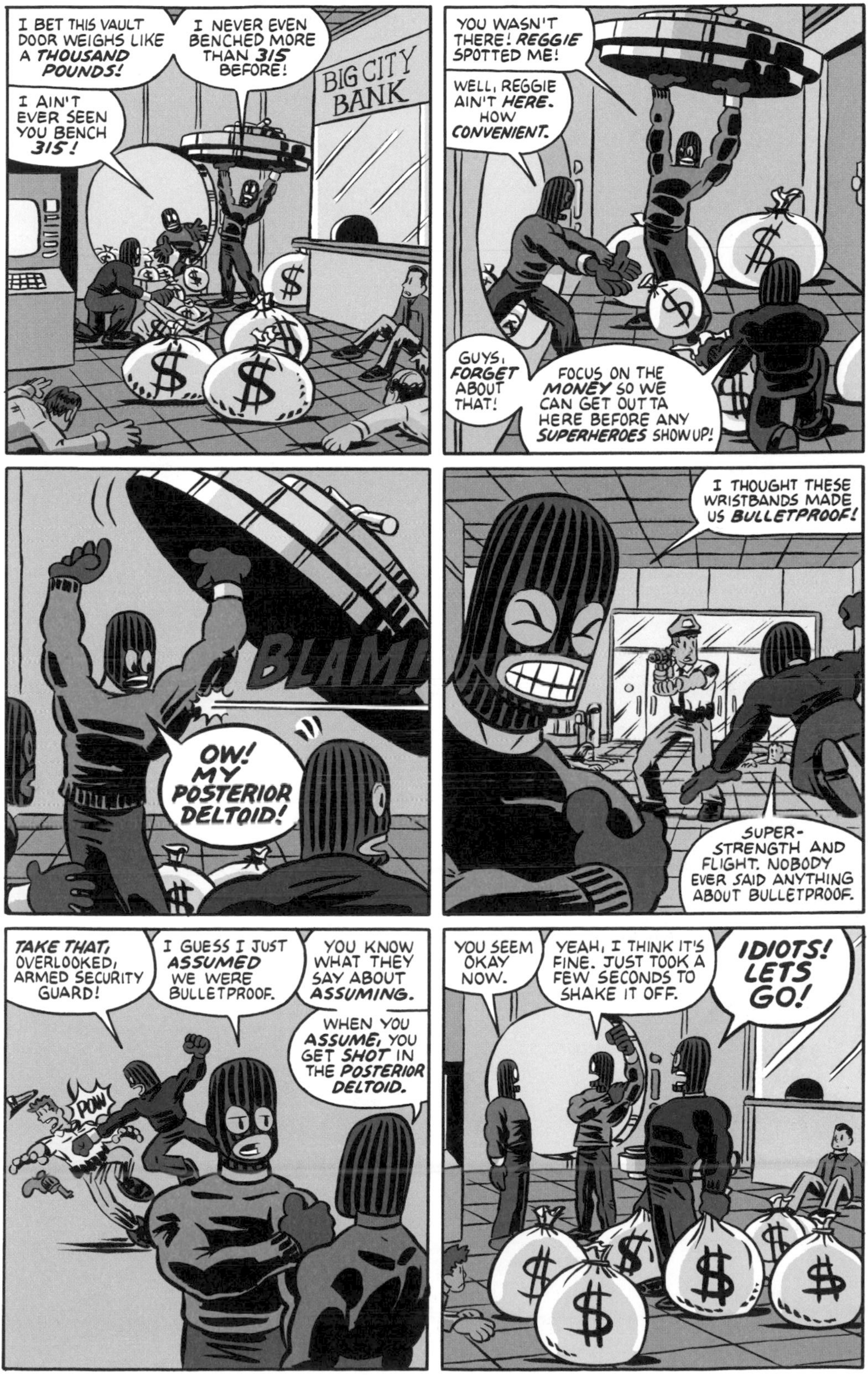
I BET THIS VAULT DOOR WEIGHS LIKE A THOUSAND POUNDS!
I NEVER EVEN BENCHED MORE THAN 315 BEFORE!
I AIN'T EVER SEEN YOU BENCH 315!
BIG CITY BANK
YOU WASN'T THERE! REGGIE SPOTTED ME!
WELL, REGGIE AIN'T HERE. HOW CONVENIENT.
GUYS, FORGET ABOUT THAT!
FOCUS ON THE MONEY SO WE CAN GET OUTTA HERE BEFORE ANY SUPERHEROES SHOW UP!
BLAM!
OW! MY POSTERIOR DELTOID!
I THOUGHT THESE WRISTBANDS MADE US BULLETPROOF!
SUPER-STRENGTH AND FLIGHT. NOBODY EVER SAID ANYTHING ABOUT BULLETPROOF.
TAKE THAT, OVERLOOKED, ARMED SECURITY GUARD!
I GUESS I JUST ASSUMED WE WERE BULLETPROOF.
YOU KNOW WHAT THEY SAY ABOUT ASSUMING.
WHEN YOU ASSUME, YOU GET SHOT IN THE POSTERIOR DELTOID.
POW
YOU SEEM OKAY NOW.
YEAH, I THINK IT'S FINE. JUST TOOK A FEW SECONDS TO SHAKE IT OFF.
IDIOTS! LETS GO!

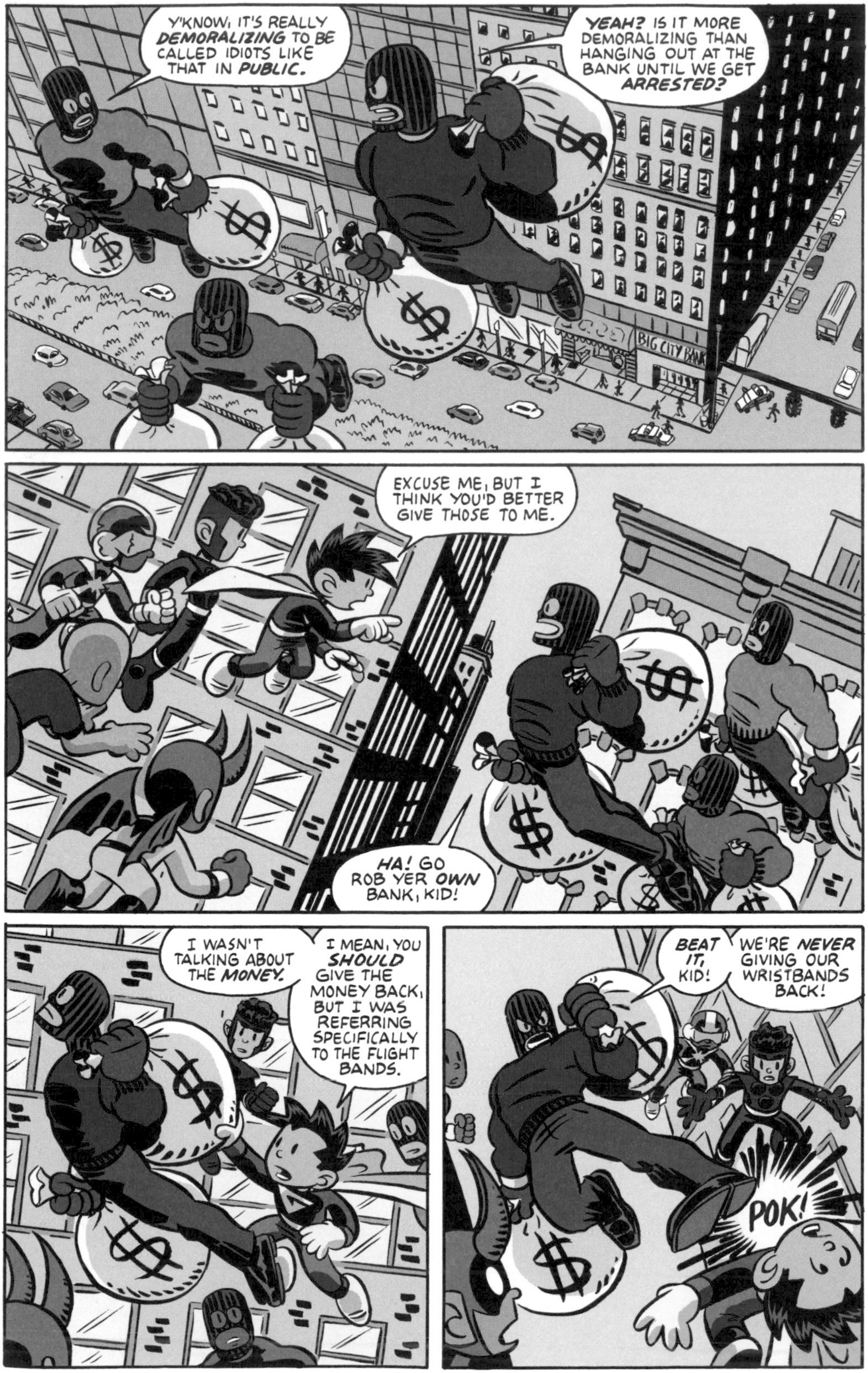

Y'KNOW, IT'S REALLY DEMORALIZING TO BE CALLED IDIOTS LIKE THAT IN PUBLIC.
YEAH? IS IT MORE DEMORALIZING THAN HANGING OUT AT THE BANK UNTIL WE GET ARRESTED?
BIG CITY BANK
EXCUSE ME, BUT I THINK YOU'D BETTER GIVE THOSE TO ME.
HA! GO ROB YER OWN BANK, KID!
I WASN'T TALKING ABOUT THE MONEY.
I MEAN, YOU SHOULD GIVE THE MONEY BACK, BUT I WAS REFERRING SPECIFICALLY TO THE FLIGHT BANDS.
BEAT IT, KID!
WE'RE NEVER GIVING OUR WRISTBANDS BACK!
POK!

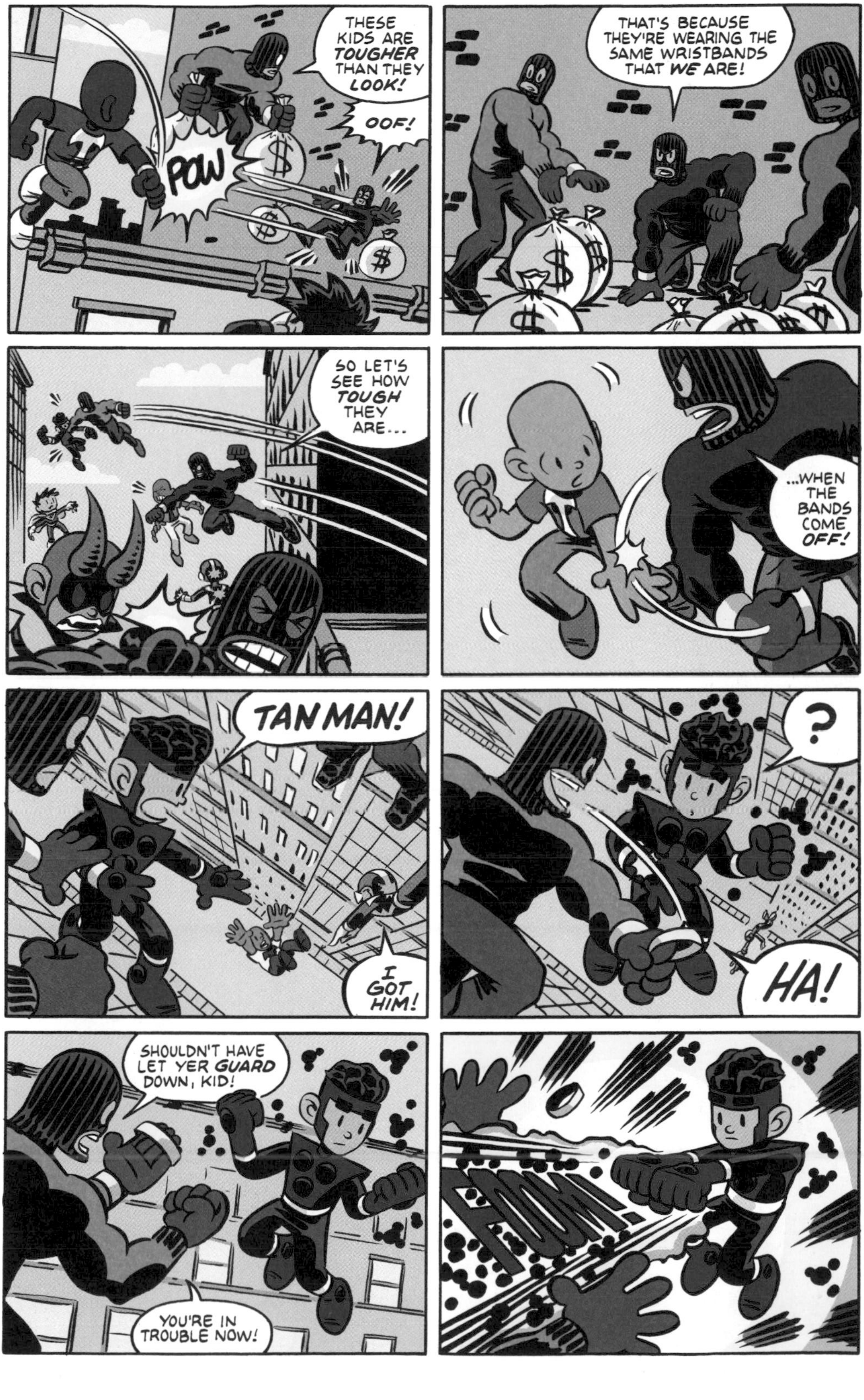
THESE KIDS ARE TOUGHER THAN THEY LOOK!
POW
OOF!
THAT'S BECAUSE THEY'RE WEARING THE SAME WRISTBANDS THAT WE ARE!
SO LET'S SEE HOW TOUGH THEY ARE...
...WHEN THE BANDS COME OFF!
TAN MAN!
I GOT HIM!
?
HA!
SHOULDN'T HAVE LET YER GUARD DOWN, KID!
YOU'RE IN TROUBLE NOW!
FOOM!

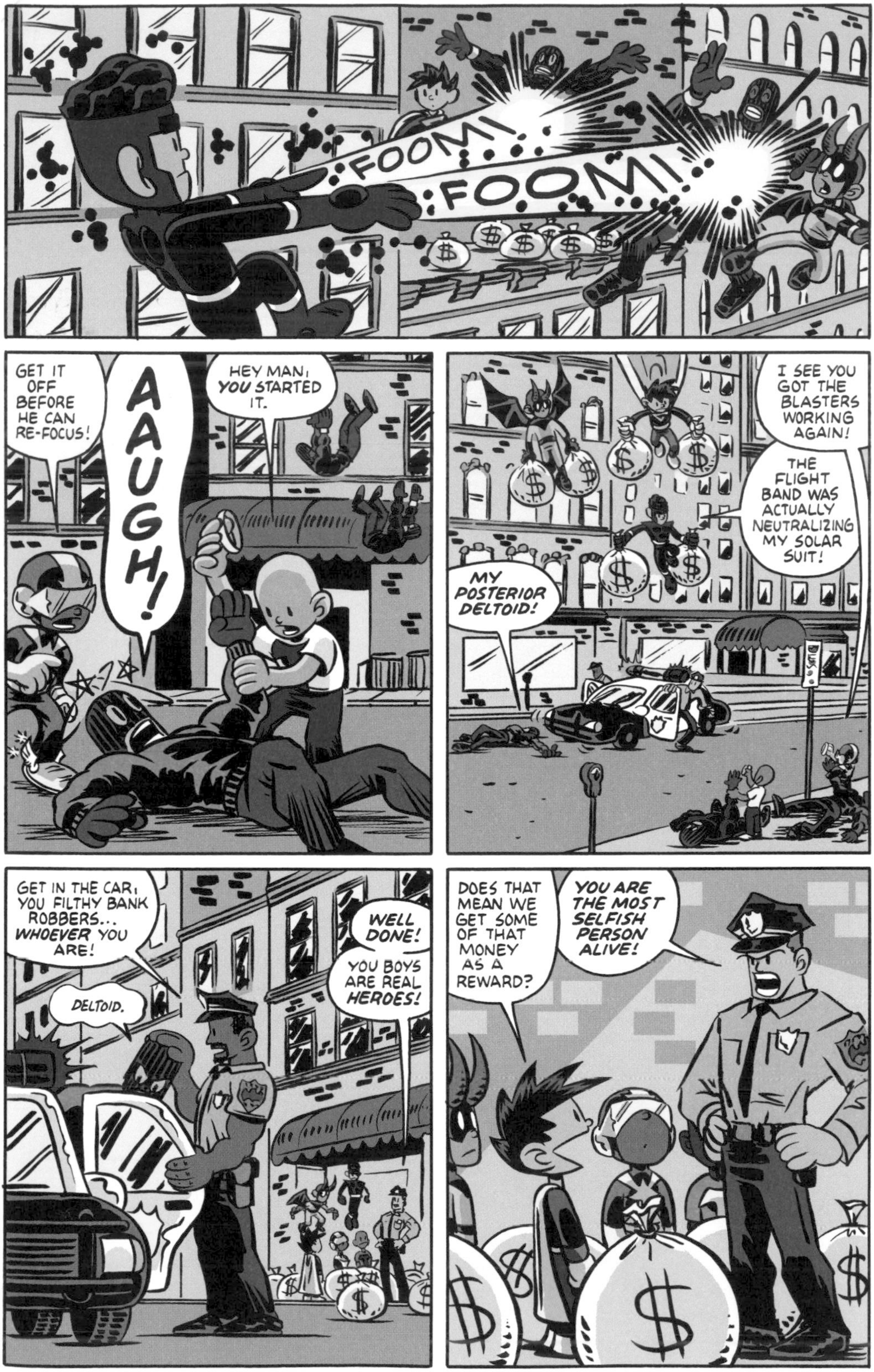
FOOM!
FOOM!
GET IT OFF BEFORE HE CAN RE-FOCUS!
AAUGH!
HEY MAN, *YOU* STARTED IT.
I SEE YOU GOT THE BLASTERS WORKING AGAIN!
THE FLIGHT BAND WAS ACTUALLY NEUTRALIZING MY SOLAR SUIT!
MY POSTERIOR DELTOID!
GET IN THE CAR, YOU FILTHY BANK ROBBERS... *WHOEVER* YOU ARE!
DELTOID.
WELL DONE!
YOU BOYS ARE REAL *HEROES!*
DOES THAT MEAN WE GET SOME OF THAT MONEY AS A REWARD?
YOU ARE THE MOST SELFISH PERSON ALIVE!

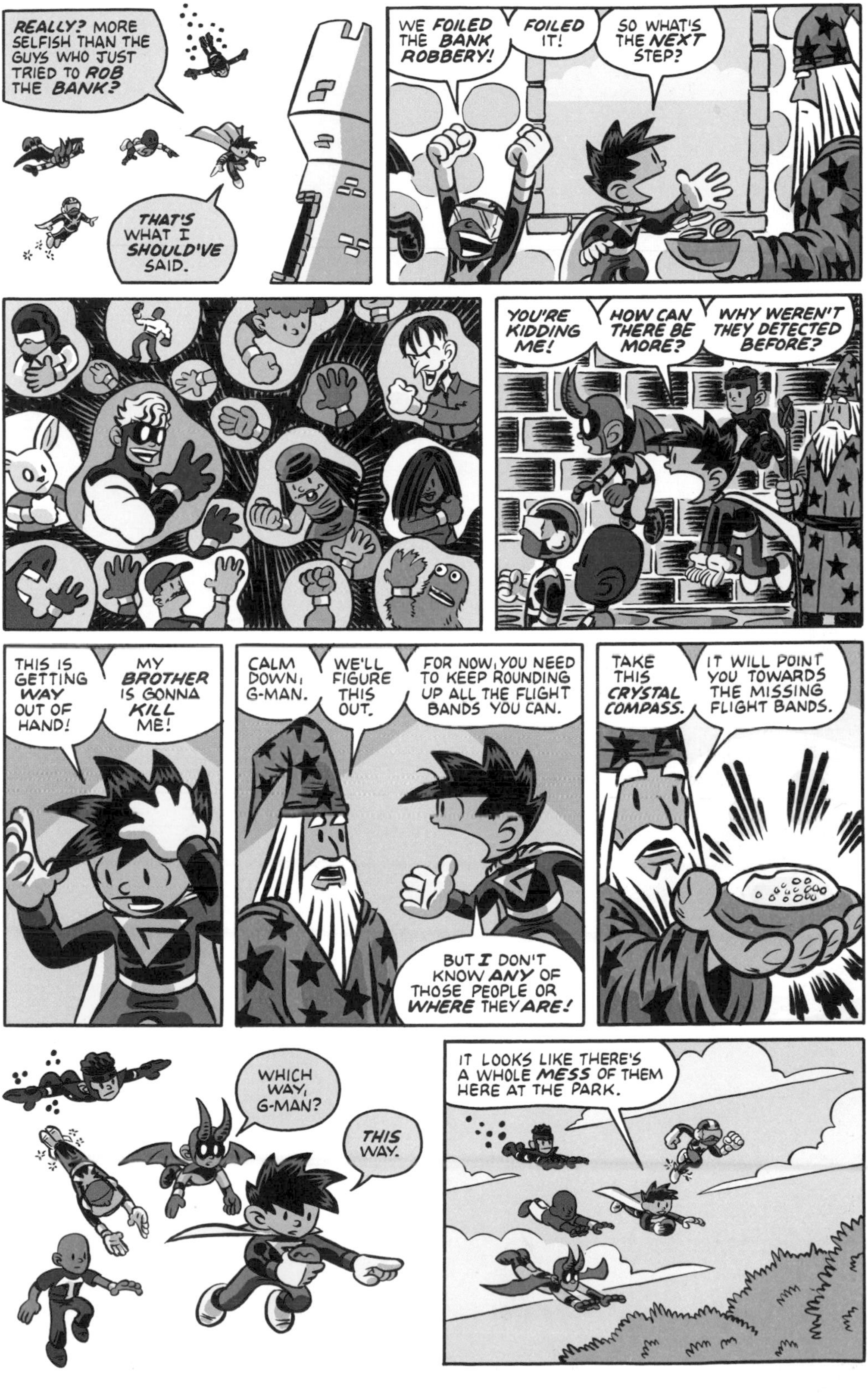
REALLY? MORE SELFISH THAN THE GUYS WHO JUST TRIED TO ROB THE BANK?
THAT'S WHAT I SHOULD'VE SAID.
WE FOILED THE BANK ROBBERY!
FOILED IT!
SO WHAT'S THE NEXT STEP?
YOU'RE KIDDING ME!
HOW CAN THERE BE MORE?
WHY WEREN'T THEY DETECTED BEFORE?
THIS IS GETTING WAY OUT OF HAND!
MY BROTHER IS GONNA KILL ME!
CALM DOWN, G-MAN.
WE'LL FIGURE THIS OUT.
FOR NOW, YOU NEED TO KEEP ROUNDING UP ALL THE FLIGHT BANDS YOU CAN.
BUT I DON'T KNOW ANY OF THOSE PEOPLE OR WHERE THEY ARE!
TAKE THIS CRYSTAL COMPASS.
IT WILL POINT YOU TOWARDS THE MISSING FLIGHT BANDS.
WHICH WAY, G-MAN?
THIS WAY.
IT LOOKS LIKE THERE'S A WHOLE MESS OF THEM HERE AT THE PARK.

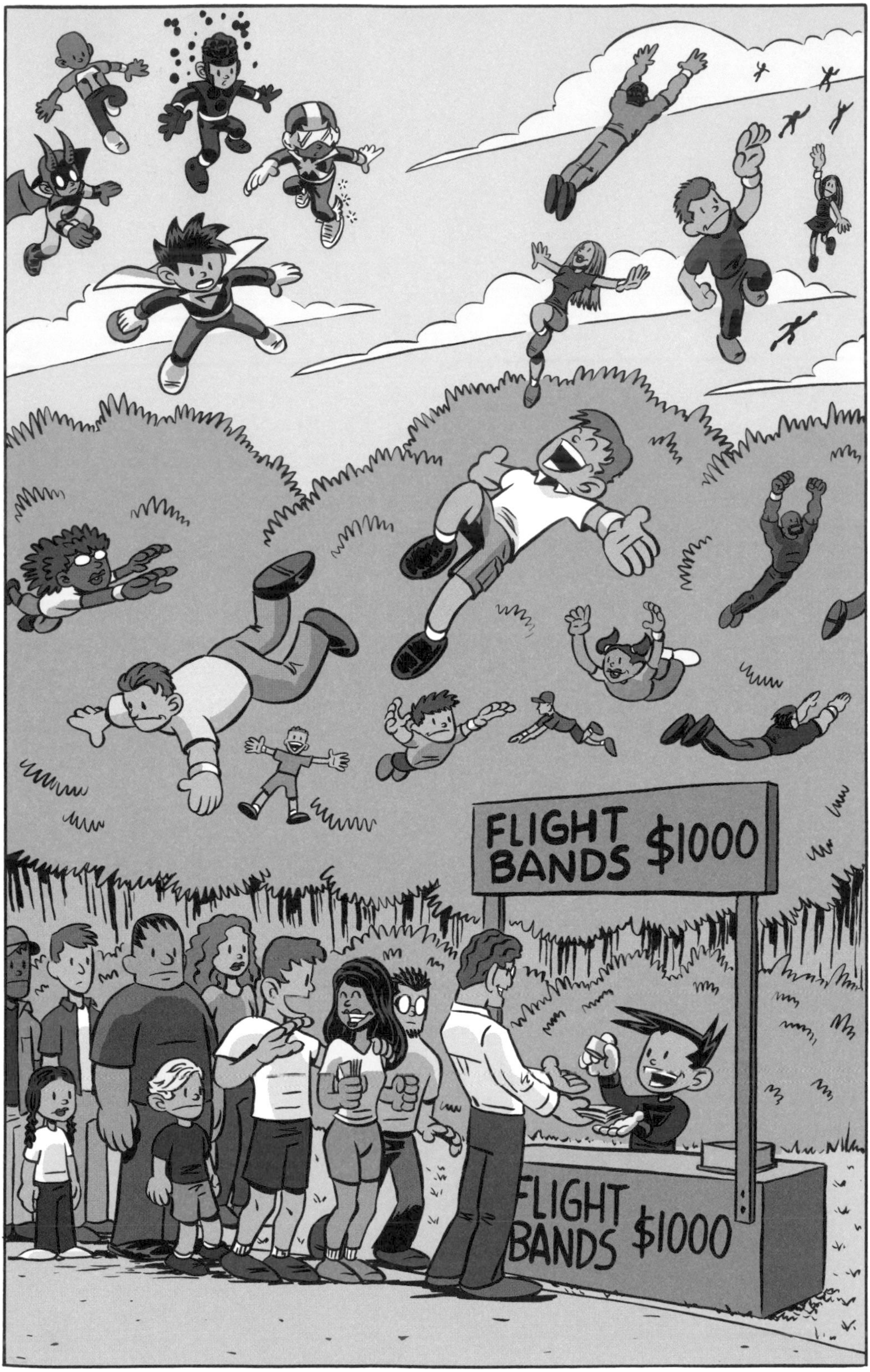
FLIGHT BANDS $1000
FLIGHT BANDS $1000

Chapter 3

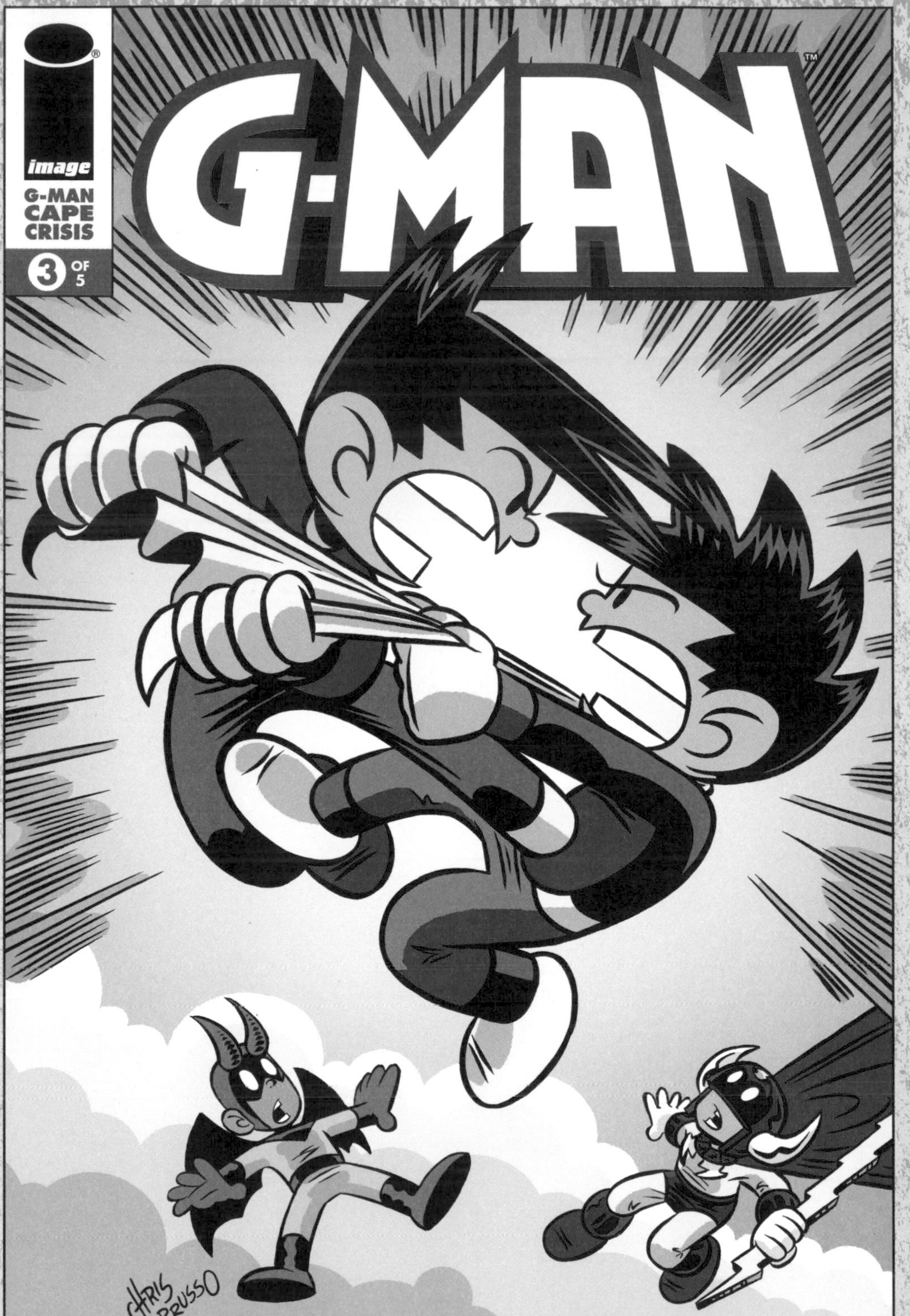
image
G-MAN
G-MAN CAPE CRISIS
3 OF 5
CHRIS GIARRUSSO

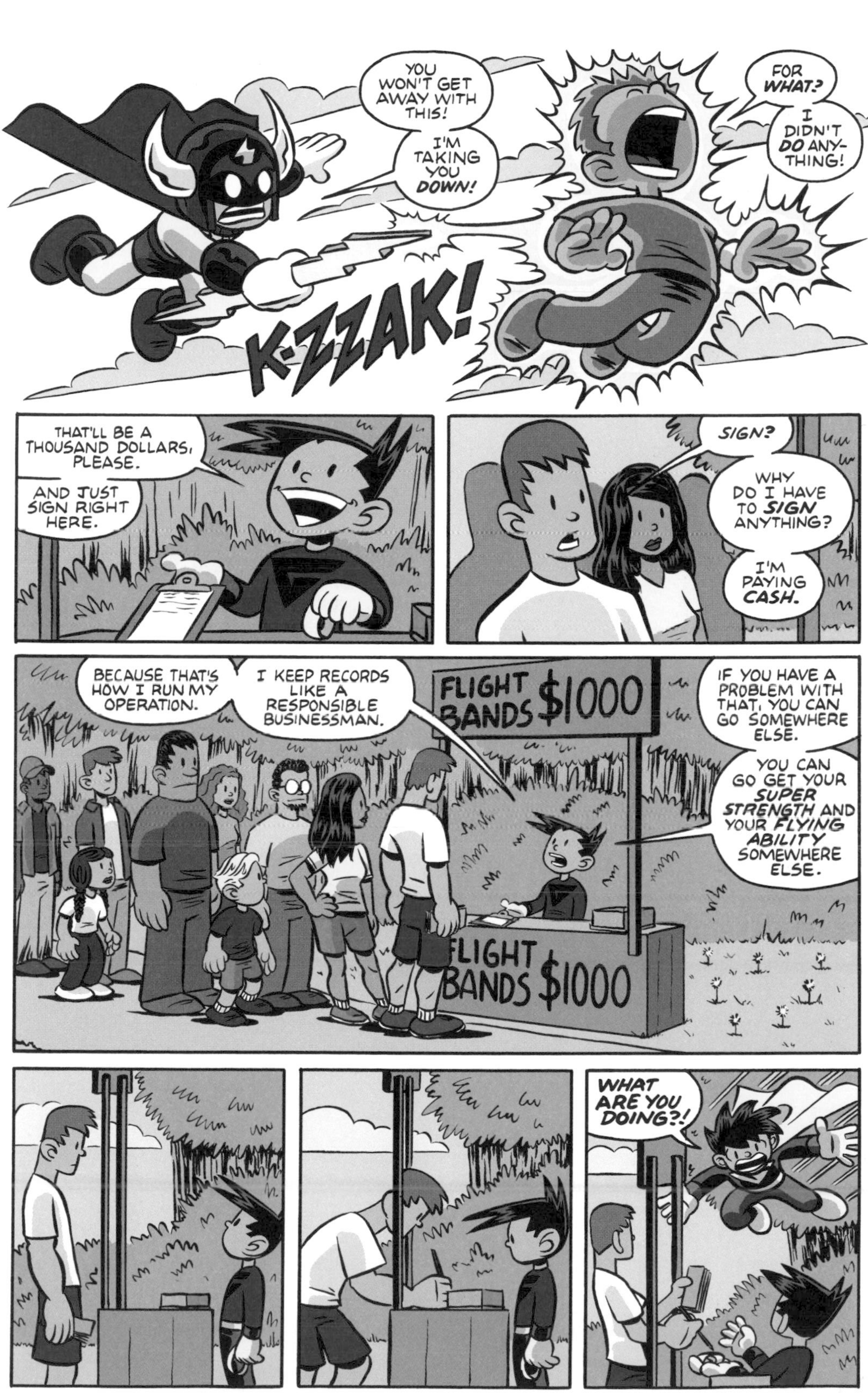
YOU WON'T GET AWAY WITH THIS!
I'M TAKING YOU DOWN!
FOR WHAT?
I DIDN'T DO ANYTHING!
K-ZZAK!
THAT'LL BE A THOUSAND DOLLARS, PLEASE.
AND JUST SIGN RIGHT HERE.
SIGN?
WHY DO I HAVE TO SIGN ANYTHING?
I'M PAYING CASH.
BECAUSE THAT'S HOW I RUN MY OPERATION.
I KEEP RECORDS LIKE A RESPONSIBLE BUSINESSMAN.
FLIGHT BANDS $1000
IF YOU HAVE A PROBLEM WITH THAT, YOU CAN GO SOMEWHERE ELSE.
YOU CAN GO GET YOUR SUPER STRENGTH AND YOUR FLYING ABILITY SOMEWHERE ELSE.
FLIGHT BANDS $1000
WHAT ARE YOU DOING?!

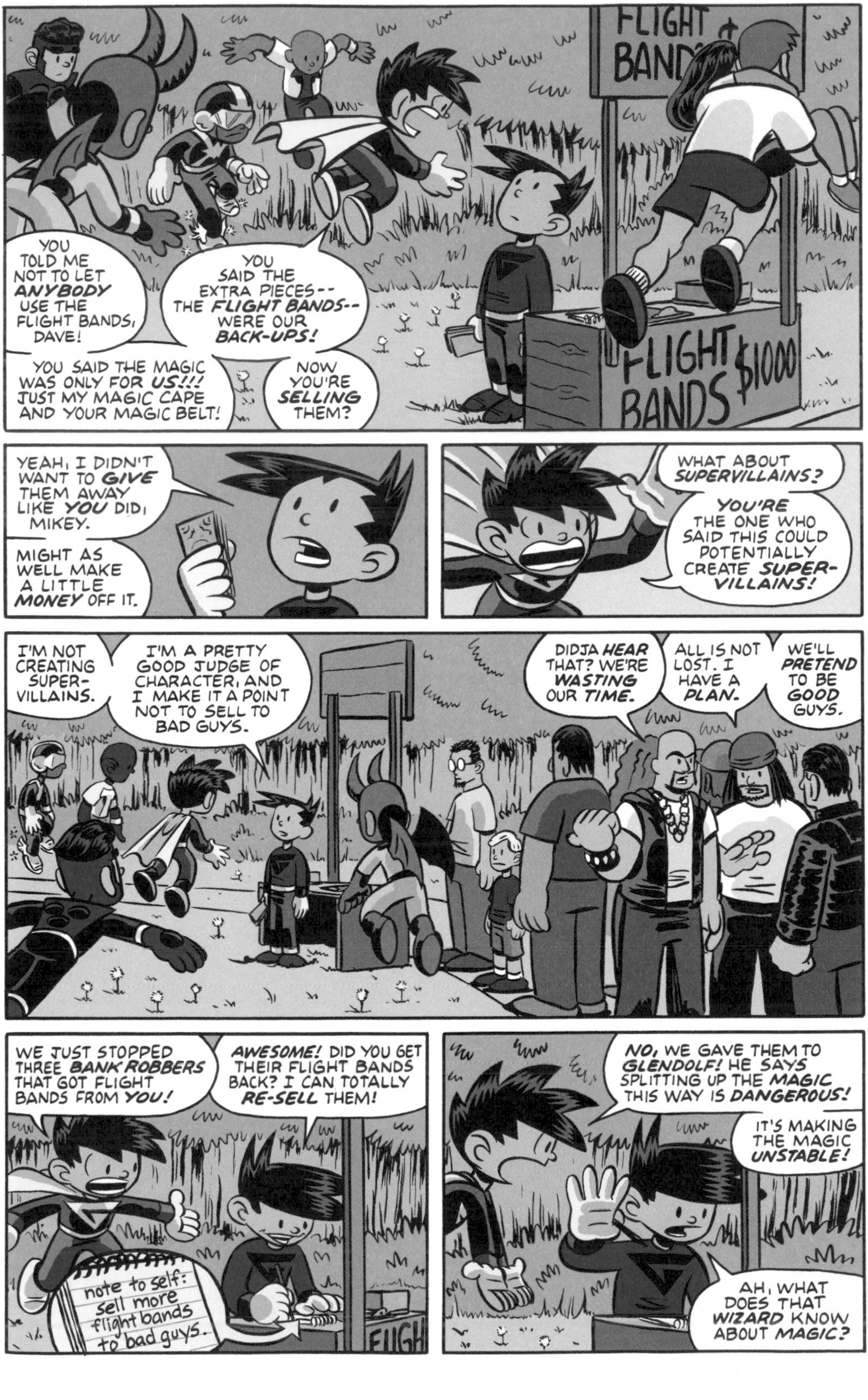
FLIGHT BANDS
YOU TOLD ME NOT TO LET ANYBODY USE THE FLIGHT BANDS, DAVE!
YOU SAID THE EXTRA PIECES-- THE FLIGHT BANDS-- WERE OUR BACK-UPS!
YOU SAID THE MAGIC WAS ONLY FOR US!!! JUST MY MAGIC CAPE AND YOUR MAGIC BELT!
NOW YOU'RE SELLING THEM?
FLIGHT BANDS $1000
YEAH, I DIDN'T WANT TO GIVE THEM AWAY LIKE YOU DID, MIKEY.
MIGHT AS WELL MAKE A LITTLE MONEY OFF IT.
WHAT ABOUT SUPERVILLAINS?
YOU'RE THE ONE WHO SAID THIS COULD POTENTIALLY CREATE SUPER-VILLAINS!
I'M NOT CREATING SUPER-VILLAINS.
I'M A PRETTY GOOD JUDGE OF CHARACTER, AND I MAKE IT A POINT NOT TO SELL TO BAD GUYS.
DIDJA HEAR THAT? WE'RE WASTING OUR TIME.
ALL IS NOT LOST. I HAVE A PLAN.
WE'LL PRETEND TO BE GOOD GUYS.
WE JUST STOPPED THREE BANK ROBBERS THAT GOT FLIGHT BANDS FROM YOU!
AWESOME! DID YOU GET THEIR FLIGHT BANDS BACK? I CAN TOTALLY RE-SELL THEM!
note to self: sell more flight bands to bad guys.
NO, WE GAVE THEM TO GLENDOLF! HE SAYS SPLITTING UP THE MAGIC THIS WAY IS DANGEROUS!
IT'S MAKING THE MAGIC UNSTABLE!
AH, WHAT DOES THAT WIZARD KNOW ABOUT MAGIC?

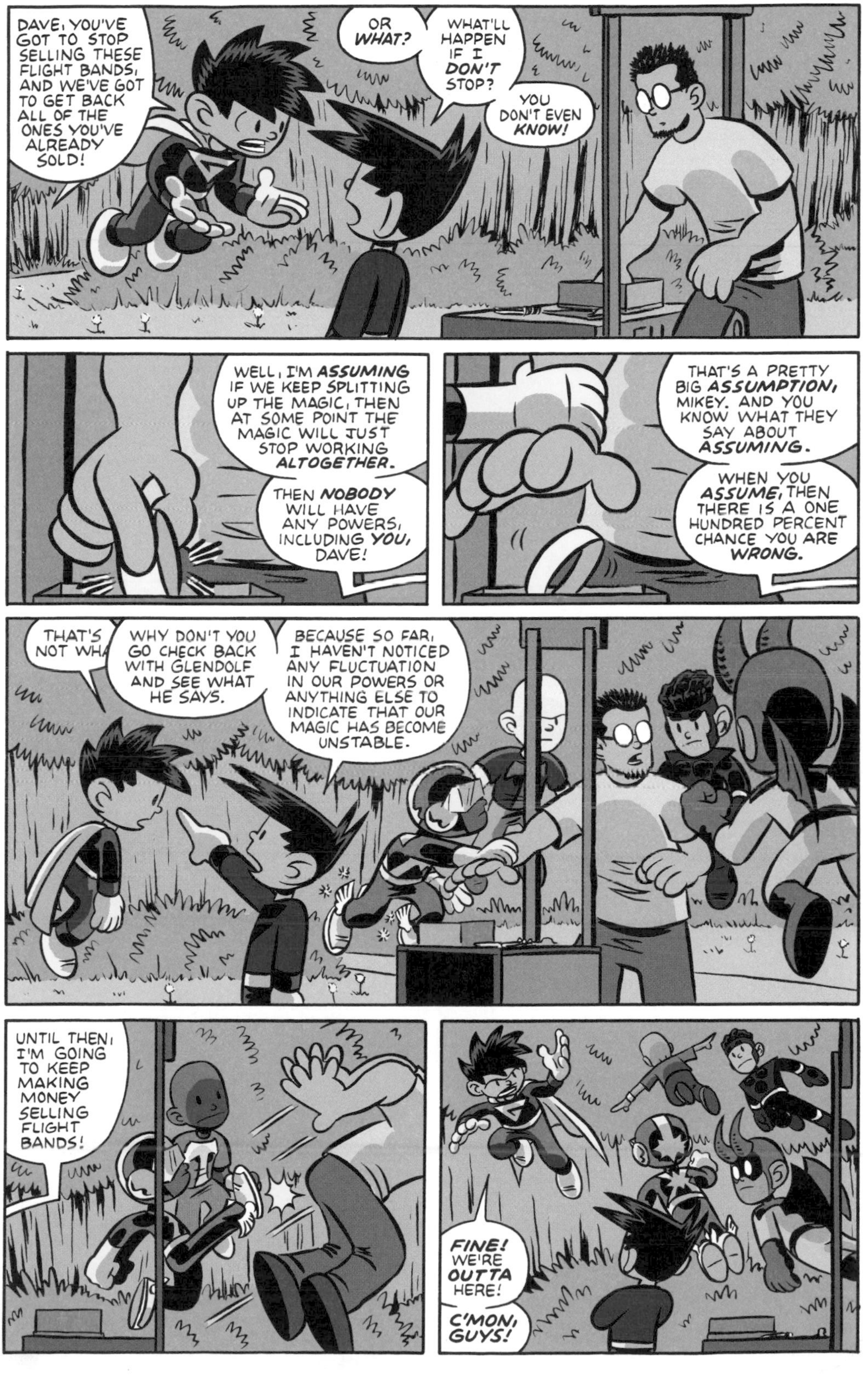
DAVE, YOU'VE GOT TO STOP SELLING THESE FLIGHT BANDS, AND WE'VE GOT TO GET BACK ALL OF THE ONES YOU'VE ALREADY SOLD!
OR WHAT?
WHAT'LL HAPPEN IF I DON'T STOP?
YOU DON'T EVEN KNOW!
WELL, I'M ASSUMING IF WE KEEP SPLITTING UP THE MAGIC, THEN AT SOME POINT THE MAGIC WILL JUST STOP WORKING ALTOGETHER.
THEN NOBODY WILL HAVE ANY POWERS, INCLUDING YOU, DAVE!
THAT'S A PRETTY BIG ASSUMPTION, MIKEY. AND YOU KNOW WHAT THEY SAY ABOUT ASSUMING.
WHEN YOU ASSUME, THEN THERE IS A ONE HUNDRED PERCENT CHANCE YOU ARE WRONG.
THAT'S NOT WHA
WHY DON'T YOU GO CHECK BACK WITH GLENDOLF AND SEE WHAT HE SAYS.
BECAUSE SO FAR, I HAVEN'T NOTICED ANY FLUCTUATION IN OUR POWERS OR ANYTHING ELSE TO INDICATE THAT OUR MAGIC HAS BECOME UNSTABLE.
UNTIL THEN, I'M GOING TO KEEP MAKING MONEY SELLING FLIGHT BANDS!
FINE! WE'RE OUTTA HERE!
C'MON, GUYS!

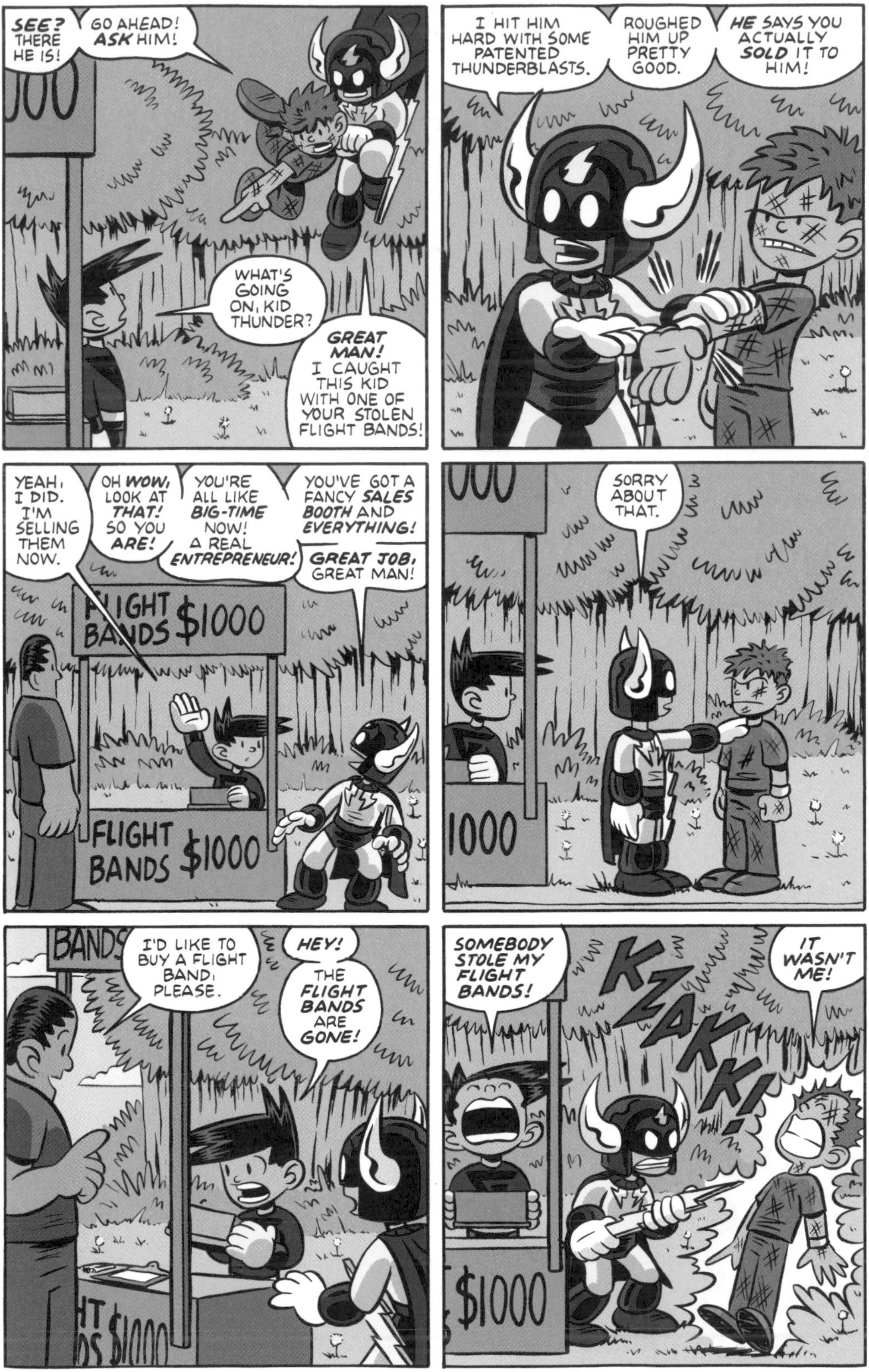
SEE? THERE HE IS!
GO AHEAD! ASK HIM!
WHAT'S GOING ON, KID THUNDER?
GREAT MAN! I CAUGHT THIS KID WITH ONE OF YOUR STOLEN FLIGHT BANDS!
I HIT HIM HARD WITH SOME PATENTED THUNDERBLASTS.
ROUGHED HIM UP PRETTY GOOD.
HE SAYS YOU ACTUALLY SOLD IT TO HIM!
YEAH, I DID. I'M SELLING THEM NOW.
OH WOW, LOOK AT THAT! SO YOU ARE!
YOU'RE ALL LIKE BIG-TIME NOW! A REAL ENTREPRENEUR!
YOU'VE GOT A FANCY SALES BOOTH AND EVERYTHING!
GREAT JOB, GREAT MAN!
FLIGHT BANDS $1000
FLIGHT BANDS $1000
SORRY ABOUT THAT.
I'D LIKE TO BUY A FLIGHT BAND, PLEASE.
HEY!
THE FLIGHT BANDS ARE GONE!
SOMEBODY STOLE MY FLIGHT BANDS!
KZAKK!
IT WASN'T ME!

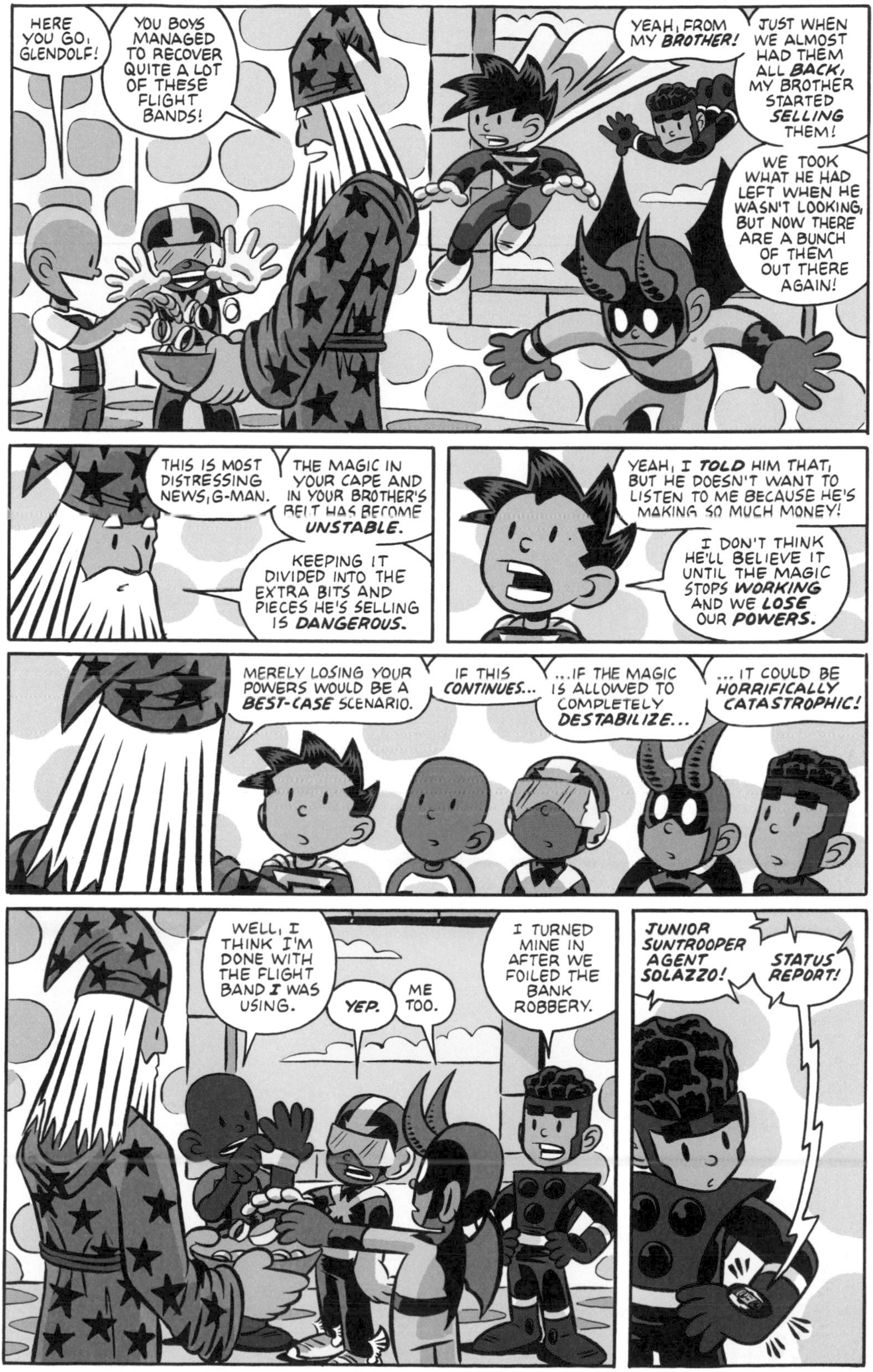
HERE YOU GO, GLENDOLF!
YOU BOYS MANAGED TO RECOVER QUITE A LOT OF THESE FLIGHT BANDS!
YEAH, FROM MY **BROTHER!**
JUST WHEN WE ALMOST HAD THEM ALL **BACK,** MY BROTHER STARTED **SELLING** THEM!
WE TOOK WHAT HE HAD LEFT WHEN HE WASN'T LOOKING, BUT NOW THERE ARE A BUNCH OF THEM OUT THERE AGAIN!
THIS IS MOST DISTRESSING NEWS, G-MAN.
THE MAGIC IN YOUR CAPE AND IN YOUR BROTHER'S BELT HAS BECOME **UNSTABLE.**
KEEPING IT DIVIDED INTO THE EXTRA BITS AND PIECES HE'S SELLING IS **DANGEROUS.**
YEAH, I **TOLD** HIM THAT, BUT HE DOESN'T WANT TO LISTEN TO ME BECAUSE HE'S MAKING SO MUCH MONEY!
I DON'T THINK HE'LL BELIEVE IT UNTIL THE MAGIC STOPS **WORKING** AND WE **LOSE** OUR **POWERS.**
MERELY LOSING YOUR POWERS WOULD BE A **BEST-CASE** SCENARIO.
IF THIS **CONTINUES...**
...IF THE MAGIC IS ALLOWED TO COMPLETELY **DESTABILIZE...**
...IT COULD BE **HORRIFICALLY CATASTROPHIC!**
WELL, I THINK I'M DONE WITH THE FLIGHT BAND **I** WAS USING.
YEP.
ME TOO.
I TURNED MINE IN AFTER WE FOILED THE BANK ROBBERY.
JUNIOR SUNTROOPER AGENT SOLAZZO!
STATUS REPORT!

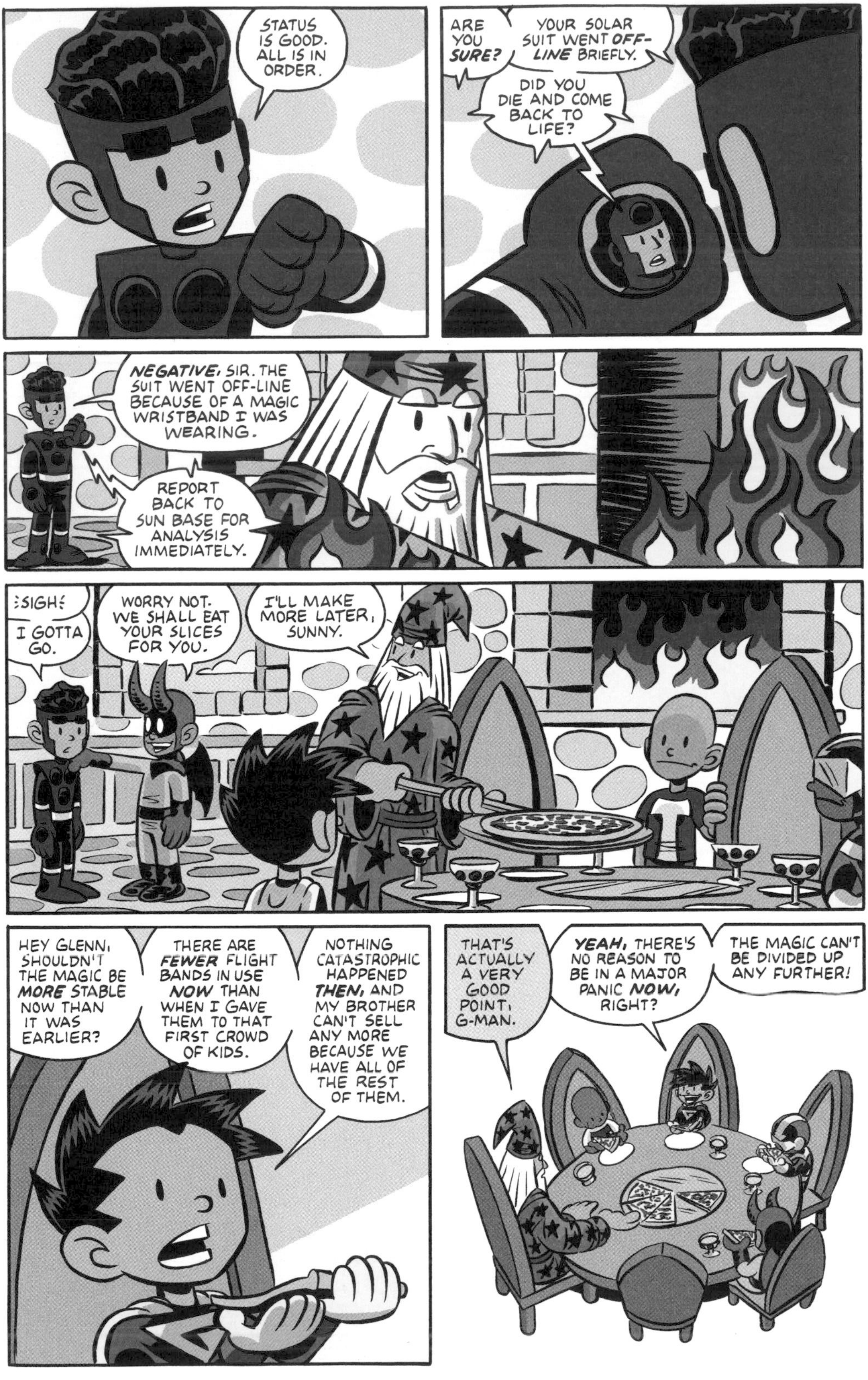
STATUS IS GOOD. ALL IS IN ORDER.
ARE YOU SURE?
YOUR SOLAR SUIT WENT OFF-LINE BRIEFLY.
DID YOU DIE AND COME BACK TO LIFE?
NEGATIVE, SIR. THE SUIT WENT OFF-LINE BECAUSE OF A MAGIC WRISTBAND I WAS WEARING.
REPORT BACK TO SUN BASE FOR ANALYSIS IMMEDIATELY.
:SIGH:
I GOTTA GO.
WORRY NOT. WE SHALL EAT YOUR SLICES FOR YOU.
I'LL MAKE MORE LATER, SUNNY.
HEY GLENN, SHOULDN'T THE MAGIC BE MORE STABLE NOW THAN IT WAS EARLIER?
THERE ARE FEWER FLIGHT BANDS IN USE NOW THAN WHEN I GAVE THEM TO THAT FIRST CROWD OF KIDS.
NOTHING CATASTROPHIC HAPPENED THEN, AND MY BROTHER CAN'T SELL ANY MORE BECAUSE WE HAVE ALL OF THE REST OF THEM.
THAT'S ACTUALLY A VERY GOOD POINT, G-MAN.
YEAH, THERE'S NO REASON TO BE IN A MAJOR PANIC NOW, RIGHT?
THE MAGIC CAN'T BE DIVIDED UP ANY FURTHER!

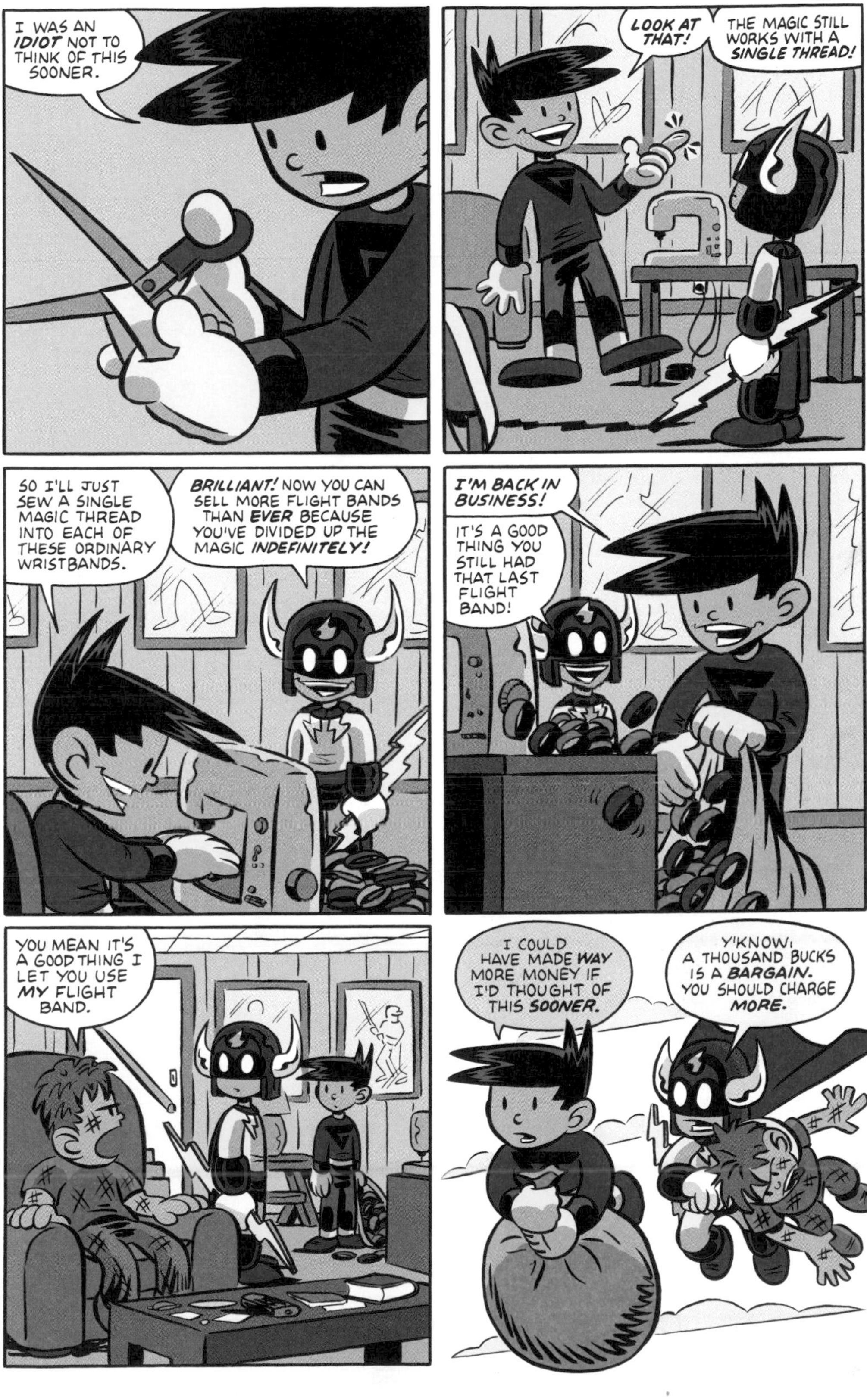
I WAS AN *IDIOT* NOT TO THINK OF THIS SOONER.
LOOK AT THAT!
THE MAGIC STILL WORKS WITH A *SINGLE THREAD!*
SO I'LL JUST SEW A SINGLE MAGIC THREAD INTO EACH OF THESE ORDINARY WRISTBANDS.
BRILLIANT! NOW YOU CAN SELL MORE FLIGHT BANDS THAN *EVER* BECAUSE YOU'VE DIVIDED UP THE MAGIC *INDEFINITELY!*
I'M BACK IN BUSINESS!
IT'S A GOOD THING YOU STILL HAD THAT LAST FLIGHT BAND!
YOU MEAN IT'S A GOOD THING I LET YOU USE *MY* FLIGHT BAND.
I COULD HAVE MADE *WAY* MORE MONEY IF I'D THOUGHT OF THIS *SOONER.*
Y'KNOW, A THOUSAND BUCKS IS A *BARGAIN.* YOU SHOULD CHARGE *MORE.*

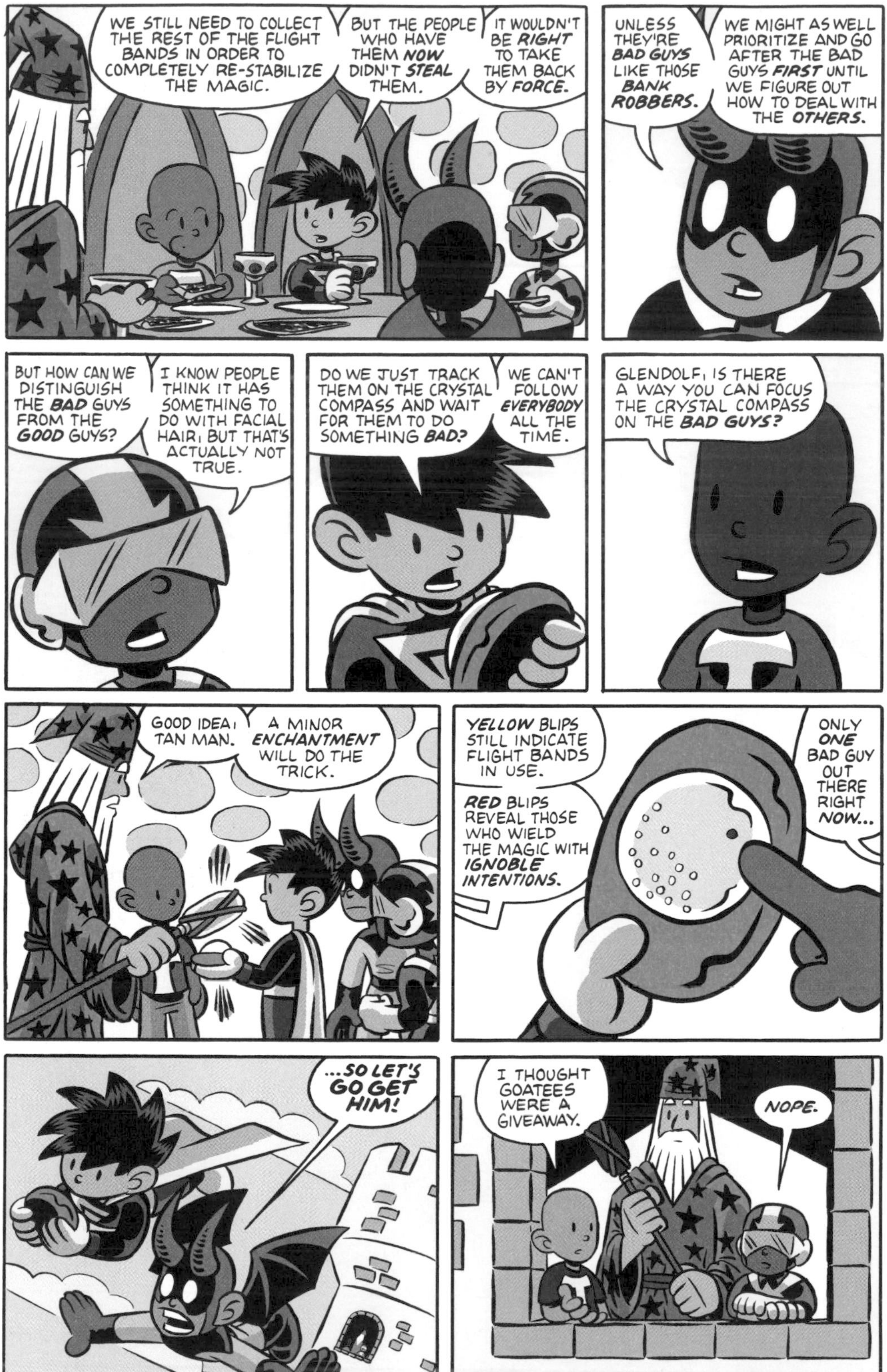
WE STILL NEED TO COLLECT THE REST OF THE FLIGHT BANDS IN ORDER TO COMPLETELY RE-STABILIZE THE MAGIC.
BUT THE PEOPLE WHO HAVE THEM NOW DIDN'T STEAL THEM.
IT WOULDN'T BE RIGHT TO TAKE THEM BACK BY FORCE.
UNLESS THEY'RE BAD GUYS LIKE THOSE BANK ROBBERS.
WE MIGHT AS WELL PRIORITIZE AND GO AFTER THE BAD GUYS FIRST UNTIL WE FIGURE OUT HOW TO DEAL WITH THE OTHERS.
BUT HOW CAN WE DISTINGUISH THE BAD GUYS FROM THE GOOD GUYS?
I KNOW PEOPLE THINK IT HAS SOMETHING TO DO WITH FACIAL HAIR, BUT THAT'S ACTUALLY NOT TRUE.
DO WE JUST TRACK THEM ON THE CRYSTAL COMPASS AND WAIT FOR THEM TO DO SOMETHING BAD?
WE CAN'T FOLLOW EVERYBODY ALL THE TIME.
GLENDOLF, IS THERE A WAY YOU CAN FOCUS THE CRYSTAL COMPASS ON THE BAD GUYS?
GOOD IDEA, TAN MAN.
A MINOR ENCHANTMENT WILL DO THE TRICK.
YELLOW BLIPS STILL INDICATE FLIGHT BANDS IN USE.
RED BLIPS REVEAL THOSE WHO WIELD THE MAGIC WITH IGNOBLE INTENTIONS.
ONLY ONE BAD GUY OUT THERE RIGHT NOW...
...SO LET'S GO GET HIM!
I THOUGHT GOATEES WERE A GIVEAWAY.
NOPE.

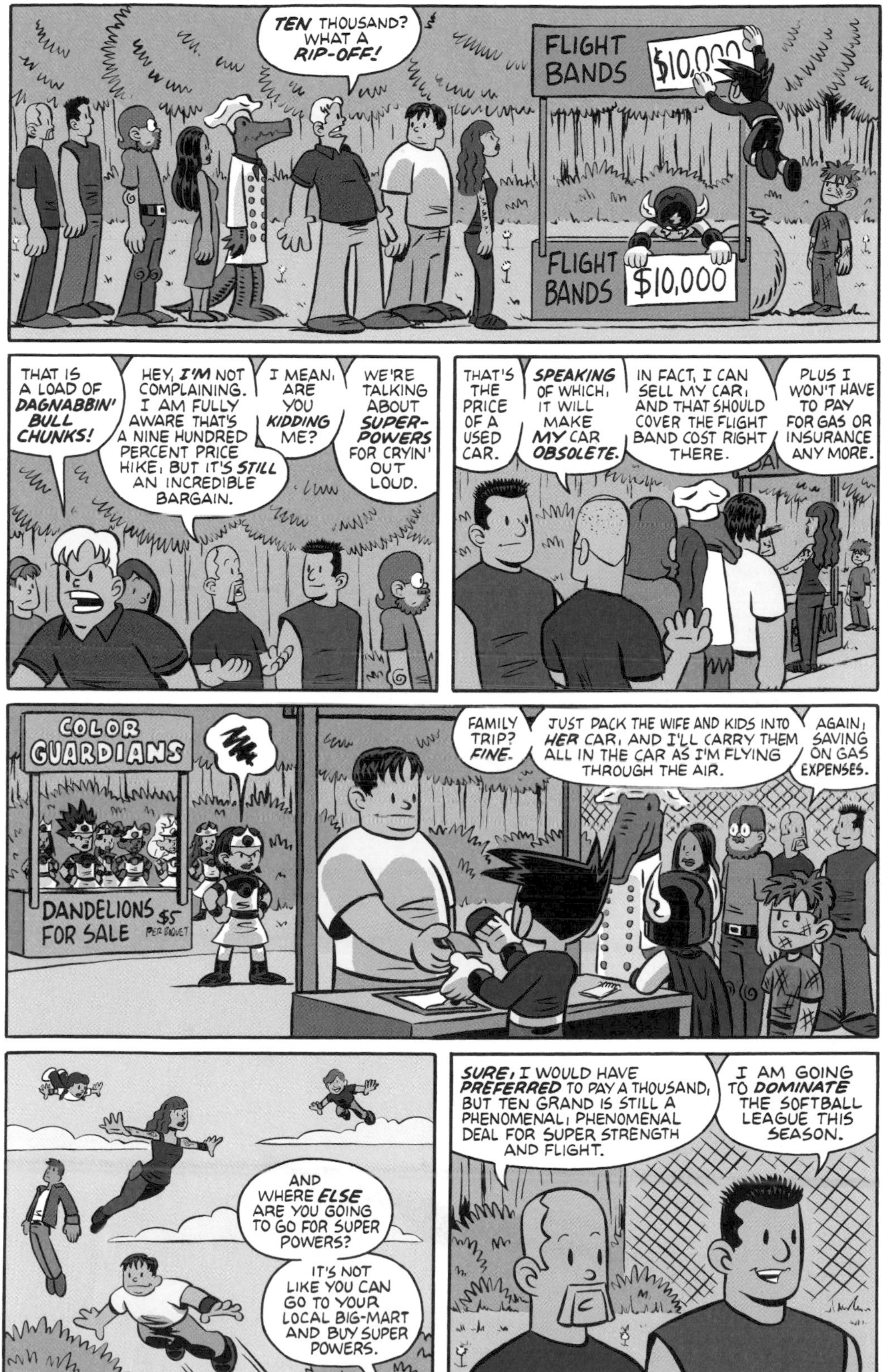

TEN THOUSAND? WHAT A RIP-OFF!
FLIGHT BANDS
$10,000
FLIGHT BANDS
$10,000
THAT IS A LOAD OF DAGNABBIN' BULL CHUNKS!
HEY, I'M NOT COMPLAINING. I AM FULLY AWARE THAT'S A NINE HUNDRED PERCENT PRICE HIKE, BUT IT'S STILL AN INCREDIBLE BARGAIN.
I MEAN, ARE YOU KIDDING ME?
WE'RE TALKING ABOUT SUPER-POWERS FOR CRYIN' OUT LOUD.
THAT'S THE PRICE OF A USED CAR.
SPEAKING OF WHICH, IT WILL MAKE MY CAR OBSOLETE.
IN FACT, I CAN SELL MY CAR, AND THAT SHOULD COVER THE FLIGHT BAND COST RIGHT THERE.
PLUS I WON'T HAVE TO PAY FOR GAS OR INSURANCE ANY MORE.
COLOR GUARDIANS
DANDELIONS $5 PER BOQUET
FOR SALE
FAMILY TRIP? FINE.
JUST PACK THE WIFE AND KIDS INTO HER CAR, AND I'LL CARRY THEM ALL IN THE CAR AS I'M FLYING THROUGH THE AIR.
AGAIN, SAVING ON GAS EXPENSES.
AND WHERE ELSE ARE YOU GOING TO GO FOR SUPER POWERS?
IT'S NOT LIKE YOU CAN GO TO YOUR LOCAL BIG-MART AND BUY SUPER POWERS.
SURE, I WOULD HAVE PREFERRED TO PAY A THOUSAND, BUT TEN GRAND IS STILL A PHENOMENAL, PHENOMENAL DEAL FOR SUPER STRENGTH AND FLIGHT.
I AM GOING TO DOMINATE THE SOFTBALL LEAGUE THIS SEASON.

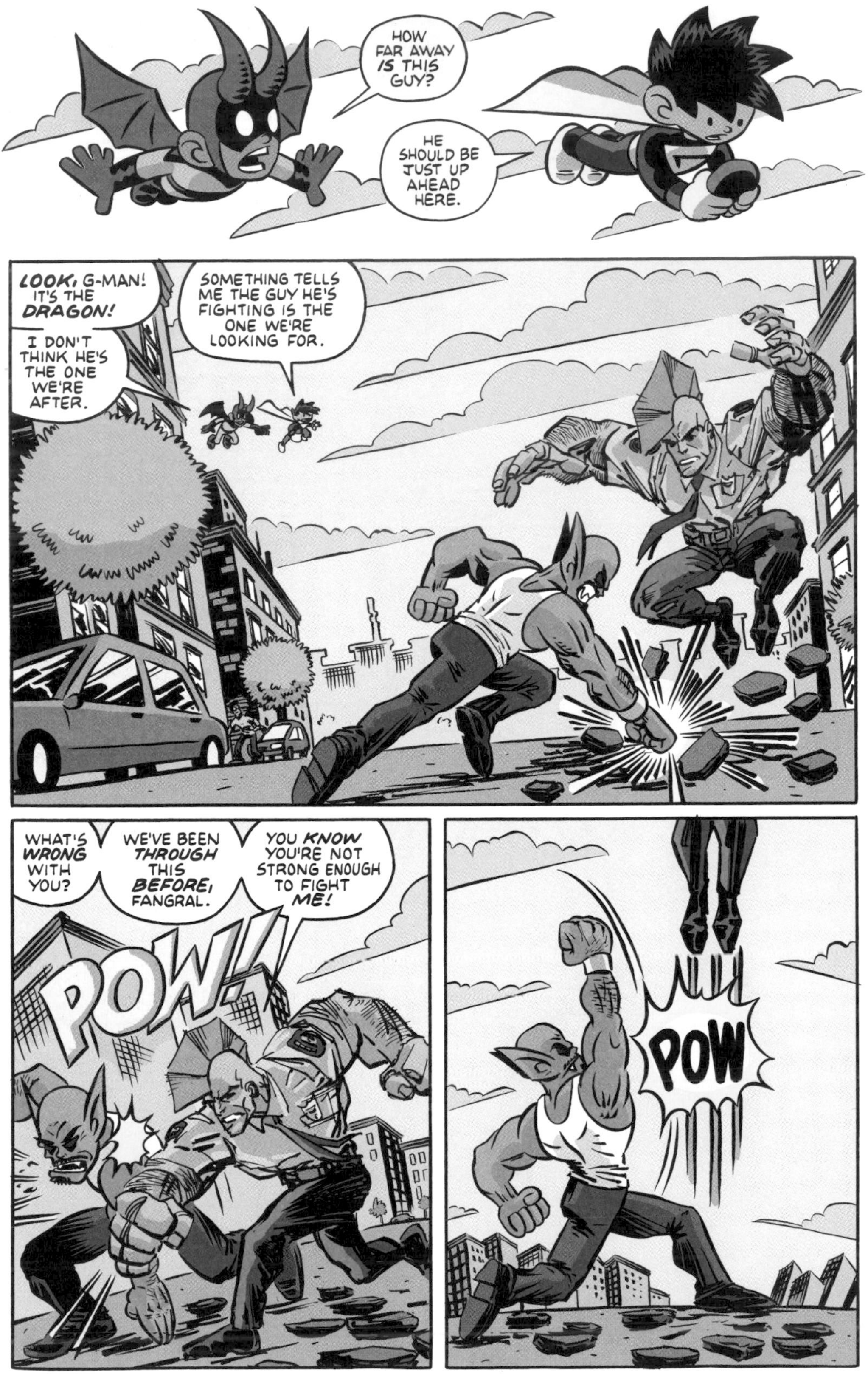
HOW FAR AWAY IS THIS GUY?
HE SHOULD BE JUST UP AHEAD HERE.
LOOK, G-MAN! IT'S THE DRAGON!
I DON'T THINK HE'S THE ONE WE'RE AFTER.
SOMETHING TELLS ME THE GUY HE'S FIGHTING IS THE ONE WE'RE LOOKING FOR.
WHAT'S WRONG WITH YOU?
WE'VE BEEN THROUGH THIS BEFORE, FANGRAL.
YOU KNOW YOU'RE NOT STRONG ENOUGH TO FIGHT ME!
POW!
POW

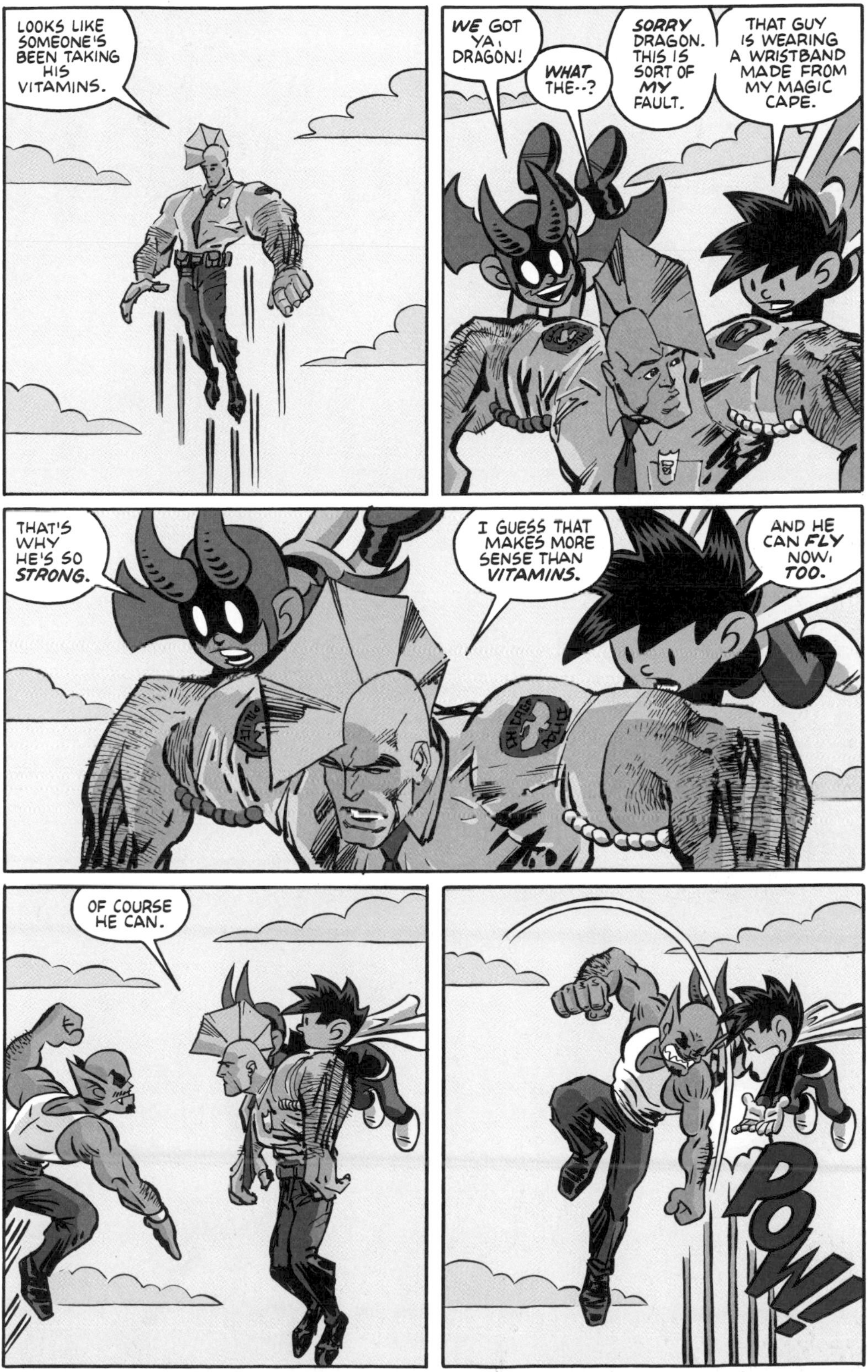
LOOKS LIKE SOMEONE'S BEEN TAKING HIS VITAMINS.
WE GOT YA, DRAGON!
WHAT THE--?
SORRY DRAGON. THIS IS SORT OF MY FAULT.
THAT GUY IS WEARING A WRISTBAND MADE FROM MY MAGIC CAPE.
THAT'S WHY HE'S SO STRONG.
I GUESS THAT MAKES MORE SENSE THAN VITAMINS.
AND HE CAN FLY NOW, TOO.
OF COURSE HE CAN.
POW!

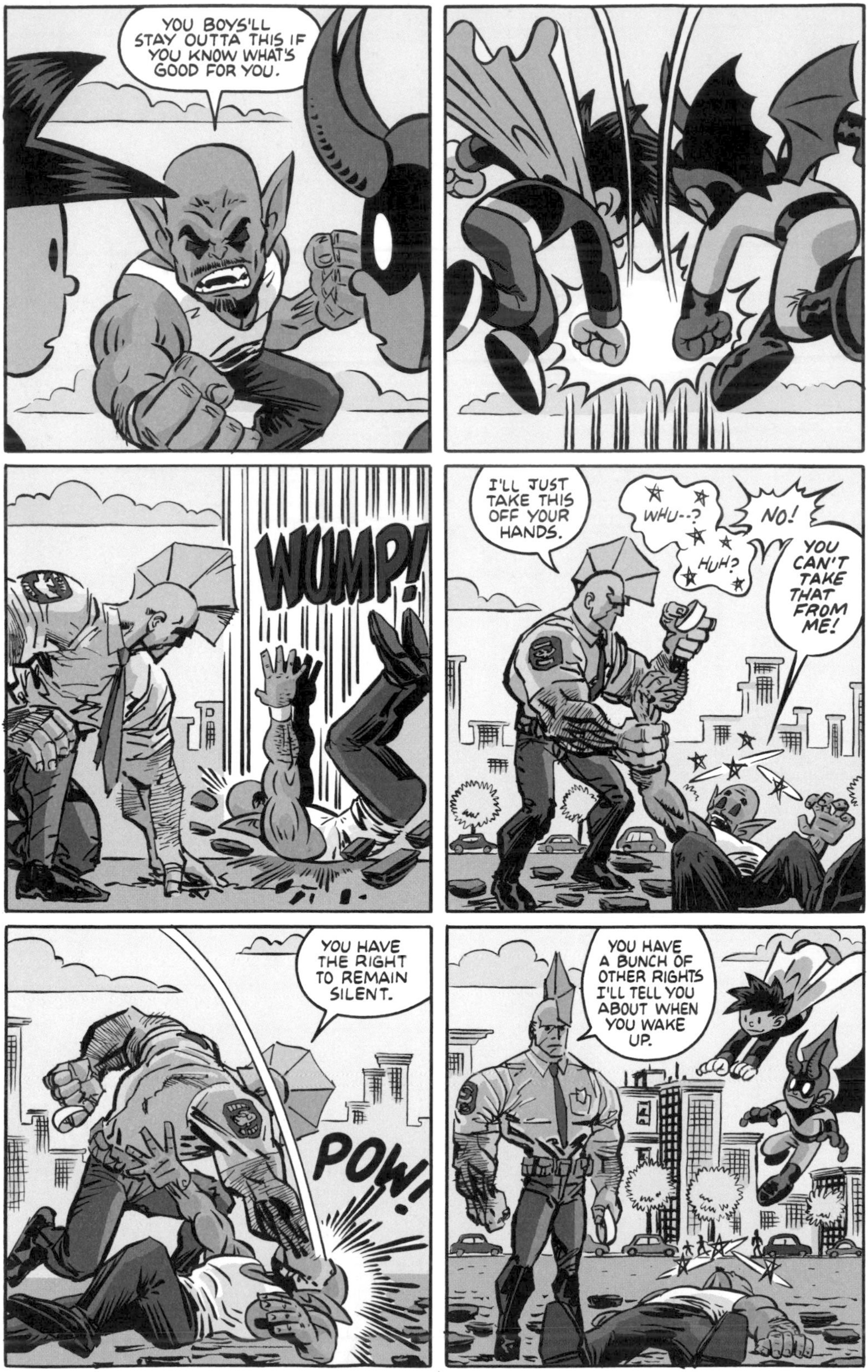
YOU BOYS'LL STAY OUTTA THIS IF YOU KNOW WHAT'S GOOD FOR YOU.
WUMP!
I'LL JUST TAKE THIS OFF YOUR HANDS.
WHU--? HUH?
NO!
YOU CAN'T TAKE THAT FROM ME!
YOU HAVE THE RIGHT TO REMAIN SILENT.
POW!
YOU HAVE A BUNCH OF OTHER RIGHTS I'LL TELL YOU ABOUT WHEN YOU WAKE UP.

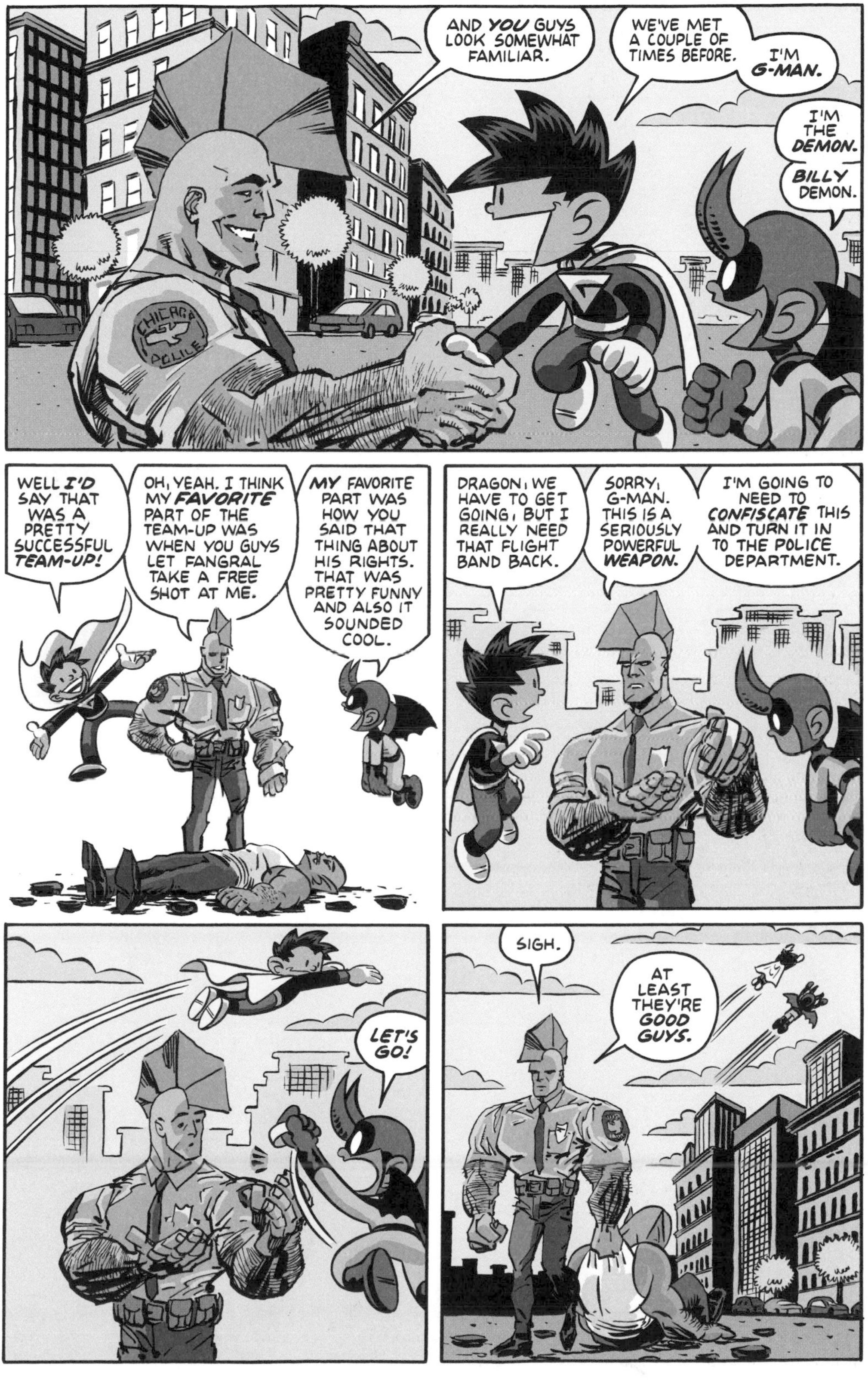
AND *YOU* GUYS LOOK SOMEWHAT FAMILIAR.
WE'VE MET A COUPLE OF TIMES BEFORE.
I'M *G-MAN.*
I'M THE *DEMON.*
BILLY DEMON.
WELL *I'D* SAY THAT WAS A PRETTY SUCCESSFUL *TEAM-UP!*
OH, YEAH. I THINK MY *FAVORITE* PART OF THE TEAM-UP WAS WHEN YOU GUYS LET FANGRAL TAKE A FREE SHOT AT ME.
MY FAVORITE PART WAS HOW YOU SAID THAT THING ABOUT HIS RIGHTS. THAT WAS PRETTY FUNNY AND ALSO IT SOUNDED COOL.
DRAGON, WE HAVE TO GET GOING, BUT I REALLY NEED THAT FLIGHT BAND BACK.
SORRY, G-MAN. THIS IS A SERIOUSLY POWERFUL *WEAPON.*
I'M GOING TO NEED TO *CONFISCATE* THIS AND TURN IT IN TO THE POLICE DEPARTMENT.
LET'S GO!
SIGH.
AT LEAST THEY'RE *GOOD GUYS.*

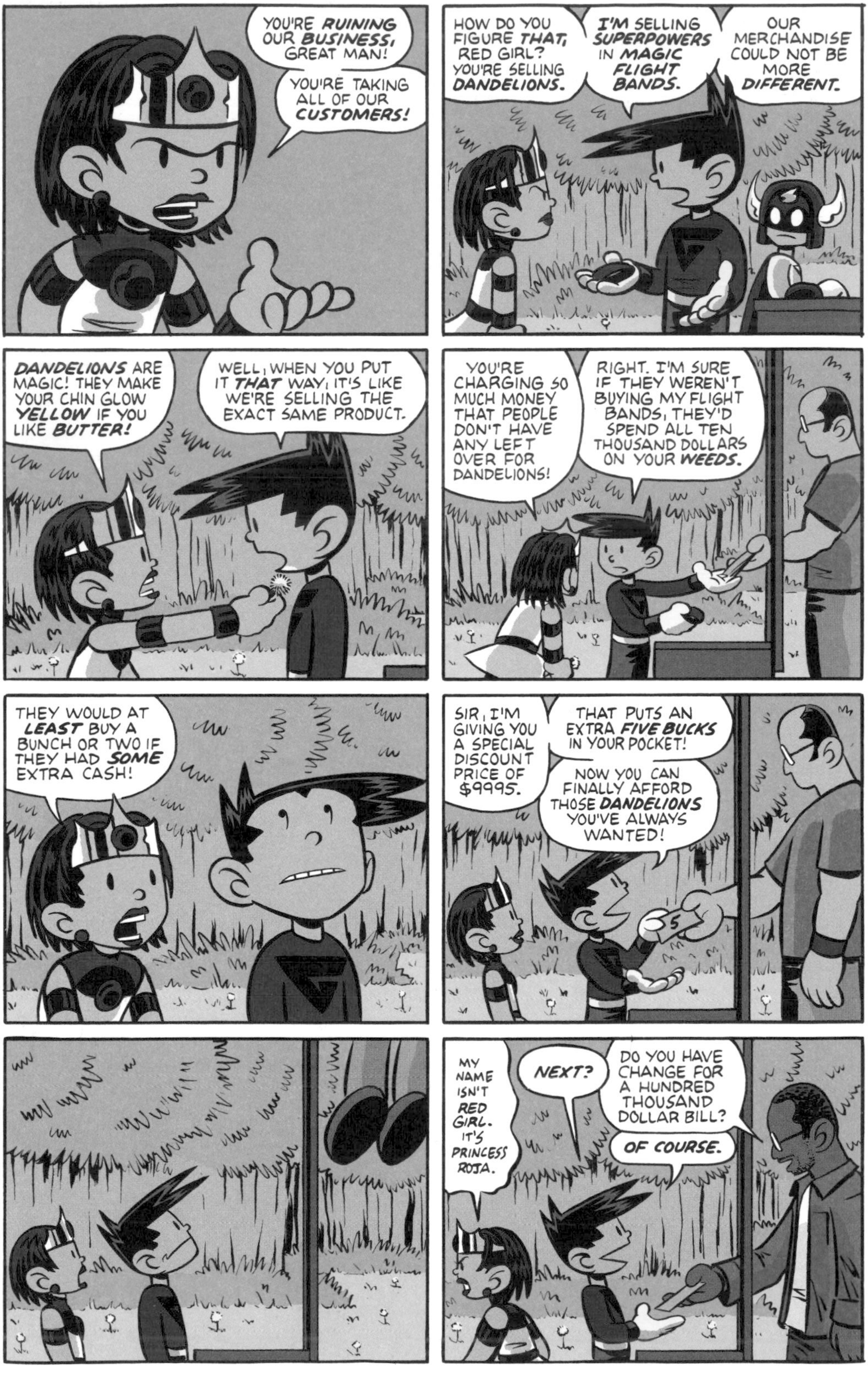
YOU'RE RUINING OUR BUSINESS, GREAT MAN!
YOU'RE TAKING ALL OF OUR CUSTOMERS!
HOW DO YOU FIGURE THAT, RED GIRL? YOU'RE SELLING DANDELIONS.
I'M SELLING SUPERPOWERS IN MAGIC FLIGHT BANDS.
OUR MERCHANDISE COULD NOT BE MORE DIFFERENT.
DANDELIONS ARE MAGIC! THEY MAKE YOUR CHIN GLOW YELLOW IF YOU LIKE BUTTER!
WELL, WHEN YOU PUT IT THAT WAY, IT'S LIKE WE'RE SELLING THE EXACT SAME PRODUCT.
YOU'RE CHARGING SO MUCH MONEY THAT PEOPLE DON'T HAVE ANY LEFT OVER FOR DANDELIONS!
RIGHT. I'M SURE IF THEY WEREN'T BUYING MY FLIGHT BANDS, THEY'D SPEND ALL TEN THOUSAND DOLLARS ON YOUR WEEDS.
THEY WOULD AT LEAST BUY A BUNCH OR TWO IF THEY HAD SOME EXTRA CASH!
SIR, I'M GIVING YOU A SPECIAL DISCOUNT PRICE OF $9995.
THAT PUTS AN EXTRA FIVE BUCKS IN YOUR POCKET!
NOW YOU CAN FINALLY AFFORD THOSE DANDELIONS YOU'VE ALWAYS WANTED!
5
MY NAME ISN'T RED GIRL. IT'S PRINCESS ROJA.
NEXT?
DO YOU HAVE CHANGE FOR A HUNDRED THOUSAND DOLLAR BILL?
OF COURSE.

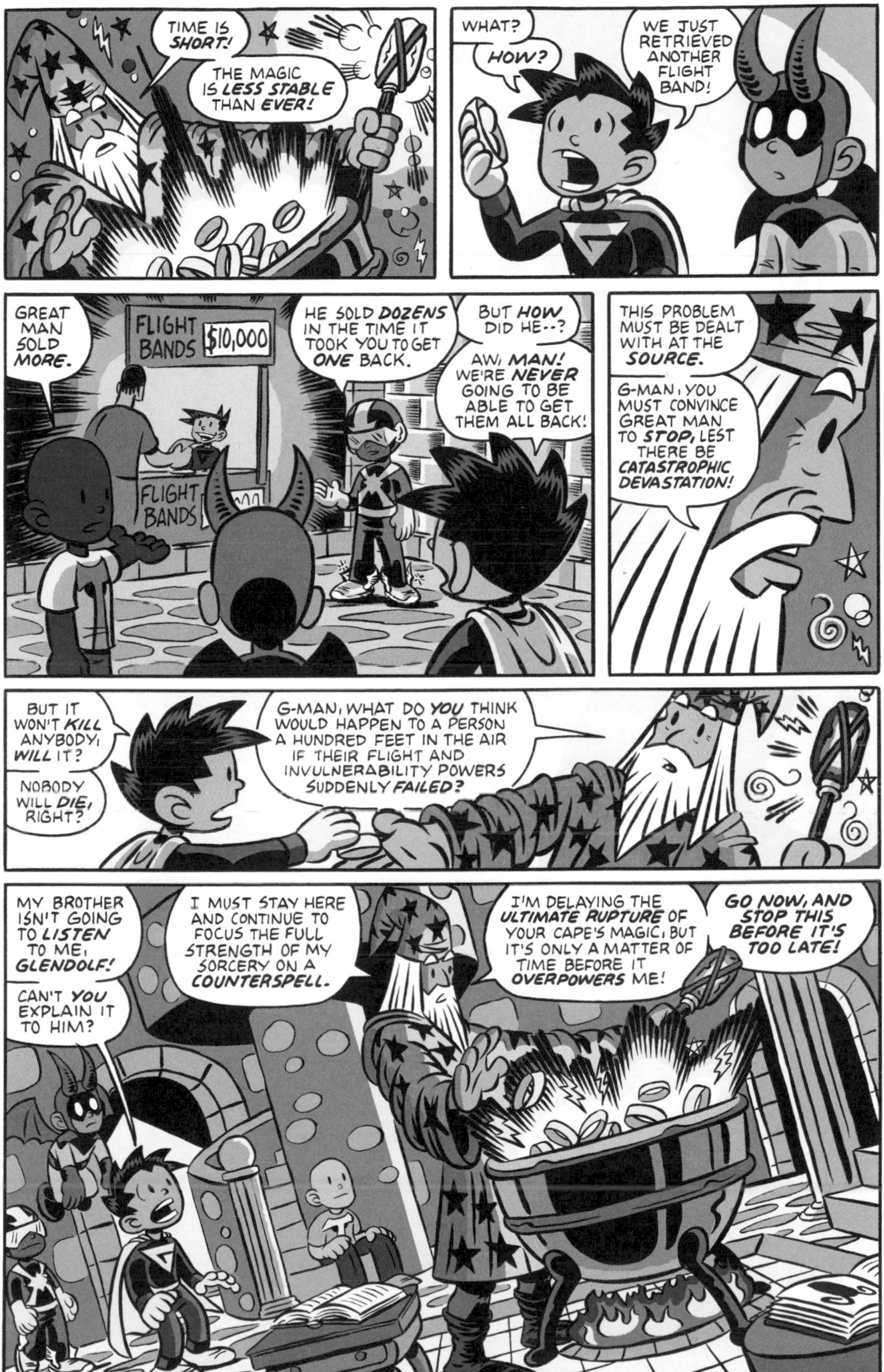

TIME IS SHORT!
THE MAGIC IS LESS STABLE THAN EVER!
WHAT? HOW?
WE JUST RETRIEVED ANOTHER FLIGHT BAND!
GREAT MAN SOLD MORE.
FLIGHT BANDS $10,000
FLIGHT BANDS
HE SOLD DOZENS IN THE TIME IT TOOK YOU TO GET ONE BACK.
BUT HOW DID HE--?
AW, MAN! WE'RE NEVER GOING TO BE ABLE TO GET THEM ALL BACK!
THIS PROBLEM MUST BE DEALT WITH AT THE SOURCE.
G-MAN, YOU MUST CONVINCE GREAT MAN TO STOP, LEST THERE BE CATASTROPHIC DEVASTATION!
BUT IT WON'T KILL ANYBODY, WILL IT?
NOBODY WILL DIE, RIGHT?
G-MAN, WHAT DO YOU THINK WOULD HAPPEN TO A PERSON A HUNDRED FEET IN THE AIR IF THEIR FLIGHT AND INVULNERABILITY POWERS SUDDENLY FAILED?
MY BROTHER ISN'T GOING TO LISTEN TO ME, GLENDOLF!
CAN'T YOU EXPLAIN IT TO HIM?
I MUST STAY HERE AND CONTINUE TO FOCUS THE FULL STRENGTH OF MY SORCERY ON A COUNTERSPELL.
I'M DELAYING THE ULTIMATE RUPTURE OF YOUR CAPE'S MAGIC, BUT IT'S ONLY A MATTER OF TIME BEFORE IT OVERPOWERS ME!
GO NOW, AND STOP THIS BEFORE IT'S TOO LATE!

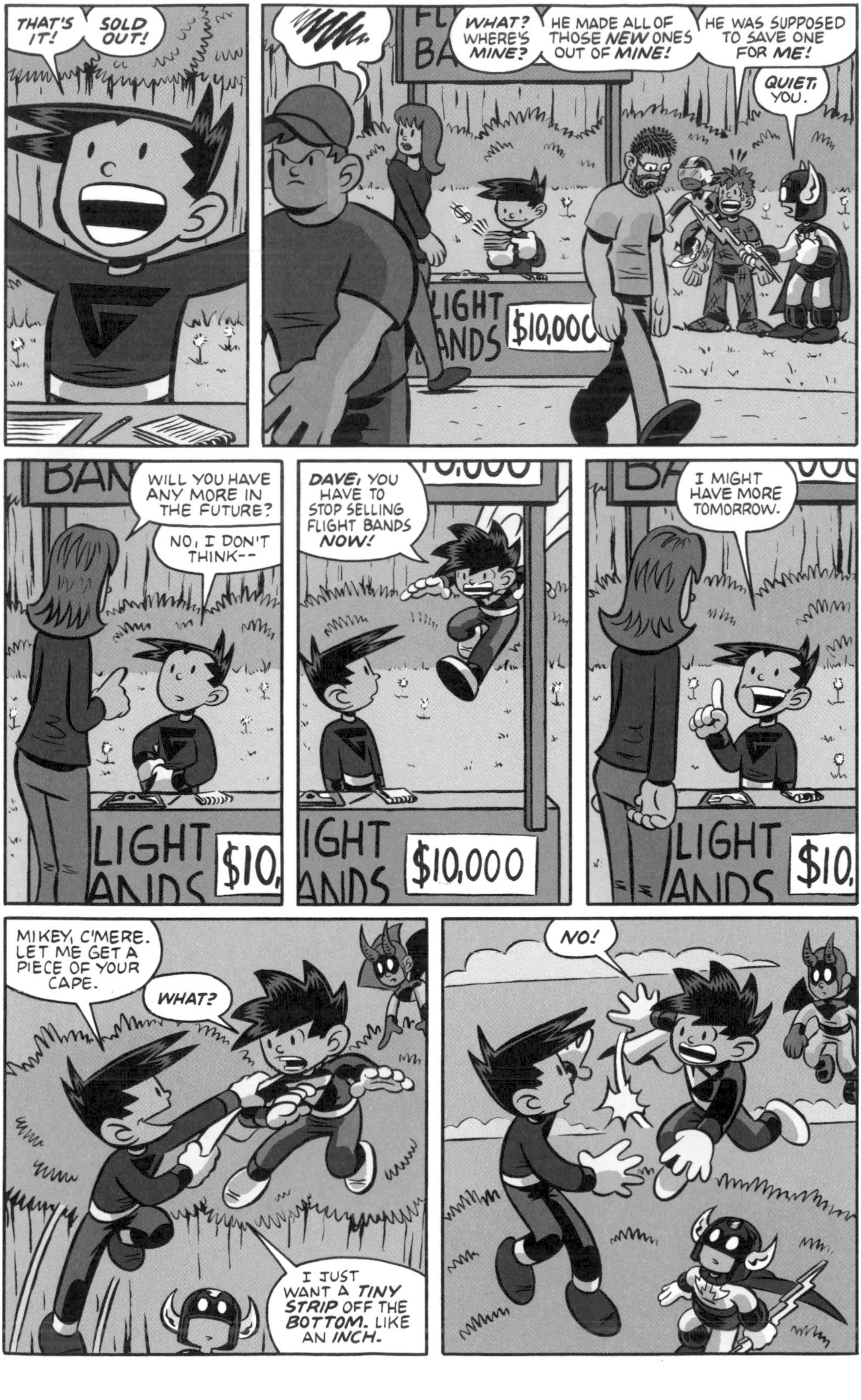
THAT'S IT!
SOLD OUT!
WHAT? WHERE'S MINE?
HE MADE ALL OF THOSE NEW ONES OUT OF MINE!
HE WAS SUPPOSED TO SAVE ONE FOR ME!
QUIET, YOU.
FLIGHT BANDS
$10,000
WILL YOU HAVE ANY MORE IN THE FUTURE?
NO, I DON'T THINK--
DAVE, YOU HAVE TO STOP SELLING FLIGHT BANDS NOW!
I MIGHT HAVE MORE TOMORROW.
MIKEY, C'MERE. LET ME GET A PIECE OF YOUR CAPE.
WHAT?
I JUST WANT A TINY STRIP OFF THE BOTTOM. LIKE AN INCH.
NO!

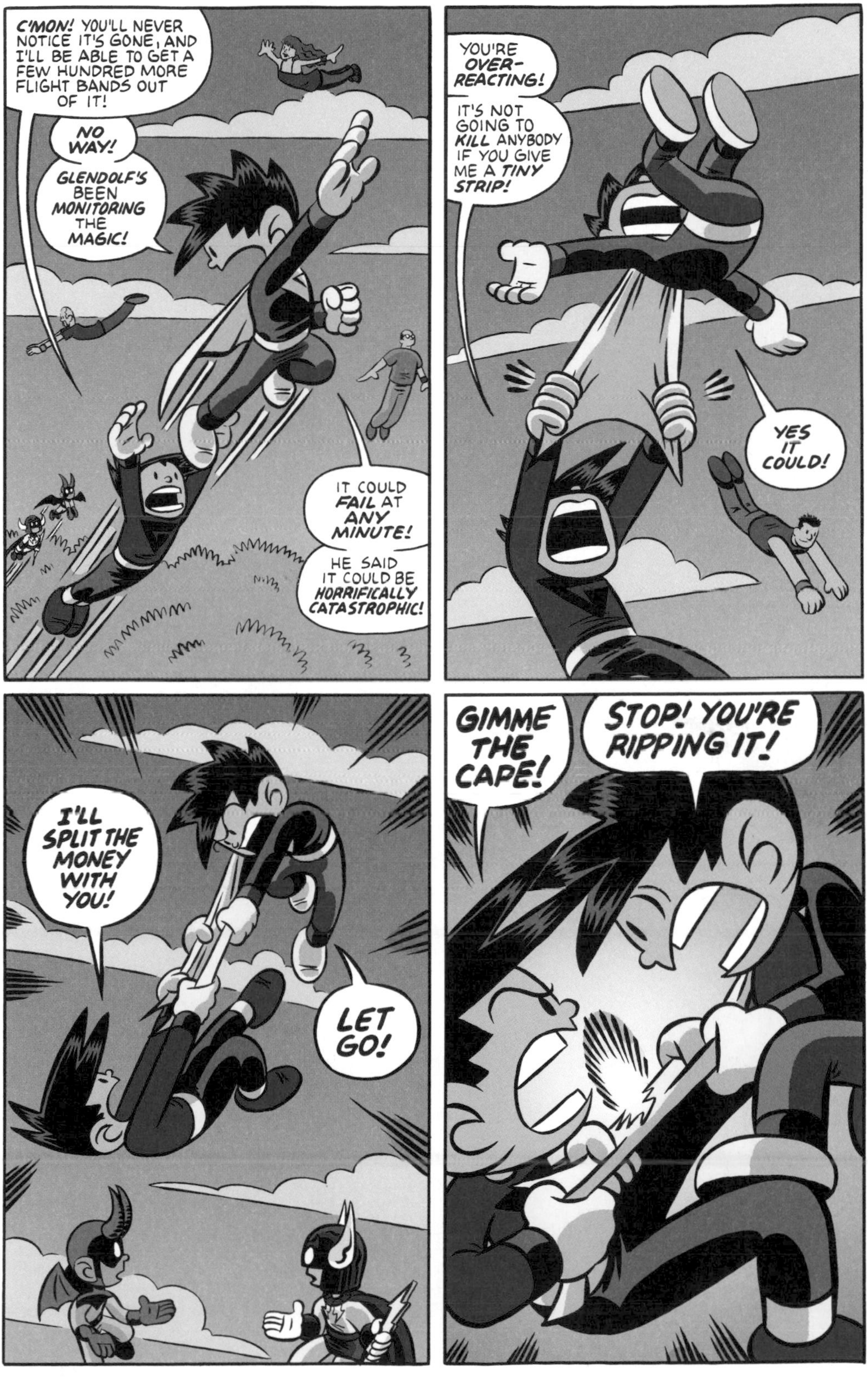
C'MON! YOU'LL NEVER NOTICE IT'S GONE, AND I'LL BE ABLE TO GET A FEW HUNDRED MORE FLIGHT BANDS OUT OF IT!
NO WAY!
GLENDOLF'S BEEN MONITORING THE MAGIC!
IT COULD FAIL AT ANY MINUTE!
HE SAID IT COULD BE HORRIFICALLY CATASTROPHIC!
YOU'RE OVER-REACTING!
IT'S NOT GOING TO KILL ANYBODY IF YOU GIVE ME A TINY STRIP!
YES IT COULD!
I'LL SPLIT THE MONEY WITH YOU!
LET GO!
GIMME THE CAPE!
STOP! YOU'RE RIPPING IT!

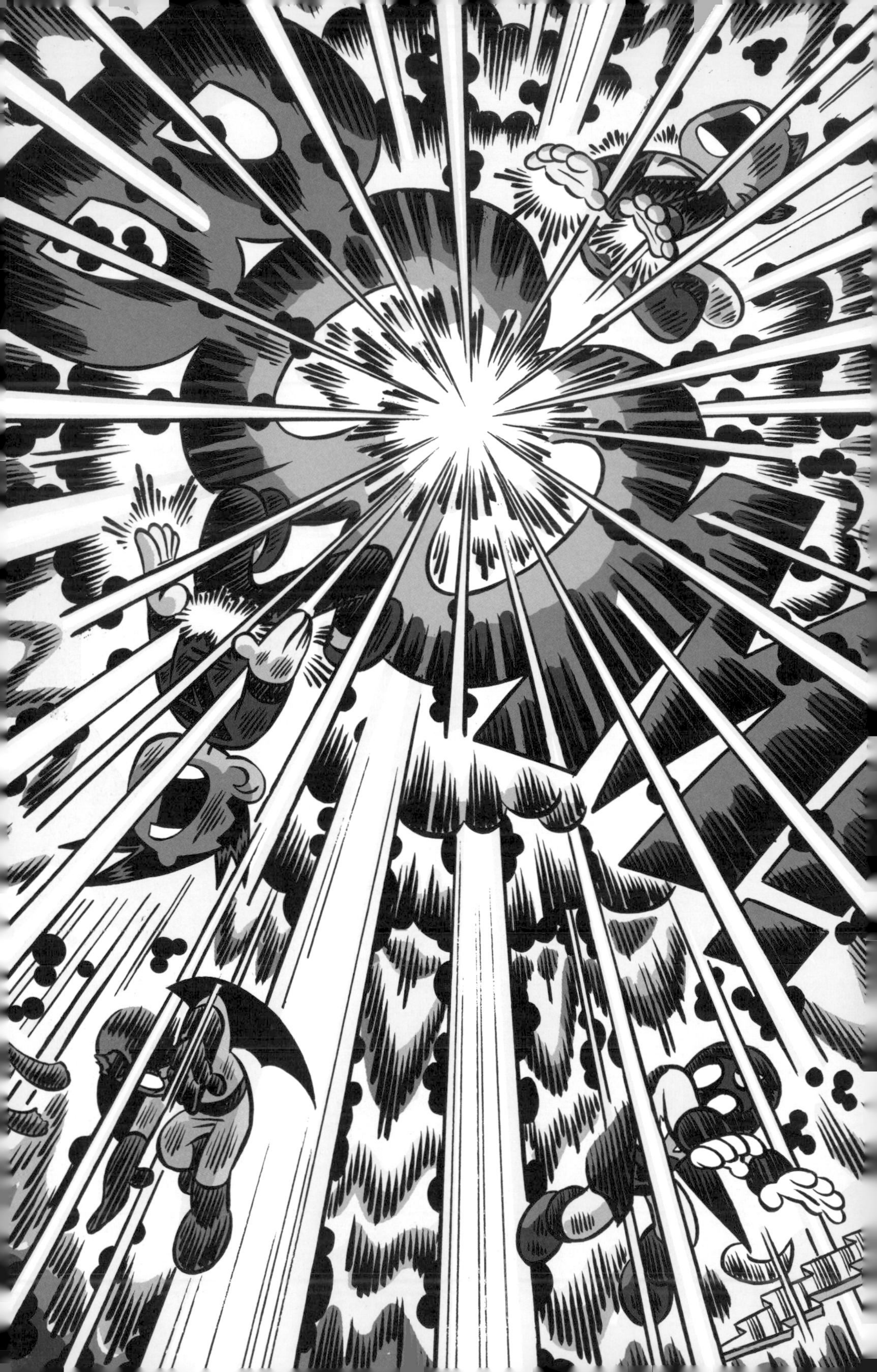

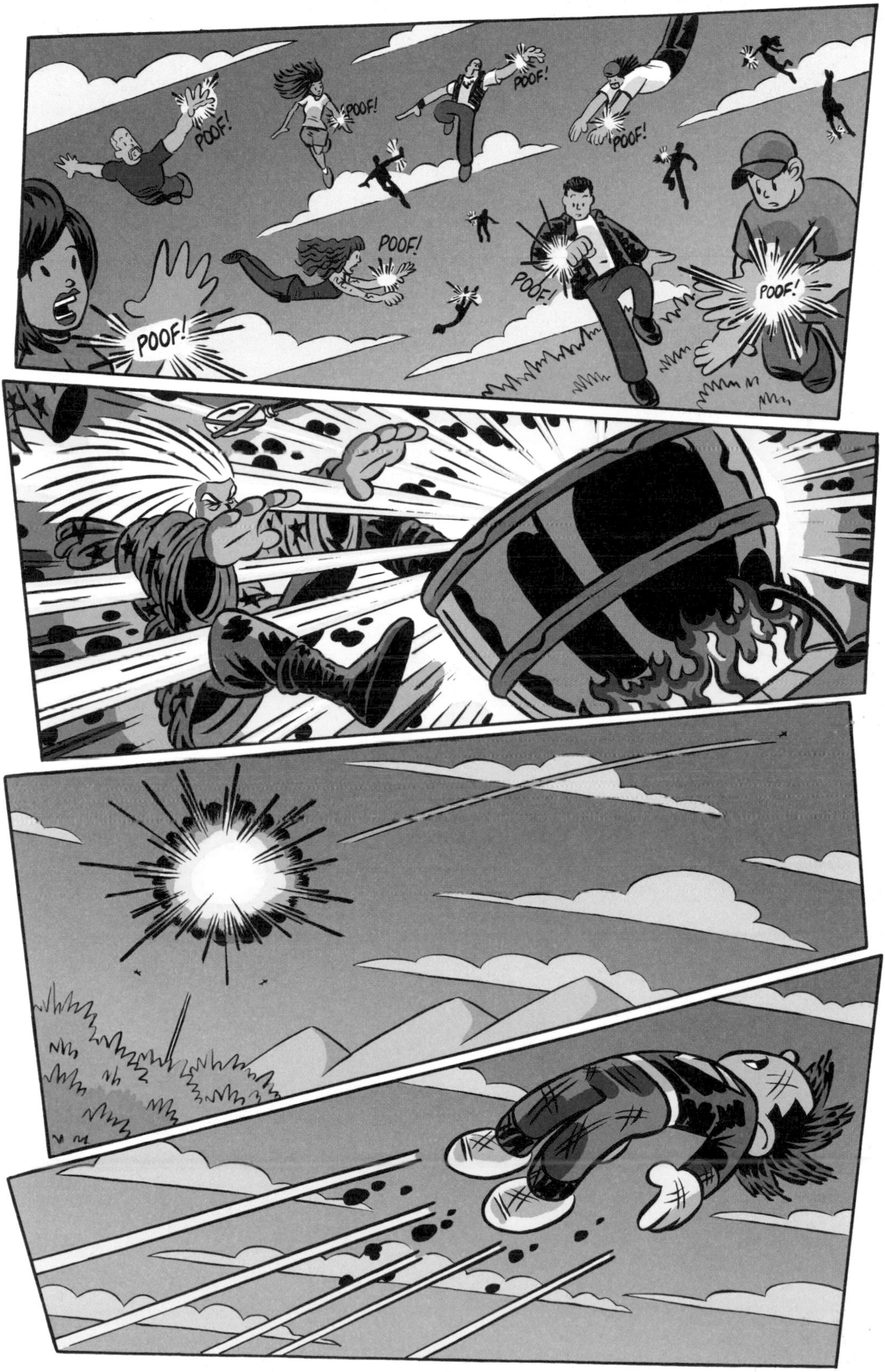
POOF!
POOF!
POOF!
POOF!
POOF!
POOF!
POOF!
POOF!

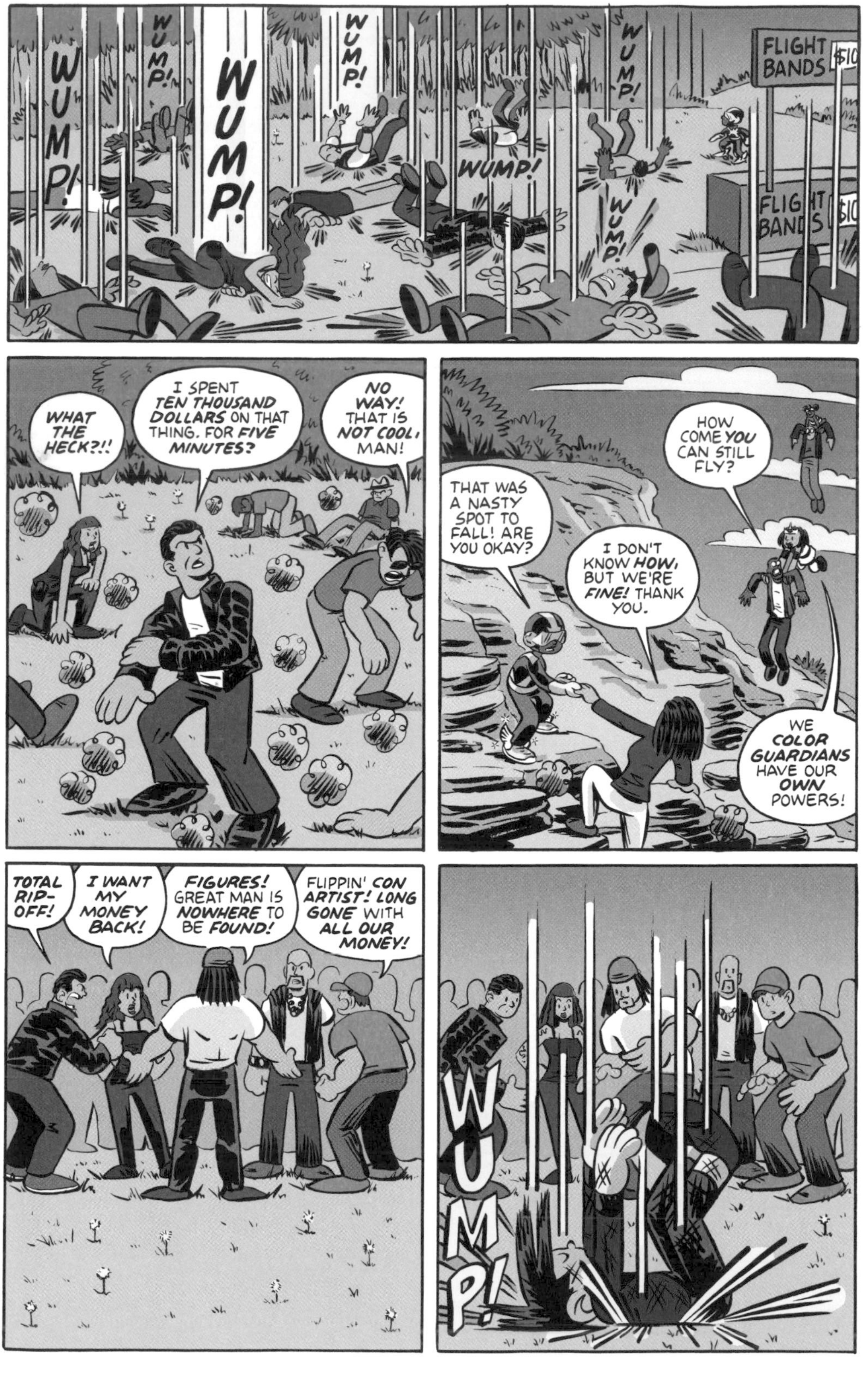
WUMP!
WUMP!
WUMP!
WUMP!
WUMP!
WUMP!
WUMP!
FLIGHT BANDS $10
FLIGHT BANDS $10
WHAT THE HECK?!!
I SPENT TEN THOUSAND DOLLARS ON THAT THING. FOR FIVE MINUTES?
NO WAY! THAT IS NOT COOL, MAN!
THAT WAS A NASTY SPOT TO FALL! ARE YOU OKAY?
HOW COME YOU CAN STILL FLY?
I DON'T KNOW HOW, BUT WE'RE FINE! THANK YOU.
WE COLOR GUARDIANS HAVE OUR OWN POWERS!
TOTAL RIP-OFF!
I WANT MY MONEY BACK!
FIGURES! GREAT MAN IS NOWHERE TO BE FOUND!
FLIPPIN' CON ARTIST! LONG GONE WITH ALL OUR MONEY!
WUMP!

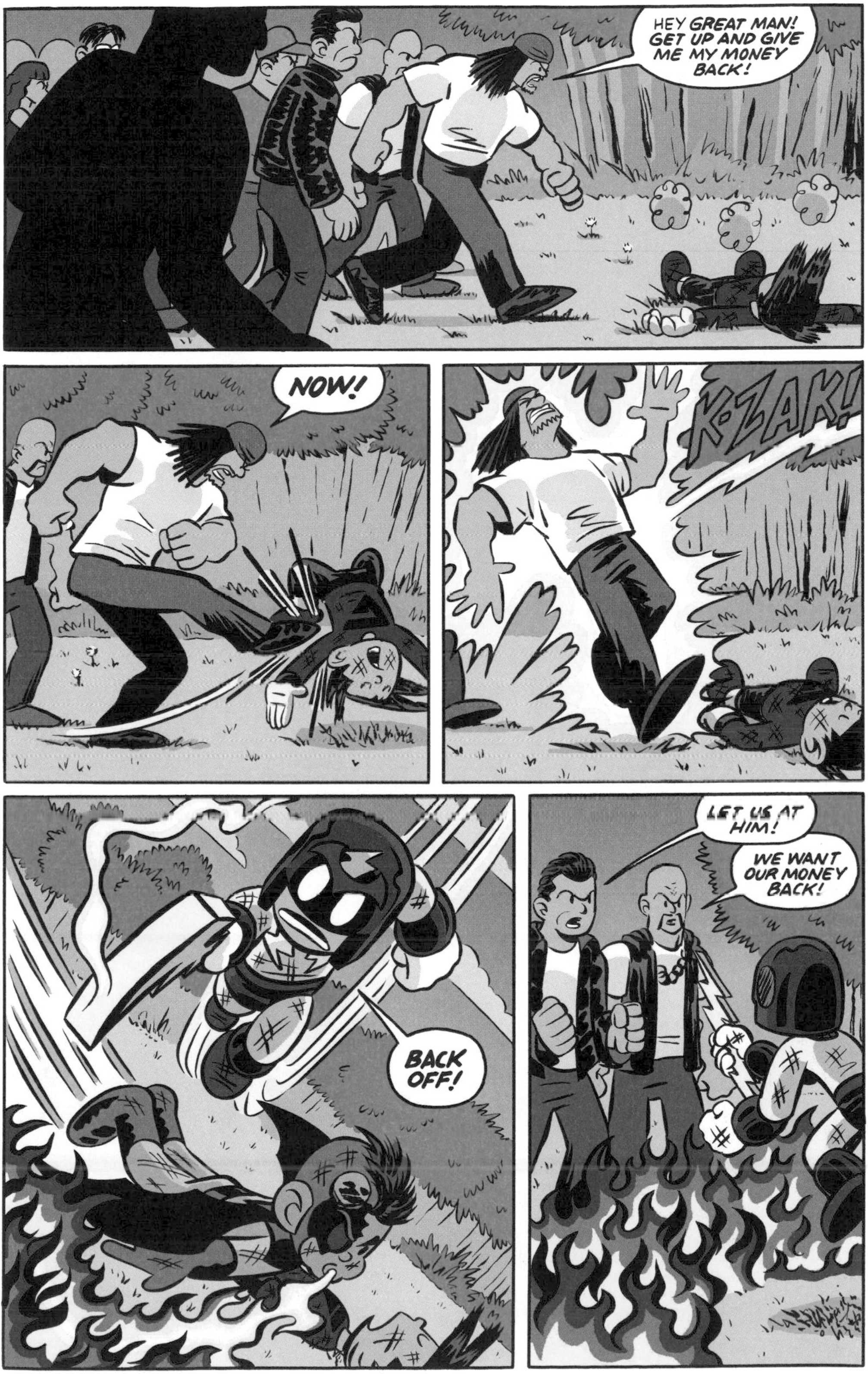
HEY GREAT MAN! GET UP AND GIVE ME MY MONEY BACK!
NOW!
K-ZAK!
BACK OFF!
LET US AT HIM!
WE WANT OUR MONEY BACK!

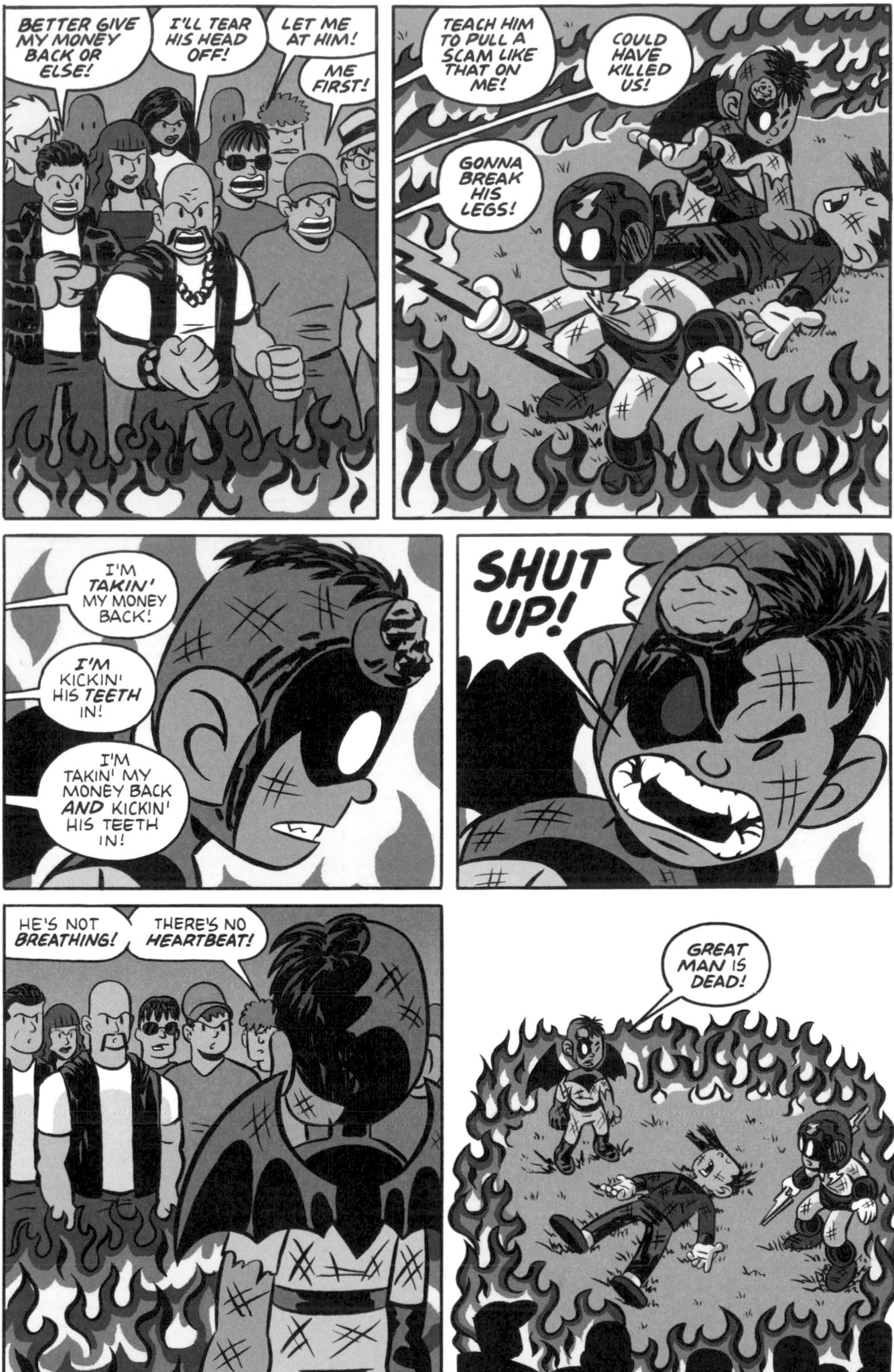
BETTER GIVE MY MONEY BACK OR ELSE!
I'LL TEAR HIS HEAD OFF!
LET ME AT HIM!
ME FIRST!
TEACH HIM TO PULL A SCAM LIKE THAT ON ME!
COULD HAVE KILLED US!
GONNA BREAK HIS LEGS!
I'M TAKIN' MY MONEY BACK!
I'M KICKIN' HIS TEETH IN!
I'M TAKIN' MY MONEY BACK AND KICKIN' HIS TEETH IN!
SHUT UP!
HE'S NOT BREATHING!
THERE'S NO HEARTBEAT!
GREAT MAN IS DEAD!

Chapter **4**

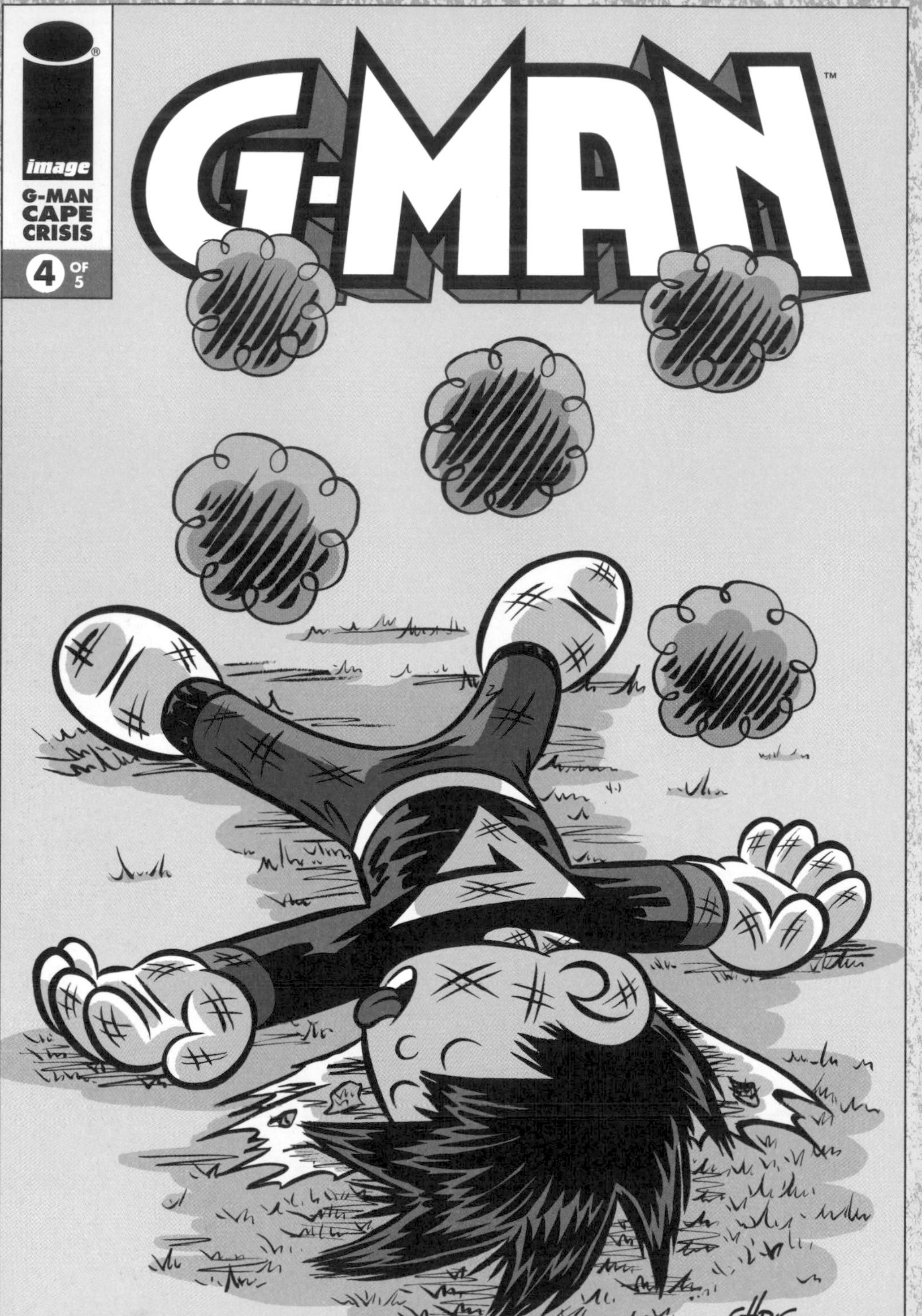
image
G-MAN
CAPE
CRISIS
4 OF 5
G-MAN™
CHRIS GIARRUSSO

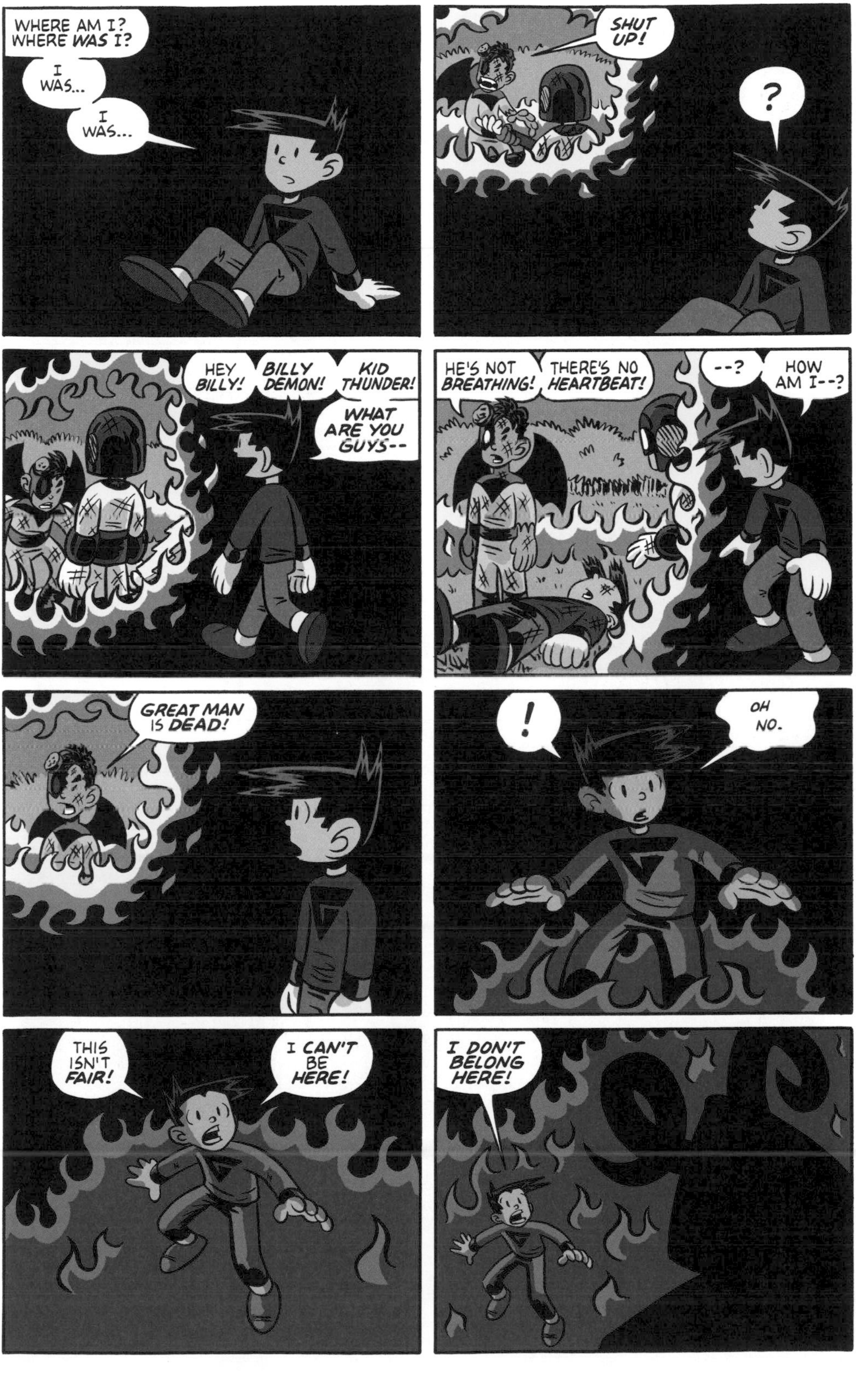
WHERE AM I? WHERE *WAS* I?
I WAS...
I WAS...
SHUT UP!
?
HEY *BILLY!*
BILLY DEMON!
KID THUNDER!
WHAT ARE YOU GUYS--
HE'S NOT *BREATHING!*
THERE'S NO *HEARTBEAT!*
--?
HOW AM I--?
GREAT MAN IS *DEAD!*
!
OH NO.
THIS ISN'T *FAIR!*
I *CAN'T* BE *HERE!*
I DON'T BELONG HERE!

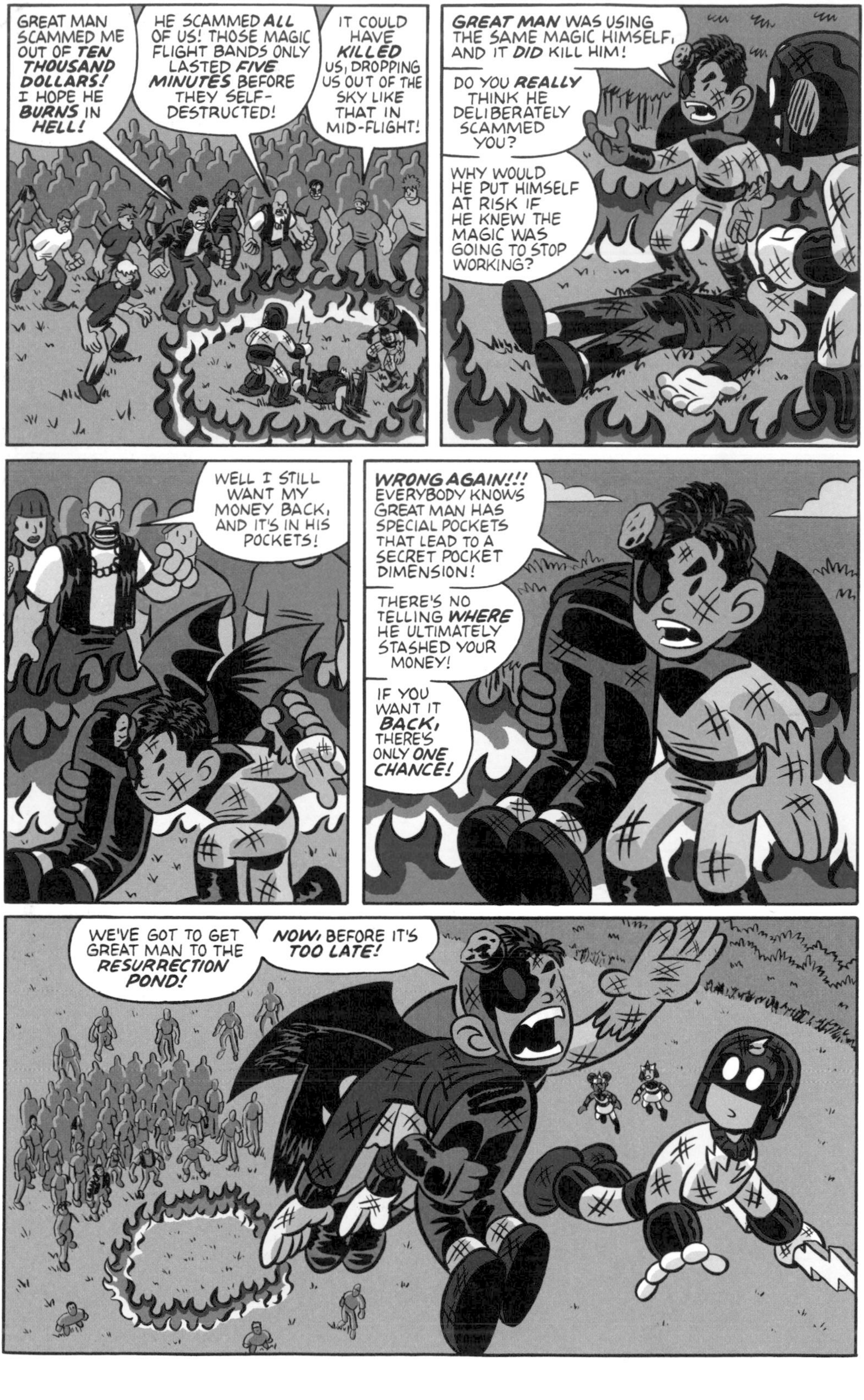
GREAT MAN SCAMMED ME OUT OF TEN THOUSAND DOLLARS! I HOPE HE BURNS IN HELL!
HE SCAMMED ALL OF US! THOSE MAGIC FLIGHT BANDS ONLY LASTED FIVE MINUTES BEFORE THEY SELF-DESTRUCTED!
IT COULD HAVE KILLED US, DROPPING US OUT OF THE SKY LIKE THAT IN MID-FLIGHT!
GREAT MAN WAS USING THE SAME MAGIC HIMSELF, AND IT DID KILL HIM!
DO YOU REALLY THINK HE DELIBERATELY SCAMMED YOU?
WHY WOULD HE PUT HIMSELF AT RISK IF HE KNEW THE MAGIC WAS GOING TO STOP WORKING?
WELL I STILL WANT MY MONEY BACK, AND IT'S IN HIS POCKETS!
WRONG AGAIN!!! EVERYBODY KNOWS GREAT MAN HAS SPECIAL POCKETS THAT LEAD TO A SECRET POCKET DIMENSION!
THERE'S NO TELLING WHERE HE ULTIMATELY STASHED YOUR MONEY!
IF YOU WANT IT BACK, THERE'S ONLY ONE CHANCE!
WE'VE GOT TO GET GREAT MAN TO THE RESURRECTION POND!
NOW, BEFORE IT'S TOO LATE!

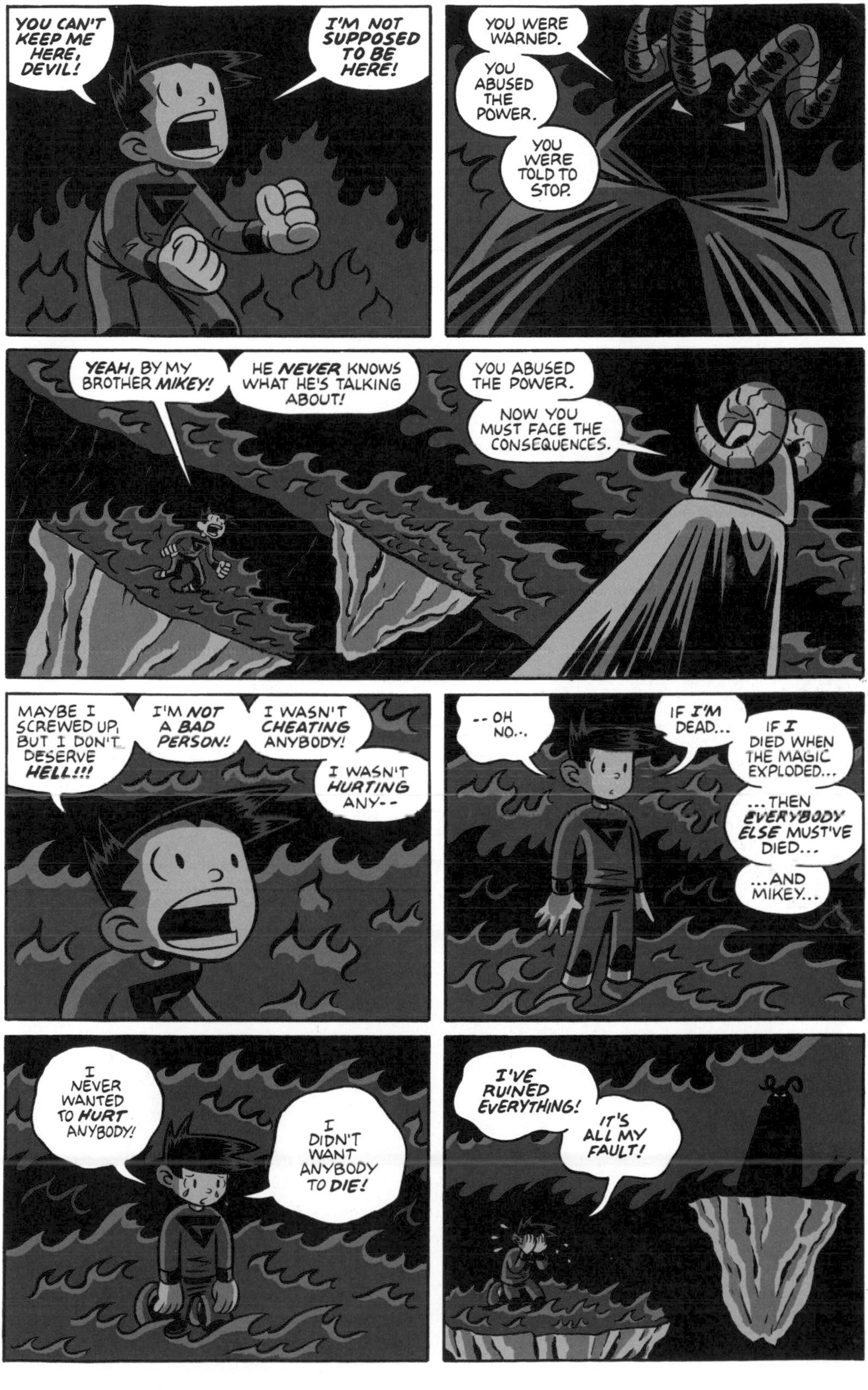
YOU CAN'T KEEP ME HERE, DEVIL!
I'M NOT SUPPOSED TO BE HERE!
YOU WERE WARNED.
YOU ABUSED THE POWER.
YOU WERE TOLD TO STOP.
YEAH, BY MY BROTHER MIKEY!
HE NEVER KNOWS WHAT HE'S TALKING ABOUT!
YOU ABUSED THE POWER.
NOW YOU MUST FACE THE CONSEQUENCES.
MAYBE I SCREWED UP, BUT I DON'T DESERVE HELL!!!
I'M NOT A BAD PERSON!
I WASN'T CHEATING ANYBODY!
I WASN'T HURTING ANY--
--OH NO...
IF I'M DEAD...
IF I DIED WHEN THE MAGIC EXPLODED...
...THEN EVERYBODY ELSE MUST'VE DIED...
...AND MIKEY...
I NEVER WANTED TO HURT ANYBODY!
I DIDN'T WANT ANYBODY TO DIE!
I'VE RUINED EVERYTHING!
IT'S ALL MY FAULT!

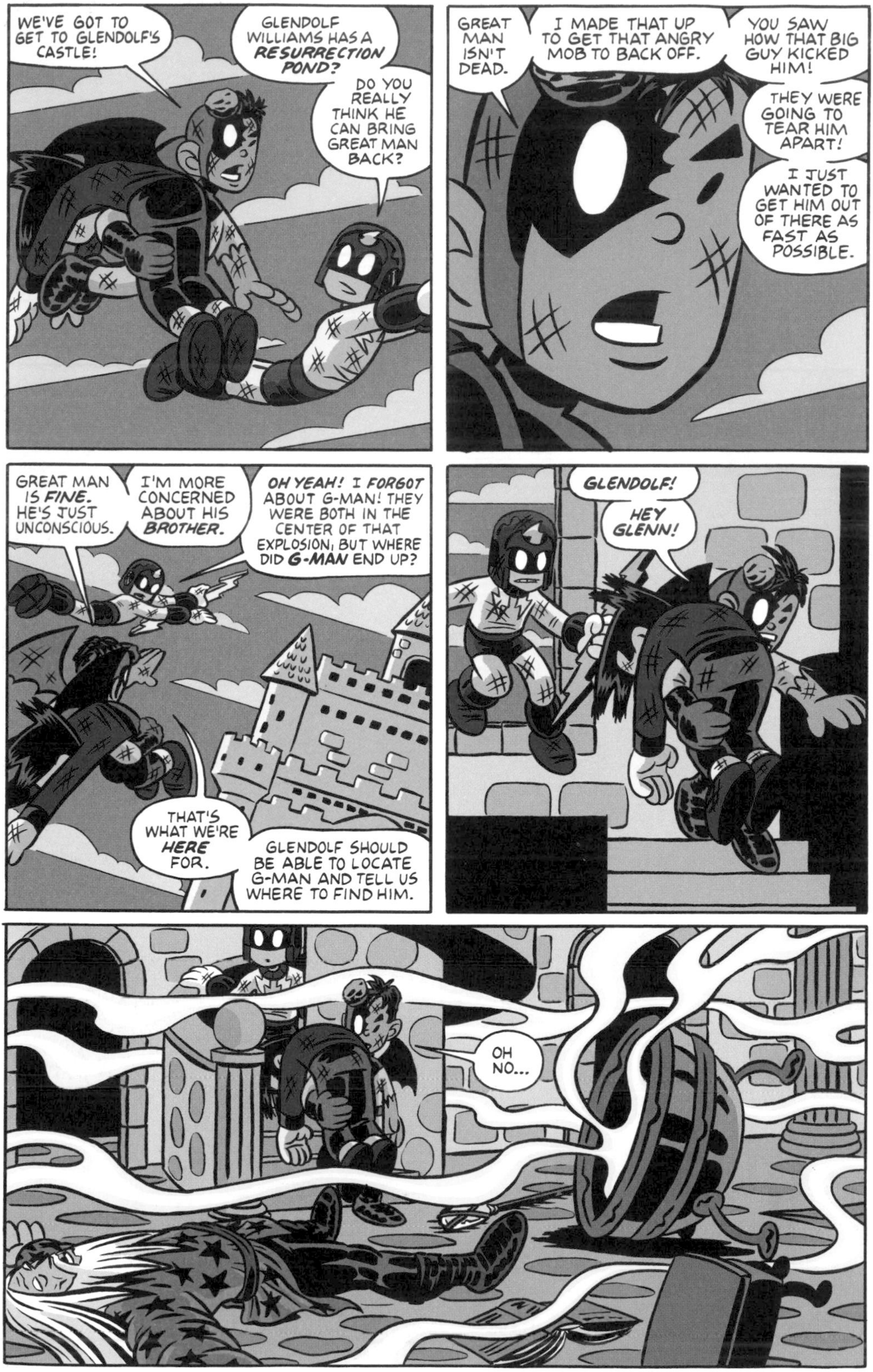
WE'VE GOT TO GET TO GLENDOLF'S CASTLE!
GLENDOLF WILLIAMS HAS A RESURRECTION POND?
DO YOU REALLY THINK HE CAN BRING GREAT MAN BACK?
GREAT MAN ISN'T DEAD.
I MADE THAT UP TO GET THAT ANGRY MOB TO BACK OFF.
YOU SAW HOW THAT BIG GUY KICKED HIM!
THEY WERE GOING TO TEAR HIM APART!
I JUST WANTED TO GET HIM OUT OF THERE AS FAST AS POSSIBLE.
GREAT MAN IS FINE. HE'S JUST UNCONSCIOUS.
I'M MORE CONCERNED ABOUT HIS BROTHER.
OH YEAH! I FORGOT ABOUT G-MAN! THEY WERE BOTH IN THE CENTER OF THAT EXPLOSION; BUT WHERE DID G-MAN END UP?
THAT'S WHAT WE'RE HERE FOR.
GLENDOLF SHOULD BE ABLE TO LOCATE G-MAN AND TELL US WHERE TO FIND HIM.
GLENDOLF!
HEY GLENN!
OH NO...

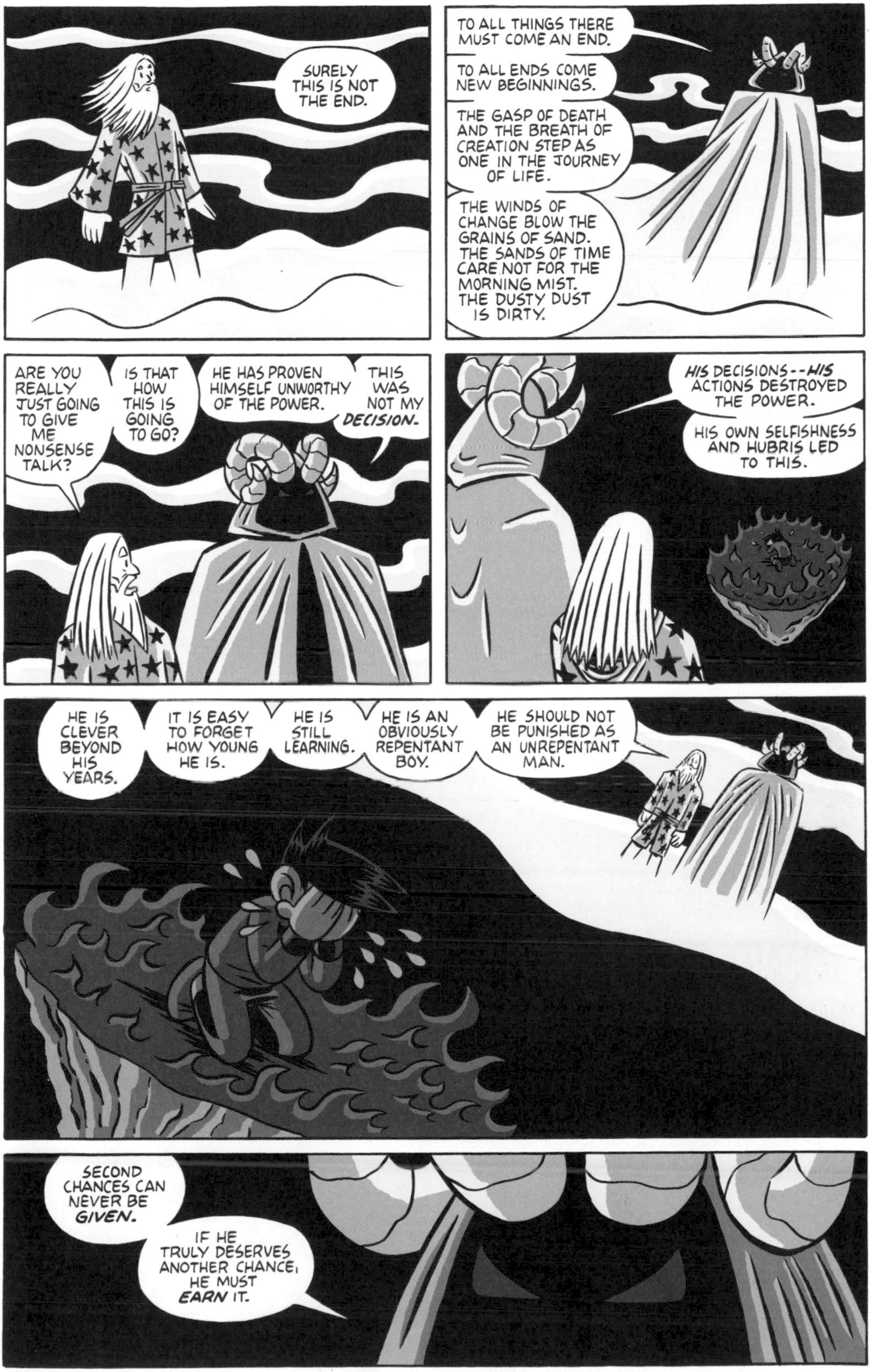
SURELY THIS IS NOT THE END.
TO ALL THINGS THERE MUST COME AN END.
TO ALL ENDS COME NEW BEGINNINGS.
THE GASP OF DEATH AND THE BREATH OF CREATION STEP AS ONE IN THE JOURNEY OF LIFE.
THE WINDS OF CHANGE BLOW THE GRAINS OF SAND. THE SANDS OF TIME CARE NOT FOR THE MORNING MIST. THE DUSTY DUST IS DIRTY.
ARE YOU REALLY JUST GOING TO GIVE ME NONSENSE TALK?
IS THAT HOW THIS IS GOING TO GO?
HE HAS PROVEN HIMSELF UNWORTHY OF THE POWER.
THIS WAS NOT MY DECISION.
HIS DECISIONS--HIS ACTIONS DESTROYED THE POWER.
HIS OWN SELFISHNESS AND HUBRIS LED TO THIS.
HE IS CLEVER BEYOND HIS YEARS.
IT IS EASY TO FORGET HOW YOUNG HE IS.
HE IS STILL LEARNING.
HE IS AN OBVIOUSLY REPENTANT BOY.
HE SHOULD NOT BE PUNISHED AS AN UNREPENTANT MAN.
SECOND CHANCES CAN NEVER BE GIVEN.
IF HE TRULY DESERVES ANOTHER CHANCE, HE MUST EARN IT.

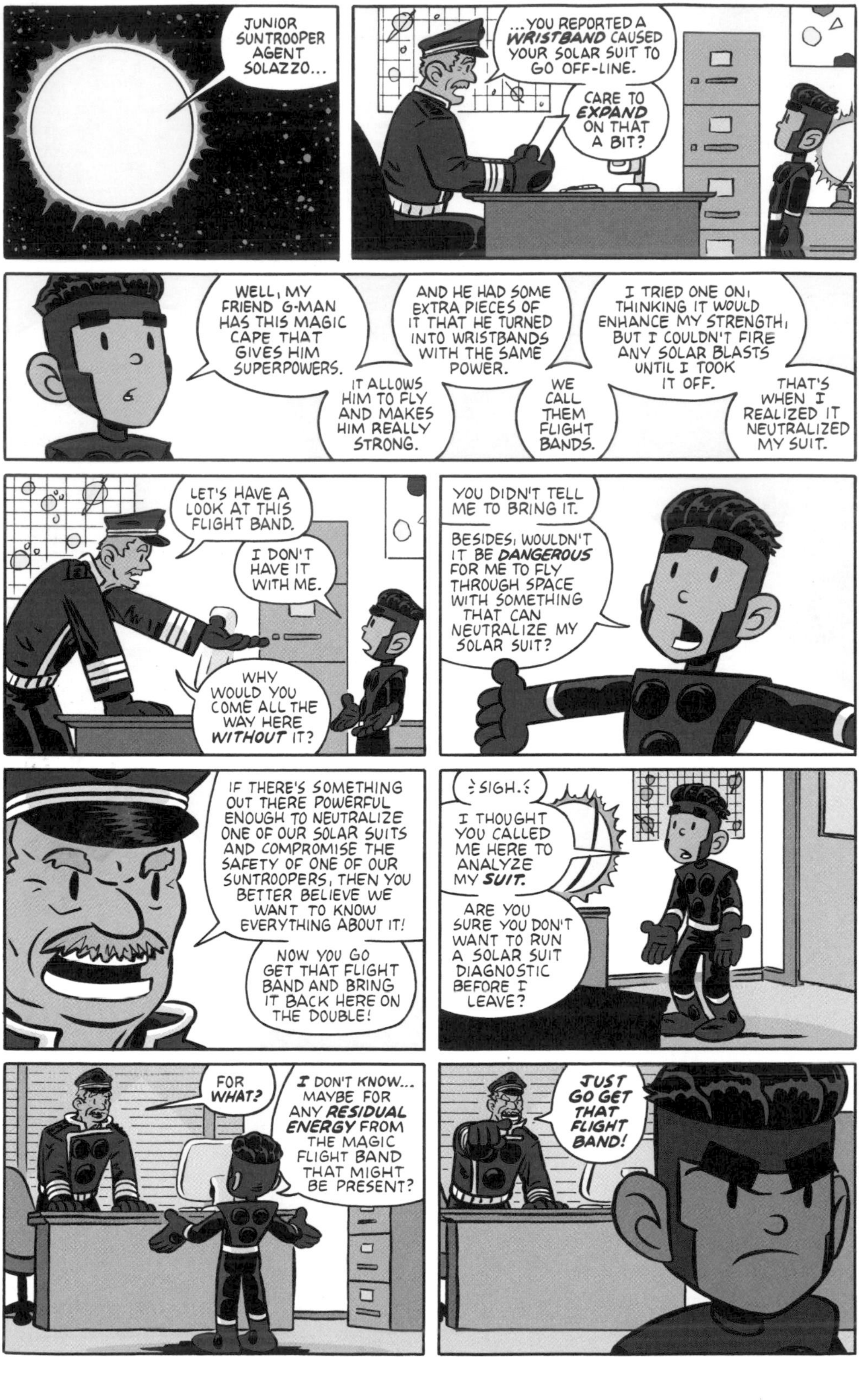

JUNIOR SUNTROOPER AGENT SOLAZZO...
...YOU REPORTED A *WRISTBAND* CAUSED YOUR SOLAR SUIT TO GO OFF-LINE.
CARE TO *EXPAND* ON THAT A BIT?
WELL, MY FRIEND G-MAN HAS THIS MAGIC CAPE THAT GIVES HIM SUPERPOWERS.
IT ALLOWS HIM TO FLY AND MAKES HIM REALLY STRONG.
AND HE HAD SOME EXTRA PIECES OF IT THAT HE TURNED INTO WRISTBANDS WITH THE SAME POWER.
WE CALL THEM FLIGHT BANDS.
I TRIED ONE ON, THINKING IT WOULD ENHANCE MY STRENGTH, BUT I COULDN'T FIRE ANY SOLAR BLASTS UNTIL I TOOK IT OFF.
THAT'S WHEN I REALIZED IT NEUTRALIZED MY SUIT.
LET'S HAVE A LOOK AT THIS FLIGHT BAND.
I DON'T HAVE IT WITH ME.
WHY WOULD YOU COME ALL THE WAY HERE *WITHOUT* IT?
YOU DIDN'T TELL ME TO BRING IT.
BESIDES, WOULDN'T IT BE *DANGEROUS* FOR ME TO FLY THROUGH SPACE WITH SOMETHING THAT CAN NEUTRALIZE MY SOLAR SUIT?
IF THERE'S SOMETHING OUT THERE POWERFUL ENOUGH TO NEUTRALIZE ONE OF OUR SOLAR SUITS AND COMPROMISE THE SAFETY OF ONE OF OUR SUNTROOPERS, THEN YOU BETTER BELIEVE WE WANT TO KNOW EVERYTHING ABOUT IT!
NOW YOU GO GET THAT FLIGHT BAND AND BRING IT BACK HERE ON THE DOUBLE!
SIGH.
I THOUGHT YOU CALLED ME HERE TO ANALYZE MY *SUIT.*
ARE YOU SURE YOU DON'T WANT TO RUN A SOLAR SUIT DIAGNOSTIC BEFORE I LEAVE?
FOR *WHAT?*
I DON'T KNOW... MAYBE FOR ANY *RESIDUAL ENERGY* FROM THE MAGIC FLIGHT BAND THAT MIGHT BE PRESENT?
JUST GO GET THAT FLIGHT BAND!

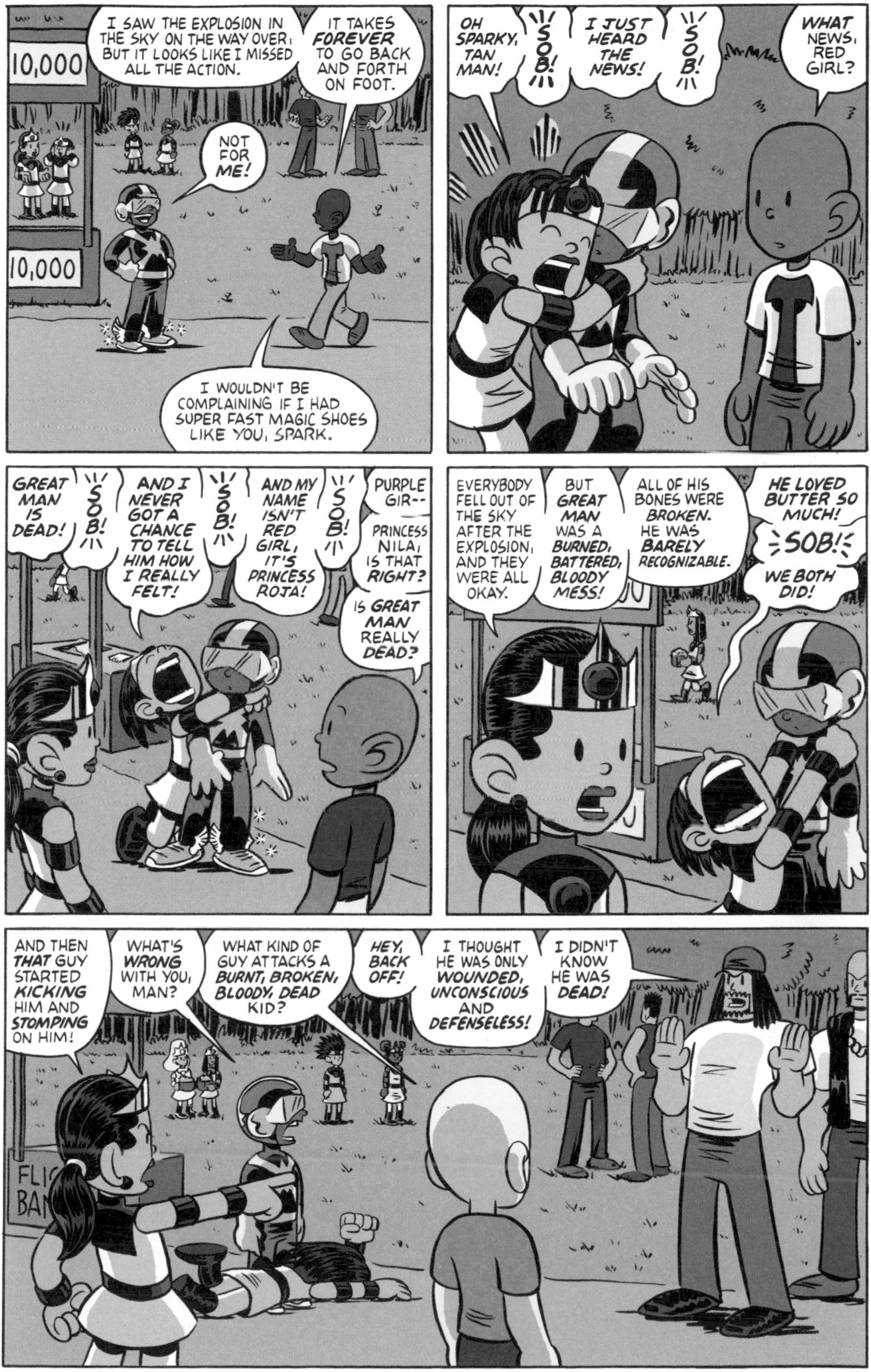
10,000
I SAW THE EXPLOSION IN THE SKY ON THE WAY OVER, BUT IT LOOKS LIKE I MISSED ALL THE ACTION.
IT TAKES FOREVER TO GO BACK AND FORTH ON FOOT.
NOT FOR ME!
10,000
I WOULDN'T BE COMPLAINING IF I HAD SUPER FAST MAGIC SHOES LIKE YOU, SPARK.
OH SPARKY, TAN MAN!
SOB!
I JUST HEARD THE NEWS!
SOB!
WHAT NEWS, RED GIRL?
GREAT MAN IS DEAD!
SOB!
AND I NEVER GOT A CHANCE TO TELL HIM HOW I REALLY FELT!
SOB!
AND MY NAME ISN'T RED GIRL, IT'S PRINCESS ROJA!
SOB!
PURPLE GIR--
PRINCESS NILA, IS THAT RIGHT?
IS GREAT MAN REALLY DEAD?
EVERYBODY FELL OUT OF THE SKY AFTER THE EXPLOSION, AND THEY WERE ALL OKAY.
BUT GREAT MAN WAS A BURNED, BATTERED, BLOODY MESS!
ALL OF HIS BONES WERE BROKEN. HE WAS BARELY RECOGNIZABLE.
HE LOVED BUTTER SO MUCH!
SOB!
WE BOTH DID!
AND THEN THAT GUY STARTED KICKING HIM AND STOMPING ON HIM!
WHAT'S WRONG WITH YOU, MAN?
WHAT KIND OF GUY ATTACKS A BURNT, BROKEN, BLOODY, DEAD KID?
HEY, BACK OFF!
I THOUGHT HE WAS ONLY WOUNDED, UNCONSCIOUS AND DEFENSELESS!
I DIDN'T KNOW HE WAS DEAD!
FLI
BA

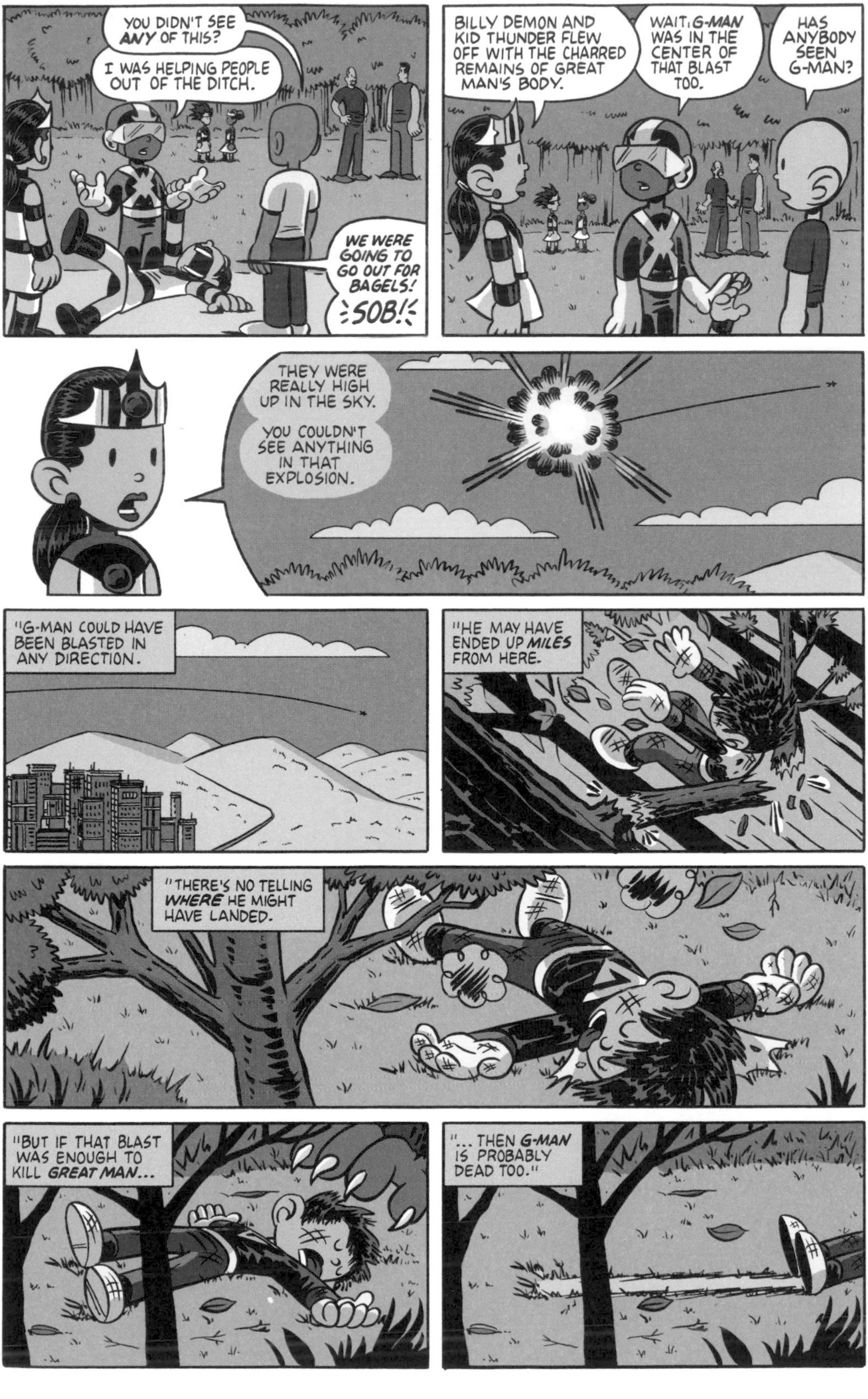
YOU DIDN'T SEE ANY OF THIS?
I WAS HELPING PEOPLE OUT OF THE DITCH.
WE WERE GOING TO GO OUT FOR BAGELS!
SOB!
BILLY DEMON AND KID THUNDER FLEW OFF WITH THE CHARRED REMAINS OF GREAT MAN'S BODY.
WAIT, G-MAN WAS IN THE CENTER OF THAT BLAST TOO.
HAS ANYBODY SEEN G-MAN?
THEY WERE REALLY HIGH UP IN THE SKY.
YOU COULDN'T SEE ANYTHING IN THAT EXPLOSION.
"G-MAN COULD HAVE BEEN BLASTED IN ANY DIRECTION.
"HE MAY HAVE ENDED UP MILES FROM HERE.
"THERE'S NO TELLING WHERE HE MIGHT HAVE LANDED.
"BUT IF THAT BLAST WAS ENOUGH TO KILL GREAT MAN...
"... THEN G-MAN IS PROBABLY DEAD TOO."

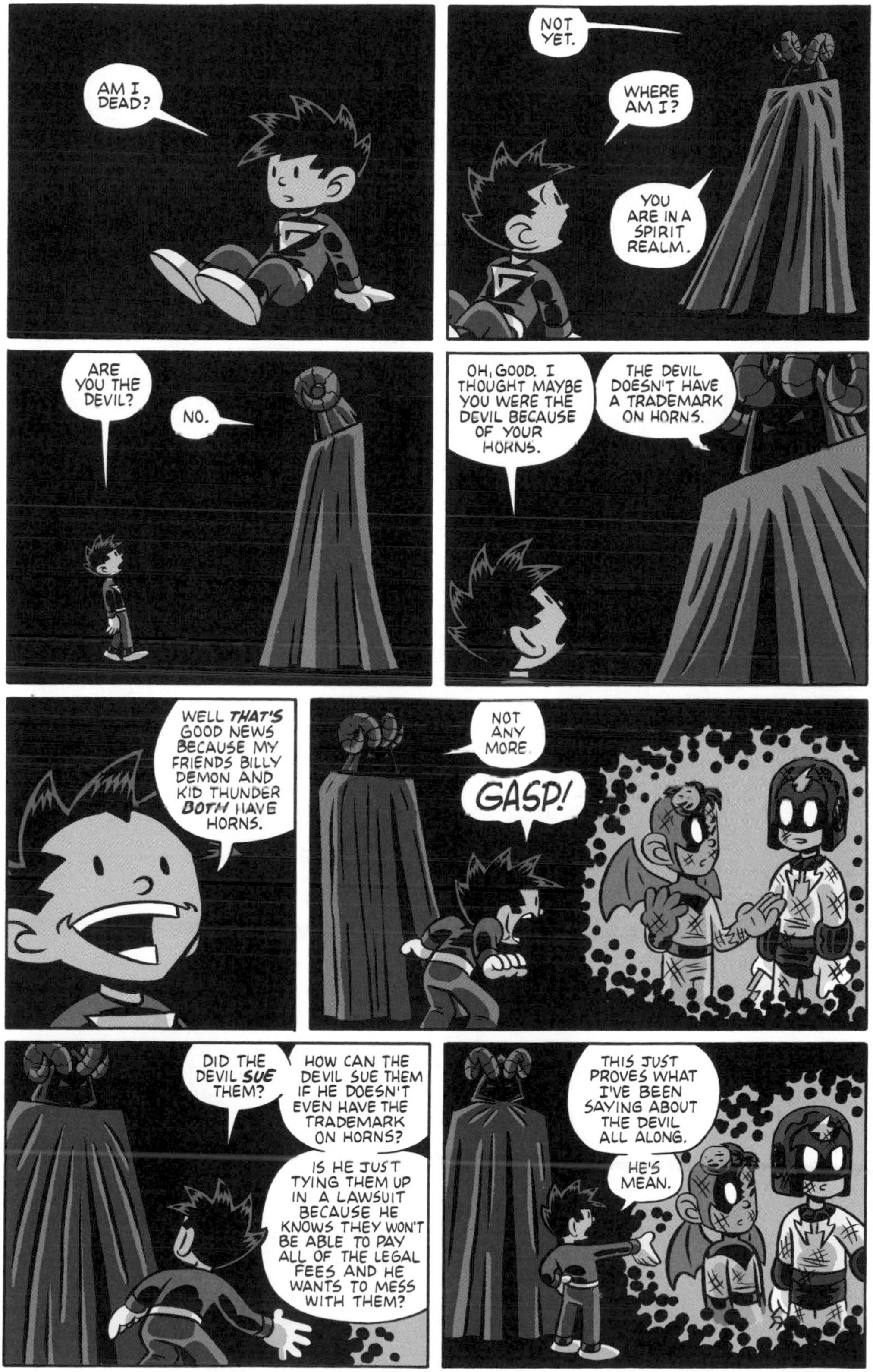
AM I DEAD?
NOT YET.
WHERE AM I?
YOU ARE IN A SPIRIT REALM.
ARE YOU THE DEVIL?
NO.
OH, GOOD. I THOUGHT MAYBE YOU WERE THE DEVIL BECAUSE OF YOUR HORNS.
THE DEVIL DOESN'T HAVE A TRADEMARK ON HORNS.
WELL THAT'S GOOD NEWS BECAUSE MY FRIENDS BILLY DEMON AND KID THUNDER BOTH HAVE HORNS.
NOT ANY MORE.
GASP!
DID THE DEVIL SUE THEM?
HOW CAN THE DEVIL SUE THEM IF HE DOESN'T EVEN HAVE THE TRADEMARK ON HORNS?
IS HE JUST TYING THEM UP IN A LAWSUIT BECAUSE HE KNOWS THEY WON'T BE ABLE TO PAY ALL OF THE LEGAL FEES AND HE WANTS TO MESS WITH THEM?
THIS JUST PROVES WHAT I'VE BEEN SAYING ABOUT THE DEVIL ALL ALONG.
HE'S MEAN.

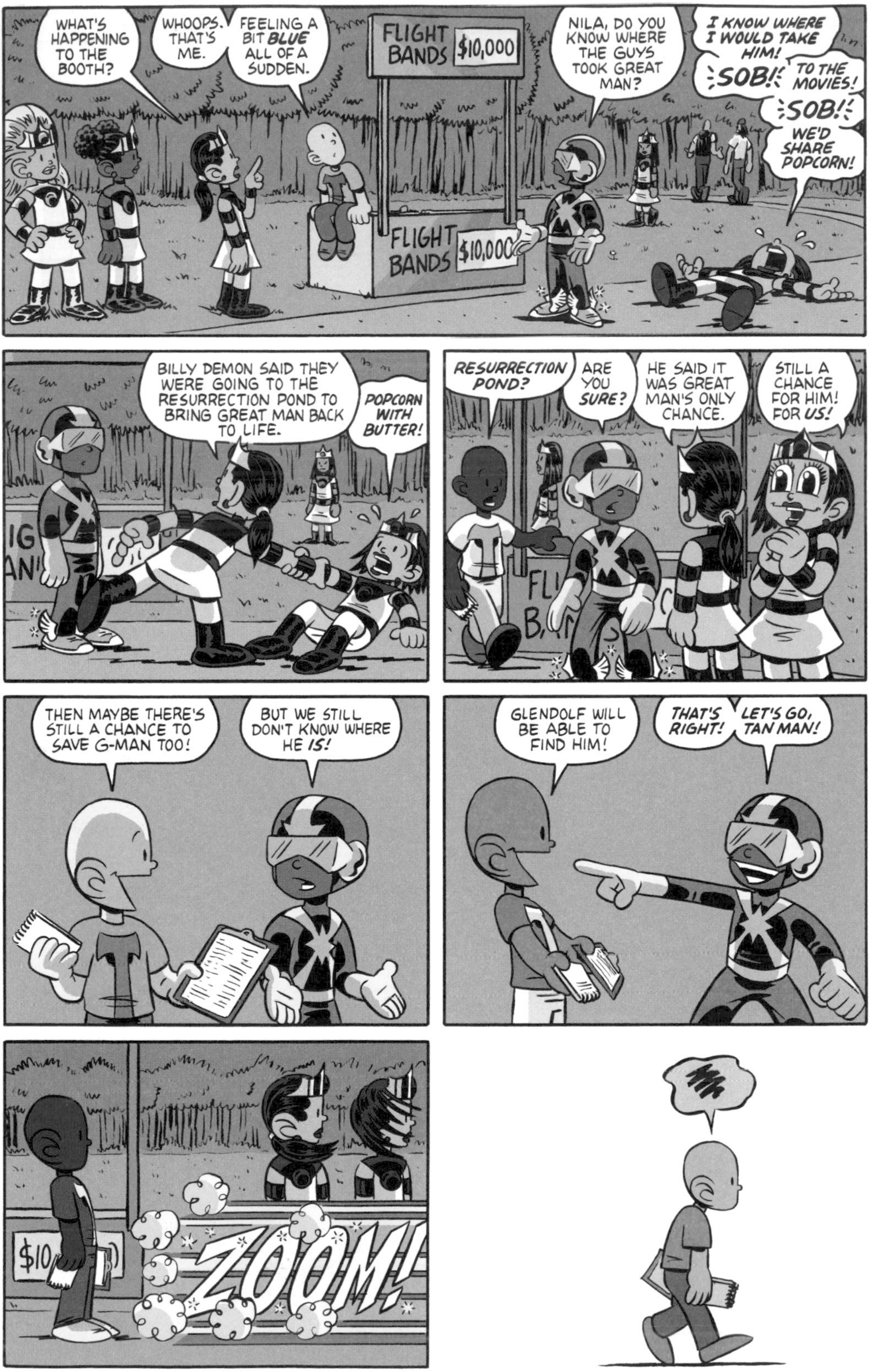

WHAT'S HAPPENING TO THE BOOTH?
WHOOPS. THAT'S ME.
FEELING A BIT BLUE ALL OF A SUDDEN.
FLIGHT BANDS $10,000
NILA, DO YOU KNOW WHERE THE GUYS TOOK GREAT MAN?
I KNOW WHERE I WOULD TAKE HIM!
SOB!
TO THE MOVIES!
SOB!
WE'D SHARE POPCORN!
FLIGHT BANDS $10,000
BILLY DEMON SAID THEY WERE GOING TO THE RESURRECTION POND TO BRING GREAT MAN BACK TO LIFE.
POPCORN WITH BUTTER!
RESURRECTION POND?
ARE YOU SURE?
HE SAID IT WAS GREAT MAN'S ONLY CHANCE.
STILL A CHANCE FOR HIM! FOR US!
THEN MAYBE THERE'S STILL A CHANCE TO SAVE G-MAN TOO!
BUT WE STILL DON'T KNOW WHERE HE IS!
GLENDOLF WILL BE ABLE TO FIND HIM!
THAT'S RIGHT!
LET'S GO, TAN MAN!
ZOOM!

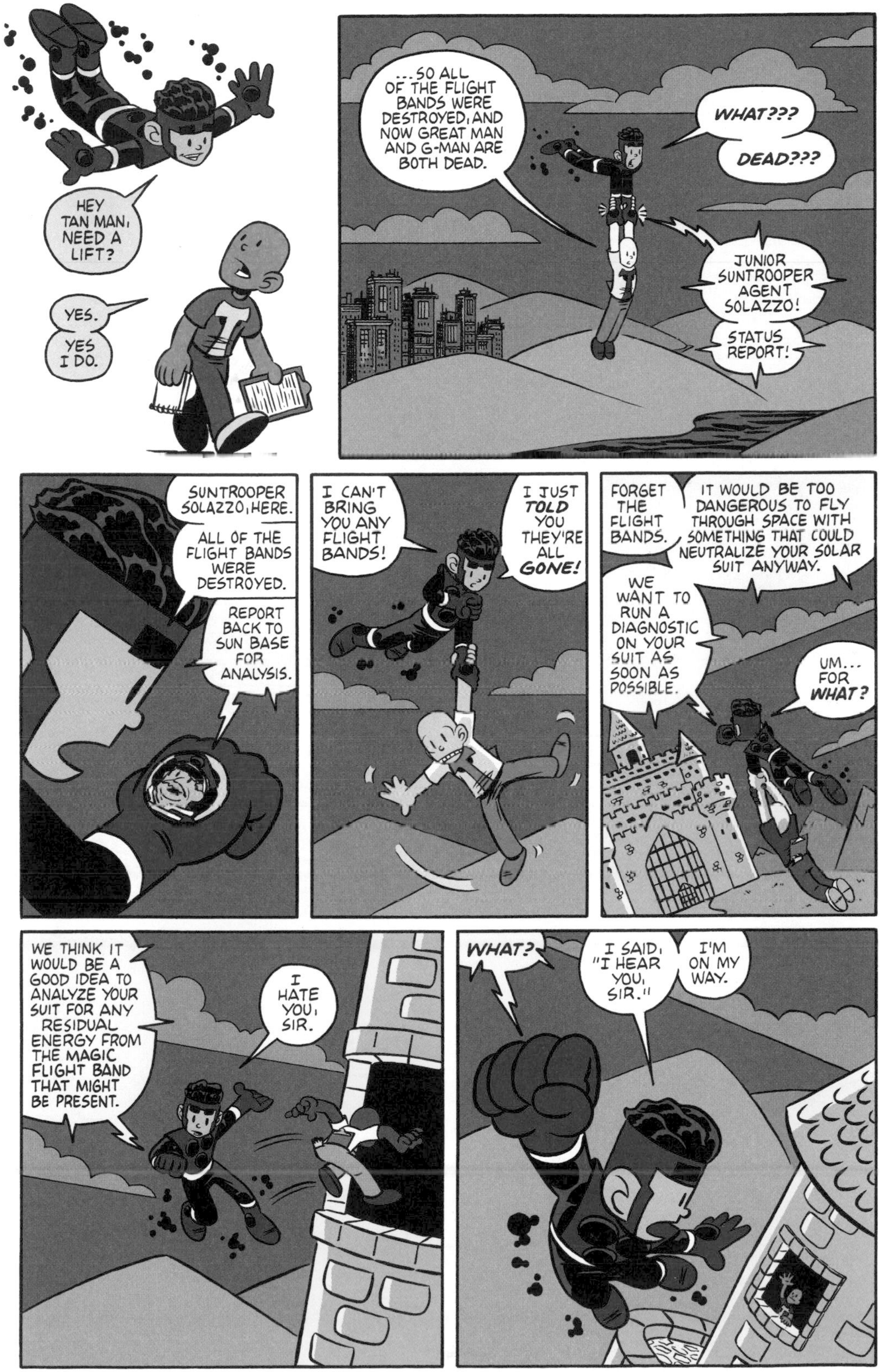
HEY TAN MAN, NEED A LIFT?
YES.
YES I DO.
...SO ALL OF THE FLIGHT BANDS WERE DESTROYED, AND NOW GREAT MAN AND G-MAN ARE BOTH DEAD.
WHAT???
DEAD???
JUNIOR SUNTROOPER AGENT SOLAZZO!
STATUS REPORT!
SUNTROOPER SOLAZZO, HERE.
ALL OF THE FLIGHT BANDS WERE DESTROYED.
REPORT BACK TO SUN BASE FOR ANALYSIS.
I CAN'T BRING YOU ANY FLIGHT BANDS!
I JUST TOLD YOU THEY'RE ALL GONE!
FORGET THE FLIGHT BANDS.
IT WOULD BE TOO DANGEROUS TO FLY THROUGH SPACE WITH SOMETHING THAT COULD NEUTRALIZE YOUR SOLAR SUIT ANYWAY.
WE WANT TO RUN A DIAGNOSTIC ON YOUR SUIT AS SOON AS POSSIBLE.
UM... FOR WHAT?
WE THINK IT WOULD BE A GOOD IDEA TO ANALYZE YOUR SUIT FOR ANY RESIDUAL ENERGY FROM THE MAGIC FLIGHT BAND THAT MIGHT BE PRESENT.
I HATE YOU, SIR.
WHAT?
I SAID, "I HEAR YOU, SIR."
I'M ON MY WAY.

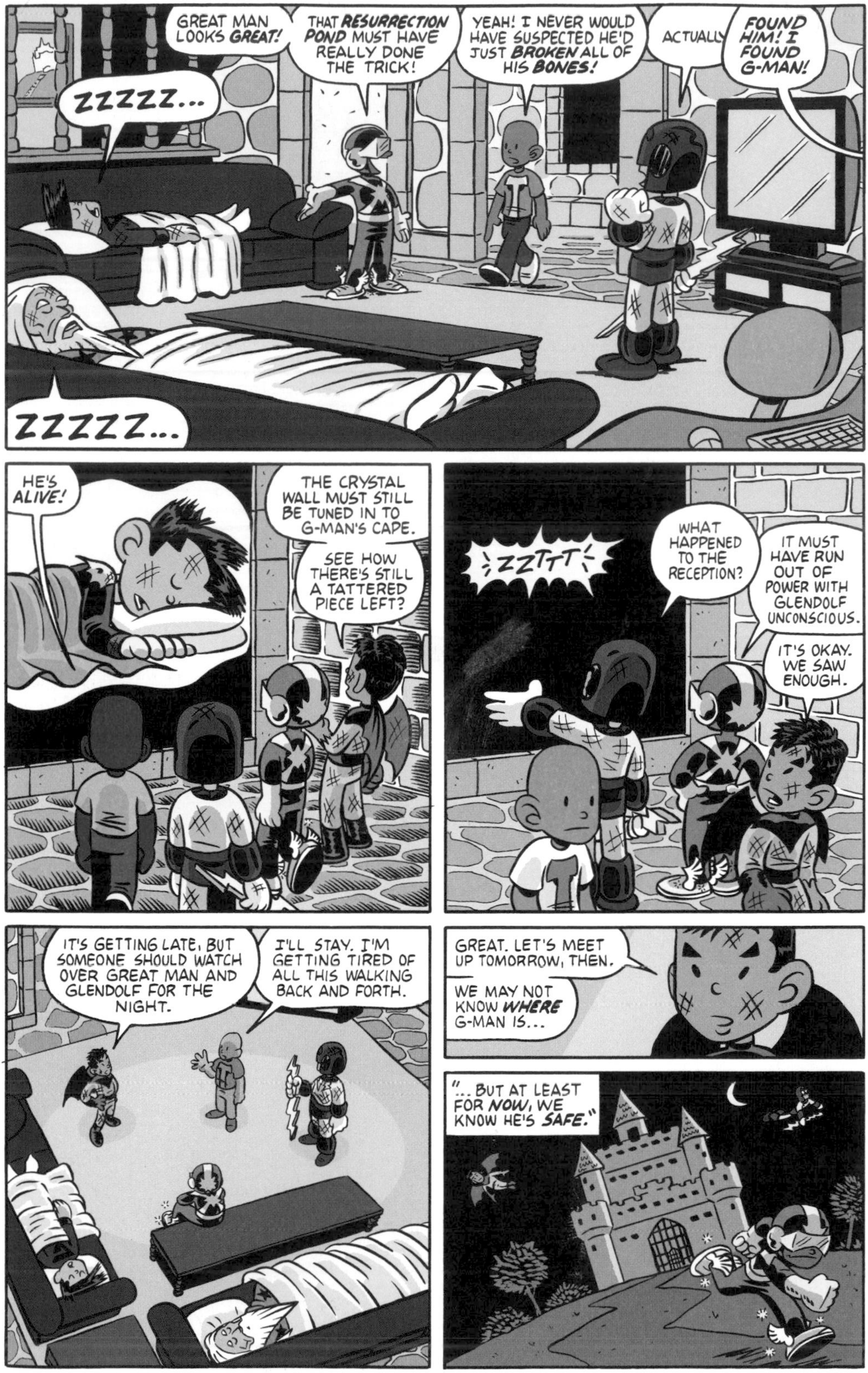
ZZZZZ...
GREAT MAN LOOKS GREAT!
THAT RESURRECTION POND MUST HAVE REALLY DONE THE TRICK!
YEAH! I NEVER WOULD HAVE SUSPECTED HE'D JUST BROKEN ALL OF HIS BONES!
ACTUALLY
FOUND HIM! I FOUND G-MAN!
ZZZZZ...
HE'S ALIVE!
THE CRYSTAL WALL MUST STILL BE TUNED IN TO G-MAN'S CAPE.
SEE HOW THERE'S STILL A TATTERED PIECE LEFT?
ZZTTT
WHAT HAPPENED TO THE RECEPTION?
IT MUST HAVE RUN OUT OF POWER WITH GLENDOLF UNCONSCIOUS.
IT'S OKAY. WE SAW ENOUGH.
IT'S GETTING LATE, BUT SOMEONE SHOULD WATCH OVER GREAT MAN AND GLENDOLF FOR THE NIGHT.
I'LL STAY. I'M GETTING TIRED OF ALL THIS WALKING BACK AND FORTH.
GREAT. LET'S MEET UP TOMORROW, THEN.
WE MAY NOT KNOW WHERE G-MAN IS...
"...BUT AT LEAST FOR NOW, WE KNOW HE'S SAFE."

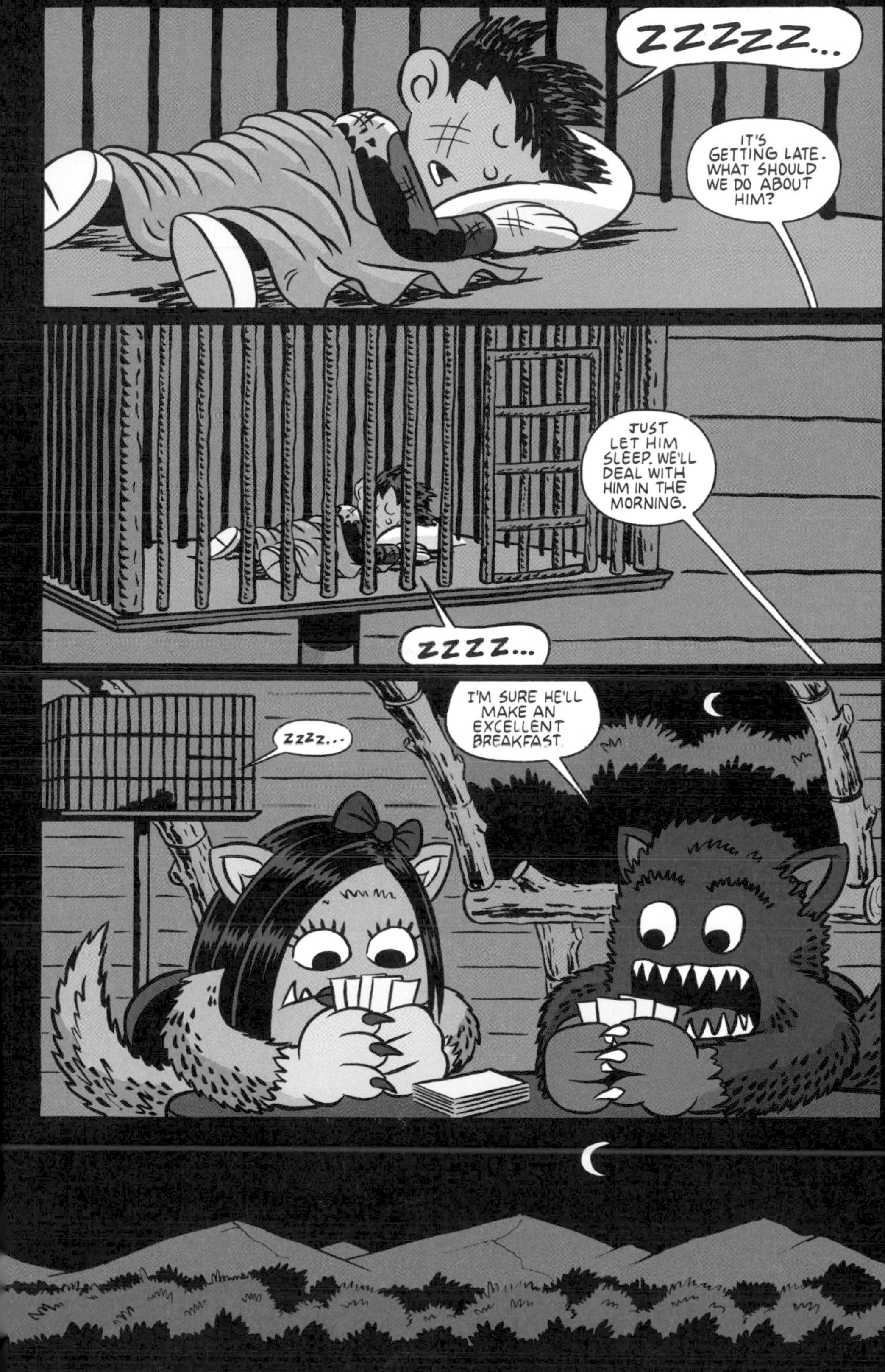
ZZZZZZ...
IT'S GETTING LATE. WHAT SHOULD WE DO ABOUT HIM?
JUST LET HIM SLEEP. WE'LL DEAL WITH HIM IN THE MORNING.
ZZZZ...
ZZZZ...
I'M SURE HE'LL MAKE AN EXCELLENT BREAKFAST.

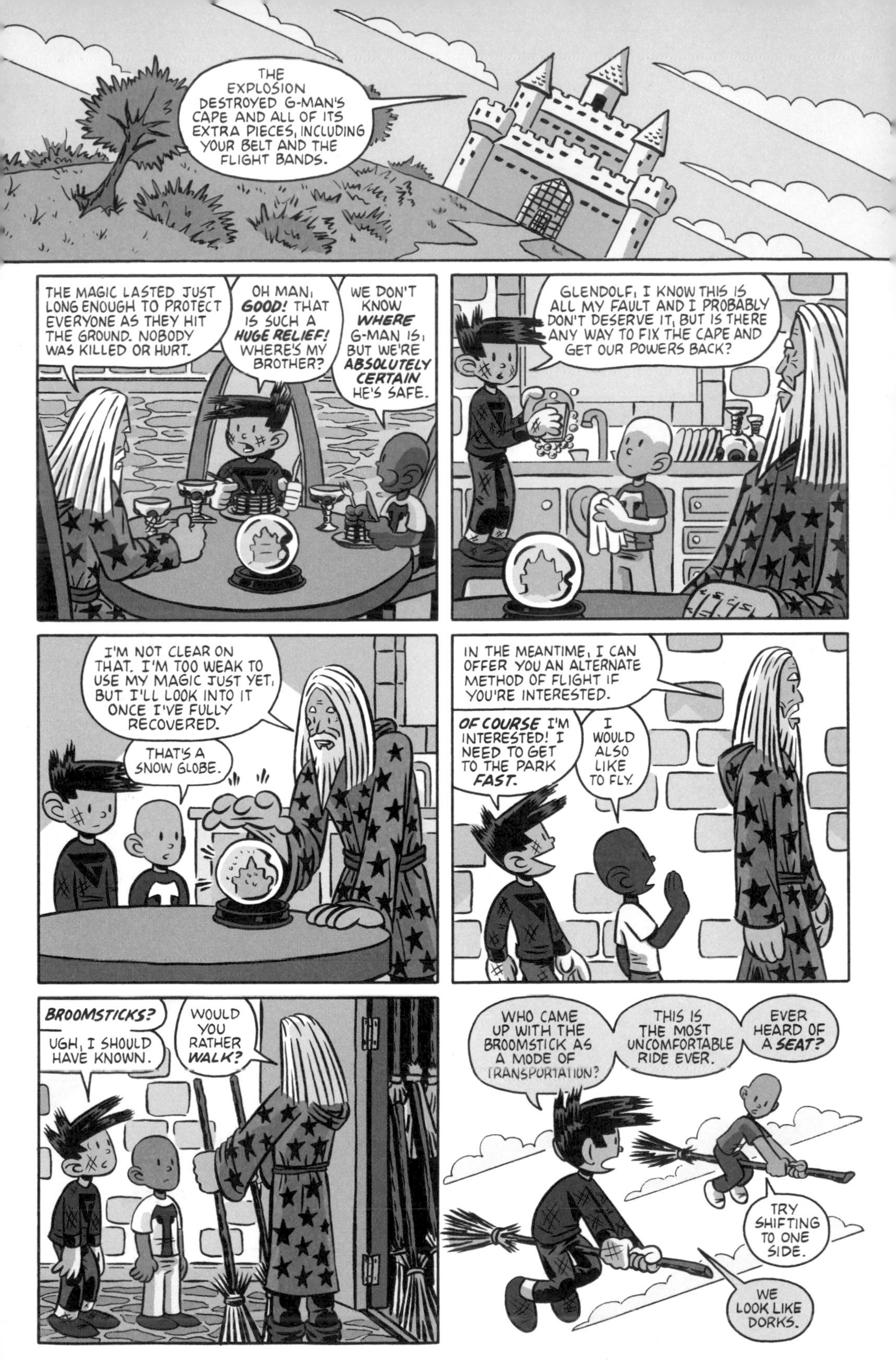
THE EXPLOSION DESTROYED G-MAN'S CAPE AND ALL OF ITS EXTRA PIECES, INCLUDING YOUR BELT AND THE FLIGHT BANDS.
THE MAGIC LASTED JUST LONG ENOUGH TO PROTECT EVERYONE AS THEY HIT THE GROUND. NOBODY WAS KILLED OR HURT.
OH MAN, GOOD! THAT IS SUCH A HUGE RELIEF! WHERE'S MY BROTHER?
WE DON'T KNOW WHERE G-MAN IS, BUT WE'RE ABSOLUTELY CERTAIN HE'S SAFE.
GLENDOLF, I KNOW THIS IS ALL MY FAULT AND I PROBABLY DON'T DESERVE IT, BUT IS THERE ANY WAY TO FIX THE CAPE AND GET OUR POWERS BACK?
I'M NOT CLEAR ON THAT. I'M TOO WEAK TO USE MY MAGIC JUST YET, BUT I'LL LOOK INTO IT ONCE I'VE FULLY RECOVERED.
THAT'S A SNOW GLOBE.
IN THE MEANTIME, I CAN OFFER YOU AN ALTERNATE METHOD OF FLIGHT IF YOU'RE INTERESTED.
OF COURSE I'M INTERESTED! I NEED TO GET TO THE PARK FAST.
I WOULD ALSO LIKE TO FLY.
BROOMSTICKS?
UGH, I SHOULD HAVE KNOWN.
WOULD YOU RATHER WALK?
WHO CAME UP WITH THE BROOMSTICK AS A MODE OF TRANSPORTATION?
THIS IS THE MOST UNCOMFORTABLE RIDE EVER.
EVER HEARD OF A SEAT?
TRY SHIFTING TO ONE SIDE.
WE LOOK LIKE DORKS.

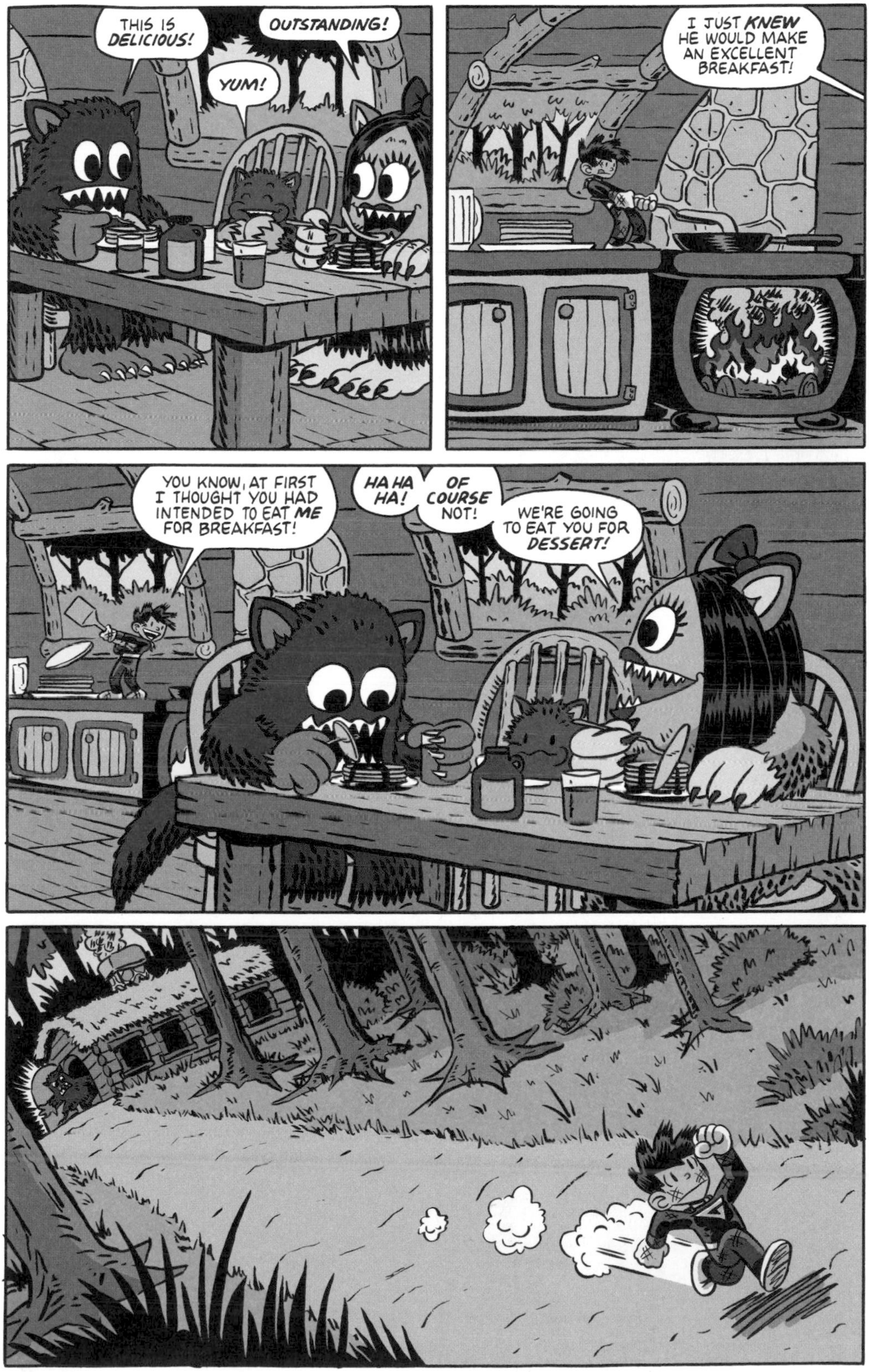
THIS IS DELICIOUS!
OUTSTANDING!
YUM!
I JUST KNEW HE WOULD MAKE AN EXCELLENT BREAKFAST!
YOU KNOW, AT FIRST I THOUGHT YOU HAD INTENDED TO EAT ME FOR BREAKFAST!
HA HA HA!
OF COURSE NOT!
WE'RE GOING TO EAT YOU FOR DESSERT!

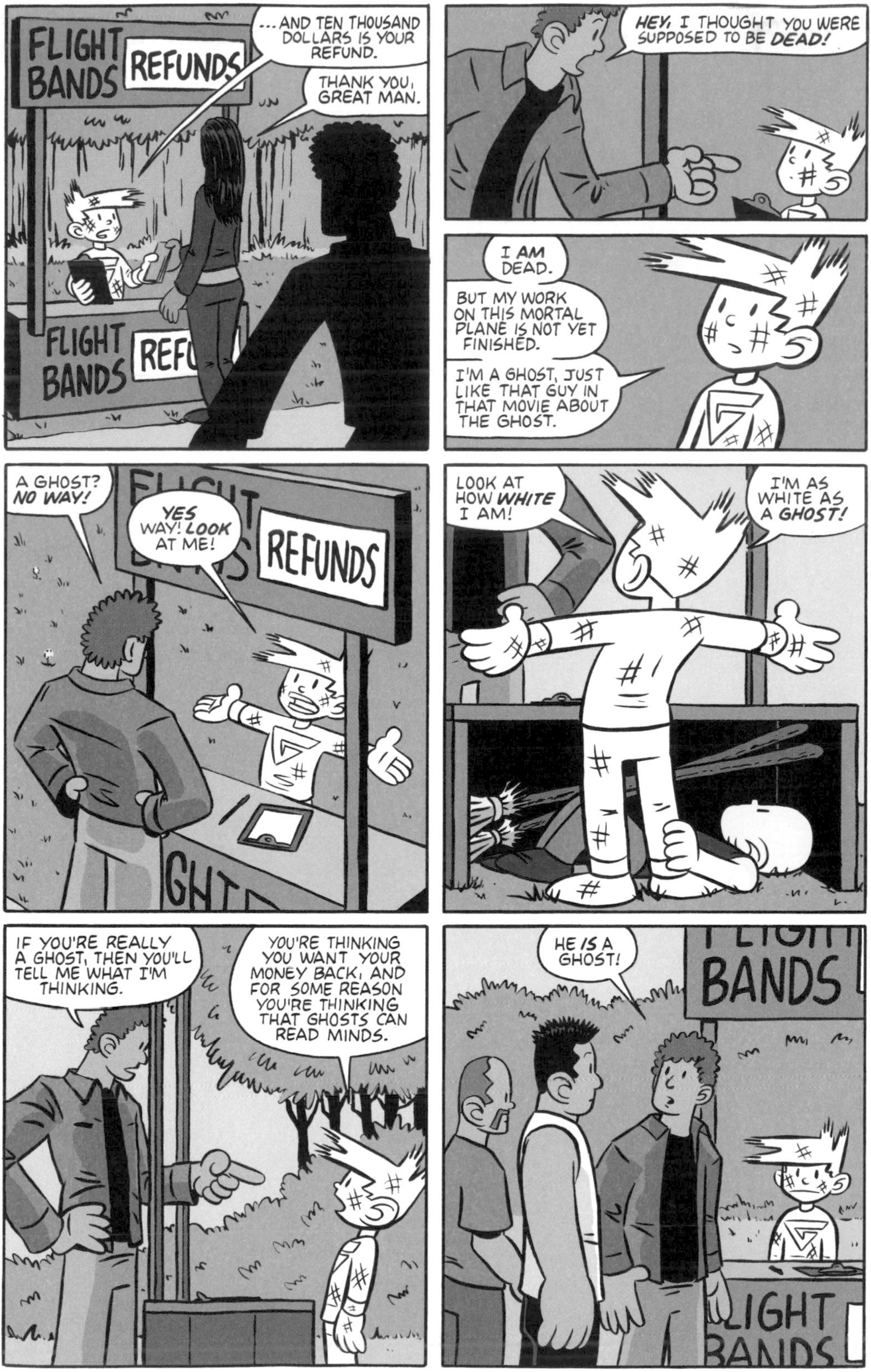
FLIGHT BANDS
REFUNDS
...AND TEN THOUSAND DOLLARS IS YOUR REFUND.
THANK YOU, GREAT MAN.
FLIGHT BANDS
HEY, I THOUGHT YOU WERE SUPPOSED TO BE DEAD!
I AM DEAD.
BUT MY WORK ON THIS MORTAL PLANE IS NOT YET FINISHED.
I'M A GHOST, JUST LIKE THAT GUY IN THAT MOVIE ABOUT THE GHOST.
A GHOST? NO WAY!
YES WAY! LOOK AT ME!
REFUNDS
LOOK AT HOW WHITE I AM!
I'M AS WHITE AS A GHOST!
IF YOU'RE REALLY A GHOST, THEN YOU'LL TELL ME WHAT I'M THINKING.
YOU'RE THINKING YOU WANT YOUR MONEY BACK, AND FOR SOME REASON YOU'RE THINKING THAT GHOSTS CAN READ MINDS.
HE IS A GHOST!
BANDS

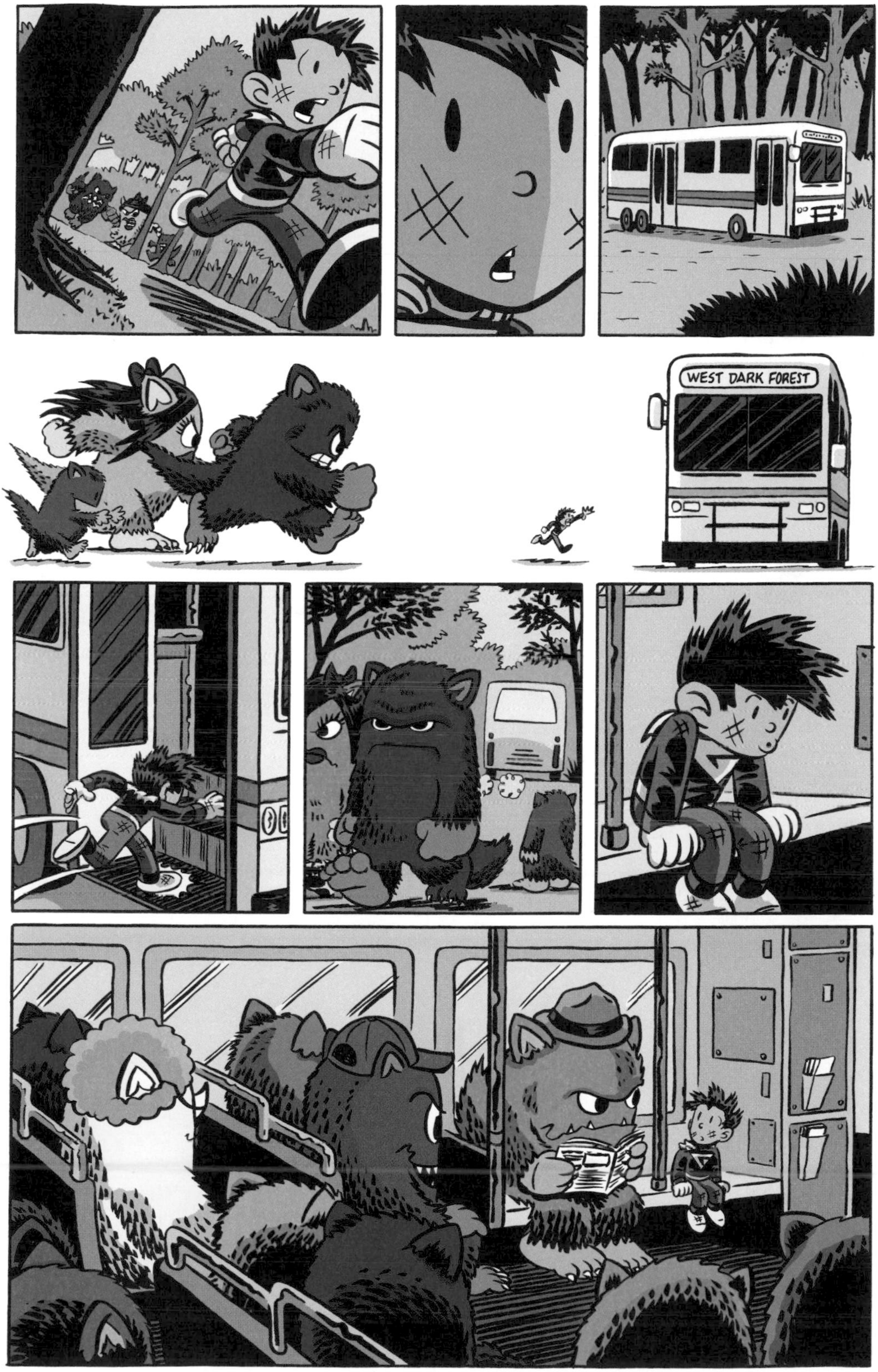
WEST DARK FOREST

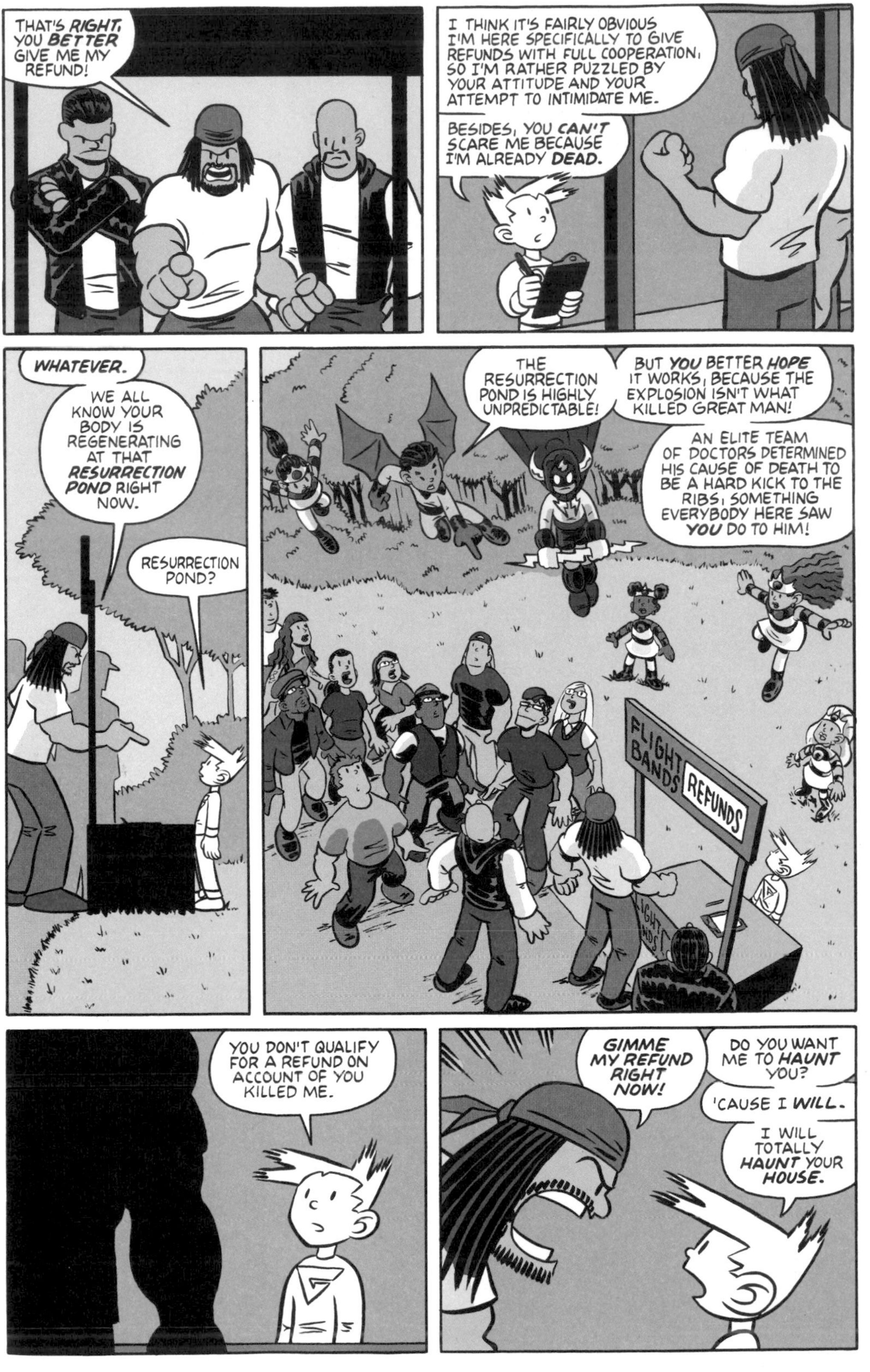
THAT'S RIGHT, YOU BETTER GIVE ME MY REFUND!
I THINK IT'S FAIRLY OBVIOUS I'M HERE SPECIFICALLY TO GIVE REFUNDS WITH FULL COOPERATION, SO I'M RATHER PUZZLED BY YOUR ATTITUDE AND YOUR ATTEMPT TO INTIMIDATE ME.
BESIDES, YOU CAN'T SCARE ME BECAUSE I'M ALREADY DEAD.
WHATEVER.
WE ALL KNOW YOUR BODY IS REGENERATING AT THAT RESURRECTION POND RIGHT NOW.
RESURRECTION POND?
THE RESURRECTION POND IS HIGHLY UNPREDICTABLE!
BUT YOU BETTER HOPE IT WORKS, BECAUSE THE EXPLOSION ISN'T WHAT KILLED GREAT MAN!
AN ELITE TEAM OF DOCTORS DETERMINED HIS CAUSE OF DEATH TO BE A HARD KICK TO THE RIBS, SOMETHING EVERYBODY HERE SAW YOU DO TO HIM!
FLIGHT BANDS
REFUNDS
YOU DON'T QUALIFY FOR A REFUND ON ACCOUNT OF YOU KILLED ME.
GIMME MY REFUND RIGHT NOW!
DO YOU WANT ME TO HAUNT YOU?
'CAUSE I WILL.
I WILL TOTALLY HAUNT YOUR HOUSE.

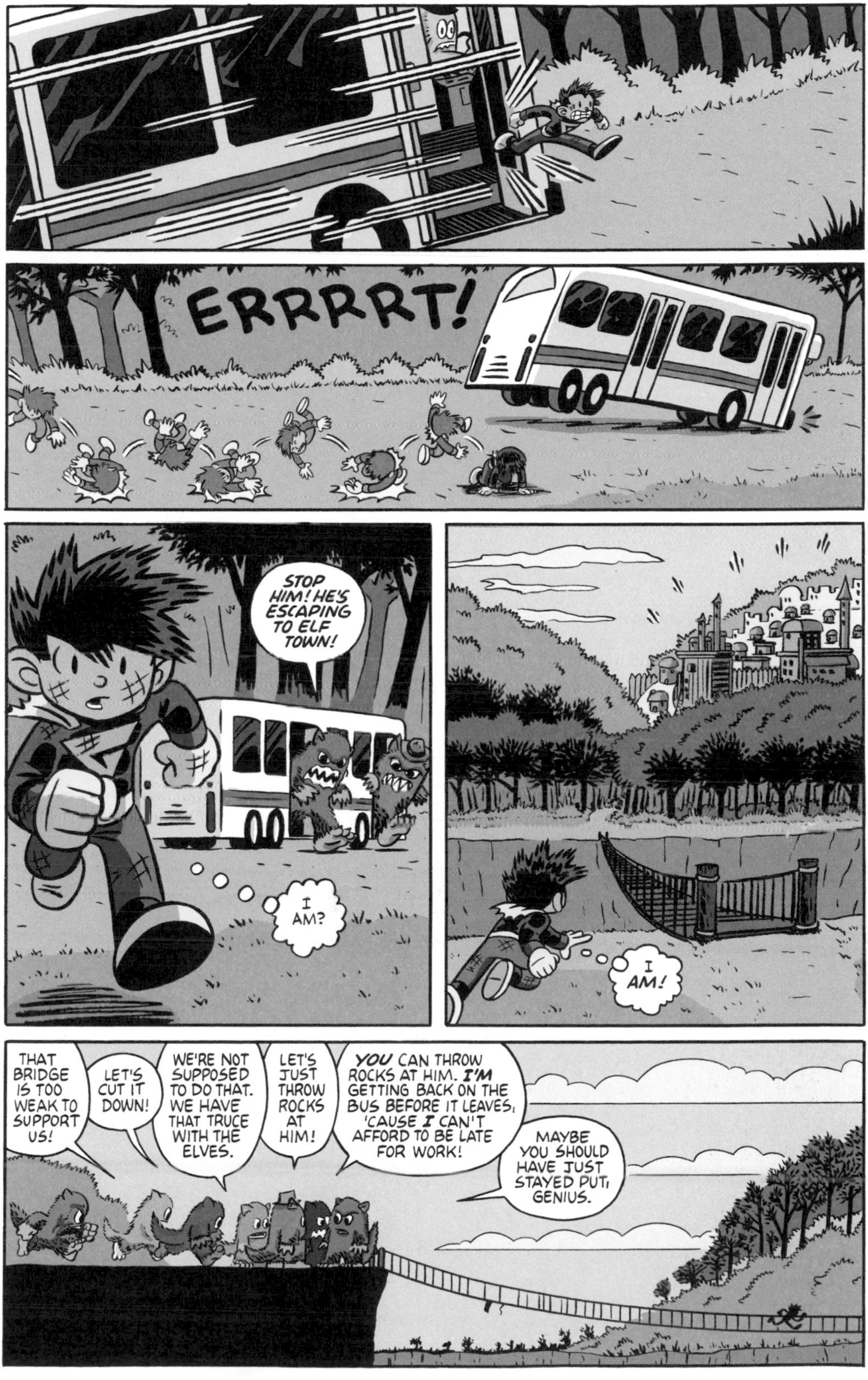
ERRRRT!
STOP HIM! HE'S ESCAPING TO ELF TOWN!
I AM?
I AM!
THAT BRIDGE IS TOO WEAK TO SUPPORT US!
LET'S CUT IT DOWN!
WE'RE NOT SUPPOSED TO DO THAT. WE HAVE THAT TRUCE WITH THE ELVES.
LET'S JUST THROW ROCKS AT HIM!
YOU CAN THROW ROCKS AT HIM. I'M GETTING BACK ON THE BUS BEFORE IT LEAVES, 'CAUSE I CAN'T AFFORD TO BE LATE FOR WORK!
MAYBE YOU SHOULD HAVE JUST STAYED PUT, GENIUS.

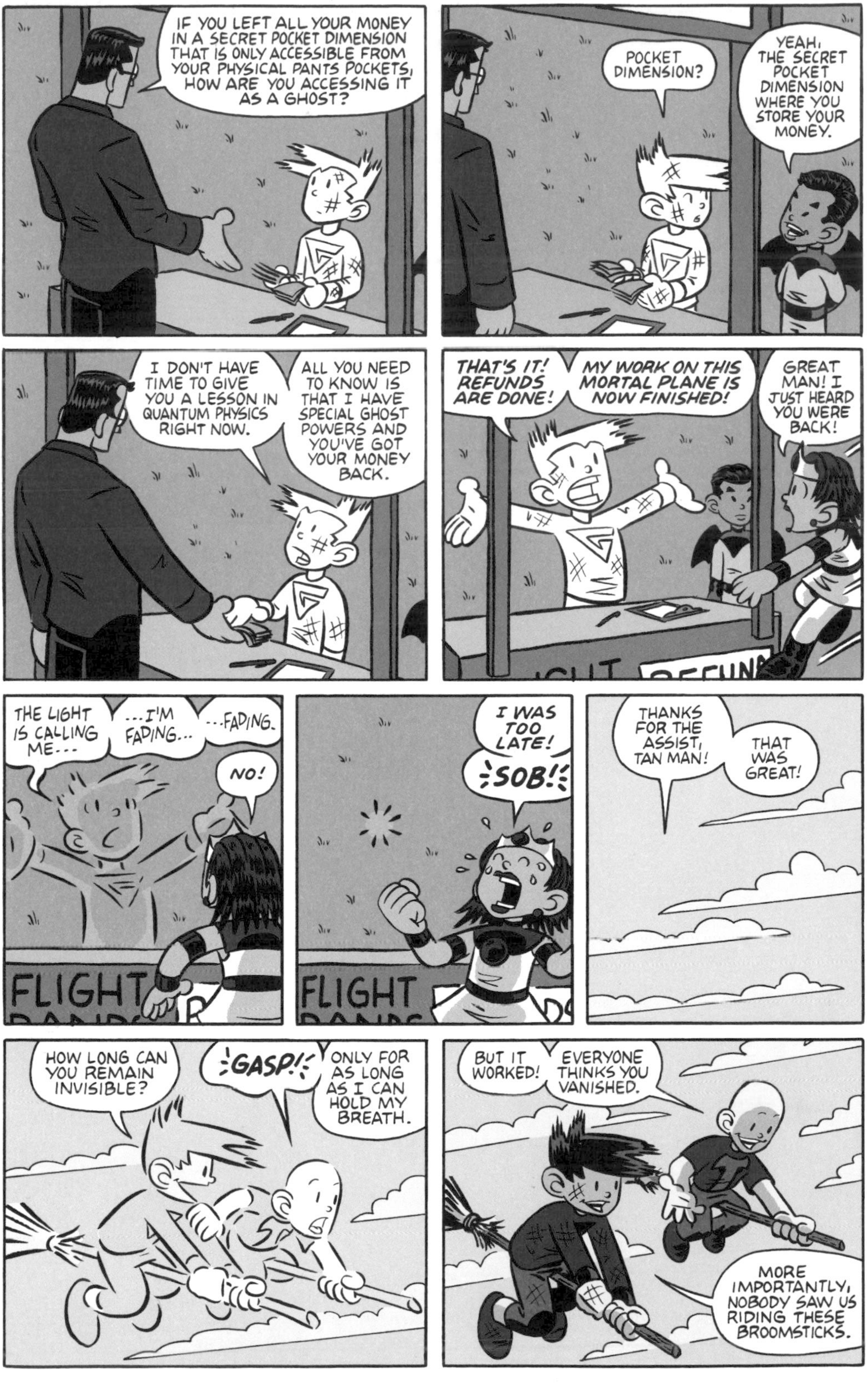
IF YOU LEFT ALL YOUR MONEY IN A SECRET POCKET DIMENSION THAT IS ONLY ACCESSIBLE FROM YOUR PHYSICAL PANTS POCKETS, HOW ARE YOU ACCESSING IT AS A GHOST?
POCKET DIMENSION?
YEAH, THE SECRET POCKET DIMENSION WHERE YOU STORE YOUR MONEY.
I DON'T HAVE TIME TO GIVE YOU A LESSON IN QUANTUM PHYSICS RIGHT NOW.
ALL YOU NEED TO KNOW IS THAT I HAVE SPECIAL GHOST POWERS AND YOU'VE GOT YOUR MONEY BACK.
THAT'S IT! REFUNDS ARE DONE!
MY WORK ON THIS MORTAL PLANE IS NOW FINISHED!
GREAT MAN! I JUST HEARD YOU WERE BACK!
THE LIGHT IS CALLING ME...
...I'M FADING...
...FADING.
NO!
FLIGHT
I WAS TOO LATE!
SOB!
FLIGHT
THANKS FOR THE ASSIST, TAN MAN!
THAT WAS GREAT!
HOW LONG CAN YOU REMAIN INVISIBLE?
GASP!
ONLY FOR AS LONG AS I CAN HOLD MY BREATH.
BUT IT WORKED!
EVERYONE THINKS YOU VANISHED.
MORE IMPORTANTLY, NOBODY SAW US RIDING THESE BROOMSTICKS.

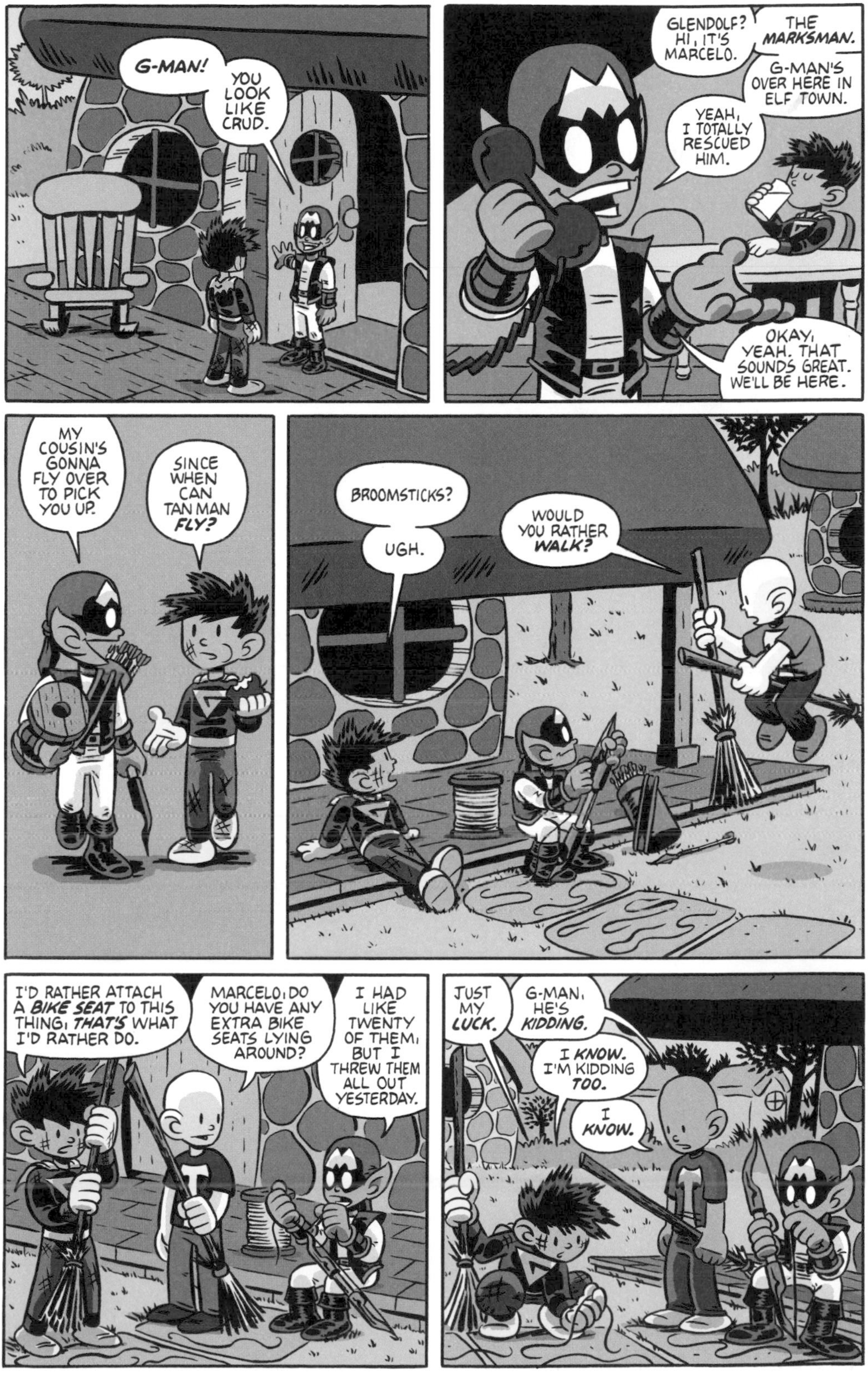
G-MAN!
YOU LOOK LIKE CRUD.
GLENDOLF? HI, IT'S MARCELO.
THE MARKSMAN.
G-MAN'S OVER HERE IN ELF TOWN.
YEAH, I TOTALLY RESCUED HIM.
OKAY, YEAH. THAT SOUNDS GREAT. WE'LL BE HERE.
MY COUSIN'S GONNA FLY OVER TO PICK YOU UP.
SINCE WHEN CAN TAN MAN FLY?
BROOMSTICKS?
UGH.
WOULD YOU RATHER WALK?
I'D RATHER ATTACH A BIKE SEAT TO THIS THING, THAT'S WHAT I'D RATHER DO.
MARCELO, DO YOU HAVE ANY EXTRA BIKE SEATS LYING AROUND?
I HAD LIKE TWENTY OF THEM, BUT I THREW THEM ALL OUT YESTERDAY.
JUST MY LUCK.
G-MAN, HE'S KIDDING.
I KNOW. I'M KIDDING TOO.
I KNOW.

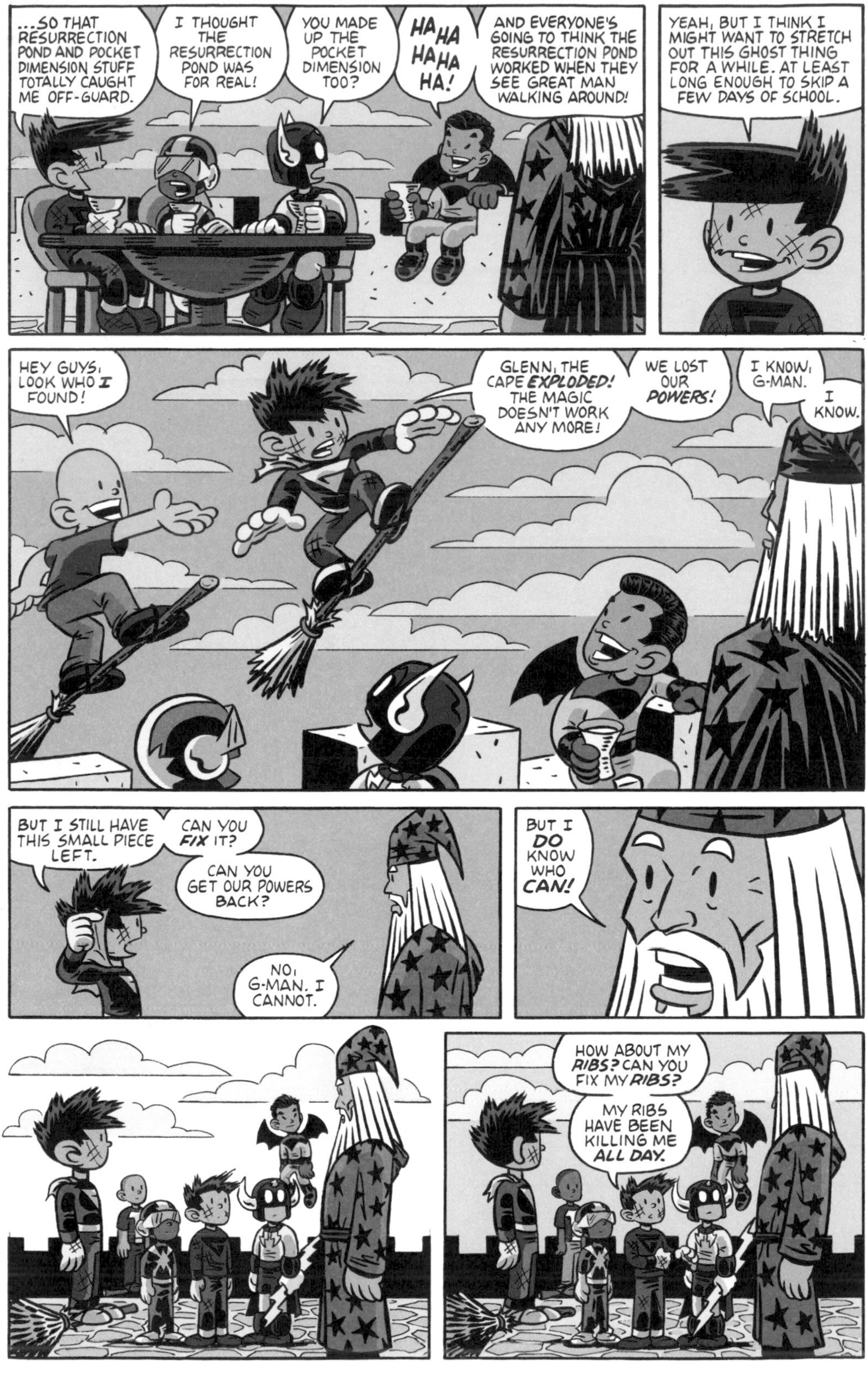
...SO THAT RESURRECTION POND AND POCKET DIMENSION STUFF TOTALLY CAUGHT ME OFF-GUARD.
I THOUGHT THE RESURRECTION POND WAS FOR REAL!
YOU MADE UP THE POCKET DIMENSION TOO?
HA HA HA HA HA!
AND EVERYONE'S GOING TO THINK THE RESURRECTION POND WORKED WHEN THEY SEE GREAT MAN WALKING AROUND!
YEAH, BUT I THINK I MIGHT WANT TO STRETCH OUT THIS GHOST THING FOR A WHILE. AT LEAST LONG ENOUGH TO SKIP A FEW DAYS OF SCHOOL.
HEY GUYS, LOOK WHO I FOUND!
GLENN, THE CAPE EXPLODED! THE MAGIC DOESN'T WORK ANY MORE!
WE LOST OUR POWERS!
I KNOW, G-MAN.
I KNOW.
BUT I STILL HAVE THIS SMALL PIECE LEFT.
CAN YOU FIX IT?
CAN YOU GET OUR POWERS BACK?
NO, G-MAN. I CANNOT.
BUT I DO KNOW WHO CAN!
HOW ABOUT MY RIBS? CAN YOU FIX MY RIBS?
MY RIBS HAVE BEEN KILLING ME ALL DAY.

Chapter 5

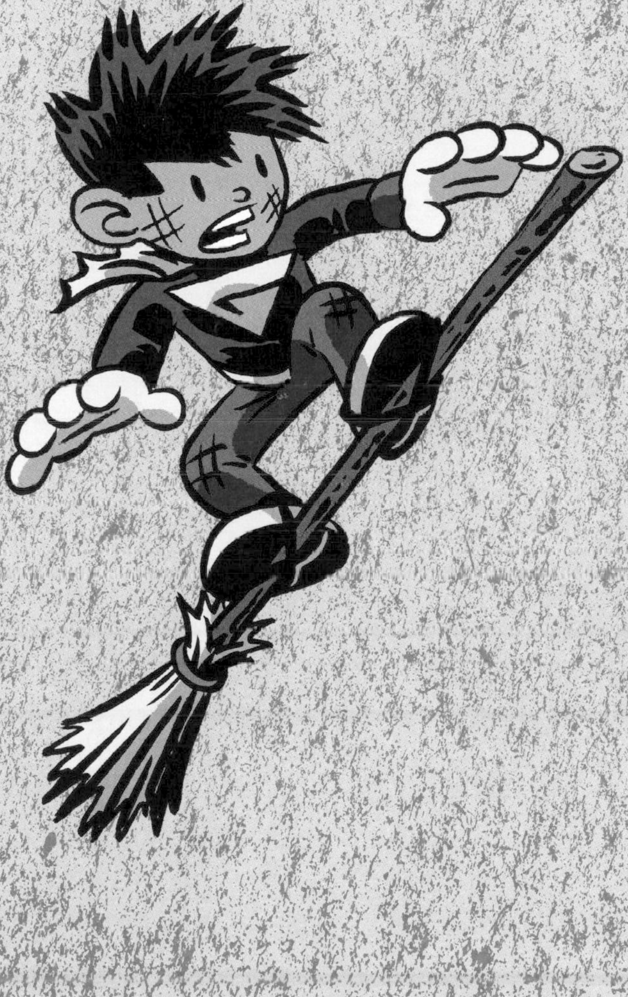

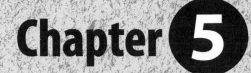

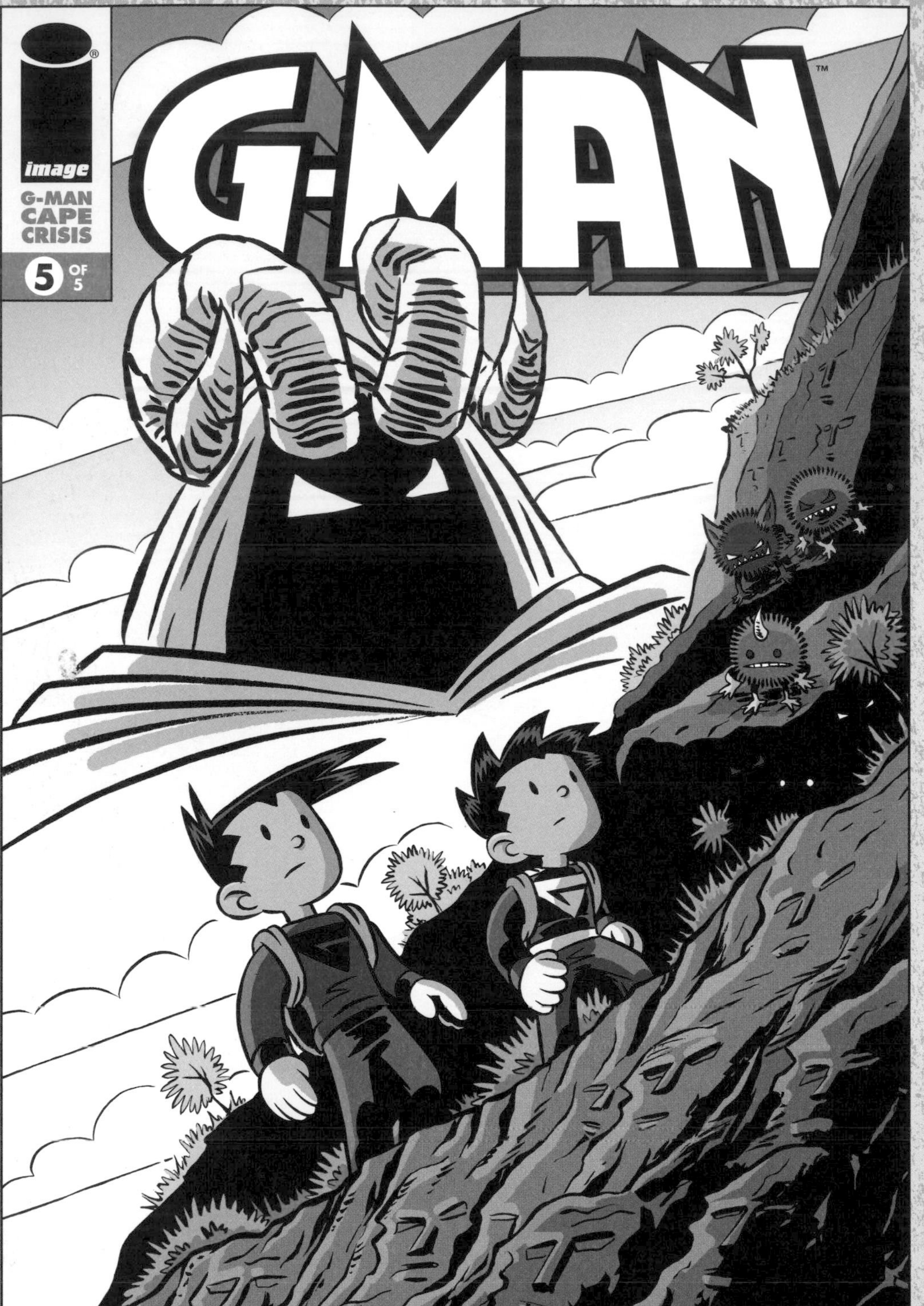
image
G-MAN
G-MAN
CAPE
CRISIS
5 OF 5
CHRIS GIARRUSSO

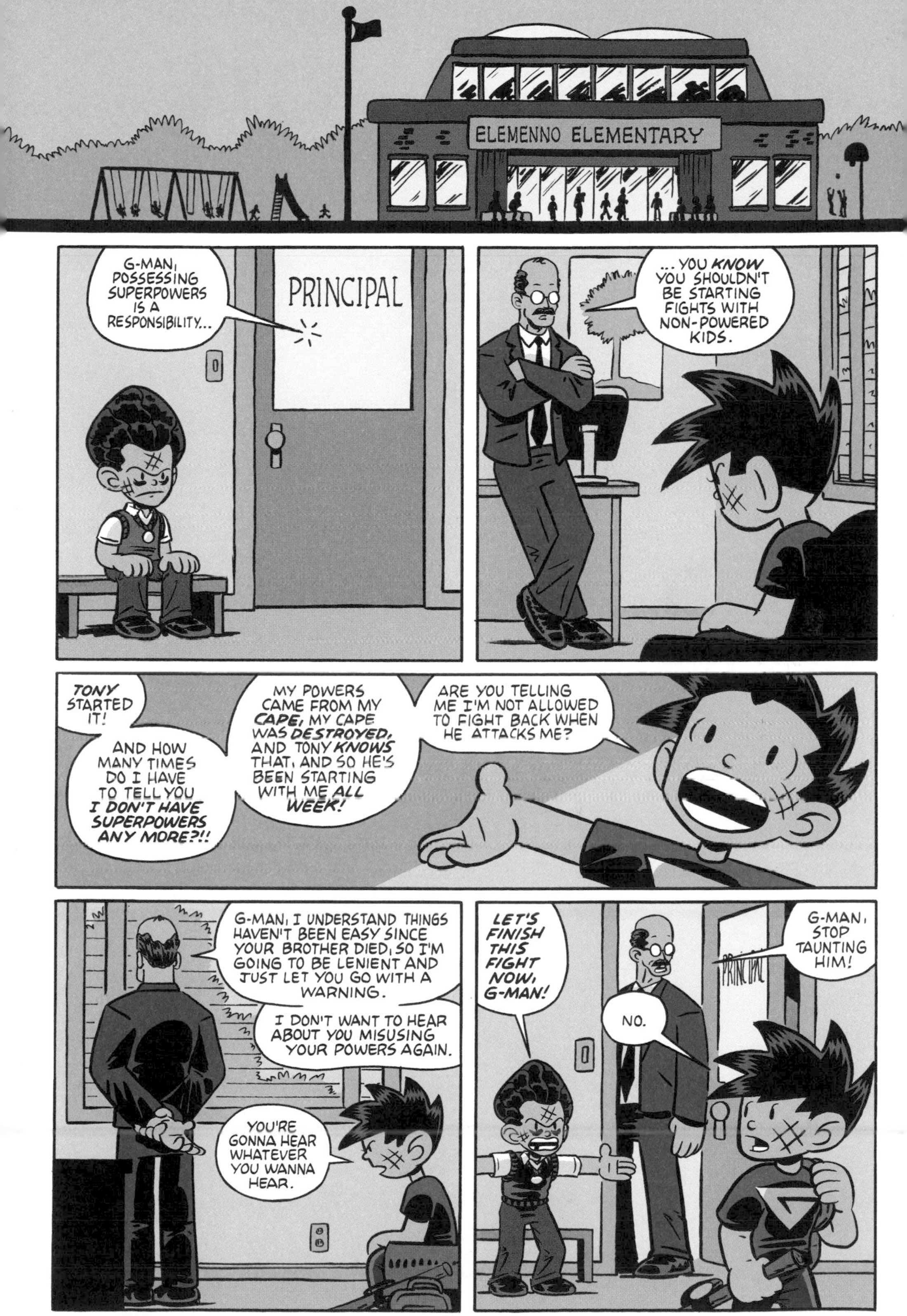
ELEMENNO ELEMENTARY
G-MAN, POSSESSING SUPERPOWERS IS A RESPONSIBILITY...
PRINCIPAL
...YOU KNOW YOU SHOULDN'T BE STARTING FIGHTS WITH NON-POWERED KIDS.
TONY STARTED IT!
AND HOW MANY TIMES DO I HAVE TO TELL YOU I DON'T HAVE SUPERPOWERS ANY MORE?!!
MY POWERS CAME FROM MY CAPE, MY CAPE WAS DESTROYED, AND TONY KNOWS THAT, AND SO HE'S BEEN STARTING WITH ME ALL WEEK!
ARE YOU TELLING ME I'M NOT ALLOWED TO FIGHT BACK WHEN HE ATTACKS ME?
G-MAN, I UNDERSTAND THINGS HAVEN'T BEEN EASY SINCE YOUR BROTHER DIED, SO I'M GOING TO BE LENIENT AND JUST LET YOU GO WITH A WARNING.
I DON'T WANT TO HEAR ABOUT YOU MISUSING YOUR POWERS AGAIN.
YOU'RE GONNA HEAR WHATEVER YOU WANNA HEAR.
LET'S FINISH THIS FIGHT NOW, G-MAN!
G-MAN, STOP TAUNTING HIM!
PRINCIPAL
NO.

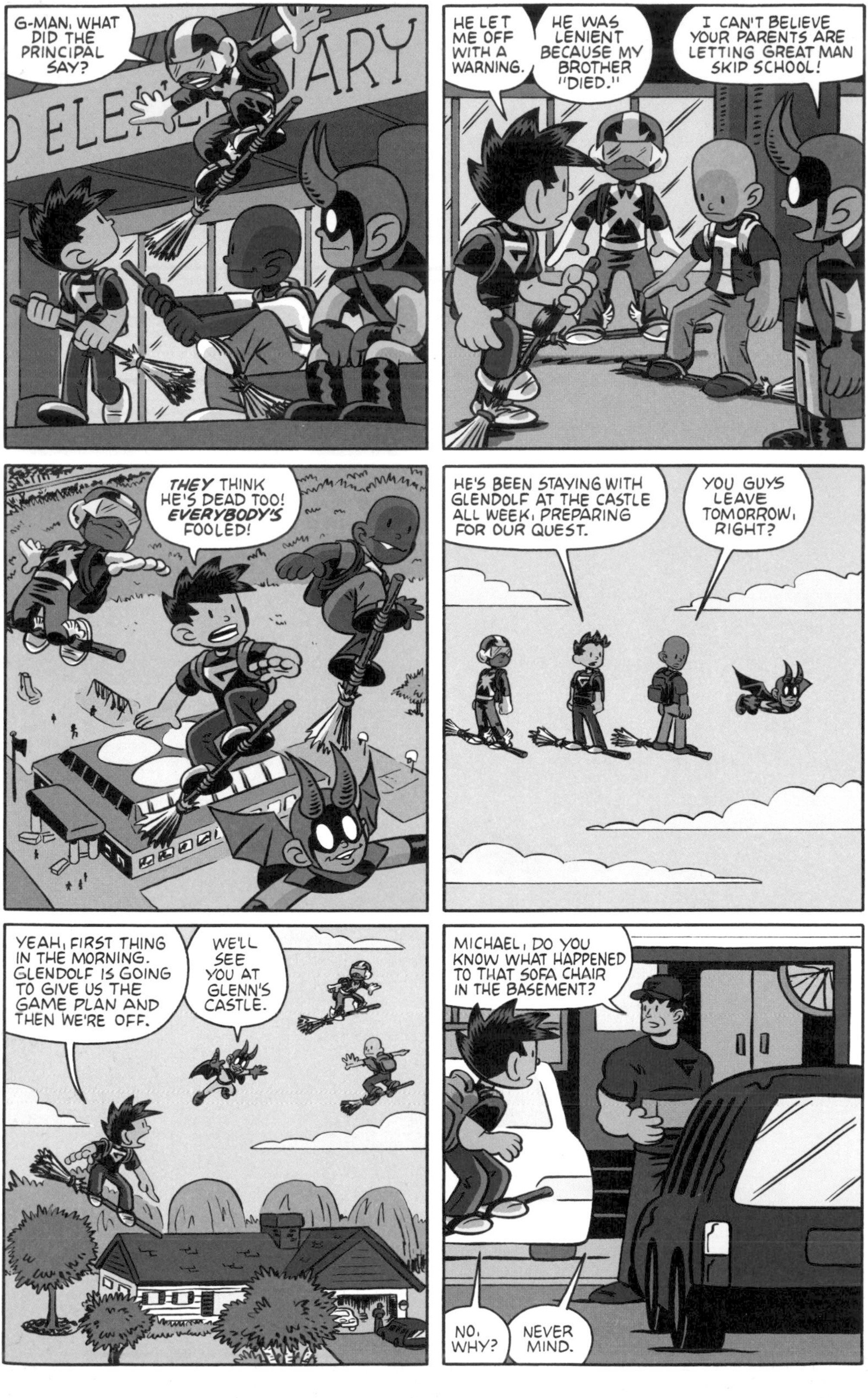
G-MAN, WHAT DID THE PRINCIPAL SAY?
HE LET ME OFF WITH A WARNING.
HE WAS LENIENT BECAUSE MY BROTHER "DIED."
I CAN'T BELIEVE YOUR PARENTS ARE LETTING GREAT MAN SKIP SCHOOL!
THEY THINK HE'S DEAD TOO! *EVERYBODY'S* FOOLED!
HE'S BEEN STAYING WITH GLENDOLF AT THE CASTLE ALL WEEK, PREPARING FOR OUR QUEST.
YOU GUYS LEAVE TOMORROW, RIGHT?
YEAH, FIRST THING IN THE MORNING. GLENDOLF IS GOING TO GIVE US THE GAME PLAN AND THEN WE'RE OFF.
WE'LL SEE YOU AT GLENN'S CASTLE.
MICHAEL, DO YOU KNOW WHAT HAPPENED TO THAT SOFA CHAIR IN THE BASEMENT?
NO, WHY?
NEVER MIND.

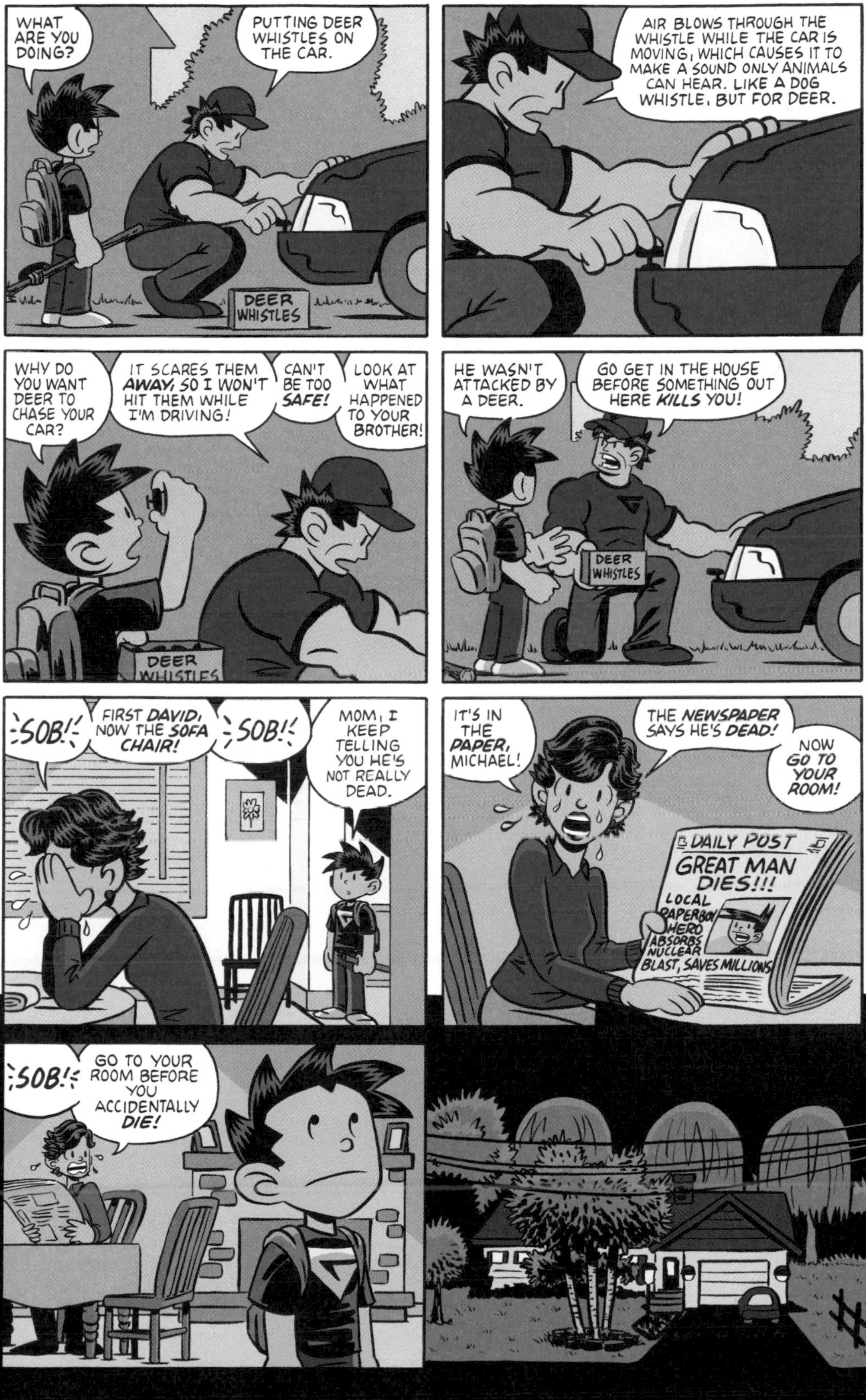
WHAT ARE YOU DOING?
PUTTING DEER WHISTLES ON THE CAR.
DEER WHISTLES
AIR BLOWS THROUGH THE WHISTLE WHILE THE CAR IS MOVING, WHICH CAUSES IT TO MAKE A SOUND ONLY ANIMALS CAN HEAR. LIKE A DOG WHISTLE, BUT FOR DEER.
WHY DO YOU WANT DEER TO CHASE YOUR CAR?
IT SCARES THEM AWAY, SO I WON'T HIT THEM WHILE I'M DRIVING!
CAN'T BE TOO SAFE!
LOOK AT WHAT HAPPENED TO YOUR BROTHER!
DEER WHISTLES
HE WASN'T ATTACKED BY A DEER.
GO GET IN THE HOUSE BEFORE SOMETHING OUT HERE KILLS YOU!
DEER WHISTLES
SOB!
FIRST DAVID, NOW THE SOFA CHAIR!
SOB!
MOM, I KEEP TELLING YOU HE'S NOT REALLY DEAD.
IT'S IN THE PAPER, MICHAEL!
THE NEWSPAPER SAYS HE'S DEAD!
NOW GO TO YOUR ROOM!
DAILY POST
GREAT MAN DIES!!!
LOCAL PAPERBOY HERO ABSORBS NUCLEAR BLAST, SAVES MILLIONS
SOB!
GO TO YOUR ROOM BEFORE YOU ACCIDENTALLY DIE!

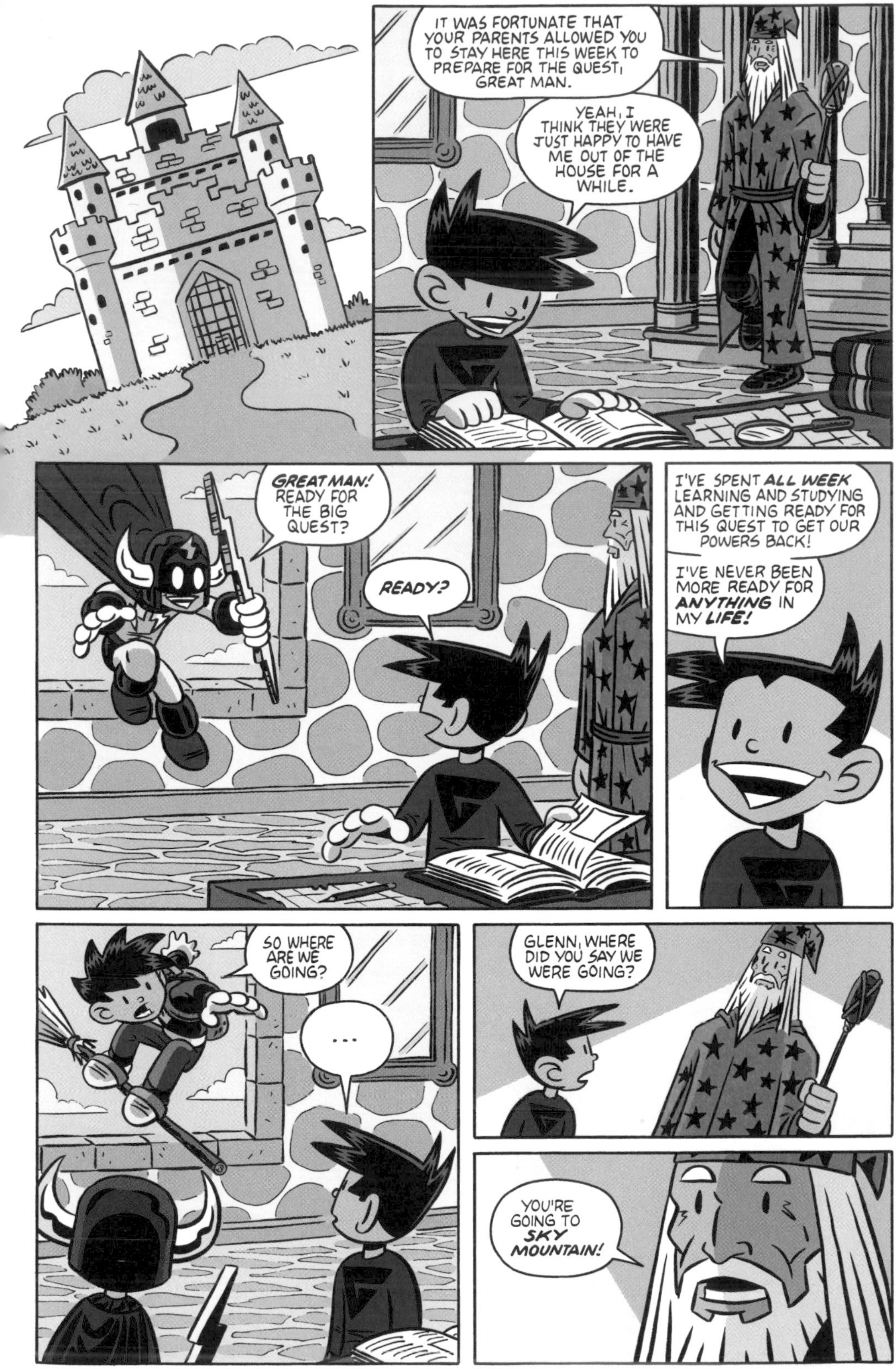
IT WAS FORTUNATE THAT YOUR PARENTS ALLOWED YOU TO STAY HERE THIS WEEK TO PREPARE FOR THE QUEST, GREAT MAN.
YEAH, I THINK THEY WERE JUST HAPPY TO HAVE ME OUT OF THE HOUSE FOR A WHILE.
GREAT MAN! READY FOR THE BIG QUEST?
READY?
I'VE SPENT ALL WEEK LEARNING AND STUDYING AND GETTING READY FOR THIS QUEST TO GET OUR POWERS BACK!
I'VE NEVER BEEN MORE READY FOR ANYTHING IN MY LIFE!
SO WHERE ARE WE GOING?
...
GLENN, WHERE DID YOU SAY WE WERE GOING?
YOU'RE GOING TO SKY MOUNTAIN!

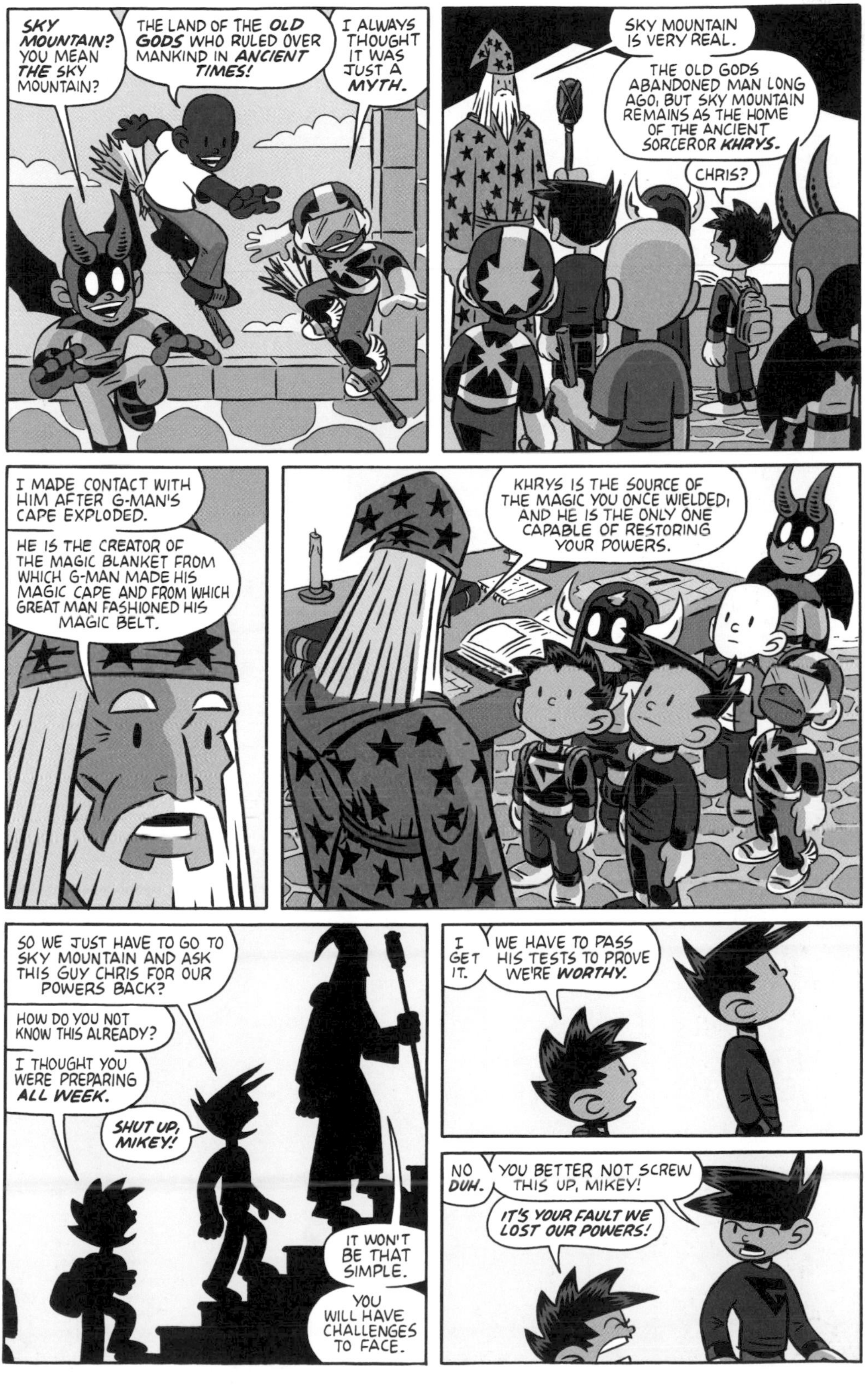
SKY MOUNTAIN? YOU MEAN THE SKY MOUNTAIN?
THE LAND OF THE OLD GODS WHO RULED OVER MANKIND IN ANCIENT TIMES!
I ALWAYS THOUGHT IT WAS JUST A MYTH.
SKY MOUNTAIN IS VERY REAL.
THE OLD GODS ABANDONED MAN LONG AGO, BUT SKY MOUNTAIN REMAINS AS THE HOME OF THE ANCIENT SORCEROR KHRYS.
CHRIS?
I MADE CONTACT WITH HIM AFTER G-MAN'S CAPE EXPLODED.
HE IS THE CREATOR OF THE MAGIC BLANKET FROM WHICH G-MAN MADE HIS MAGIC CAPE AND FROM WHICH GREAT MAN FASHIONED HIS MAGIC BELT.
KHRYS IS THE SOURCE OF THE MAGIC YOU ONCE WIELDED, AND HE IS THE ONLY ONE CAPABLE OF RESTORING YOUR POWERS.
SO WE JUST HAVE TO GO TO SKY MOUNTAIN AND ASK THIS GUY CHRIS FOR OUR POWERS BACK?
HOW DO YOU NOT KNOW THIS ALREADY?
I THOUGHT YOU WERE PREPARING ALL WEEK.
SHUT UP, MIKEY!
IT WON'T BE THAT SIMPLE.
YOU WILL HAVE CHALLENGES TO FACE.
I GET IT.
WE HAVE TO PASS HIS TESTS TO PROVE WE'RE WORTHY.
NO DUH.
YOU BETTER NOT SCREW THIS UP, MIKEY!
IT'S YOUR FAULT WE LOST OUR POWERS!

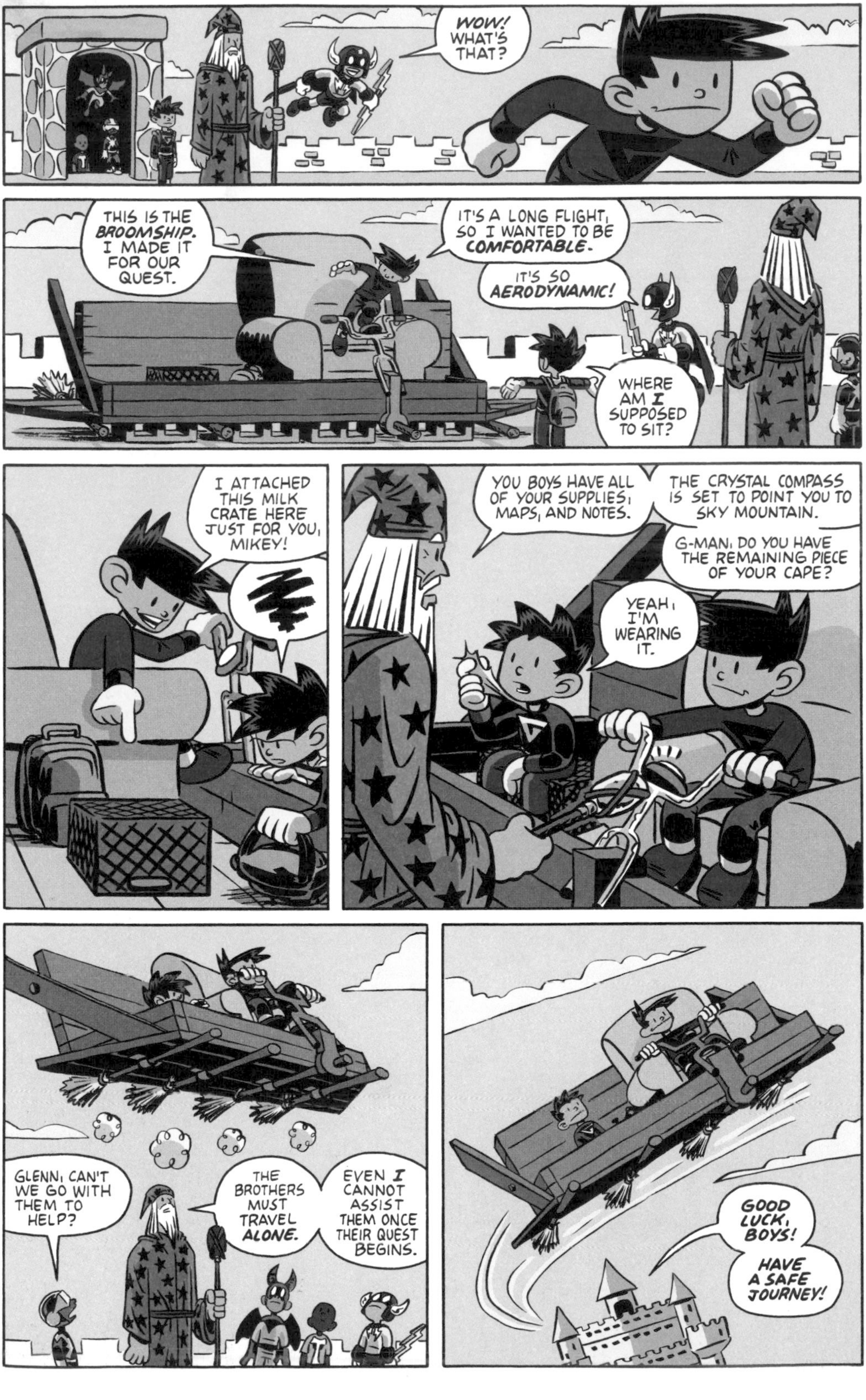

WOW! WHAT'S THAT?
THIS IS THE BROOMSHIP. I MADE IT FOR OUR QUEST.
IT'S A LONG FLIGHT, SO I WANTED TO BE COMFORTABLE.
IT'S SO AERODYNAMIC!
WHERE AM I SUPPOSED TO SIT?
I ATTACHED THIS MILK CRATE HERE JUST FOR YOU, MIKEY!
YOU BOYS HAVE ALL OF YOUR SUPPLIES, MAPS, AND NOTES.
THE CRYSTAL COMPASS IS SET TO POINT YOU TO SKY MOUNTAIN.
G-MAN, DO YOU HAVE THE REMAINING PIECE OF YOUR CAPE?
YEAH, I'M WEARING IT.
GLENN, CAN'T WE GO WITH THEM TO HELP?
THE BROTHERS MUST TRAVEL ALONE.
EVEN I CANNOT ASSIST THEM ONCE THEIR QUEST BEGINS.
GOOD LUCK, BOYS!
HAVE A SAFE JOURNEY!

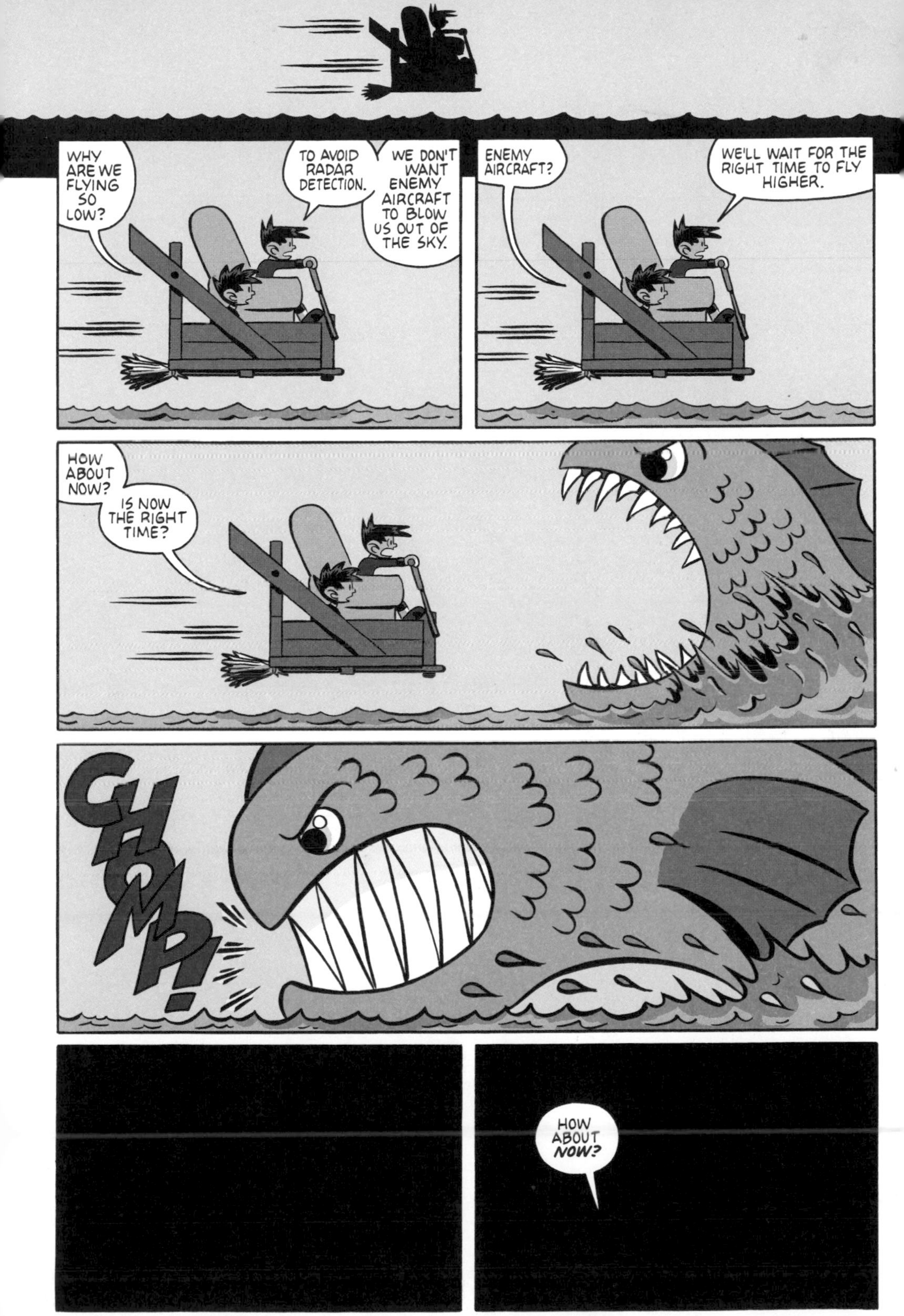
WHY ARE WE FLYING SO LOW?
TO AVOID RADAR DETECTION.
WE DON'T WANT ENEMY AIRCRAFT TO BLOW US OUT OF THE SKY.
ENEMY AIRCRAFT?
WE'LL WAIT FOR THE RIGHT TIME TO FLY HIGHER.
HOW ABOUT NOW?
IS NOW THE RIGHT TIME?
CHOMP!
HOW ABOUT *NOW?*

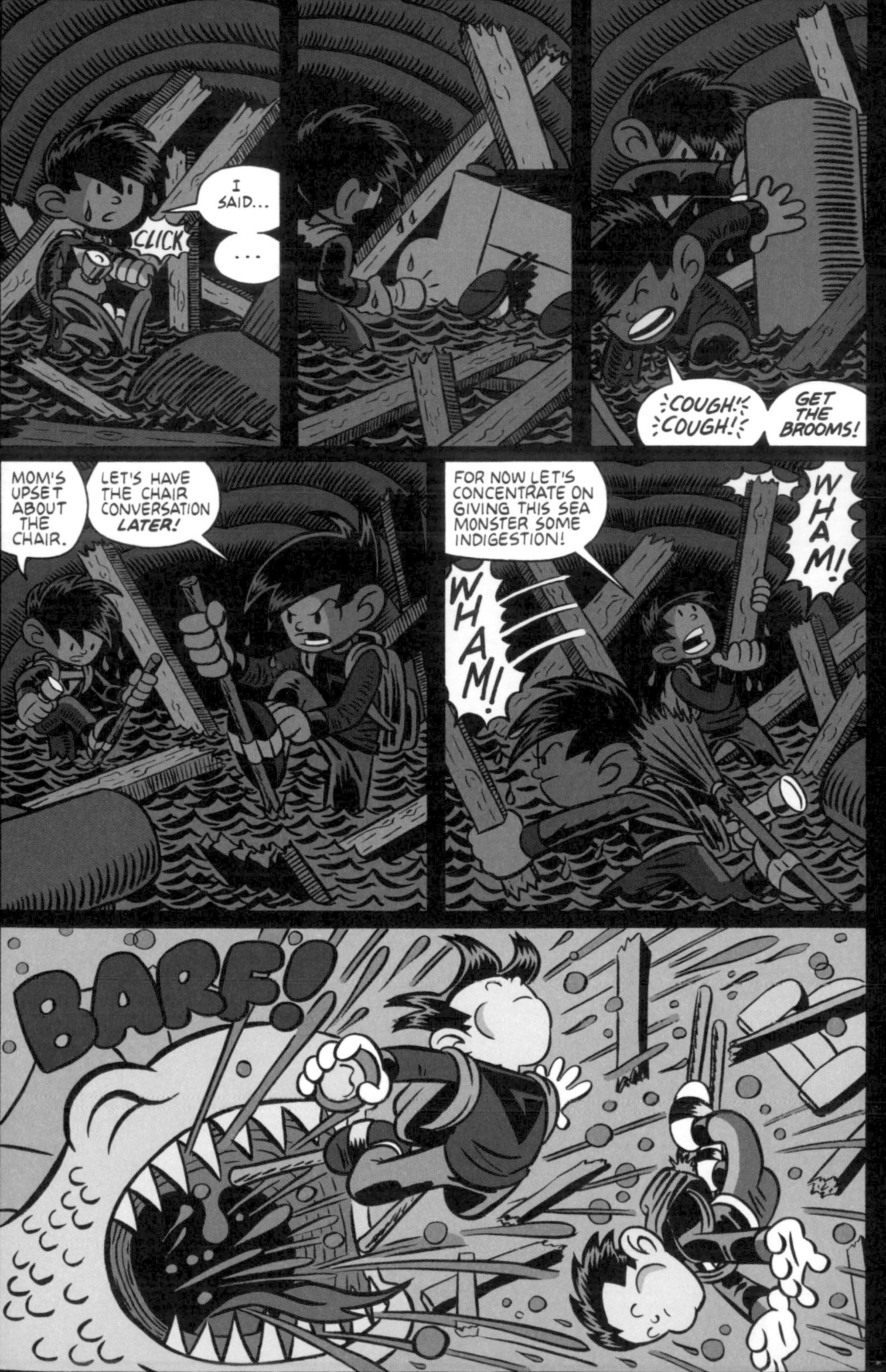

I SAID...
...
CLICK
COUGH! COUGH!
GET THE BROOMS!
MOM'S UPSET ABOUT THE CHAIR.
LET'S HAVE THE CHAIR CONVERSATION *LATER!*
FOR NOW LET'S CONCENTRATE ON GIVING THIS SEA MONSTER SOME INDIGESTION!
WHAM!
WHAM!
BARF!

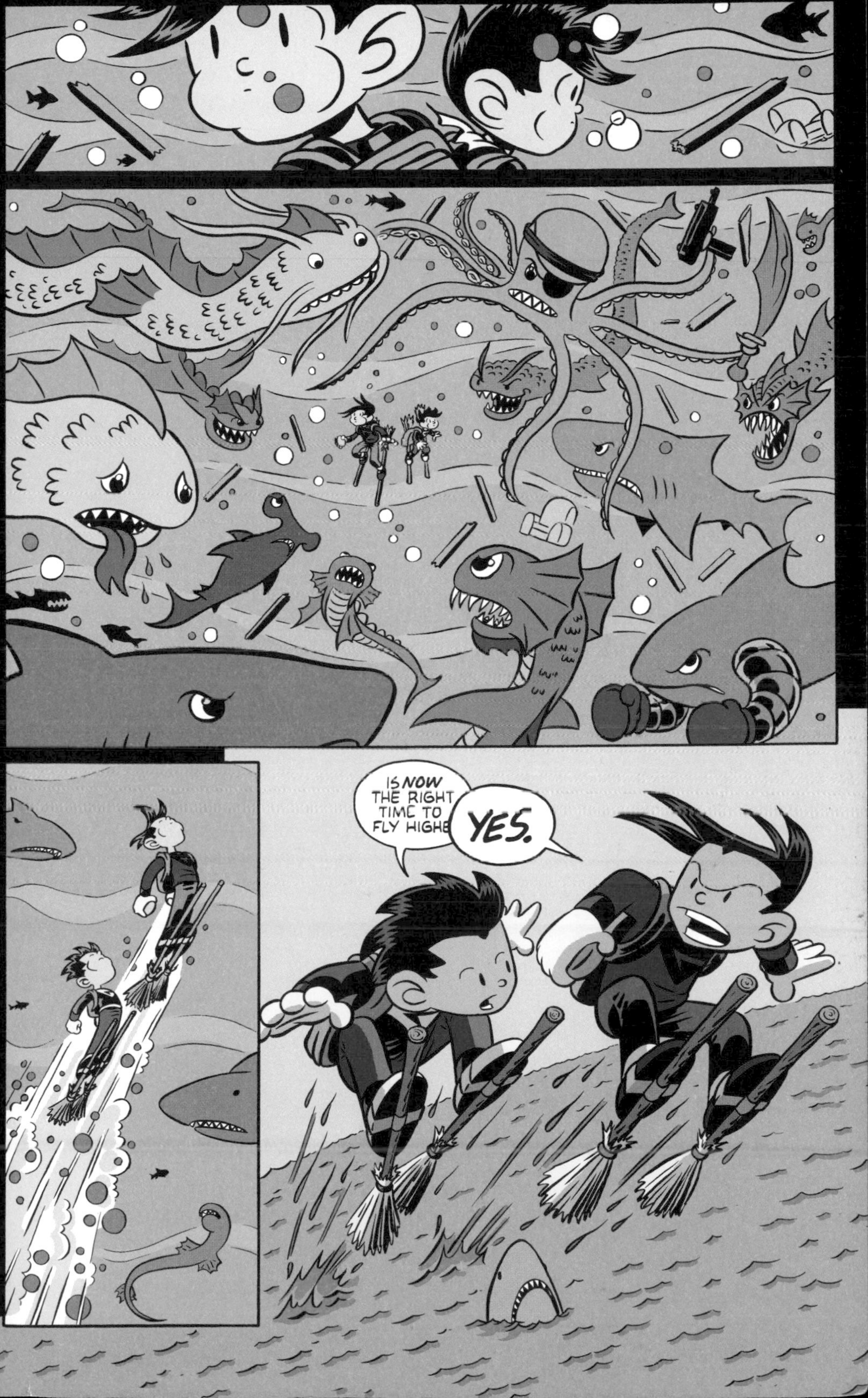
IS NOW THE RIGHT TIME TO FLY HIGHE
YES.

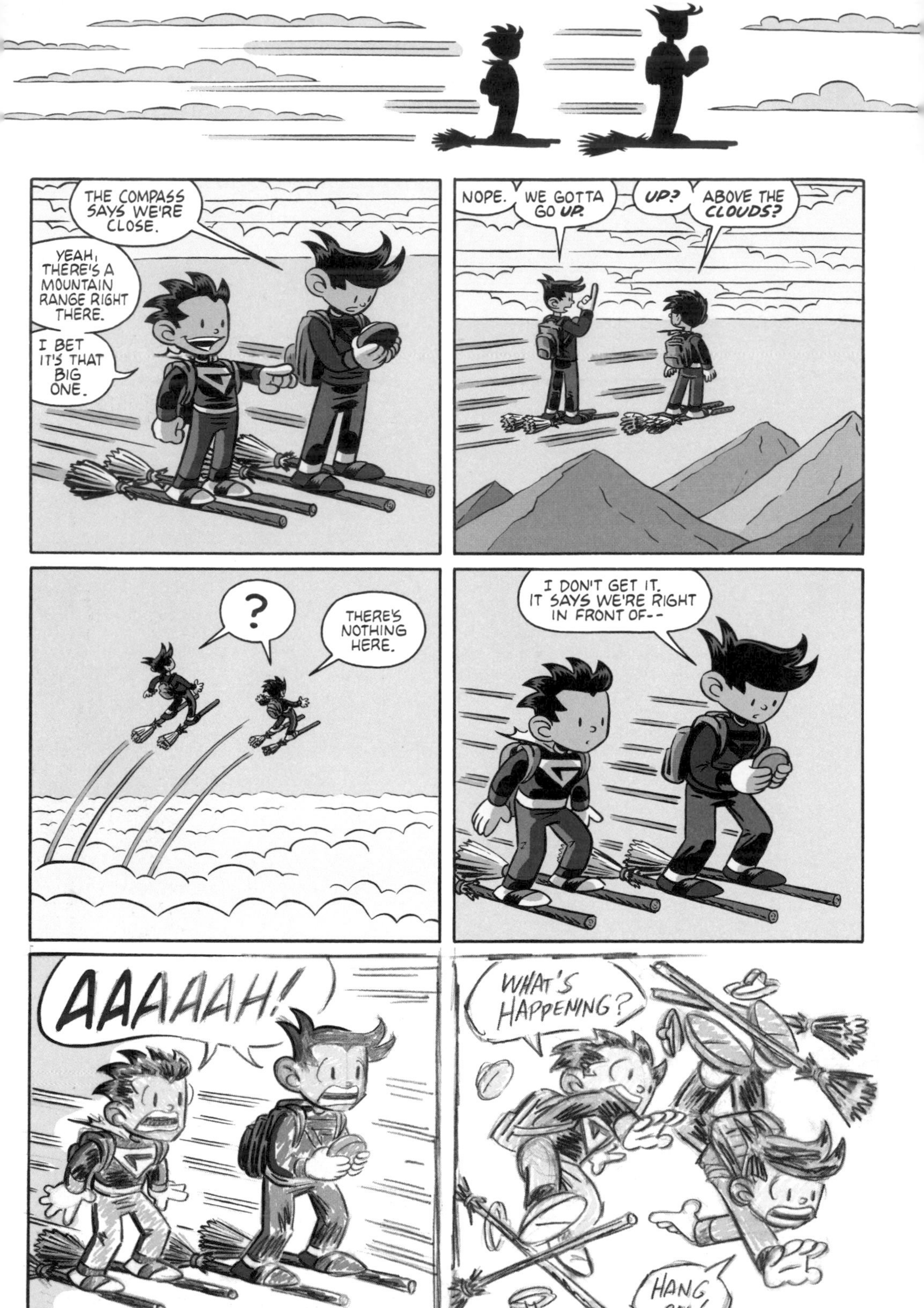
THE COMPASS SAYS WE'RE CLOSE.
YEAH, THERE'S A MOUNTAIN RANGE RIGHT THERE.
I BET IT'S THAT BIG ONE.
NOPE.
WE GOTTA GO UP.
UP?
ABOVE THE CLOUDS?
?
THERE'S NOTHING HERE.
I DON'T GET IT. IT SAYS WE'RE RIGHT IN FRONT OF--
AAAAAH!
WHAT'S HAPPENING?
HANG ON!

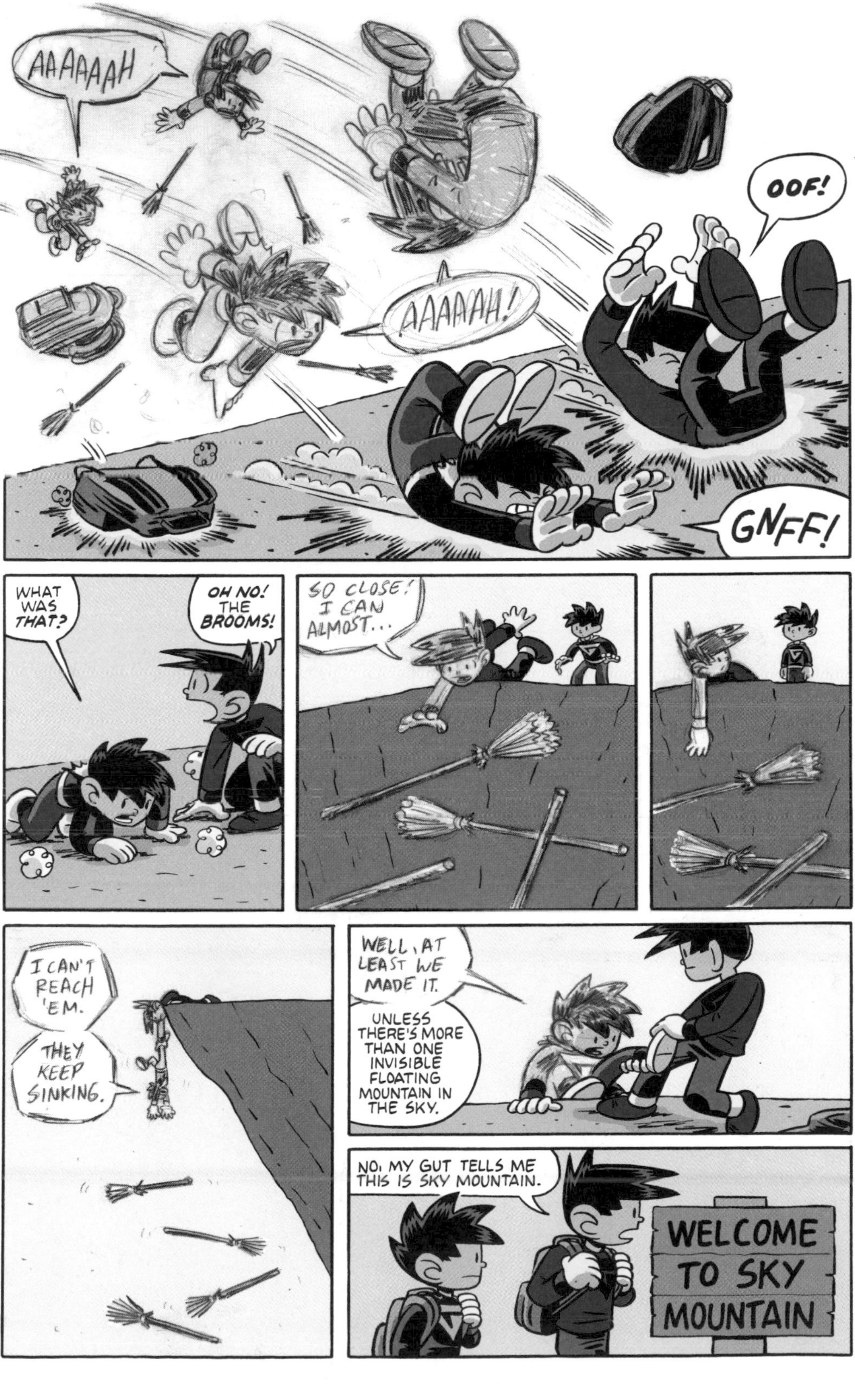
AAAAAAH
OOF!
AAAAAH!
GNFF!
WHAT WAS THAT?
OH NO! THE BROOMS!
SO CLOSE! I CAN ALMOST...
I CAN'T REACH 'EM.
THEY KEEP SINKING.
WELL, AT LEAST WE MADE IT.
UNLESS THERE'S MORE THAN ONE INVISIBLE FLOATING MOUNTAIN IN THE SKY.
NO, MY GUT TELLS ME THIS IS SKY MOUNTAIN.
WELCOME TO SKY MOUNTAIN

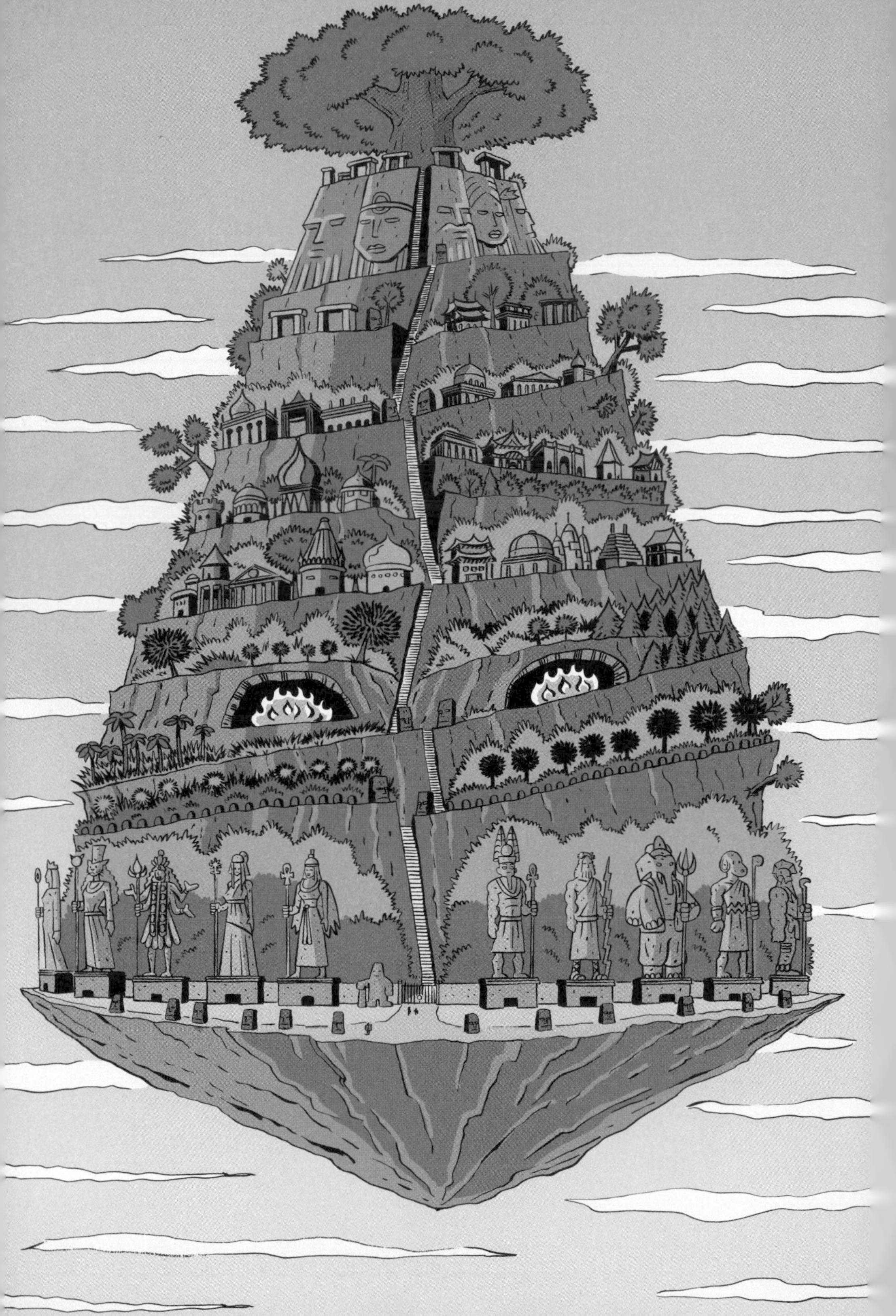

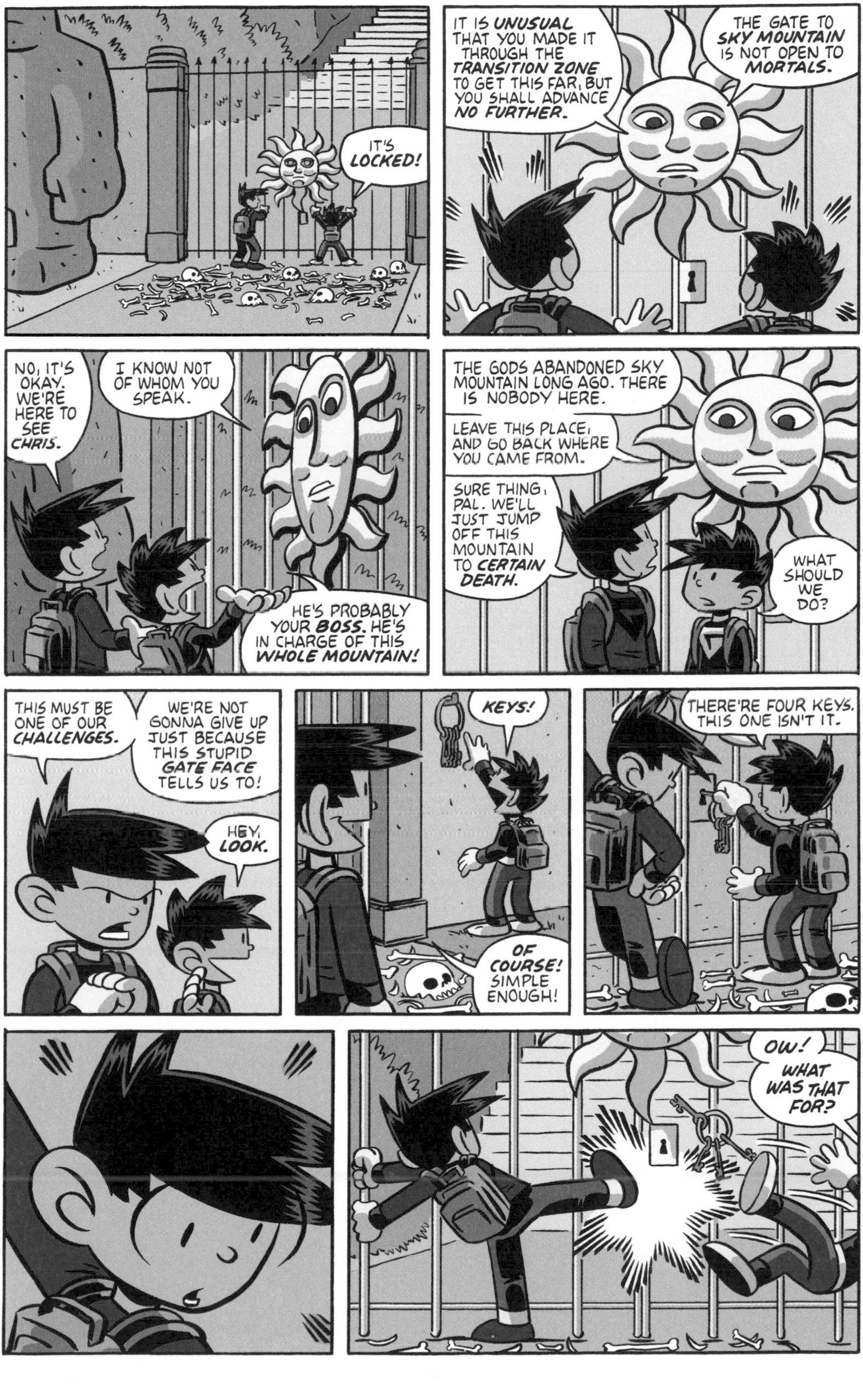
IT'S LOCKED!
IT IS UNUSUAL THAT YOU MADE IT THROUGH THE TRANSITION ZONE TO GET THIS FAR, BUT YOU SHALL ADVANCE NO FURTHER.
THE GATE TO SKY MOUNTAIN IS NOT OPEN TO MORTALS.
NO, IT'S OKAY. WE'RE HERE TO SEE CHRIS.
I KNOW NOT OF WHOM YOU SPEAK.
HE'S PROBABLY YOUR BOSS. HE'S IN CHARGE OF THIS WHOLE MOUNTAIN!
THE GODS ABANDONED SKY MOUNTAIN LONG AGO. THERE IS NOBODY HERE.
LEAVE THIS PLACE, AND GO BACK WHERE YOU CAME FROM.
SURE THING, PAL. WE'LL JUST JUMP OFF THIS MOUNTAIN TO CERTAIN DEATH.
WHAT SHOULD WE DO?
THIS MUST BE ONE OF OUR CHALLENGES.
WE'RE NOT GONNA GIVE UP JUST BECAUSE THIS STUPID GATE FACE TELLS US TO!
HEY, LOOK.
KEYS!
OF COURSE! SIMPLE ENOUGH!
THERE'RE FOUR KEYS. THIS ONE ISN'T IT.
OW! WHAT WAS THAT FOR?

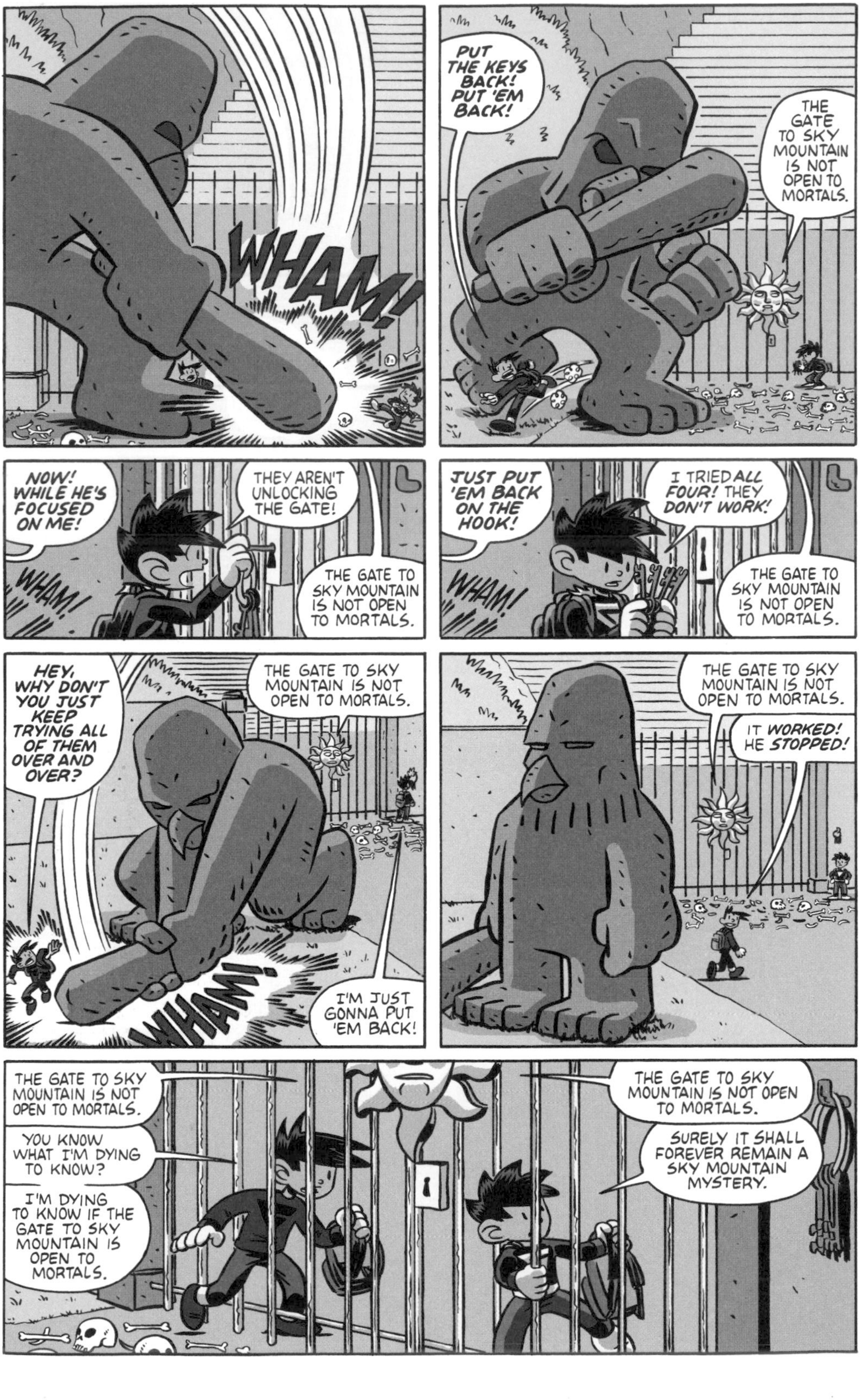
WHAM!
PUT THE KEYS BACK! PUT 'EM BACK!
THE GATE TO SKY MOUNTAIN IS NOT OPEN TO MORTALS.
NOW! WHILE HE'S FOCUSED ON ME!
THEY AREN'T UNLOCKING THE GATE!
WHAM!
THE GATE TO SKY MOUNTAIN IS NOT OPEN TO MORTALS.
JUST PUT 'EM BACK ON THE HOOK!
I TRIED ALL FOUR! THEY DON'T WORK!
WHAM!
THE GATE TO SKY MOUNTAIN IS NOT OPEN TO MORTALS.
HEY, WHY DON'T YOU JUST KEEP TRYING ALL OF THEM OVER AND OVER?
THE GATE TO SKY MOUNTAIN IS NOT OPEN TO MORTALS.
WHAM!
I'M JUST GONNA PUT 'EM BACK!
THE GATE TO SKY MOUNTAIN IS NOT OPEN TO MORTALS.
IT WORKED! HE STOPPED!
THE GATE TO SKY MOUNTAIN IS NOT OPEN TO MORTALS.
YOU KNOW WHAT I'M DYING TO KNOW?
I'M DYING TO KNOW IF THE GATE TO SKY MOUNTAIN IS OPEN TO MORTALS.
THE GATE TO SKY MOUNTAIN IS NOT OPEN TO MORTALS.
SURELY IT SHALL FOREVER REMAIN A SKY MOUNTAIN MYSTERY.

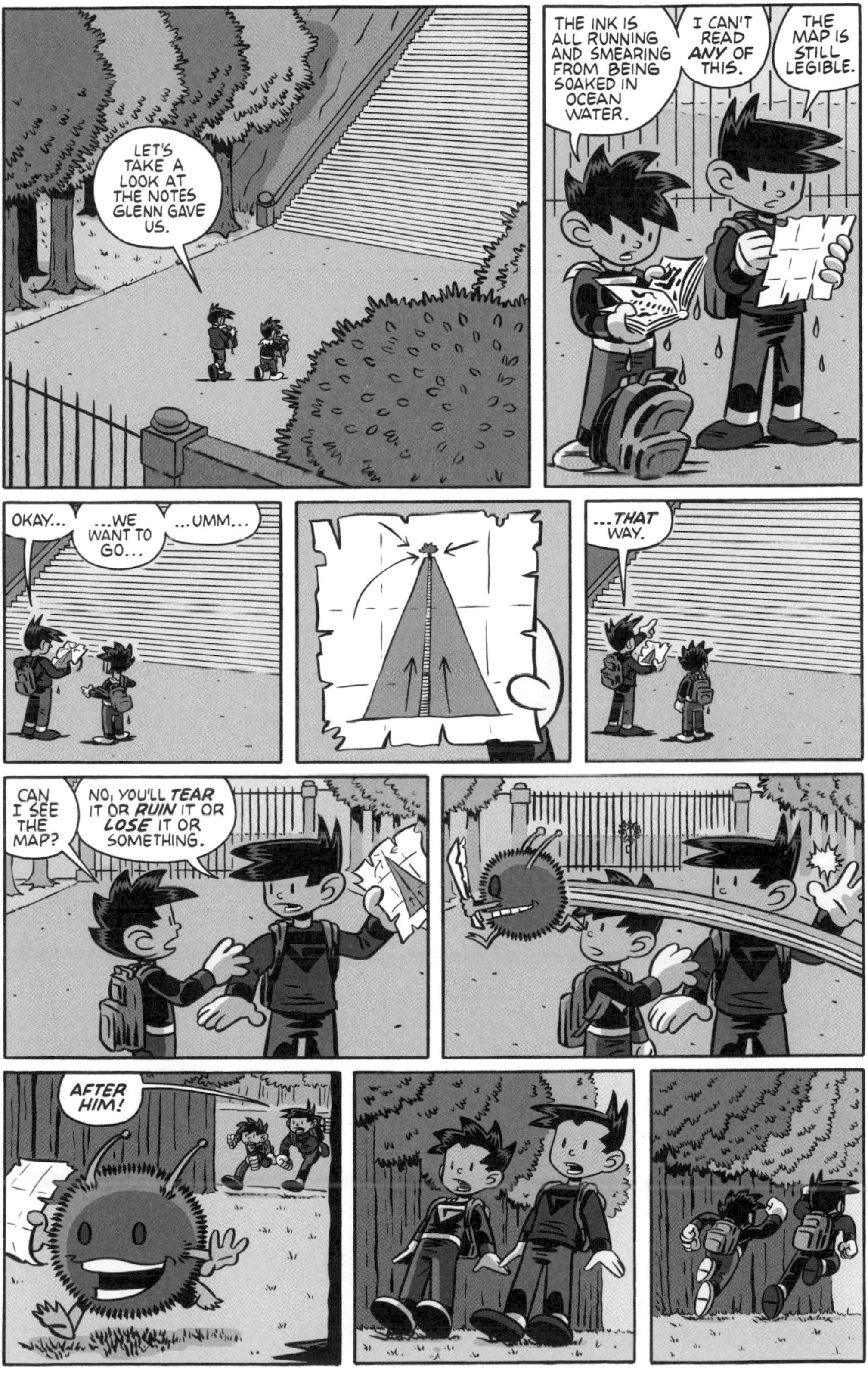
LET'S TAKE A LOOK AT THE NOTES GLENN GAVE US.
THE INK IS ALL RUNNING AND SMEARING FROM BEING SOAKED IN OCEAN WATER.
I CAN'T READ ANY OF THIS.
THE MAP IS STILL LEGIBLE.
OKAY...
...WE WANT TO GO...
...UMM...
...THAT WAY.
CAN I SEE THE MAP?
NO, YOU'LL TEAR IT OR RUIN IT OR LOSE IT OR SOMETHING.
AFTER HIM!

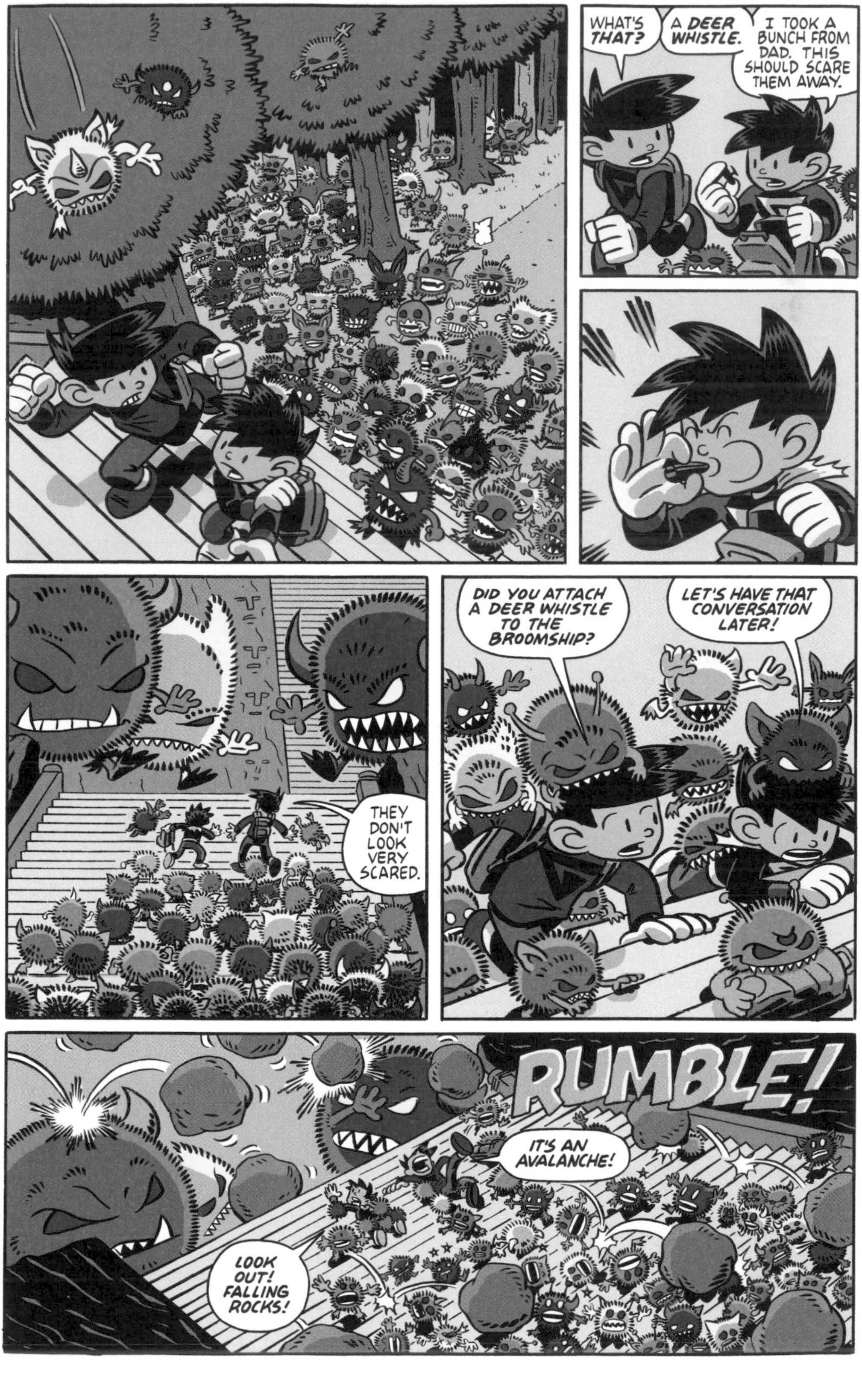
WHAT'S THAT?
A DEER WHISTLE.
I TOOK A BUNCH FROM DAD. THIS SHOULD SCARE THEM AWAY.
THEY DON'T LOOK VERY SCARED.
DID YOU ATTACH A DEER WHISTLE TO THE BROOMSHIP?
LET'S HAVE THAT CONVERSATION LATER!
RUMBLE!
IT'S AN AVALANCHE!
LOOK OUT! FALLING ROCKS!

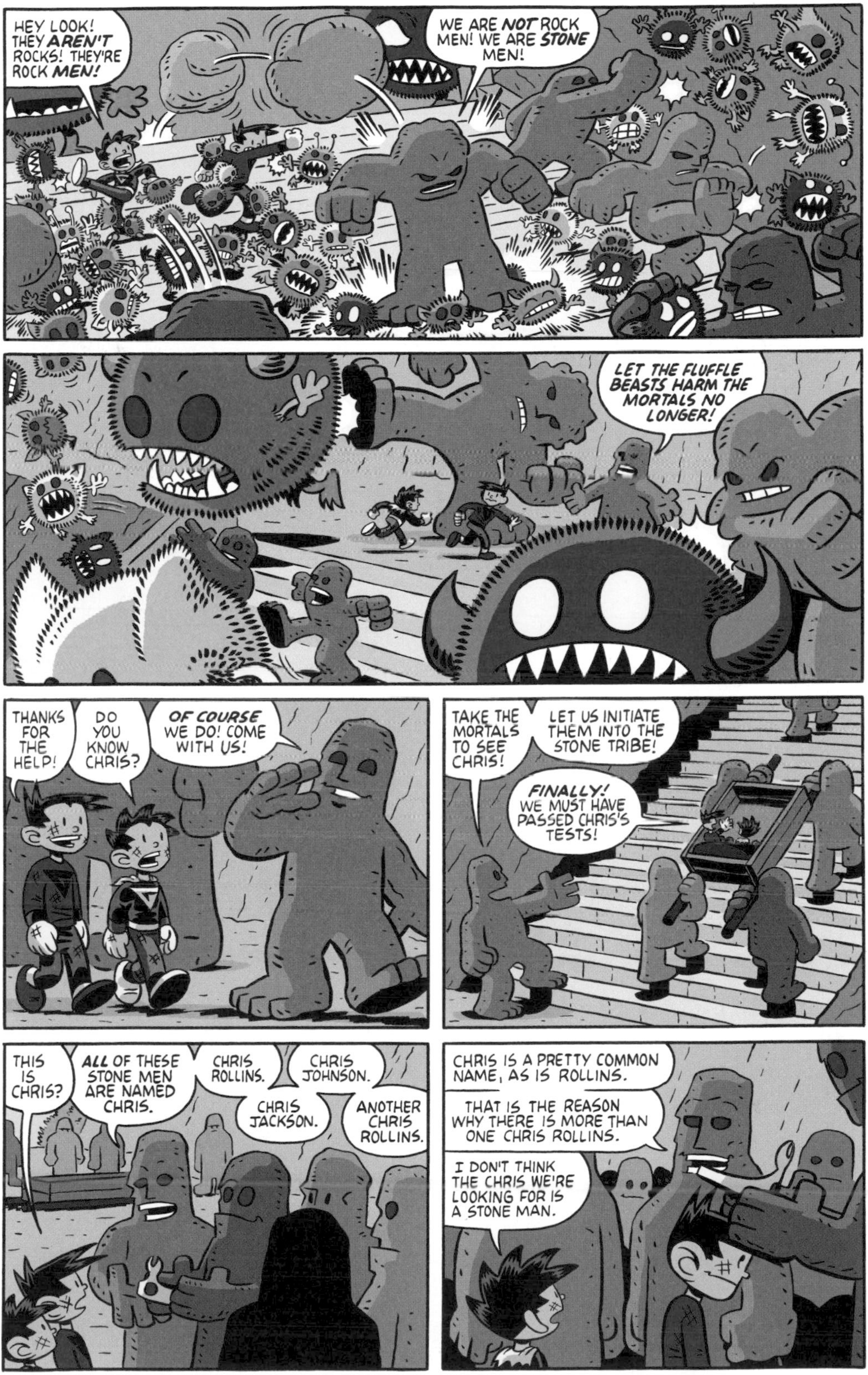
HEY LOOK! THEY AREN'T ROCKS! THEY'RE ROCK MEN!
WE ARE NOT ROCK MEN! WE ARE STONE MEN!
LET THE FLUFFLE BEASTS HARM THE MORTALS NO LONGER!
THANKS FOR THE HELP!
DO YOU KNOW CHRIS?
OF COURSE WE DO! COME WITH US!
TAKE THE MORTALS TO SEE CHRIS!
LET US INITIATE THEM INTO THE STONE TRIBE!
FINALLY! WE MUST HAVE PASSED CHRIS'S TESTS!
THIS IS CHRIS?
ALL OF THESE STONE MEN ARE NAMED CHRIS.
CHRIS ROLLINS.
CHRIS JOHNSON.
CHRIS JACKSON.
ANOTHER CHRIS ROLLINS.
CHRIS IS A PRETTY COMMON NAME, AS IS ROLLINS.
THAT IS THE REASON WHY THERE IS MORE THAN ONE CHRIS ROLLINS.
I DON'T THINK THE CHRIS WE'RE LOOKING FOR IS A STONE MAN.

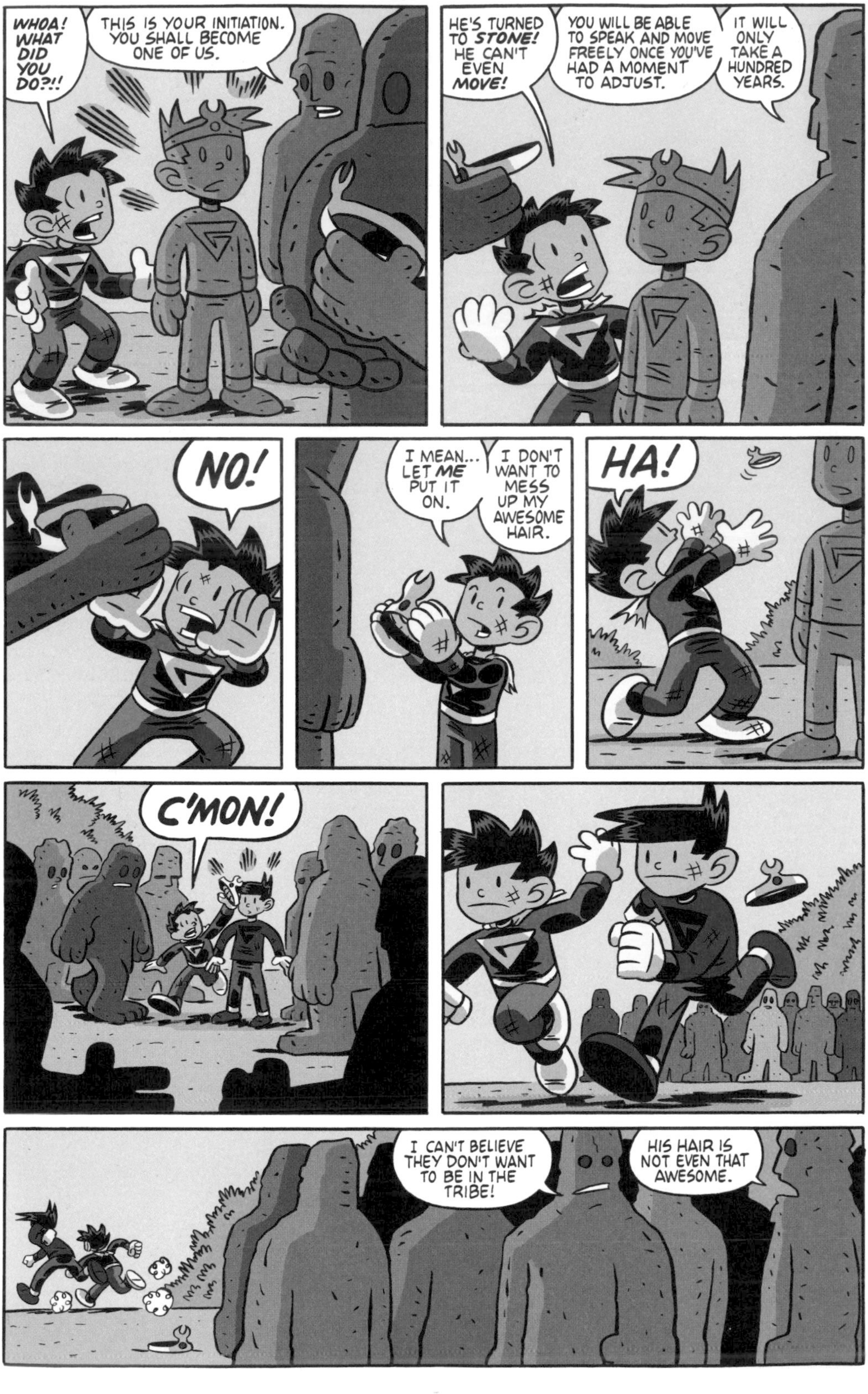
WHOA! WHAT DID YOU DO?!!
THIS IS YOUR INITIATION. YOU SHALL BECOME ONE OF US.
HE'S TURNED TO STONE! HE CAN'T EVEN MOVE!
YOU WILL BE ABLE TO SPEAK AND MOVE FREELY ONCE YOU'VE HAD A MOMENT TO ADJUST.
IT WILL ONLY TAKE A HUNDRED YEARS.
NO!
I MEAN... LET ME PUT IT ON.
I DON'T WANT TO MESS UP MY AWESOME HAIR.
HA!
C'MON!
I CAN'T BELIEVE THEY DON'T WANT TO BE IN THE TRIBE!
HIS HAIR IS NOT EVEN THAT AWESOME.

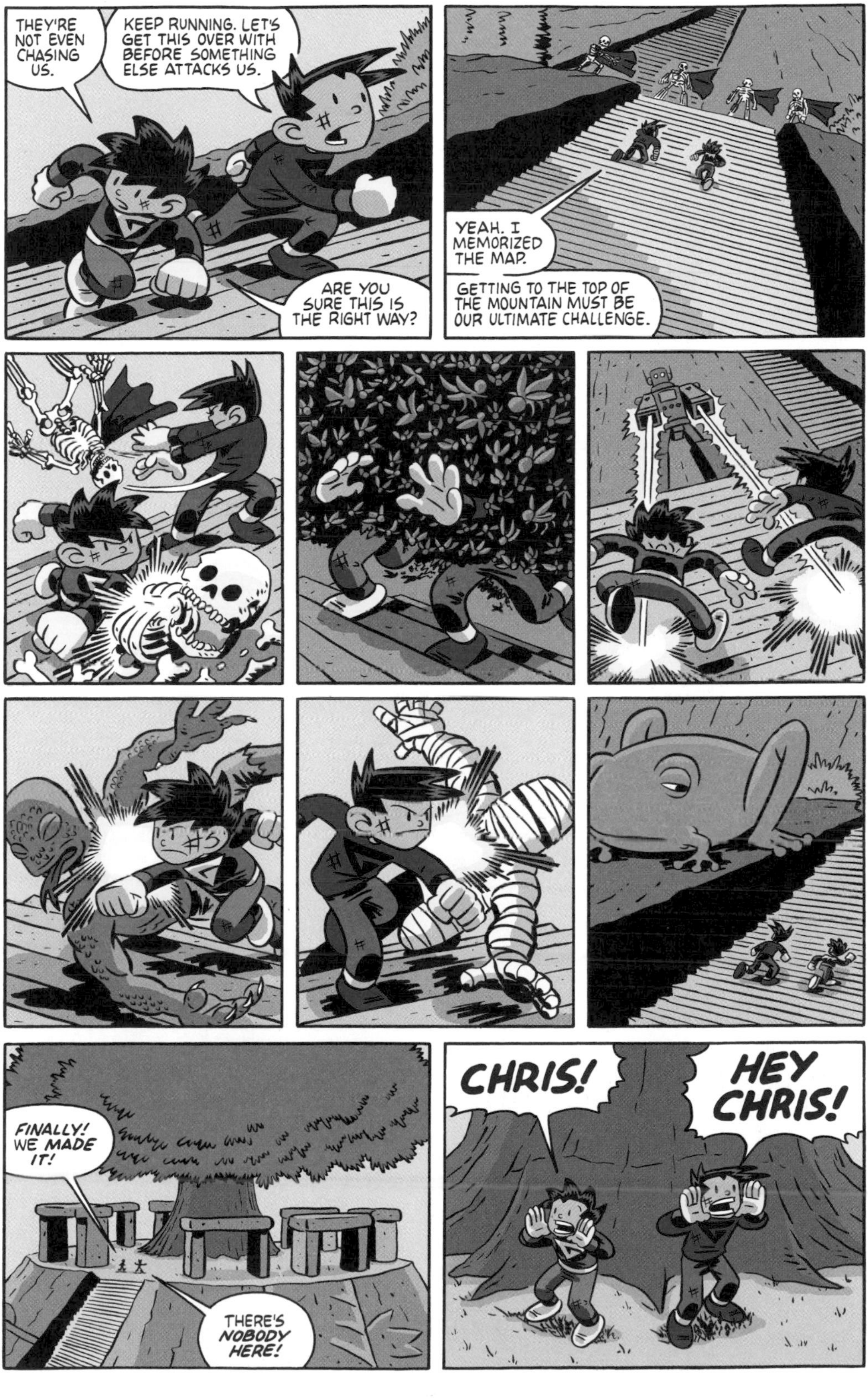
THEY'RE NOT EVEN CHASING US.
KEEP RUNNING. LET'S GET THIS OVER WITH BEFORE SOMETHING ELSE ATTACKS US.
ARE YOU SURE THIS IS THE RIGHT WAY?
YEAH. I MEMORIZED THE MAP.
GETTING TO THE TOP OF THE MOUNTAIN MUST BE OUR ULTIMATE CHALLENGE.
FINALLY! WE MADE IT!
THERE'S NOBODY HERE!
CHRIS!
HEY CHRIS!

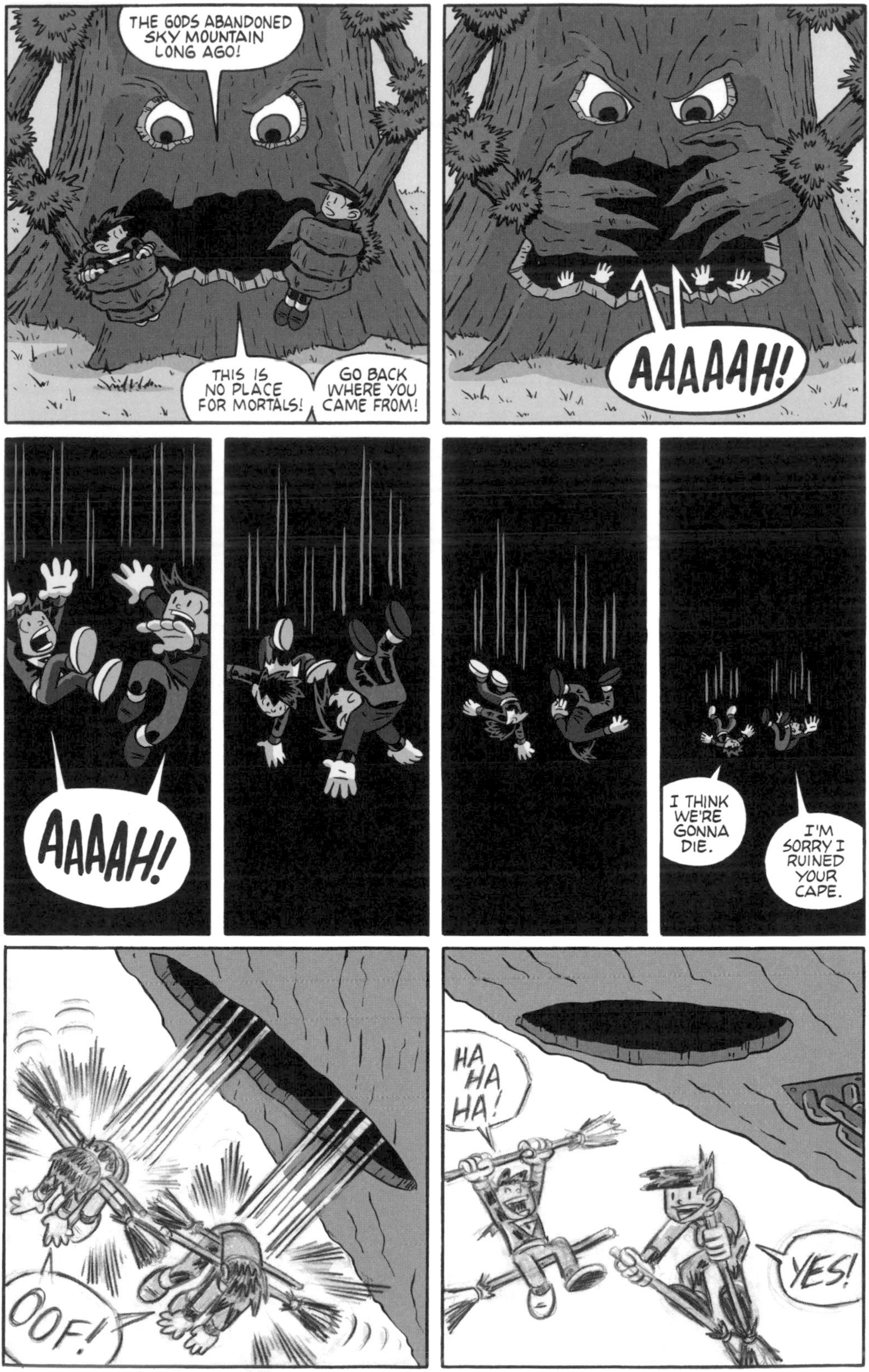
THE GODS ABANDONED SKY MOUNTAIN LONG AGO!
THIS IS NO PLACE FOR MORTALS!
GO BACK WHERE YOU CAME FROM!
AAAAAH!
AAAAH!
I THINK WE'RE GONNA DIE.
I'M SORRY I RUINED YOUR CAPE.
OOF!
HA HA HA!
YES!

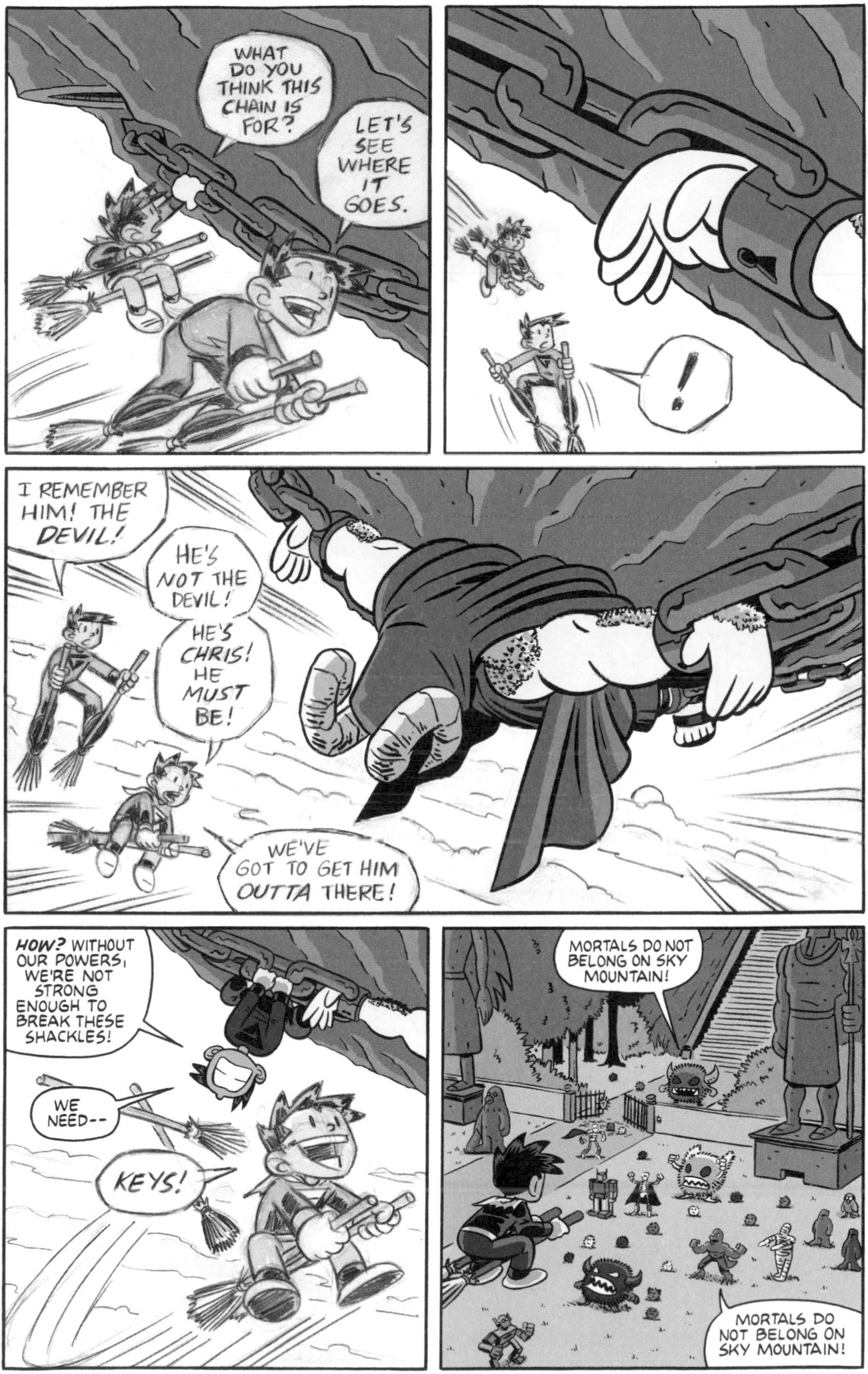
WHAT DO YOU THINK THIS CHAIN IS FOR?
LET'S SEE WHERE IT GOES.
!
I REMEMBER HIM! THE DEVIL!
HE'S NOT THE DEVIL!
HE'S CHRIS! HE MUST BE!
WE'VE GOT TO GET HIM OUTTA THERE!
HOW? WITHOUT OUR POWERS, WE'RE NOT STRONG ENOUGH TO BREAK THESE SHACKLES!
WE NEED--
KEYS!
MORTALS DO NOT BELONG ON SKY MOUNTAIN!
MORTALS DO NOT BELONG ON SKY MOUNTAIN!

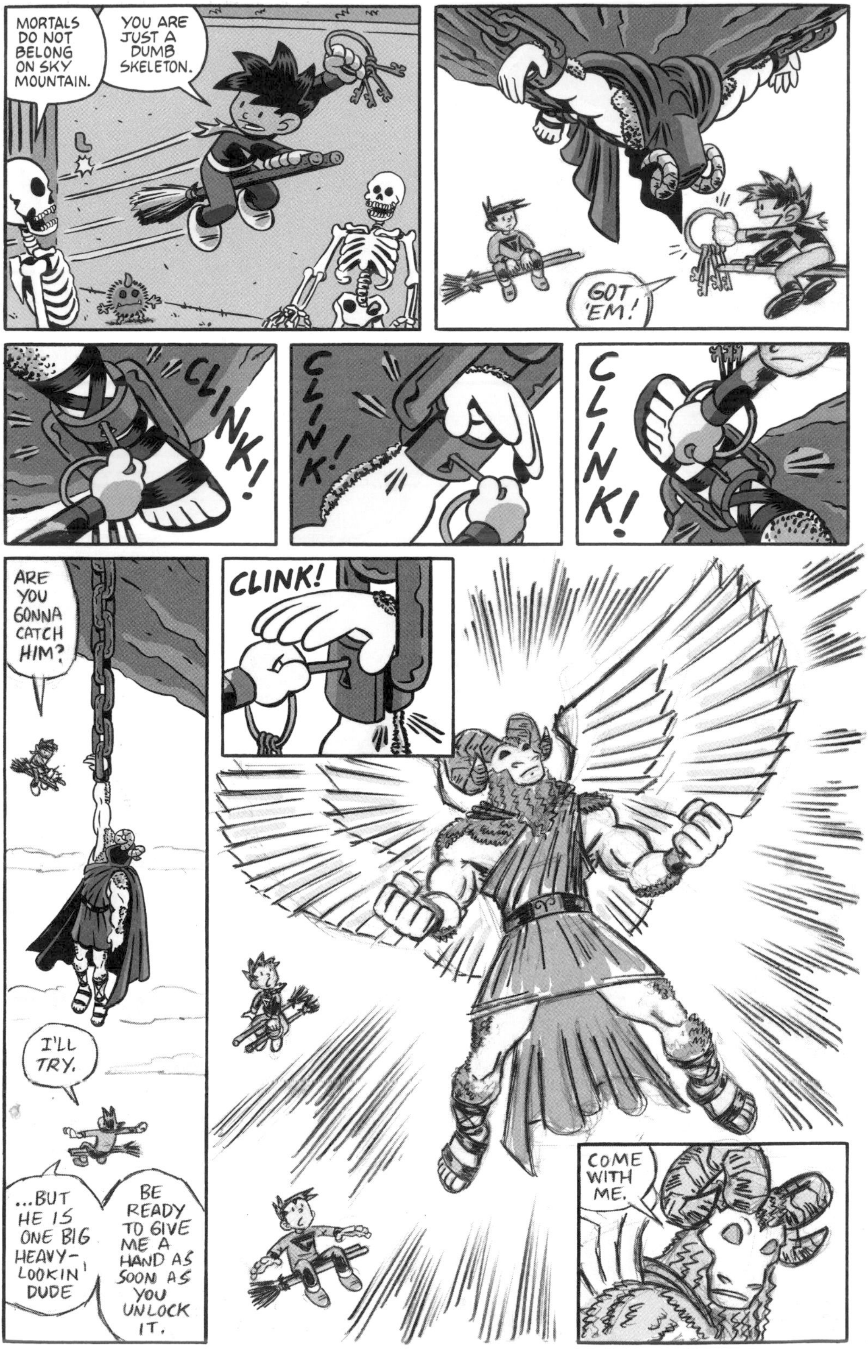

MORTALS DO NOT BELONG ON SKY MOUNTAIN.
YOU ARE JUST A DUMB SKELETON.
GOT 'EM!
CLINK!
CLINK!
CLINK!
ARE YOU GONNA CATCH HIM?
I'LL TRY.
...BUT HE IS ONE BIG HEAVY-LOOKIN' DUDE
BE READY TO GIVE ME A HAND AS SOON AS YOU UNLOCK IT.
CLINK!
COME WITH ME.

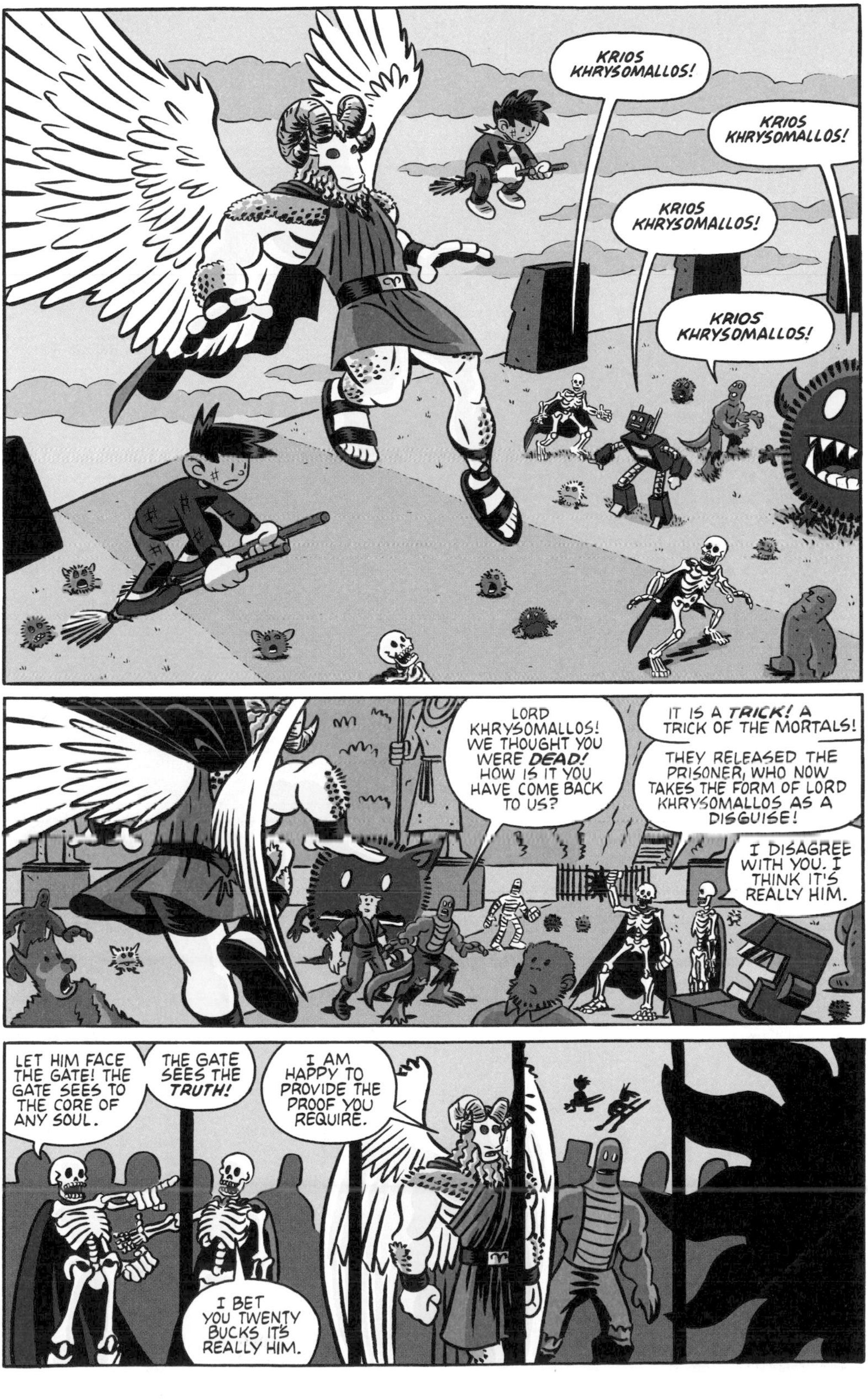
KRIOS KHRYSOMALLOS!
KRIOS KHRYSOMALLOS!
KRIOS KHRYSOMALLOS!
KRIOS KHRYSOMALLOS!
LORD KHRYSOMALLOS! WE THOUGHT YOU WERE DEAD! HOW IS IT YOU HAVE COME BACK TO US?
IT IS A TRICK! A TRICK OF THE MORTALS!
THEY RELEASED THE PRISONER, WHO NOW TAKES THE FORM OF LORD KHRYSOMALLOS AS A DISGUISE!
I DISAGREE WITH YOU. I THINK IT'S REALLY HIM.
LET HIM FACE THE GATE! THE GATE SEES TO THE CORE OF ANY SOUL.
THE GATE SEES THE TRUTH!
I BET YOU TWENTY BUCKS IT'S REALLY HIM.
I AM HAPPY TO PROVIDE THE PROOF YOU REQUIRE.

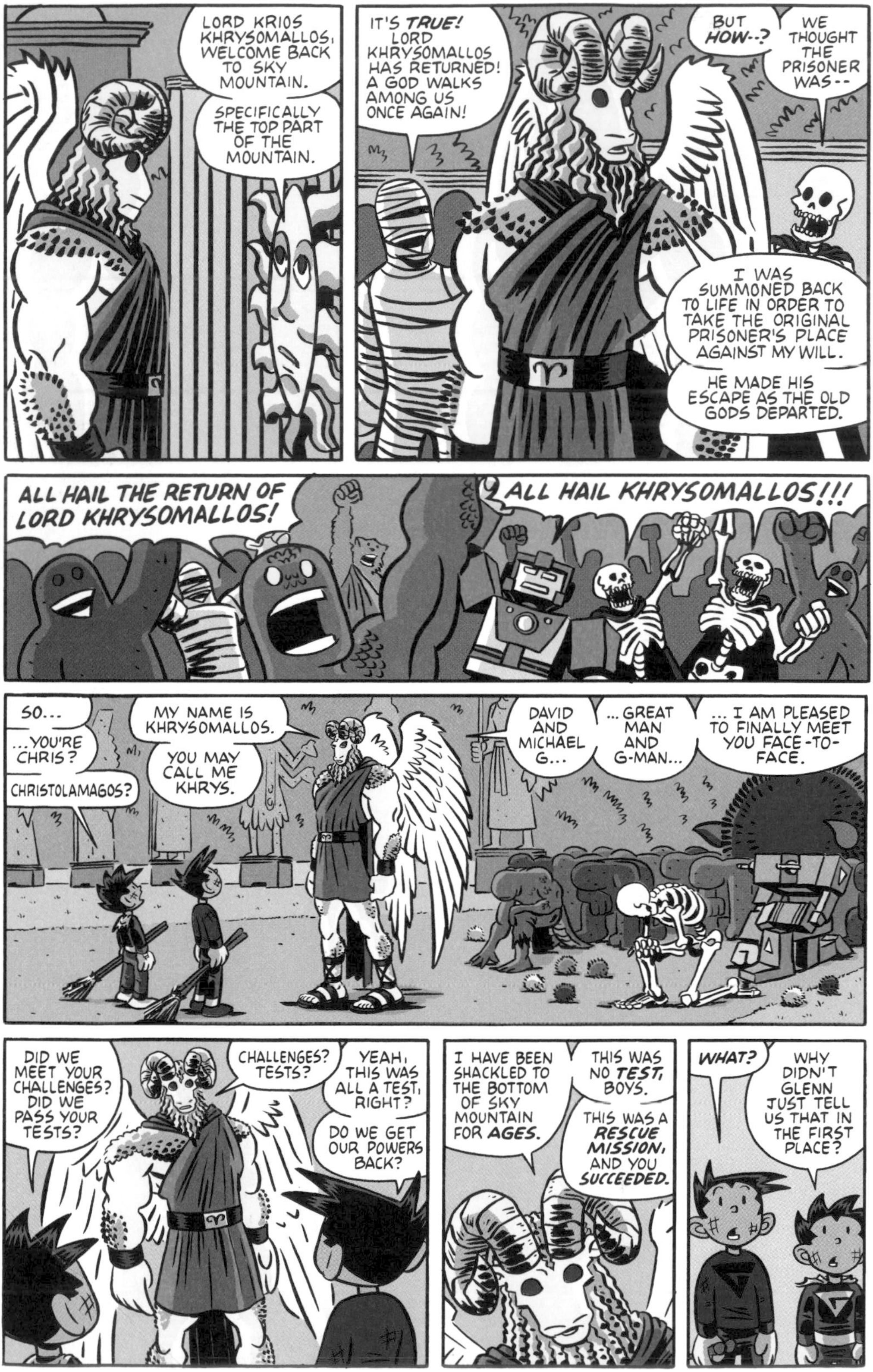
LORD KRIOS KHRYSOMALLOS, WELCOME BACK TO SKY MOUNTAIN.
SPECIFICALLY THE TOP PART OF THE MOUNTAIN.
IT'S TRUE! LORD KHRYSOMALLOS HAS RETURNED! A GOD WALKS AMONG US ONCE AGAIN!
BUT HOW--?
WE THOUGHT THE PRISONER WAS--
I WAS SUMMONED BACK TO LIFE IN ORDER TO TAKE THE ORIGINAL PRISONER'S PLACE AGAINST MY WILL.
HE MADE HIS ESCAPE AS THE OLD GODS DEPARTED.
ALL HAIL THE RETURN OF LORD KHRYSOMALLOS!
ALL HAIL KHRYSOMALLOS!!!
SO...
...YOU'RE CHRIS?
CHRISTOLAMAGOS?
MY NAME IS KHRYSOMALLOS.
YOU MAY CALL ME KHRYS.
DAVID AND MICHAEL G...
...GREAT MAN AND G-MAN...
...I AM PLEASED TO FINALLY MEET YOU FACE-TO-FACE.
DID WE MEET YOUR CHALLENGES? DID WE PASS YOUR TESTS?
CHALLENGES? TESTS?
YEAH, THIS WAS ALL A TEST, RIGHT?
DO WE GET OUR POWERS BACK?
I HAVE BEEN SHACKLED TO THE BOTTOM OF SKY MOUNTAIN FOR AGES.
THIS WAS NO TEST, BOYS.
THIS WAS A RESCUE MISSION, AND YOU SUCCEEDED.
WHAT?
WHY DIDN'T GLENN JUST TELL US THAT IN THE FIRST PLACE?

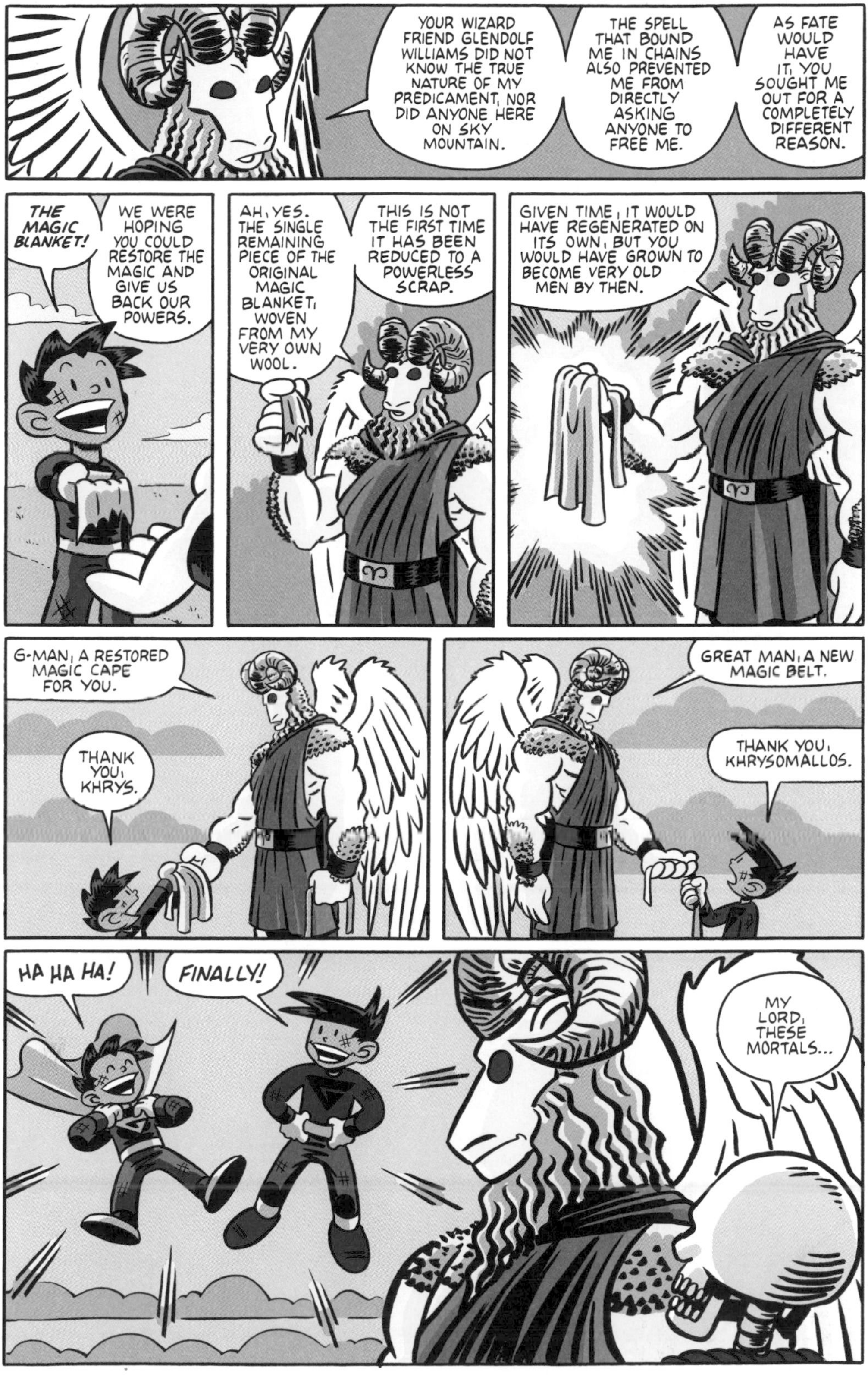
YOUR WIZARD FRIEND GLENDOLF WILLIAMS DID NOT KNOW THE TRUE NATURE OF MY PREDICAMENT, NOR DID ANYONE HERE ON SKY MOUNTAIN.
THE SPELL THAT BOUND ME IN CHAINS ALSO PREVENTED ME FROM DIRECTLY ASKING ANYONE TO FREE ME.
AS FATE WOULD HAVE IT, YOU SOUGHT ME OUT FOR A COMPLETELY DIFFERENT REASON.
THE MAGIC BLANKET!
WE WERE HOPING YOU COULD RESTORE THE MAGIC AND GIVE US BACK OUR POWERS.
AH, YES. THE SINGLE REMAINING PIECE OF THE ORIGINAL MAGIC BLANKET, WOVEN FROM MY VERY OWN WOOL.
THIS IS NOT THE FIRST TIME IT HAS BEEN REDUCED TO A POWERLESS SCRAP.
GIVEN TIME, IT WOULD HAVE REGENERATED ON ITS OWN, BUT YOU WOULD HAVE GROWN TO BECOME VERY OLD MEN BY THEN.
G-MAN, A RESTORED MAGIC CAPE FOR YOU.
THANK YOU, KHRYS.
GREAT MAN, A NEW MAGIC BELT.
THANK YOU, KHRYSOMALLOS.
HA HA HA!
FINALLY!
MY LORD, THESE MORTALS...

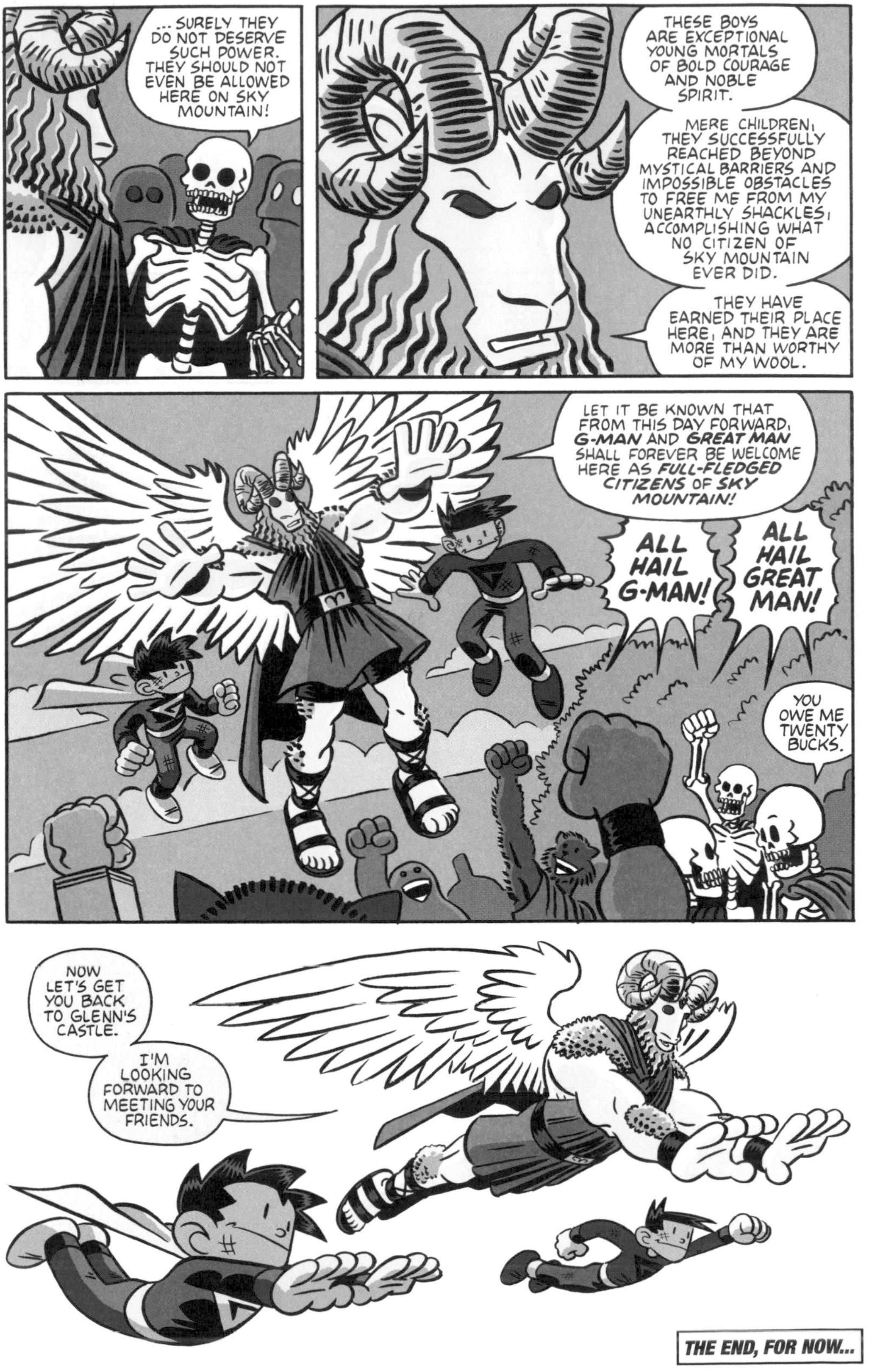
...SURELY THEY DO NOT DESERVE SUCH POWER. THEY SHOULD NOT EVEN BE ALLOWED HERE ON SKY MOUNTAIN!
THESE BOYS ARE EXCEPTIONAL YOUNG MORTALS OF BOLD COURAGE AND NOBLE SPIRIT.
MERE CHILDREN, THEY SUCCESSFULLY REACHED BEYOND MYSTICAL BARRIERS AND IMPOSSIBLE OBSTACLES TO FREE ME FROM MY UNEARTHLY SHACKLES, ACCOMPLISHING WHAT NO CITIZEN OF SKY MOUNTAIN EVER DID.
THEY HAVE EARNED THEIR PLACE HERE, AND THEY ARE MORE THAN WORTHY OF MY WOOL.
LET IT BE KNOWN THAT FROM THIS DAY FORWARD, G-MAN AND GREAT MAN SHALL FOREVER BE WELCOME HERE AS FULL-FLEDGED CITIZENS OF SKY MOUNTAIN!
ALL HAIL G-MAN!
ALL HAIL GREAT MAN!
YOU OWE ME TWENTY BUCKS.
NOW LET'S GET YOU BACK TO GLENN'S CASTLE.
I'M LOOKING FORWARD TO MEETING YOUR FRIENDS.
THE END, FOR NOW...

CHRIS G's CAPE CRISIS SKETCHBOOK

Here's a look at some of the work that went into drawing the original comic covers for GMAN: CAPE CRISIS.

I usually do tiny, rough thumbnail sketches before I begin working on a final drawing. For issue 1, I was pretty confident I could draw what I had in my head, so I only did one rough thumbnail before I went to full pencils.

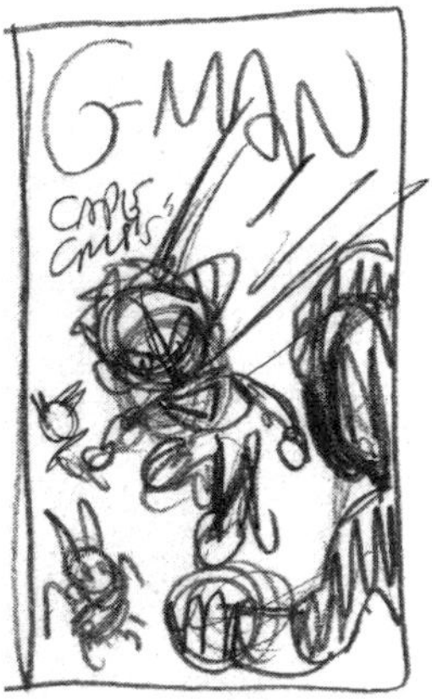

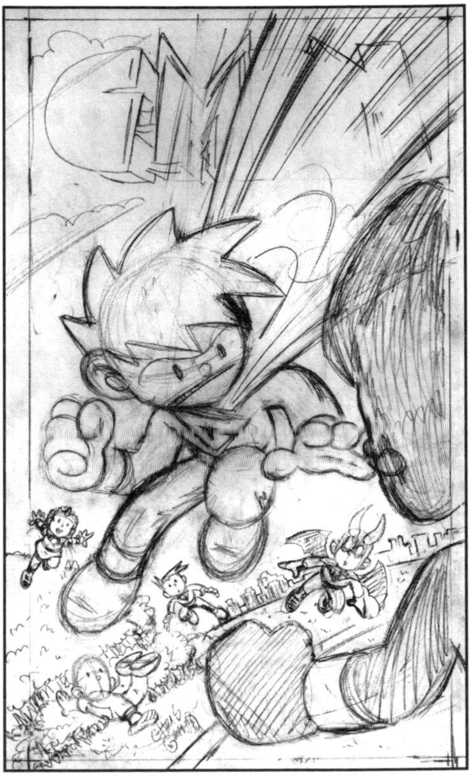

I spent a lot more time thumbnailing the cover for issue 2, sketching and re-sketching until I felt I was ready to attack the final piece.

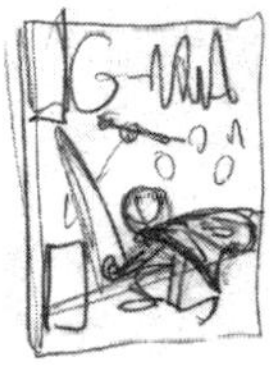

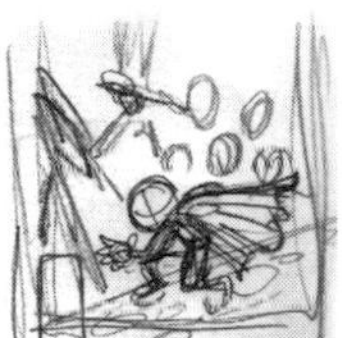

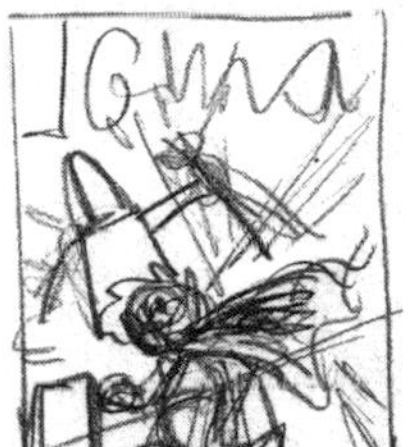

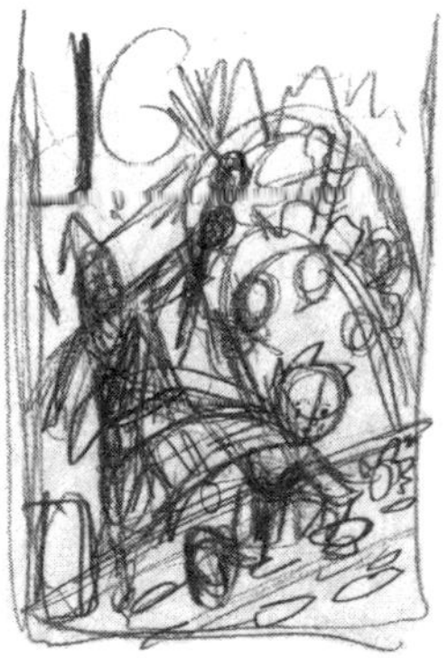

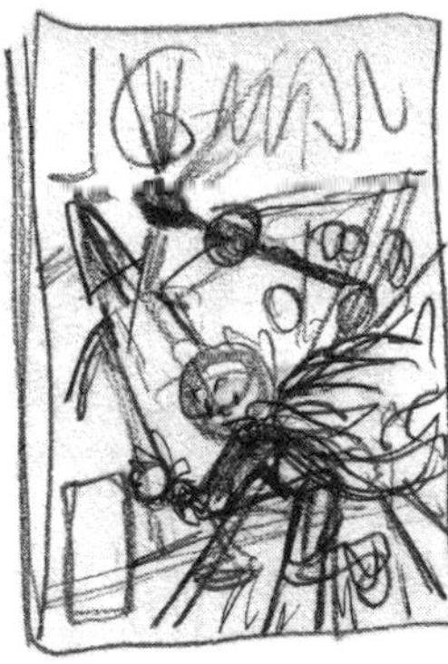

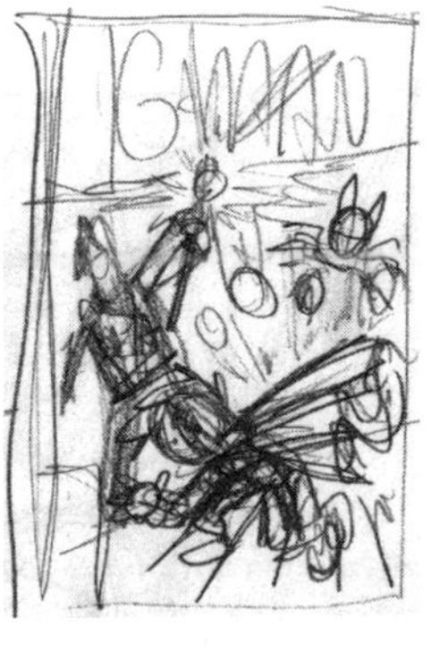

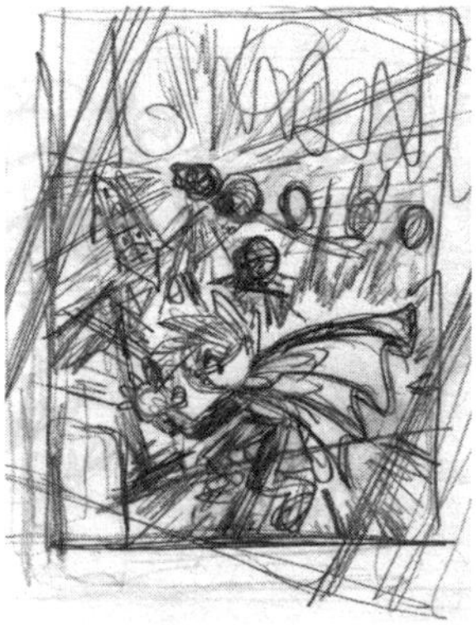

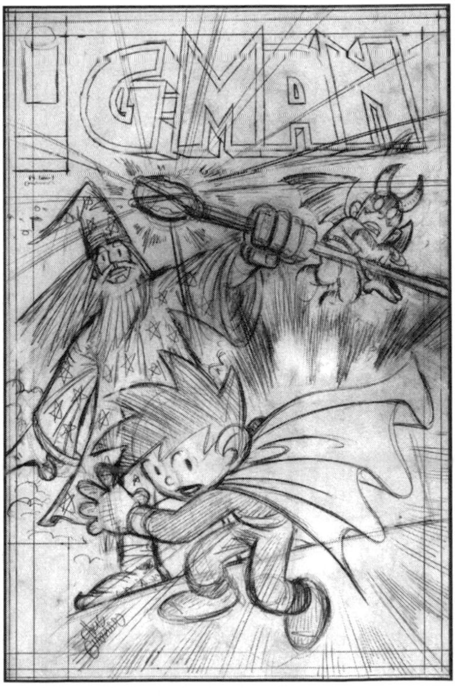

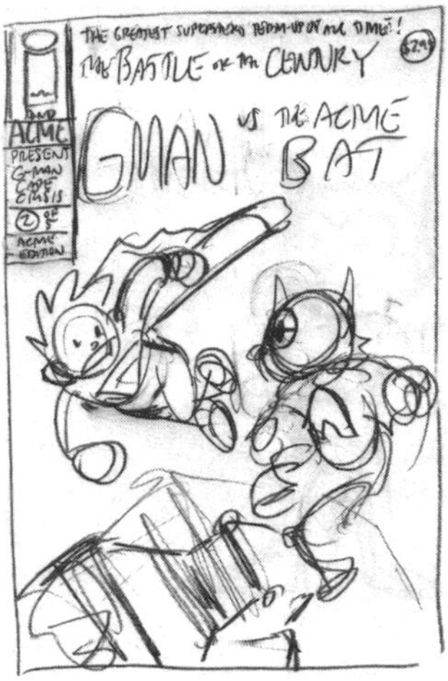

G MAN
VS THE ACME BAT

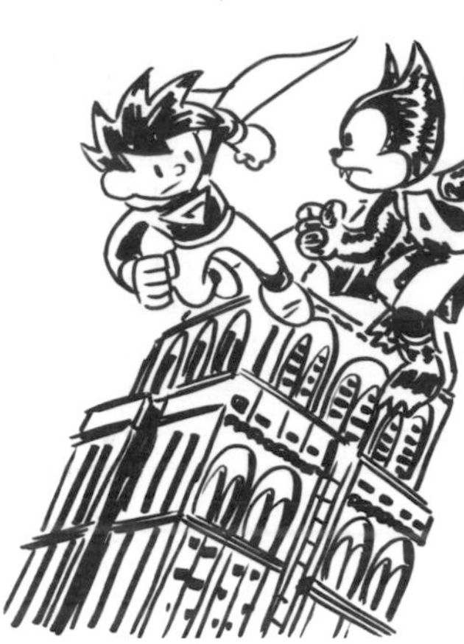

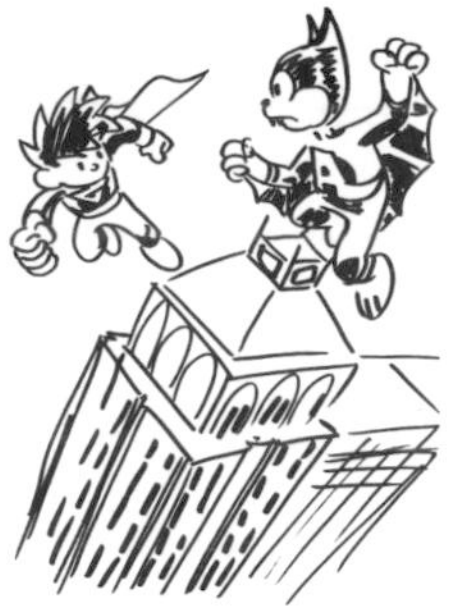

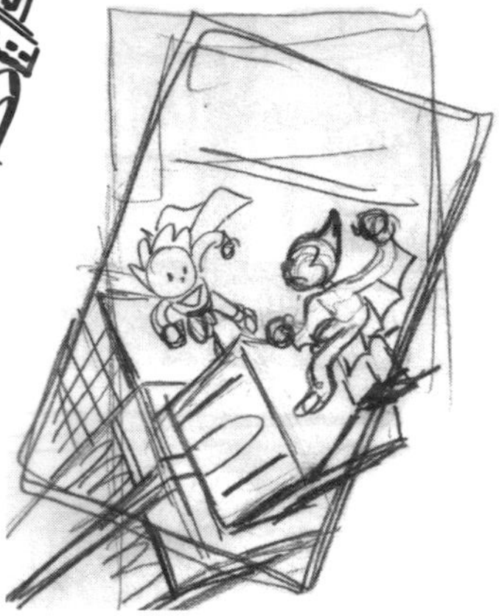

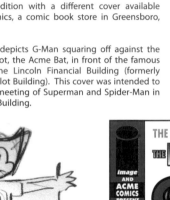

Issue 2 had a special edition with a different cover available exclusively at Acme Comics, a comic book store in Greensboro, North Carolina.

The Acme variant cover depicts G-Man squaring off against the Acme Comics store mascot, the Acme Bat, in front of the famous Greensboro landmark, the Lincoln Financial Building (formerly known as the Jefferson Pilot Building). This cover was intended to pay homage to the first meeting of Superman and Spider-Man in front of the Empire State Building.

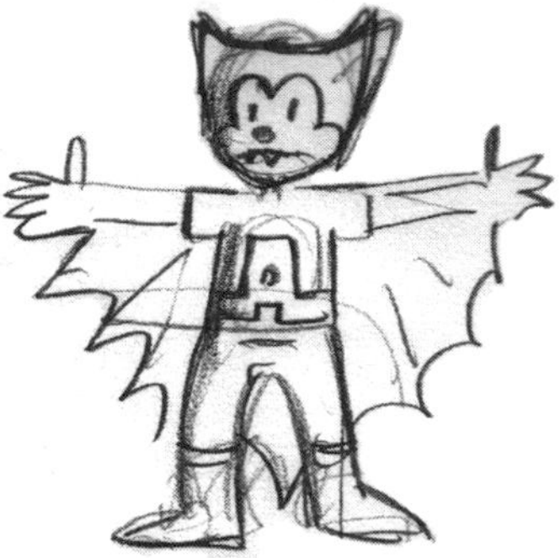

Some preliminary sketches of the Acme Bat, as I adapted his design to my style.

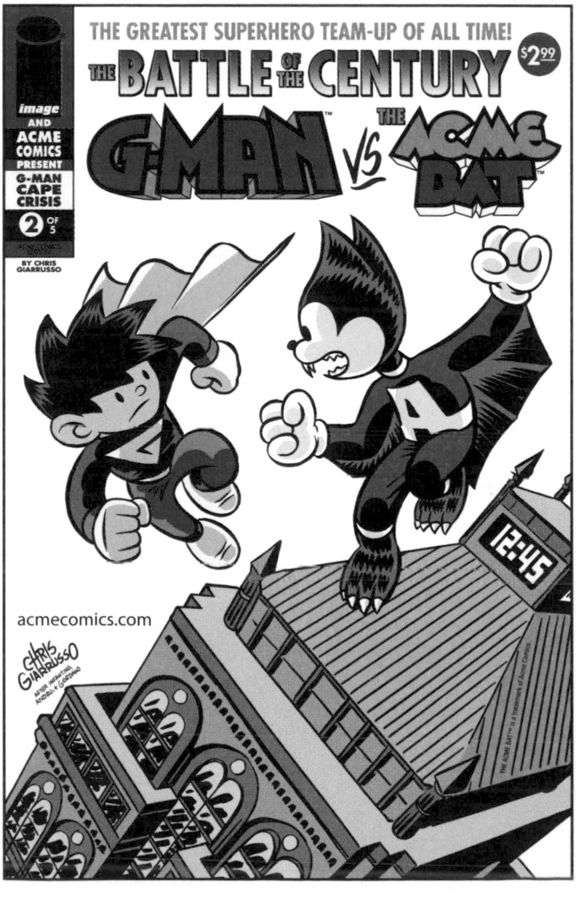

THE GREATEST SUPERHERO TEAM-UP OF ALL TIME!
THE BATTLE OF THE CENTURY
$2.99
image
AND
ACME COMICS
PRESENT
G-MAN CAPE CRISIS
2 OF 5
BY CHRIS GIARRUSSO
G-MAN™ VS THE ACME BAT™
12:45
acmecomics.com
CHRIS GIARRUSSO

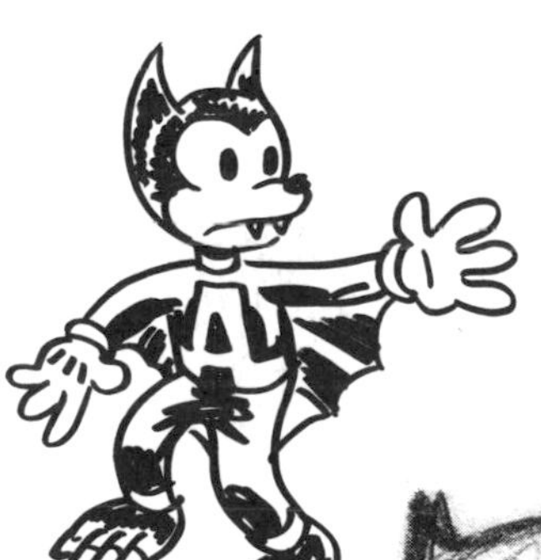

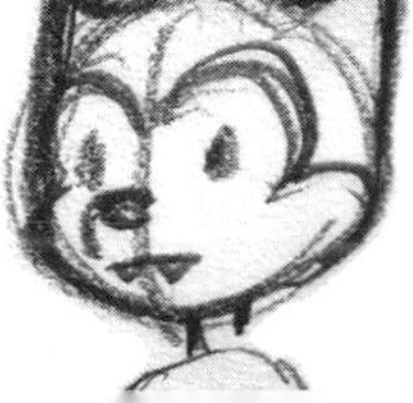

Cover thumbnails and pencils for Cape Crisis issues 3 and 4.

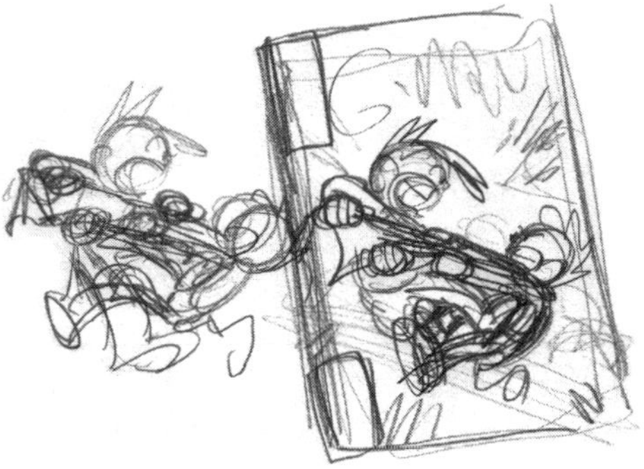

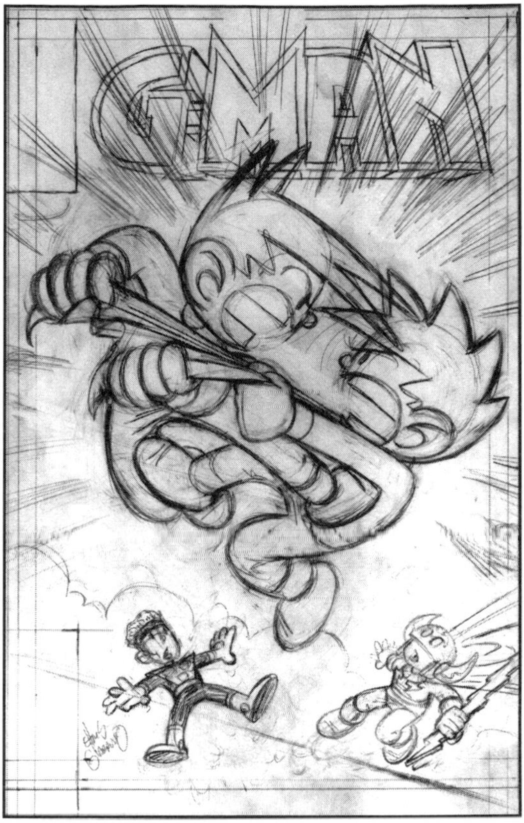

Issue 3 originally had Sunny the Suntrooper on the cover (as shown here in the pencils), but by the time I figured out exactly what was going to happen in the story, I realized Sunny was going to be off-planet during this scene. I substituted Billy Demon in for Sunny on the final cover.

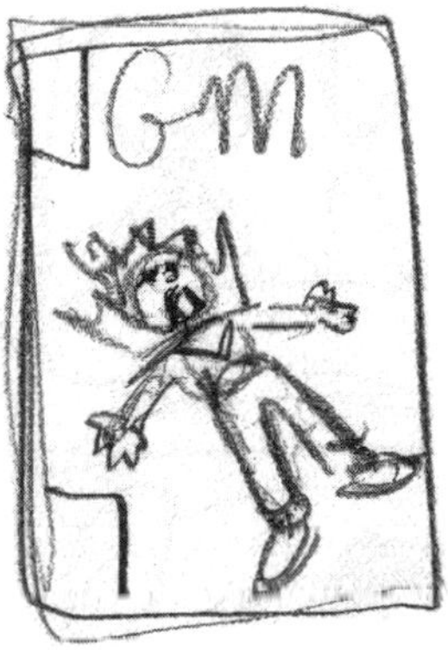

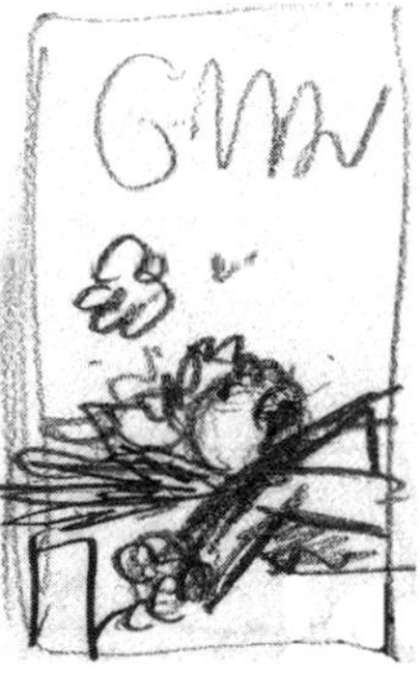

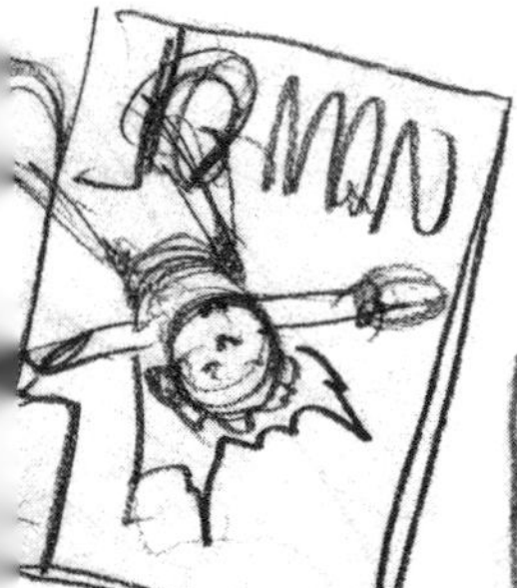

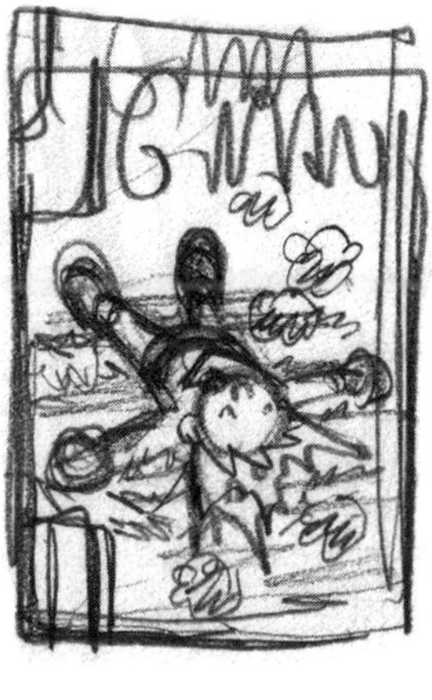

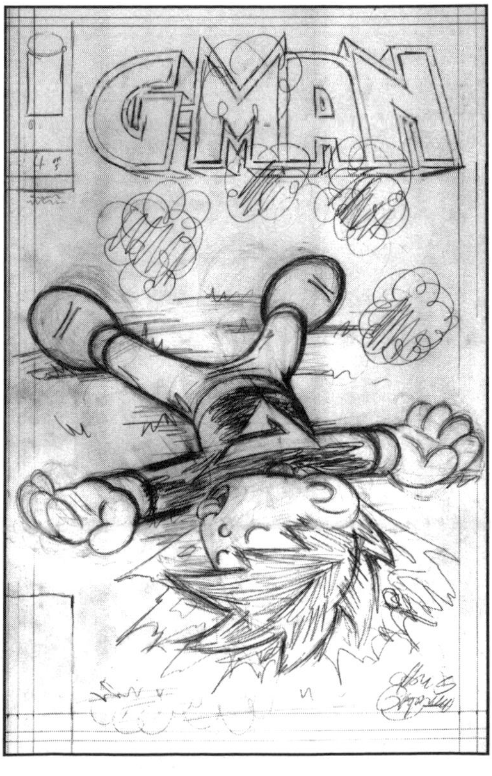

Cover thumbnails and pencils for issue 5.

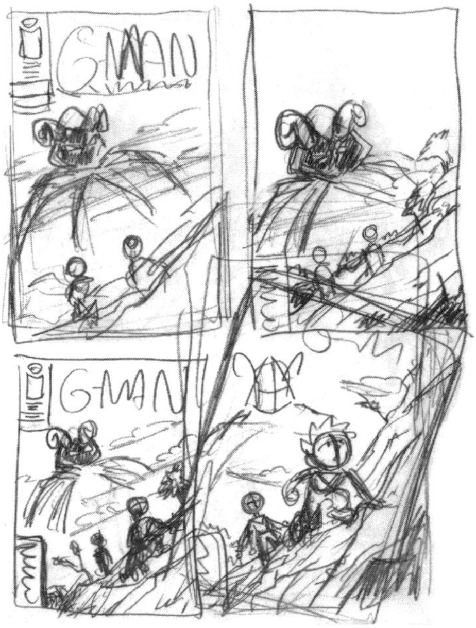
G-MAN
G-MAN

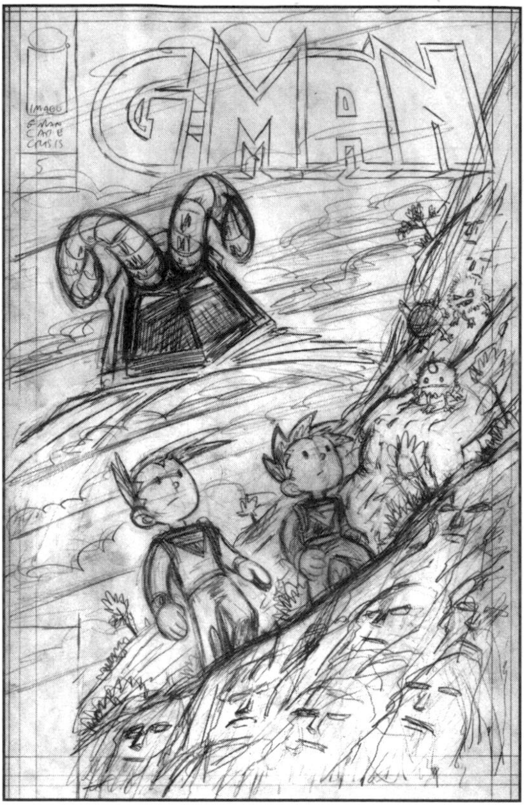
GMAN

Issue 5 featured the first clear look at Khrysomallos without his robes and hood shrowding him in mystery. Far outside of my standard kid superhero comfort zone, Khrysomallos was a challenge to design.

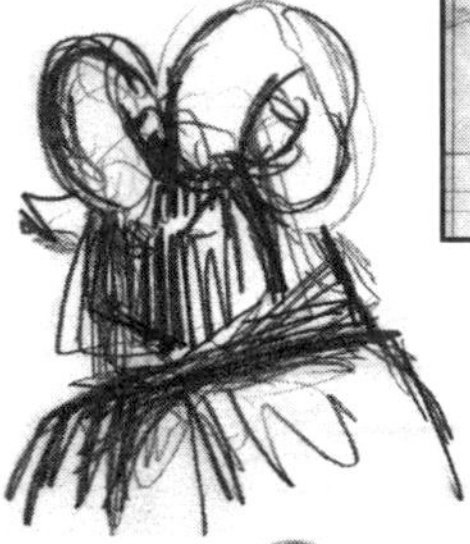

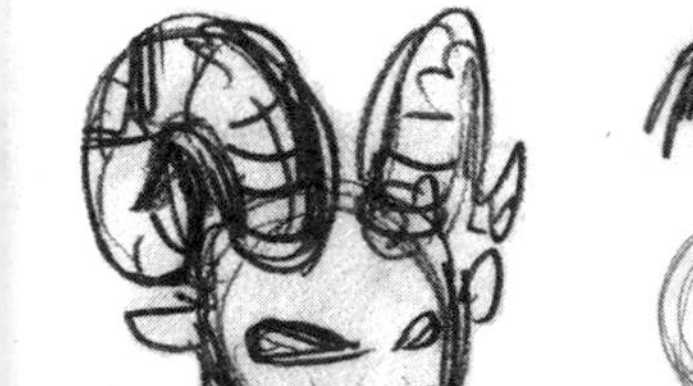

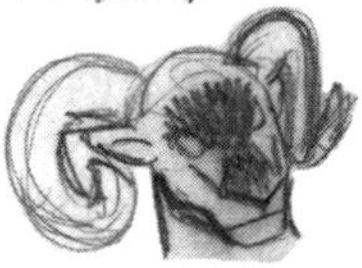

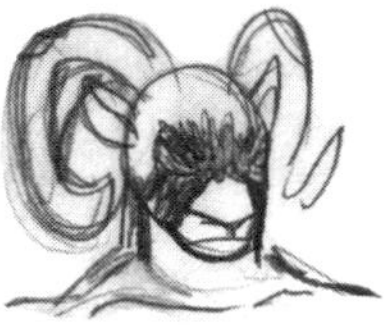

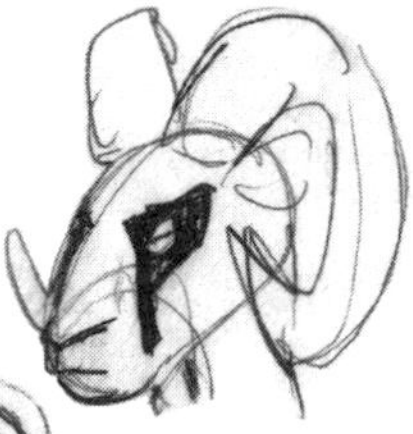

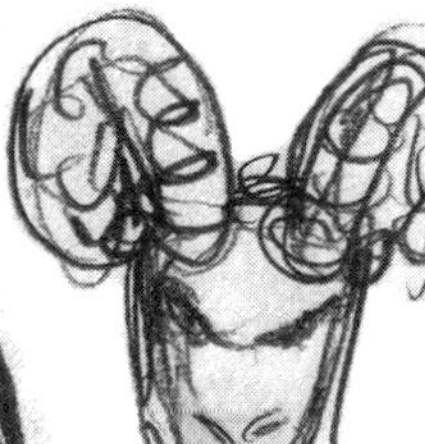

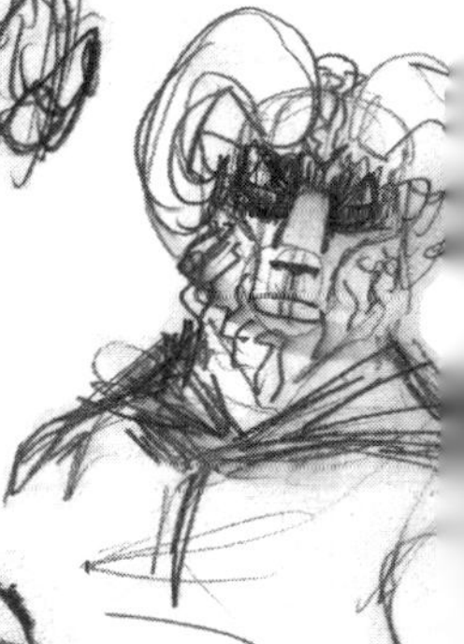

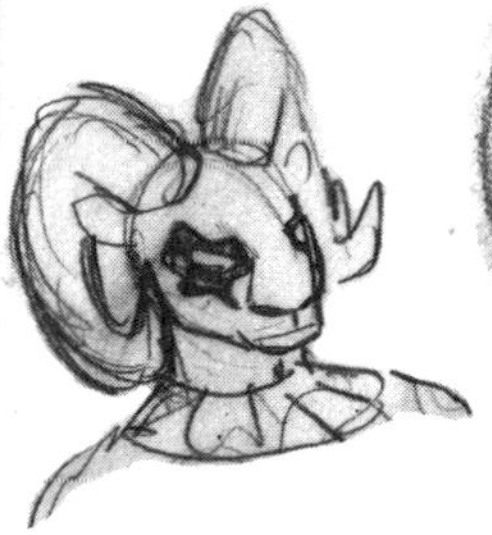

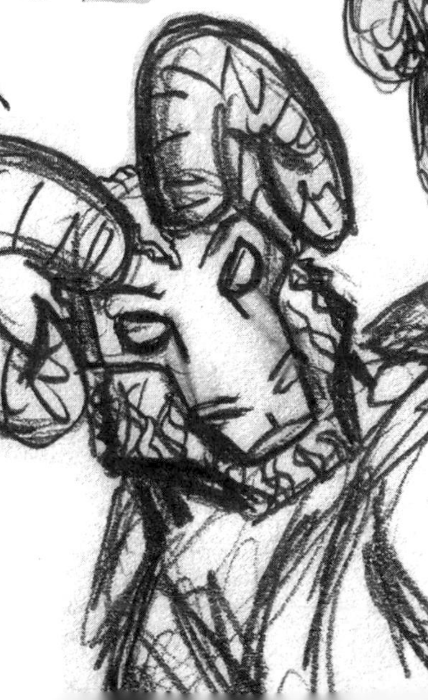

Khyrsomallos was always meant to have the head of a ram, but it was the addition of the wooly beard that finally gave him the regal, majestic look of an immortal.